THE BONES OF THE PAST

THE BONES OF THE PAST

CRAIG A. MUNRO

INKSHARES

Published by Inkshares, Inc., San Francisco, California
www.inkshares.com

Edited and designed by Girl Friday Productions
www.girlfridayproductions.com

Cover design by Scott Barrie
Celtic skull design by Joanna Moran and Design Clinic
Map design by John Robin

ISBN: 9781942645337
e-ISBN: 9781942645344
Library of Congress Control Number: 2016942386

For Margo, who gave me a pen and a new reason to write.

LIST OF CHARACTERS
BY PRIMARY LOCATION

BIALTA

Altog, a Night Guardsman

Banjax, an unlicensed mage and companion of the Prince

Brolt, a Night Guard Godchosen

Corfon Tilden, Arcanum archmage and member of the Closed Council

Dantic, Arcanum archmage of the Eighth Order

Dwyn, a Night Guard squad leader

Felkin, a general of the Bialtan Southern Army

Grae, a Night Guard scout

Greal, a Night Guardsman

Gurtraven Calmosin, aka Gurt, commander of the Night Guard

Gustave, an archmage and adviser to the king

Holit Nobesid, an Arcanum special investigator

Inksharud, a Night captain, leader of the Korsten City Night Guard

Jalim Bagwin, an Arcanum crafter

Jeb, a palace servant

King Arlon, ruler of Bialta

Kishan Nikhil, kladic of the Oviyan tribe
Krigare, weapons master of the Night Guard
Lera, a Night Guard archmage
Lord Harold Irem, a Bialtan nobleman
Matchstick, a magical construct, Dantic's servant
Min, a Night Guardsman
Neskin, second to General Solten
Nesrine, an Arcanum archmage and member of the Closed
    Council
Nial, a child mage
Salt, a Night Guard recruit
Seely, a Night Guard
Shade, an unlicensed mage
Sigmond, King Arlon's herald
Skeg, a merchant catering to unlicensed mages
Skye, a Night Guardsman
Solten, a general of the Bialtan Eastern Army
Tassos, a Night Guard scout
Tsoba, a Night Guard squad leader
Urit, a Night Guardsman
Wheeze, a Night Guard medic
Yajel, aka the Prince, a crime lord
Zulaxrak, aka Zuly, a Karethin demoness

TOLRAHK ESAL

Alyre Manek, a Warchosen
Betar, a merchant and slave owner
Carver, a fleshcarver
Drokga, tyrant of Tolrahk Esal
Gruig Berrahd Tolrahk, eldest son of the Drokga
Maran Vras, a slave gladiator

Nasaka Jadoo, the Drokga's mage hunter
Old Man, a gladiator champion
Roga, Carver's slave and assistant
Sigian, a slave
Urotan Oskmen Tolrahk, supreme commander of the
Tolrahkali armies

SACRAL

Beren, a master runesmith
Brek, a Warchosen
Corwin the Magnificent, an illusionist and entertainer
Gerald, Maura and Beren's son
Gorsek, a Warchosen
Harrow, a Warchosen
Jenus Chenton, champion of Sacral, bodyguard to the king
and commander of his armies
Jerik, a master armorer and weaponsmith
Kabol, an envoy from the nation of Aboleth
Karim, a retired veteran
King Ansyl, an archmage and ruler of Sacral
Marean, a battlemage
Maura, Beren's wife
Molt, a squad leader
Orik, a priest of the White Mother
Serim, a senior priest of the White Mother
Sevren, a battlemage
Sien, a Warchosen
Traven, a Warchosen and second to Jenus
Vegard, a Warchosen
Yeltos Rogayen, high priest of the White Mother
Zorat, a Warchosen from Aboleth

ISCHIA

Cyril, an undead assassin, a Crow
Dead King, ruler of Ischia
Grodol, a Gling'Ar Warchosen
Masul, a Gling'Ar mage
Rahz the Insane, master assassin and leader of the Dead
    King's Crows
Sonum, the Gling'Ar warchief

DRETH

Lamek, a Dreth pureblood
Nok Dreth, ruler of the Dreth
Nokor Ben Akyum, a Dreth pureblood and envoy to Bialta
Thirat Bel Thammar, a Dreth pureblood and forge master

DEITIES

Amarok, a wolf god
Amon Kareth, demon lord of the Karethin realm
Basat, Bialtan god of pleasure
Bernolk the Golden, god of wealth, commerce, and marriage
Deceiver, god of lies, enemy of the White Mother
Helual, god of science and medicine
She Who Feeds, goddess of decay
Silent God, god of death
White Mother, patron goddess of Sacral

PROLOGUE

The wind whipped grit around Rahz as he crouched in a rocky crevasse. The blasted desert known as the Wastes was one of the most desolate places on the continent, but tonight he was just one watcher among many scattered around the plain. *It is almost time.*

Sacral, Rahz's former home, would be making its return to the world, just as his master had predicted. The city had been taken by a betrayer—a former friend—who tore it out of the world to somewhere *other*, even as she ascended to godhood on a wave of stolen power.

A flicker in the valley, then a flash of light in the distance—a great black wall now stood a few hundred paces from Rahz, as familiar as the back of his own hand though he hadn't seen it in centuries. The great city-state of Sacral had indeed returned. Tens of thousands of its inhabitants crowded the battlements of the outer wall clamoring for a look *outside*. Rahz felt the commotion the appearance triggered among the other watchers in the Wastes. A host of minds and talents reached out to the great city, eager to learn more. And were slapped back by a surprisingly powerful surge of magic. The message was clear—lives could have been taken. Posturing or truth, Rahz would need to find out. His master was eager for news. But it seemed as though at least one worthwhile opponent still lived in the city; whether that person was a friend of old or a new player remained to be seen.

Brief skirmishes broke out across the Wastes, opportunists taking advantage of their rivals' distraction to strike or simply spies stumbling across each other and reacting violently. *No need to let others have all the fun.* Rahz gestured and a dozen dark-clothed forms detached themselves from the shadows and rushed off into the darkness.

It didn't take long for the crowds of Sacral to lose interest in the fields of black rock beyond their battlements. Some of them wandered atop the wall for a while, but none seemed willing to open the gates and venture outside in the dark. As the moons set, they slowly drifted back to their homes until only the odd patrol was visible passing by.

Time to see what they've done to the place. Rahz moved in fits and bursts, as silent and unpredictable as the shadow of a bat under the twin moons. He slipped over the wall unseen and moved into the broad expanse of farmland that separated the outer wall from the inner. He ran silently through long fields of grains and vegetables, pastureland and tight groves of trees—everything Sacral needed to feed and clothe its huge population.

The inner wall was even taller than the outer, designed as the last line of defense for the original inhabitants of the great city. It was as lightly guarded as the outer had been. *Wherever the city was, I guess they didn't have much to guard against,* Rahz thought as he moved into the city proper. True to her name, the White Mother's followers had repainted every black basalt building he could see white and kept everything meticulously clean. All the statues and murals Rahz remembered were gone as well, replaced by depictions of their goddess triumphing over Death—a skeleton wearing a crown—or battling a shadowy figure called the Deceiver. Rahz grunted in amusement. *Looks like she's managed to come up with a new enemy to blame her problems on.* Though he wouldn't admit it, being back in Sacral was unsettling. Everything was as he remembered it but strangely distorted, like a reflection in an imperfect mirror.

Rahz chose one of the main thoroughfares that would take him to the heart of the city—to the Great Temple. There weren't many people about at this late hour and it wasn't difficult to travel quickly without being seen. He didn't even bother taking to the rooftops as he would have in the past. Still, it was a long way and, even moving at speed, the sun was threatening to rise by the time the temple came into view.

A few early risers were starting to emerge from the houses, and Rahz was forced to hide. He saw people passing by the Great Temple—it too repainted and covered with elaborate murals of the goddess. Few of the people acknowledged the building. Those who did made only a token gesture of obeisance as they passed by. *The fires of piety have cooled here.* For a city so overfilled with religious imagery, it was surprising to see the people treat the focus of their faith as nothing more than a habit or even with indifference. *She never understood faith herself when she was mortal, so there's little surprise that she couldn't instill it in her followers.*

He settled in to his hiding place atop a large house. He would watch and wait until his master decided to act. When the time came, Rahz would move through Sacral with his Crows and reap bloody murder.

PART I

CHAPTER 1

For Maura, as for many of the inhabitants of Sacral, the return was a disappointment. The Wastes weren't much of an improvement over the featureless gray nothing that had ringed their home for so long. The priests had been talking about it for as long as anyone could remember, reminding them that the White Mother had moved the great city to reward her followers with a thousand years of peace. But now the fated day had finally come, and it was time to reclaim their rightful place in the world.

Maura joined the crowds, as eager as any of them for a look beyond their borders. She walked along the wall for a time, arm in arm with her husband, Beren, hoping to see something more, but the same featureless landscape seemed to totally surround the lush valley that housed their city. They gave up shortly before midnight and followed the stream of people who were starting the long walk back to their homes. *If the thousand years of peace are over, what does that mean for us really? And what exactly are we returning to besides rocks and dust?*

The next morning, Maura joined a few brave souls who set out to explore a little farther. The guards opened the West Gate and allowed the people to walk outside for the first time. People were excited and cheerful despite the barren landscape—until they found a corpse. A man dressed in dark leathers had been eviscerated and left in a shallow dip between two large boulders. There was blood everywhere, and flies swarmed around the remains. The excitement and curiosity in the crowd vanished in an instant, and the people all clamored to be allowed back inside. Soldiers were sent out to do a sweep of the surrounding area—they found a number of additional bodies, men and women of various descriptions, all dressed for concealment among the rocks. The number of soldiers patrolling the walls was tripled after that, and few if any citizens of the great city ventured outside the gates again. Even when merchants from foreign lands started to arrive in the following weeks, they were greeted with equal amounts of curiosity and distrust. The goods they brought were neither of a quality superior to those made locally or were far too ostentatious to appeal to the local, conservative tastes. Few returned. And for the most part, the people of Sacral went back to ignoring the existence of anything beyond their borders.

"Are you going to those damned games again?" said Maura.

". . . I am. But only because the king will be there," Beren answered.

"The king? Attending those barbaric games? I think not. Besides, it's Gerald's turn to have a day off."

"But dear, you know—"

"Between the endless hours you spend in your workshop and running off to those bloody games, it's a wonder I still recognize you. If our son weren't working for you, he'd have forgotten who you are by now."

"*Dear*, you know I have to see how my work holds up in combat. It's part of my job. Besides, most of my good ideas have occurred to me while I'm watching. And it *is* true. The priests have been shouting it all over the city this morning—the king is making an announcement at the end of the games. We can't very well miss his first public appearance in over ten years, can we? I hear it might have something to do with the last group of outsiders who've arrived. Apparently they're envoys of some sort, not merchants at all."

Maura turned her back on him, both to feign anger and to hide the smile that bubbled to the surface.

"I was about to ask you to join us, actually. I had Jerik get us some good seats so we'd be close enough to see the king."

Maura turned back to him, smiling. She did so enjoy teasing him. "Why, thank you, love. It's about time you got around to inviting me. So let's be off, shall we? Jerik dropped by an hour ago and gave me our passes."

Beren blinked at the sudden change, a momentary look of frustration flashing across his face, followed by a sheepish grin. "I was wondering why you were out here and not in the house," he admitted. "Let's get going then. We need to hurry if we're going to see the early matches." Beren grabbed Maura's hand and practically dragged her through the streets toward the arena. "Besides, my sweet, the contests are not really barbaric. Not a single competitor has died since Orik took over as arena master three years ago." Maura rolled her eyes. He just didn't know when to quit. Her husband loved his family and his work, but almost nothing got him as excited as a trip to the *contests* as he called them. "Besides, Orik is a priest of the White Mother. He wouldn't have agreed to the post if the Mother herself didn't approve of the games."

"Now, Beren, my sweet, you know he only did it to save himself the bother of walking down to the arena every week to heal the poor wounded fighters."

Beren stopped and glanced back at his wife to make sure she was joking. She smiled and he couldn't keep a straight face either. They walked on with their arms linked, both feeling lucky to have the other.

They arrived at the arena well ahead of the starting time, but the place was already busy. Hawkers were selling every conceivable food, drink, and trinket. The arena was one of the largest buildings in the city, able to accommodate ten thousand people. It was, like everything in the city, gleaming white in honor of the White Mother who had founded Sacral. The arena floor was so heavily enchanted that it could be changed to mimic different terrain types and weather conditions. Combatants squared off with real weapons here—often runed or even enchanted. When a mortal blow was about to land, the "fallen" was teleported to healing chambers below, where various priests and herbalists immediately started work on repairing whatever damage had been done. The king himself was said to have had a part in perfecting the enchantment. Control of the great magic was given over to the designated arena master.

Beren and Maura had to push their way through the crowd to get to the main entrance. Lots of people recognized Beren and waved. Many tried to ask him for tips or information about his clients. As one of the premier runesmiths in Sacral, Beren and his smith partner, Jerik, provided arms and armor for many of the contestants.

Beren wouldn't stop to talk. He had learned to stay quiet anywhere near the arena until the games were well and truly over for the week, after a stray comment from him had caused a swarm of betting in favor of one of his clients last year. *It wouldn't have been so bad if the man hadn't lost,* Maura mused.

Historically, matters of honor between any two citizens of Sacral could be settled in the arena. But as time went on, the number of grievances citizens wanted to settle in safe but real combat led the king to impose a rather hefty ring fee to anyone who wasn't a recognized member of the city guard or the army.

They took their seats. A few minutes later, Jerik arrived and sat next to Beren.

"Glad to see you both made it early."

"Hi, Jerik. You know I wouldn't miss a matchup like this. Captain Sien and Captain Gorsek! They'll be talking about this one for years."

"Big turnout by any standard. I heard people have come from farms as far away as the outer wall to hear what the king has to say. A good few I spoke to didn't even care about the contests!"

"Well, if the king's announcement was enough to draw my lovely wife here, I'll not be surprised if people are crowding outside the arena for news." Jerik grunted in amusement as Maura dug her elbow into her husband's ribs.

Maura looked on as the two men chatted about the evening's competitors. Jerik's massive frame, grizzled gray beard, and piercing blue eyes were in contrast to her bookish, absent-minded husband. Still, they were as close as brothers, and Maura couldn't imagine a better friend for Beren. She tuned out the men's conversation and looked at the royal box to their left. They were seated so close to the king himself!

Beren might not have a very good head for money, always squandering any extra he put aside on new tools or materials for his workshop, but he was very well respected and never failed to provide for his family. Unlike most of the *talented* merchants of Sacral, they did not live in a manse on the hill surrounded by servants. He paid Jerik an even share of the profits, gave generous wages to his assistant, and was generally quite free with his money. He would never be rich, and Maura loved him all the more for it.

The talented of Sacral were said to be more numerous than in any other city. Still, they were by no means common. Twenty-eight talented merchants plied their trades in the city-state of nearly three hundred thousand. There were also a hundred or so mages of varying disciplines and abilities, and rarest of them all, the Warchosen. They were warriors whose talent fueled their combat abilities and gave them superhuman strength, speed, and agility. Only sixteen true Warchosen were known to live in Sacral. They all served in the Royal Guard as bodyguards to the king, tasked with guarding the royal person and commanding his armies in the field.

The first few combats, or *contests*, Maura reminded herself, were straightforward, one-on-one fights between warriors favoring a wide variety of weapons. Most of these were low-ranking soldiers using standard-issue weaponry and armor: steel chain or scale armor and high-quality steel weapons bearing a rune. They glowed clearly as the combatants' life forces gave power to the runes.

Despite her husband's reassurances that no one would be permanently injured or killed, Maura saw warriors spray blood from a dozen wounds, and one man even had his arm severed at the elbow. Beren winced but insisted that Orik would have the poor man healed up in no time.

The last of the preliminary combats finished and horns sounded. The Speaker called out the names of the various teams and squads that would be competing, as well as the six Warchosen who would be dueling at the end of the event. The crowd cheered the combatants as they entered. The sound rose to deafening heights as the Warchosen stepped onto the arena sand and bowed first to one another, then to the assembled warriors who would compete that evening.

The sound faltered as the crowd's attention shifted, and then the cheers redoubled. The royal box was suddenly full. The king himself, the ancient archmage of Sacral, was calmly sitting back in his seat. Those who sat with him all wore varying looks of shock and disbelief.

Teleportation was the rarest of magical arts. Only a few legendary mages had ever truly mastered the incredibly complex weavings and control it required. Maura felt a flush of pride as she looked at their ruler. Though his hair was pure white and his face lined, his bearing was regal. He showed absolute confidence with his every gesture. King Ansyl was old, even for a mage. His five-hundredth birthday had been the celebration of the year. Still, he looked no different to Maura than he had a decade ago when he last addressed the public directly.

To the king's right was the high priest of the White Mother, Yeltos Rogayen. Standing behind the king was Jenus Chenton, the captain of the Royal Guard, anointed champion of the White Mother, and commander of Sacral's armies. The last two individuals were unfamiliar and clearly not locals. Both the man and the woman were heavily armored. And judging by the number of empty scabbards strapped to them, they were used to being heavily armed as well. The most shocking thing about them was the color they wore. Their breastplates were lacquered a deep blood red, as were the links of their mail. Even the leather underpadding they wore had been tinted with the unlucky color.

The games resumed. Teams of two or three faced each other, followed by full squads.

Despite herself, Maura found she was raptly watching the struggles, all the while silently cheering for the combatants who were her husband's customers. Two full companies, the Third and the Ninth, faced off in the final group battles. Each was split into a number of perfect square formations and armed with identical swords, spears, and shields. Maura noticed the two foreigners in the king's box speaking softly in their strange language. Still, their meaning was clear, and the look of mild disgust on the woman's face was unmistakable, as were her dismissive gestures.

Beren and Jerik alternately congratulated each other or shook their heads in shared disappointment as the men and women carrying their weapons and armor onto the sands won or lost. Between bouts they chatted about what had worked and what hadn't and discussed ways of improving their wares.

The excitement in the arena swelled when the Warchosen matches began. Each of these incredible warriors had the ability to single-handedly turn the tide of a battle. They traded blows with dizzying speed, riposting and parrying attacks that would have felled a lesser warrior. Each of these exceptional men and women had become legends in the city. All of them had legions of loyal fans who had come to support them, and the crowd's cheers never faltered during a match.

Again Maura looked over at the foreigners and caught the woman's sour look as she watched the combatants. The man gave her a small nod and turned to address the king. His voice was soft and had an unfamiliar lilt to it, but the words carried easily to those seated near the royal box.

"Your Majesty, you honor us with this display. Your soldiers are masters of their arts. . . . Still, one would have to wonder at their efficacy when life is truly at stake—"

The king cut him off. "I have no doubts about the abilities of Sacral's bravest sons and daughters, Kabol. And I would guess that your ruler agrees or he would not have sent you here to *beg* our aid."

The man the king had called Kabol stood and bowed deeply. "Your Majesty, I meant no disrespect. I merely wanted to suggest one final combat for this evening's entertainment.

Watching Sacral's mighty fighters has made my own companion eager to test herself against such formidable opponents. Might I suggest that sword-mistress Zorat be allowed to duel your own bodyguard?"

The king's face betrayed a flicker of concern before his mouth spread into a wide smile. He rose to his feet and spoke: "The esteemed envoy Kabol from the land of Aboleth has asked to see our champion face his own in the arena!" The crowd roared in response. "Shall we agree to this final demonstration of our might?" The crowd shouted and screamed, as chants of "Jenus" broke out from all corners. It was a rare thing for the champion to take to the sands. In his last combat he had defeated two of the Warchosen simultaneously. One of the Warchosen moved into the royal box to take up guard over the king.

The king waved his arm, and both Jenus and Zorat found themselves standing on the arena floor. Maura looked down at the man who had been Sacral's champion for nearly ten years, though he was barely into his thirties. Jenus, tall and confident, looked every inch the champion of a great nation. His chiseled features and deep-blue eyes left many a woman with a dreamy look on her face. The whole city loved him. Maura had never heard anyone say a thing against him.

Beside her Beren muttered, "That's hardly fair." Jerik grunted his agreement.

Maura raised a questioning eyebrow at him. He looked at her for a second before realizing she had no idea what he was talking about.

"Jenus is wearing his field armor. It's more heavily worked than anything else made since the founding. He usually wears standard issue to compete . . ." Beren's words trailed off as his eyes bulged. "By the White Mother and all the gods! He's unsheathing the Lightbringer!"

"The king must really want to make a point," said Jerik.

"Whatever that point is," Maura said.

It was said that the Lightbringer could only be unsheathed in defense of Sacral. The White Mother herself had given it to her first champion and charged him with the protection of her people. None living had seen it used, but the stories about the legendary blade were many. The priests claimed that the White Mother had used it to slay Death itself and thereby granted her followers eternity in her care. Now it was being drawn against a supposed ally on the arena floor.

Jenus wore a look of reverent ecstasy as he pulled the massive blade from the sheath on his back. Zorat took an involuntary step back as the weight of the ancient artifact registered. Then she shook herself like a dog shedding water and drew her two midsized blades. Somewhere between a long knife and a shortsword, the blades were oddly curved and the guards bore evil-looking barbs. The two walked slowly to their marks, staring at each other. The air between them was electric. Jenus pulled on his helm and raised his blade.

The king's voice rose above the noise of the arena again: "Begin!"

The crowd watched in awe as the two fought like forces of nature. Jenus was like a tidal wave, all fluid economy of movement and blows powerful enough to split a mountain. But if he was a tidal wave, then Zorat was a hurricane, spinning fury and lightning-fast attacks coming from every direction. She danced and dodged and spun around the champion, evading his every attack and forcing him to parry again and again. After Jenus deflected yet another series of attacks, he lunged forward, sweeping the Lightbringer across in front of him. The crowd cheered as Zorat threw herself back and the blade passed within a whisper of her chest.

Neither fighter seemed able to gain an advantage. Minutes passed. Zorat would dart forward with a flurry, which the champion would dodge and parry. Then she would throw herself out of the way of his powerful counter.

Zorat dove toward one of Jenus's thrusts. Locking her crossguards around his blade, she flipped right over the Lightbringer and swept both her swords across his chest as she came back to her feet. His white tabard was torn from him completely, and all could see the twin blackened scars etched across his breastplate. But the enchanted metal held, and the blows didn't slow the champion in the least. Zorat blocked the inevitable counterattack with both blades.

She sorely underestimated the power of the man swinging the sword, everyone would later say. Her own weapons were snapped back against her chest, and she was sent flying across the sand. She rolled when she hit the ground and came to a sudden stop against the arena wall. Both her swords lay lost in the dust. Zorat struggled to get back to her feet, but her own weapons had pierced her armor and severed her clavicles. Her arms were not responding properly. Wisps of smoke rose from the wounds. Jenus walked over to her calmly and prepared to deliver the final blow that would send her to the healing chambers below. He looked up at the crowd as the cheers redoubled.

Zorat clenched her teeth in obvious fury, and with a pained grunt threw a small knife toward the champion. Jenus flinched aside just in time. The blade barely missed his right eye. It entered the eye-slit of his helm and split the skin from the end of his eyebrow to his ear.

Jenus tore out the knife and threw it to the sand at his feet. Then he pulled off his helm and threw it at Zorat. It hit her in the face and knocked her head back against the wall. Blood poured down from a dozen cuts on her face. He then walked up to her and impaled her through the stomach. She let out a grunt of pain and vanished as he wrenched the blade out.

The crowd cheered around her, but Maura was troubled. This unknown woman had scored two hits on their greatest champion. Whether the others wanted to admit it or not, Jenus owed his victory only to his armor.

"Your champion has quite a temper, Your Majesty," said Kabol.

"He has every right to be angered. We are allies, are we not? Your woman dishonored herself breaking the rules of the arena and our city. This is a place of honorable combat. We do not abide by coward's weapons thrown to steal victory."

"Quite so, Your Majesty. I will reprimand her. Though your champion seems to have punished her sufficiently." He stood and bowed. "An impressive display in any case. Jenus is truly an exceptional man."

The king stood and spoke again: "A fine display, my champion; you have our thanks."

His voice grew louder then: "People of Sacral, the envoys from Aboleth have come to beg our aid. Their homes are under attack by vicious inhuman savages. Though they have thus far acquitted themselves honorably, they lack the numbers needed to both defend their homes and to take the fight to the enemy." The king paused and waited for the people to absorb his words. Then with a slight nod in the direction of the high priest he continued: "The White Mother herself has asked that we help these noble foreigners as best we can. After much discussion with my councillors, it has been decided that Jenus himself will lead four companies of our brave soldiers to aid our new friends."

Maura felt like she had swallowed a stone. The king didn't look happy with his own declaration. *This is all wrong. How can he send away nearly half our soldiers?* Questions swirled in her head. "The temple of the White Mother has promised to send priests and novices versed in the healing arts to care for the bodies and souls of our brave fighting men and women. So you need not fear for the well-being of your friends or family members as they go off to remind the outside world of our glory!" The crowd's cheers went on and on. The king listened for a long time before he waved them to silence.

"Now, my loyal people, I must take my leave of you. I will see you all in four days' time. I will employ my arts to speed our brave fighters to the city of Sariah." And with a slight nod of his head he was gone. The royal box was empty. The silence held for less than a second before every person in the arena started speaking.

Maura, Beren, and Jerik slowly made their way through the crowd. Looks exchanged between them were enough for Maura to know that both her husband and Jerik were as unsettled by the announcement as she was. Three quiet people in a sea of conversations. Some were excited at the prospect of a real battle; others were busy reliving the fight between Jenus and Zorat. Maura felt cut off from the people around her like never before. Surely some of them must feel as she did? But none of the faces around her betrayed the least concern. Beren led her out of the crowd at the front of the arena.

"Do you mind going home alone, my love? Jerik and I need to get back to the shop. I think we're about to get a few hundred last-minute orders from whichever companies get chosen to go."

"Of course. Go on and have fun, but don't keep Gerald there too late," she answered, trying to sound upbeat. She forced a smile onto her face. Beren looked into her eyes for a minute before nodding.

"I'll be home as soon as I can."

Maura watched him go before turning and walking quickly home.

***

Nial looked out the window and watched the moon set over the merchant quarter of Darien City. It wouldn't be long now. Her father would be home soon, drunk with today's earnings. He would be angry to find there was nothing to eat. Every day got a little worse. He spent less time at his anvil, made less money, and beat her more. The day he heard that Smith Calderson's apprentices were getting paid more for their work than he was himself, he had nearly beaten her to death. Her jaw still popped when she moved it side to side.

Nial had borrowed all she could from their neighbors to help keep them fed. She did chores and ran errands for them, but the harvests had been poor this year. Prices had gone up and few families had anything to spare. The neighbors took pity on little Nial, but they weren't willing to see their own families go without to feed a drunkard and his ten-year-old daughter. The box that had held her mother's three silver spoons and her wedding necklace had been empty for months. There was nothing left, not a scrap of food. Nothing left, and no one to turn to for help. No one was willing to confront her father. A lifetime of work at his anvil had given him prodigious strength. His huge frame and drink-maddened eyes would give a rampaging bull pause. *All in all, I'm lucky he hasn't killed me yet.* Her mind wandered as she looked out the small window. Her father came home later these nights. The taverns in the merchant quarter had all barred him from coming back, so he stomped off to the slums to drink. Now he returned in an even worse mood, feeling humiliated and angry. Nial couldn't quite bring herself to hate him for it. She could remember clearly how he had been when her mother was still alive. A laughing giant, always kind to his little daughter and doting on his beautiful wife. She could remember him boasting that they had almost saved enough money for him to be able to build a full forge. No more cold-hammering simple goods. He would be able to compete with Calderson or even Bran, the most famous smith in the city.

All that had changed when her mother got a sickness in her lungs. Her body bent double with the force of her coughing, blood staining her lips. She wasted away in just a few short days.

Nial's father spent all their savings on medicines and potions. He then prayed in the temple of Helual, the god of science and medicine, until he was asked to leave when the priests realized he didn't have enough money for a proper donation.

The door slammed and shook her out of her reverie. Nial turned away from the window and waited for him to walk to the bedroom.

"Where's my dinner, you miserable brat?" he bellowed. His voice slurred from too much cheap ale. "D'you think I work all day to come home and starve?"

Nial didn't bother answering. She had learned long ago that arguing with him was pointless. She just stood up and waited for the first blow to fall. Her lack of fear only made him angrier. He beat her harder and longer than he ever had before. When he stopped, his fists were wet with her blood.

He stumbled over to his pallet, vomited, and passed out in his own mess. Nial's mind had gone numb with the first punch. She barely felt the beating, she was so light-headed from hunger and misery. *This time is different.* Her body was going cold. But that was fine. The blood pooling under her was lovely and warm. It reminded her of the times her mother would heat pot after pot of water and they would each take a hot bath in the spare rain barrel. She couldn't wait for the water to rise and warm the rest of her cold body. Her mind went strangely blank, and she felt herself reaching out for the memory of her mother.

Nial! She struggled to move. Was that her mother calling?

My poor sweet Nial, answer me. It was a woman's voice, but it wasn't her mother. It carried a desperation of its own. Nial wanted to get up and warn the nice lady. Her father would be angry if a stranger came into the house. But it was no use, she was too weak. She couldn't move. A warm feeling flowed over her whole body.

I am like you, Nial. Weak, and my family treats me harshly. Nial felt sad for the nice woman. *There is strength within us both. If we share with each other, we will be strong indeed!* Nial smiled. It would be nice to be strong. *Our hearts will warm each other. We will never be cold or alone again. Just open yourself to me.* Nial tried to ask "How?" but her mouth wouldn't work. She almost panicked. Would her nice new friend think she didn't want to help her? *Dearest Nial, don't worry. I will never leave you alone. Now, open your heart and your mind to me. I am Zulaxrak. Take my name into your heart as I have taken yours. We will become one.*

Nial thought of the strange name. She repeated it in her mind over and over again. She offered all the love in her heart and desperately wished for Zulaxrak to love her in return. Then came a wave of ecstasy. Nial joined with another being in a way that few ever can. They shared consciousness, knowledge, and lives as the essence of Zulaxrak was drawn into Nial's body.

Nial gasped as a seemingly endless stream of images and memories flooded into her mind. She understood now that Zulaxrak was a demon. *Zuly,* she thought affectionately. A fledgling succubus. Bigger, stronger demons had often tormented her. She had fled her world into the void just as a great brute of a Scar demon was about to devour her. In Zuly's mind,

Nial saw the demon world she had come from. A dark waste. Stone, dust, and desolation. Various demons mated or were raped and spawned young in the fetid pools that dotted the stony landscape. The demons that hatched were as varied in their forms as their parents had been. From the moment they hatched, the battle to survive began and never ended. Demons consumed, used, or enslaved each other to grow in power. They did not require food or water to live. But the hunger to grow, the hunger for more strength and power, was more intense by far. The strong dominated while the weak ended up as dinner. With each new kind of demon they consumed, they would evolve, gaining some of the powers of the fallen. The greatest demons were those that managed to find a way to a mortal realm to consume souls. The souls became bound within the demon—even if the demon was defeated and banished back to the demon world. A demon grew mighty with just a single soul. Amon Kareth, the archdemon of this world, had consumed thousands.

Zuly shuddered in pleasure at the rush of power. She saw how Nial and her parents lived and how her mother died. She saw the beatings in the child's memories and understood. Their worlds were different in many ways, but the rule of strength was the same. She had thought to offer the child all kinds of things to allow her to enter, to bind her wasted essence to Nial's body to save herself. But Nial had pulled her in deeply, had shared her body with Zuly completely and without hesitation. Pushed to desperation, they had each found a comfort and kinship in the other. The bond they had formed was a strange one. Zuly didn't understand it very well. She thought they had each become the other's familiar. Zuly herself was surprised by the fading of her hunger. For the first time in her existence she felt safe and almost at peace.

Nial, you are a mage of great power. You might not have known what you were doing, but you called me here. You helped me open the way. Our talents will feed off each other and we will become mighty. No one will ever hurt us again.

Nial felt the blood being drawn back into her body. *Your blood is far too precious. We mustn't waste a single drop.* Nial pulled herself to her feet and walked over to her own pallet. She drifted off to sleep with a smile on her lips.

Nial woke up long before her father and started to clean the house as she had done every day since her mother had died. She thought of the previous night, not sure if it had been a dream.

Her skin was unmarked. She looked at her reflection in the rain barrel and saw that her face wasn't even bruised. She whispered, "Zuly?"

I am here with you, Nial. I will always be here. The voice came from inside her head.

"Zuly! I was afraid you were only a dream."

I'm happy to say sometimes dreams come true.

Nial sighed in relief and continued chatting happily with her new friend as she went about her chores. An hour past midday, as she was sweeping the leaves from their lane, she heard her father fumbling around in the kitchen, looking for food and drink.

"Nial! Where are you? You worthless child!" She had never heard him so angry when he wasn't drunk. Fear kept her standing outside.

Don't fear, sweet Nial. Remember, you are no longer alone.

"Thank you, Zuly! It's just that he's so angry."

You have nothing to fear. Now let's go inside and deal with your father where no one else can see.

Nial let the twig broom fall in the dust and walked into the house. She was not alone now. She would not be afraid, not ever again. Her father was breaking empty jugs and plates, building up his temper.

"First no dinner and now no breakfast?!" Zuly and Nial looked back at him from inside their shared body, not bowing her head as he had expected.

"If you didn't spend every coin on cheap drink, maybe I'd be able to buy food." His bloodshot eyes went wide with surprise. "And if you woke up earlier, I wouldn't have to tell your customers to take their money somewhere else." The girls could see shame and anger warring in his eyes. Anger won.

"You sniveling little bitch! How dare you speak to me that way! I should sell you! Then I wouldn't be wasting half my food on you." The back of his hand cracked against her face. The girls stumbled back. Their mouth was bleeding, but they were smiling.

"That was the last time you will ever hit me, Father."

Zuly came forward and showed Nial how to use the magic inside her. Invisible power reached out and grabbed Nial's father as he was about to swing again. His eyes bulged as his arms were slowly twisted behind his back. Slowly the girls increased the pressure until he groaned in pain.

"Now, *Father*," said Zuly. "I will explain how our new lives will be. You will get up at dawn every morning. You will stand on the street at the end of the lane and shout out your services like a street hawker until two hours past dusk. Any and all coin you receive, you will hand directly to me. I will continue to clean and cook, but I'm through doing it without you doing your part." The girls dropped him in a heap on the floor. He stared at Nial. The voice and body were those of his daughter, but the words were more mature by far.

"Freak! Witch! Possessed! I'll have the priests burn you alive!"

Zuly just laughed. "The drunkard who beats his daughter is afraid because the child is making him do his work? Who would believe you? Now, enough talking. Get outside to the rain barrel and clean yourself up. You have work to do." He just sat on the floor staring dumbly at her.

"I wasn't asking, Father." Zuly's power flowed out, gripped him around the head, and dragged him toward the door. He was whimpering as urine stained his breeches and ran down to the floor. "And, Father, if a single drop of ale or wine passes your lips, you will suffer for it. Do we understand each other?" Without waiting for an answer, Nial opened the door and threw him outside. With a smile on her face and a spring in her steps, she went back to her chores.

Nial, I'm bored . . . Let's go out and play!

"But I haven't finished cleaning yet."

You clean every day. It's clean already. And you need a break.

"Father has been working hard; I just want to do my part too."

I know you're a good girl, Nial, but he did nothing for years. And the house really isn't going to get any cleaner no matter how long you scrub it. We'll only go out for an hour, all right?

"I guess an hour would be fine. It would be nice to play in the sun."

As they left the house, Nial could hear her father's hammer ringing clearly through the early afternoon bustle of the merchant quarter. It was a happy sound. It made her think of times when her mother had still been alive. He had taken Zuly's warning to heart and didn't drink a drop. He worked every day until he was exhausted. With Nial's permission he used some of his earnings to buy extra metals and worked them into a variety of shapes to hawk on the street while he looked for more customers. Word was getting around about the quality of his work, and more and more customers came down the lane to see him. Building a real forge was becoming a goal again.

"This was a good idea, Zuly. We haven't been out for anything but going to the market in weeks."

I want to show you something, Nial. I've been exploring the city at night. While you sleep my mind is free to wander. Memories played out for Nial of a small door at the end of an alley. All kinds of strangely dressed people were going in and out of the place. *This is where I want to go.*

"Of course, Zuly." Nial smiled and skipped down the street. Some of the people Zuly had shown her looked really funny. Passersby smiled at the happy little girl hopping down the street talking to herself.

Zuly guided them down several smaller and darker streets until they came out into a muddy little alley. The smell was foul. Refuse was piled in the streets.

"What is this place, Zuly? It smells bad."

This is where your father used to come to drink. These are the slums, or the Muds. The poorest people in the city live here.

"The slums are a bad place. My mother always told me bad people live here."

Not all of them are bad, sweet Nial. The really bad people mostly only come out at night when they don't have to try so hard to hide what they do. But the place I sensed isn't far.

They walked through several more filthy streets. The ground was nothing but a squelching mess of mud and worse. The sewers didn't even extend into this part of the city. Rats scurried around, darting away from mud-caked urchins. Every second door seemed to be a brothel or a run-down drinking house. Overly thin, tired women looked out of windows and tried to catch the attention of passing men. On the street there were few people. The children she saw moved quickly and looked over their shoulders often. There were some older prostitutes, men and women both, past their best earning years and cast out of the brothels, wandering around with lost looks. They called out to the few men who walked by in threadbare clothing.

Nial was shocked. Her home in the merchant quarter, modest as it was, had not prepared her for this squalor. How could people who were so terribly poor and sad live just a few minutes' walk from her house?

We're almost there, said Zuly. *We just need to go to the end of this street and take the next right.* Nial walked faster, eager to get this little errand of Zuly's out of the way. As they reached the end of the street and turned into the little alley on the right, they saw a man looking at them strangely. He was wearing a brown cloak with the hood up even on this nice sunny summer day. Other than the mud stains around the hem, it looked far cleaner and newer than the clothes everyone else was wearing. They couldn't see his face clearly, but he made Nial's skin crawl looking at her the way he was. They rushed past him and walked down to the end of the alley. It was a dead end. Only a single dingy-looking wood door marked the muddy brick walls.

"Lost are you, little bird?" They spun around. The man had followed them. He sounded like the few customers Nial's father had who wore really nice clothes. But it made her feel dirty having this man talk to them, even more than walking barefoot through all the filth.

"How lucky for both of us that I was the one to find you."

"I'm not lost, sir. I'm just out for a walk," Nial said as she backed away from him.

"Of course you are. Now come here, little bird. I'll take good care of you." He sounded angry now. He stepped closer. They could see his face in the shadows of his hood. A normal-looking man that Nial wouldn't have noticed if he hadn't been looking at her with such a scary, hungry look. He dashed forward and tried to grab Nial but came up short. He looked back, wondering what was holding him back, but he couldn't see anything. Zuly had stopped him with her magic. She tightened it all around him, forcing his arms to his sides.

"What . . . ?" He started to shout before Zuly snapped his mouth shut. His eyes were wide now. The hunger in them had fled. Nial could see only terror.

I'm sorry, Nial. I really thought we'd get here without attracting so much attention during the day. But I guess it's for the best. This horrible man will give us something to trade with.

"Trade with?" asked Nial. *Yes, this place is a store. A very special store. We have to hurry. We can't be seen out here like this.*

Zuly reached out and pushed on the wood door with their magic. It swung inward silently. They walked into the strangest shop Nial had ever seen. There were bundles of herbs and plants all around the room like in the apothecary she had visited with her father when her mother was sick. But all kinds of other strange things were scattered around as well: pieces of animals, dried or floating in jars like pickles; jagged pieces of stone or metal; small statues; and even some jewelry hanging from hooks on the wall behind the counter. A man entered the room from the far side. He was totally hairless and wore only a pair of knee-length breeches. The rest of his body was covered with a dizzying pattern of tattoos and scars. Seemingly random objects—glass, metal, and even small tools—pierced any patch of skin he could conceivably reach.

His dark eyes were bright as he welcomed Nial to his store: "Welcome, little lady. What can old Skeg do for you this fine day?" His voice was raspy, each word strangely drawn out. He seemed to be totally ignoring the man floating behind them.

"Hello, Mister Skeg," answered Zuly. "We're looking for a sphere of polished obsidian. About twice the size of my fist should do."

Skeg's eyes widened slightly when Zuly said "we," and he looked at them intently for a moment before answering. "I think I have something that could do the trick. Obsidian is not widely used in this city so you're lucky." He stepped around the counter and through a curtain. "I won't be a moment."

He reappeared a minute later with a black glassy orb in his hands. The reflections off it were faintly green. "Will this do?"

"It's perfect," said Zuly. "Do you have tools to carve it as well?"

"I might have something here somewhere." He ran his hands over his body and pulled two sharp little glass carving tools out of the skin on the small of his back. Both the tools were faintly wet with blood. Zuly nodded.

"Now about payment. . . . I assume the gentleman behind you will be handling that part of our transaction?" Zuly nodded again.

"He will, but only his body. His soul is ours."

Skeg's eyes widened so much that Nial thought they would fall out of his head. ". . . and you can do that?" he asked.

"We can. But we'll need a safe place to do it. We don't want to get noticed." She stared at him.

"Of course, of course. The back room is fully warded. You should be able to do whatever you need there." He gestured for her to follow him and walked back through the curtain behind the counter.

The back room was musty and bare. The whitewash was mildewed, and a small, rickety staircase was set against the back wall. A tattered straw rug covered the floor. Skeg knelt down and rolled it up. Beneath it, the stone floor had been carved with a wide swirl of strange letters and shapes that radiated out from a central point almost to the walls.

"Some customers need to use this from time to time. It should mask near anything a single talent can whip up, should keep any noise in as well," said Skeg. "Is this going to be messy?"

"It might be," answered Zuly. "If you bring me a basin, I should be able to keep most of the blood in it."

Skeg nodded and rushed back out to the store. Nial was sure she had seen his hands shaking.

He came back in with a large wood washbasin. "Where would you like it?"

Zuly pointed to the center of the circle. He nodded and set it down, then gave a little nod and walked back out into the store. Zuly used their power and made the man they had caught float over the basin. *Nial? You may not want to watch this part. I'm going to hurt this bad man.*

"Is he really so bad?" Nial answered out loud. *I can taste it coming off him, my sweet Nial. I can tell what kind of person he is. He has caused a lot of pain to those around him, especially girls. Worse, he likes it. And wants nothing more than to do it again and again.* Nial nodded, accepting what Zuly told her. Her mother had been harsh but fair. Punishment was something she understood.

"Okay, Zuly. I'll try not to watch." *That's good, Nial. But even if you peek, remember what I am going to do to this monster is not nearly as bad as he deserves.* Zuly relaxed part of her binding and released the man's jaw.

"I will give you one chance to make this quick and painless." The man stared at her, his eyes wild.

"Please! Please!" he screamed. "I won't do it again, I swear! I've got money! I have rich friends! I could get you gold if you let me go!"

Zuly looked at him impassively. "You will repeat after me: I grant you power over my soul."

"You're mad!" the man screeched.

"You will say it, little man. And you will mean it with your whole being. I will know when you do. Till then . . ." She gestured and a small cut appeared across his cheek. Slowly the cut lengthened and branched into two. Each new cut branched again and extended down under his tunic. The man's desperate screams changed pitch as the pain hit him. Zuly gestured impatiently, and his clothes split along the seams and floated across the room to land in a heap. The cuts continued to grow and to multiply. Blood started to drip down into the washbasin. "Say the words and I will end your pain," said Zuly.

Skeg paced back and forth in his shop after the little girl had taken the man in the back room. He traded in some dark things, being one of the only merchants in the city who catered to unlicensed mages. He had also seen his share of corpses and even one or two people killed in front of him. But the child treating the man she carried around like nothing more than meat, and the intent to butcher him like an animal, left him unnerved to say the least. He did not judge his customers. He wouldn't have survived long if he had. But what was stopping the girl from doing the same to him? She said she didn't want to be noticed. Maybe that would be enough to keep him safe. His own feeble talent was nothing compared to hers. He could barely move a cup of water across a table, much less float around a grown man with barely a thought. He'd never turned on a customer before, but he might have to send a note to the Night Guard about this one.

An interminable wait later, the girl walked back out. She had the orb clutched tightly in one hand. Skeg could see a spark moving around inside it. There wasn't a drop of blood on her.

"Mister Skeg?" she called, the voice now that of a child. "We're done. We left things as neat as we could. You can keep his clothes and his purse." Skeg nodded and walked them out. It was almost an hour before he worked up the nerve to cross through the curtain. He gaped at what he saw. The body had been left floating above the basin. Its skin had been removed in a single ragged piece and was folded neatly next to the man's clothing. Not a drop of blood had been spilled outside the basin. Skeg shivered and got to work. He'd have little trouble selling the dead man to one of the less official cults in the city or to any one of a dozen aspiring necromancers, but he could only guess how long it would be till the buyers would come to collect. He'd have to take him down to the cold cellar, but how was he going to get him down?

Outside in the empty alley, Zuly lifted up the sphere and watched the spark dance around inside it. *Look at it, Nial! Isn't it pretty?* Nial traced a finger across the sphere following the light.

"It's very pretty."

Once I have time to carve and enchant the stone, we can draw on its power. Each soul we claim will make us stronger. Nial could feel the hunger in Zuly. It had faded since they joined and was scarcely comparable to what she had felt from Zuly's memories of *before*, but still it gnawed at her.

"So we have to find another bad man?"

Any souls will do, my sweet Nial. But for you, we will only hunt the wicked. People like that man come to the slums to hurt people no one cares about. The city guards don't come to the Muds unless they have to, and people disappear around here every day. We can turn their game on them.

Nial considered silently for a moment "All right, Zuly. We can go out again. But not until next week and only if we've finished our chores."

Oh, thank you, Nial! I hoped you'd understand! The happy little girl skipped back home smiling, carrying a man's soul like a firefly dancing in a jar.

CHAPTER 2

Salt walked through the dock district like he owned the place. Every time he returned to Darien City, the great capital of Bialta, after another stint at sea, he felt like the world was his. He was free to do as he pleased, and the coins in his pocket were enough to see him well fed and housed for a month. The stench from the vomit and less identifiable wastes clogging the gutters of the port streets was simply a welcome break from the different stinks and cramped quarters of the merchant ship's hold.

The port was a riot of colors and smells. As one of the largest port cities in the North as well as the seat of the Arcanum— Bialta's famed school of magic—Darien attracted a dizzying assortment of visitors from all over the known world. Salt heard dozens of languages being spoken and walked around the usual profusion of beggars without stopping.

With luck I might not have to ship out again for a week. Not that he was really worried. He had a good reputation with the city's captains. It never took him more than a day or two to find work again. He worked hard and rarely let drink interfere with his duties or his life. His weakness was soft company in his bed. He knew from experience that the ladies in the dockside brothels could empty his pockets in a matter of hours given half the chance. And letting them do so was certainly tempting after nearly four months at sea.

No. I need to try and make my money last a little this time. I really need some new clothes and a room at the very least before I spend anything else. Determined, Salt passed the cheap taverns and brothels where most of his shipmates were happily being relieved of their wages.

He walked past a particularly wretched-looking hole called the Empty Barrel. A drunkard burst out of the place yelling something unintelligible and collided with Salt. Salt reached down to make sure his coins were still in his pocket. The man bit back an angry outburst when he looked up at Salt's imposing frame. He stood nearly a head taller than the drunk, and his broad body was hardened by long months at sea. His rough wiry red beard and ragged hair gave him a wild appearance.

He growled down at the smaller man until a woman walked past, her mesmerizing blue-green eyes interrupting his thoughts. He nearly tripped over a heap of empty crates as he watched her pass by. With a curse he pushed the drunkard aside and looked back at her, but the woman was just disappearing into a side street. He was sure he had heard her laugh as he stumbled.

His good intentions quickly forgotten, Salt set off after her through a maze of filth-ridden streets and alleyways, always just catching sight of her gray cloak disappearing around the next corner. Each time, he thought he heard the sound of soft laughter.

Salt's blood was up. He was jogging now, a wide grin on his face, eager to catch this strange beauty who wanted to play with him. His smile widened when he jumped around a corner, certain that he had finally caught her in a dead-end alley. He was half right—it was a dead end. But the woman wasn't there. The alley was dark, but unquestionably empty. He looked down at the moldy stacks of junk and a dead rat, wondering where she could possibly have gone.

"How in all the hells . . . ," he cursed under his breath. He turned away and almost collided with her. She was standing directly behind him, hands on her hips, a smile on her lips.

"Hi, sailor. Were you following me?" Salt couldn't answer her just yet. She smelled wonderful, even in this stink pit of an alley. A subtle fragrance that made him think of cookies and soft soap. Nothing at all like the chokingly sweet scents the brothels girls wore. Her gray cloak was certainly well made. Her skin was pale and clear, her teeth perfect. Her dark-brown hair was pulled back from her face, most of it hidden beneath her hood.

Shaking himself, he stammered, ". . . Er, y-y-yes, I was . . ." He felt horribly unsure of himself now—a child in front of this beautiful woman.

"Well? Why were you following me, sailor boy?" The word *boy* stung him into action. He wrapped his arms around her. His mouth moved to hers. Her reaction was all that he'd hoped for and more. Her soft lips opened to him and her tongue met his. Her mouth was so sweet he never wanted the kiss to end. Her body melted into his, her soft curves pressed up against his whole body. His mind was spinning, his blood on fire.

"Come with me," she whispered, her breath hot on his ear. "I have a room nearby."

All Salt could do was grunt his agreement. He wasn't thinking about the rest of the month anymore, or even his next meal. She quickly led him to a worn door with peeling green paint, little different from any other in these back alleys. She pushed it open. Stumbling inside, Salt barely kept himself from gawking at what he saw. The peeling paint ended at the door frame. The inside was freshly whitewashed. Red and white flowers were set in large clay vases about the single room. Almost the entire space was taken up by a massive feather bed, the likes of which Salt had never even dreamed of sleeping in. The room was dimly lit by an oil lamp set on a small table next to the bed. The mystery woman wasted no time, pushing Salt onto the bed and dropping her cloak. She wore nothing underneath. She stood there for a moment, allowing him to admire the perfection of her body, before throwing herself on top of him.

What followed was the most passionate, most intense, and by far the most amazing sexual encounter Salt had ever dreamed of. He didn't know how much time had passed when he dropped into an exhausted sleep, blissfully content in the wonderfully soft bed with the beautiful stranger next to him.

Salt opened his eyes at the feel of a light slap on his face. The mysterious woman was straddling his hips. His arms and legs had been expertly tied to the four bedposts, and the lamp had been lit again. At first he thought this might be another game—he was tied down naked, and she was still naked too. Then he saw the knife in her hand.

"Awake yet, lover?" She slapped him again, harder this time. She slowly ran the jagged edge of the knife across the skin of his chest. "I want you to be fully awake and aware. I wouldn't want you to miss a second of what's coming. You fulfilled your first task admirably. Now we'll see how you are at satisfying a darker need within me."

Salt began to pull against the ropes again; fear and helplessness were taking over.

"Oh, don't fight it, my sweet sailor. You gave me great pleasure. Your body is unexpectedly clean and healthy, and your spirit is strong indeed. I am not only going to kill you and feed on your flesh—though that is part of it, I admit; I also am sac-rificing you to my mistress, She Who Feeds."

Salt began to struggle in earnest now. "Let me go! You crazy bitch! You can't do this!"

"Now now," she said, easily keeping her place on top of him. "You said last night that the joy you found in my arms was worth any price. I am exacting that price. I will feast on your flesh and send your soul to my mistress. You will serve as her consort for the coming year. You will sire a new clutch of eggs for her just as you have sired a new child within me. You will be granted a full year of ecstasy in her realm before she consumes your soul. Laying a full clutch of eggs will leave her weak-ened and you can't blame her for being hungry after all." She grinned, enjoying his panic. Without further warning she drew the blade down his chest along his sternum. Salt screamed and struggled even harder. His wrists and ankles were bleeding as freely as his chest, staining the white bed linens crimson. The priestess just smiled and leaned down to lick the blood that ran down to his stomach.

The door exploded off its hinges, smashing to splinters against the opposite wall.

"You won't escape this time, witch!" came a shout from outside. A crossbow bolt took her in the side of the neck. She didn't scream as the bolt hit her. Cracks radiated out across her skin from where it had pierced her skin, grubs and maggots spilling out. The priestess howled in fury. She raised the blade, intent on finishing off Salt. Instead, she fell apart, her once smooth skin dissolving in an instant into a revolting mass of insects. Salt screamed in disgust as the mess skittered, crawled, and slithered across his body, each small creature fleeing.

A grizzled-looking city guardsman rushed into the room. A bulky, middle-aged woman in stained dark-blue robes was right on his heels. A wall of fire sealed the doorway behind her.

The guardsman was stomping on as many of the crawling things as he could as they rushed away in every direction. The woman began to bang the iron foot of her staff against the floor. With each blow, growing waves of fire swept out along the floorboards from the impact.

"Gurt, you fool, you know you shouldn't have gone in ahead of me. Now I have to cleanse you again."

"Dammit, we got the bitch this time, let me enjoy it!"

The floorboards were blackening under the pulses of fire. The underside of the bed was beginning to smoke. Gurt looked down at Salt.

"Looks like we got here just in time, eh, lad?"

"Just get him off the bed, Gurt; I'll have to burn it and cleanse him as well."

Gurt pulled a dagger from his belt and cut the ropes restraining Salt. Staggering to his feet, Salt clutched the cut across his chest. "It's all right, lad, the cut isn't deep. Now hurry up and walk through the doorway. We'll have a healer see to you outside."

Salt rushed toward the door but hesitated before stepping into the flames.

"Go on, it won't hurt you, though you won't have much hair left on the other side," said Gurt, just before shoving the dazed sailor through the fire. Salt felt a wave of heat followed by the stench of burning hair, and then cool night air. It looked to be about an hour before dawn. The sky was a deep purple just beginning to lighten to blue. A half-dozen soldiers were standing in a loose arc around the doorway, crossbows and spears trained on him. Gurt stepped out behind him. His leather armor fell off him into a heap of ash and metal buckles. He stood unashamedly in front of the soldiers rubbing his hand over his newly bald head.

"Wheeze! Come see to the lad's scratch. Seely, stop gawking and get me some clothes or a blanket or something. Find something for the lad while you're at it."

A harried-looking soldier in his forties jogged over, breathing heavily. He sounded like he was about to pass out as he struggled to draw each gasping breath. In one hand he held a bag, which he set down at Salt's feet before he started to examine his wound. The soldier didn't say a word. *Probably can't spare the breath with all his wheezing.* A girl who couldn't have been more than sixteen handed Salt an old blanket while trying her best not to look anywhere near him and blushing furiously. *And that must be Seely.*

Salt wrapped the blanket around his hips, nodding thanks to the girl. The medic put a simple bandage on Salt's chest and rushed off. His wheezing never changed pitch. Salt ran his hands across his body and over his head. Nothing but clean skin. His wild hair and straggly beard, even his eyebrows and lashes were gone. His skin had never felt so smooth. *I wonder if that mage woman is going to charge me for the shave and haircut.* He started laughing. Low at first, but the laughter just kept bubbling up until tears were running down his face. Gurt, now dressed in a blanket similar to Salt's own, took him by the arm.

"Come on, lad. It's been a rough night. You've had a real shock, but you've come through it with nothing more than a scratch. Why not join me and my men in a little victory celebration?" Salt muffled his laughs in his arm and managed a nod. Gurt turned back to the waiting soldiers.

"Tell Krigare to take a couple lads and clean up when Lera finishes inside. Shouldn't be long. You can join us at the Red Rat when you're done." The soldiers nodded and went about their work.

Salt followed Gurt's lead. He didn't know or care where they were going. After a few minutes, they came to a large tavern that obviously catered to soldiers. Nearly every man or woman in the place was wearing a uniform from the city guard, or one of the other branches of the Bialtan military.

Gurt and the others were quickly recognized. Many greeted them by name when they arrived, some commenting sarcastically about blankets becoming their new uniform. Within minutes, two long tables were cleared for the new arrivals as several soldiers congratulated them and offered to buy them celebratory pints. *Recognized and respected,* thought Salt. Still, he didn't ask any questions. He just drained the tankard that was set in front of him. More drinks followed. Lera and the other soldiers joined them, and one of soldiers had brought Salt his coins from the wreckage of the priestess's home; then even more drinks followed. Salt didn't take much notice of the conversation beyond the repeated toasts and cheers of "We got the bitch!" and "The bloody bitch is finally gone for good!" Gurt didn't seem the least uncomfortable sitting there dressed only in his blanket, and Salt let himself relax as he poured down the succession of drinks that were placed in front of him.

Salt woke up in the morning with a groan. His head was splitting with the worst hangover he could remember. The room spun around him. *Room?* Where was he anyway? The narrow bed he lay in was hard, the sheets rough but not unpleasantly so. The room was dark. He could only vaguely see the stone wall next to him and the hint of a large dark space around him. Now that he was thinking past the pain in his head he could hear other people in the darkness beyond, at least a couple breathing deeply and one snoring softly.

He thought back to the previous night. He could remember pints, a lot of them. He couldn't be sure just how many. There was something else too, some half-remembered drunken heart-to-heart with Gurt.

Salt reached up and gingerly touched his chest. A bandage was tightly bound over the cut, but it didn't hurt too much. His wrists were also covered in scabs from struggling against the ropes the priestess had bound him with. He sat up and fumbled in the darkness for a light. His hand found a heavy curtain against the wall above his bed. A quick tug and he was blinded by the afternoon sun. He blinked against the glare and saw a large courtyard below him.

"Gods, lad!" He heard Gurt's sleepy voice. "Close that bloody curtain. Some of us are still trying to sleep off last night's celebration."

Salt looked around at a barracks. A group of soldiers were glaring at him through half-open eyes. Salt closed the curtain. "Sorry," he croaked, his voice raw.

"S'okay, lad, but try to get back to sleep. We start your training tonight."

Salt let his head fall back to the pillow before the words sunk in. Last night's conversation returned to him in striking clarity—an invitation to join some group called the Night Guard. Warnings of it being a tough path to walk and lots of talk of hunting the hunters. *Fuck me blind. . . . I went and joined the army.*

***

The Tolrahkali had come to the continent almost five centuries ago according to the local histories. Where they came from, no one could quite agree on, not even the Tolrahkali themselves. Their skin, unlike the other humans living on the continent, was a deep golden brown. Tales told of a fleet of great ships that arrived with a storm one night. Dozens of the ships were wrecked as they collided with the rocky coast. It was to their credit that any of them survived on the shore of the

Great Desert. Barely a handful of date palms grew out of the earth, drinking up what little water passed beneath the sands. On one point all the historians agree though: the Tolrahkali found a way to control the Korant ants that lived in the area. Korant ants were about the size of large dogs. As the Tolrahkali builders, the ants burrowed deep below the earth to dig for resources for their masters. They carried impossibly heavy stones and built for them the great city that the current king of the Tolrahkali, or the Drokga, as he styled himself, still ruled.

The city of Tolrahk Esal, meaning literally Tolrahk home, stood on a wide plain on the southern edge of the Great Desert, known locally as the Green Sea. Its strangely organic architecture and smooth, slick buildings made it unique in all the known world.

If the North had a common refuse pit, then Tolrahk Esal was it. The city, last and least of the Free Cities, was a moldering sore on the edge of civilization. The Tolrahkali had no farmlands or mines beyond those of the Korant ants. No great craftsmen like the Dreth, no great scholars and mages like the Bialtans, no great priests like the Abolians, or famous artists like the Keralans. The Tolrahkali had only themselves, but they were happy to trade. From the first, the greatest exports of the city-state were slaves, prostitutes, and mercenaries. The mercenary companies that sold their services in the city were now countless, as were the pleasure palaces. The slave markets were always crowded, and the blood sports in the city's many arenas always attracted large crowds. Though slavery was illegal in most of the northern nations, many were the rich and powerful who imported a handful of the wretches for a variety of unsavory tasks.

Carver had only been in Tolrahk Esal a few hours. He looked out over the city from a balcony in a modest inn and waited with a patience that seemed unnatural. His thinning gray hair hung in a lank mess in front of his wrinkled, gray-skinned face. He constantly had to brush it aside to see, a task made difficult by his twisted spine and weak legs. He was never without a sturdy walking stick and, because of it, could never use more than one hand for anything while standing. Physically, he well knew, he was the object of pity at best, revulsion at worst. He watched multitudes of people scurry around like the oversized insects that served them. Their meaningless lives were devoted to the trivial pursuits of wealth and self-indulgence.

Carver's sworn enemy was disorder. Disorder created the corruption, pain, and death that mortals brought to one another time and again. Following the example of his former master, he was striving to find a solution, a way of fixing civilization, of creating something truly eternal. He had yet to find a solution in his thousand years of searching. But what was time to him? He had conquered death, and one day, he was sure, he would remake the world.

He looked down at the people, free men or slaves, going about their business, none more significant than a worm to him. *Strange that the very things I loathe most make it easier for me to carry out my work.* Tolrahk Esal sickened him. Nothing would give Carver greater satisfaction than to grind the whole corrupt mess to dust. *There will be time enough for that later. For now, the Tolrahkali offer unique opportunities and resources. And I'll have to worm my way into the favor of their tyrant to get them.*

The Tolrahkali themselves, those golden-skinned descendants of the original seafaring people, were not half as self-indulgent as the multitudes of visitors and foreign residents. They were warriors all. The only thing they respected was strength, and the greatest soldiers and generals among them were given a level of respect that the local temples could only dream of.

There were other paths to power in the city though. Carver had seen the adulation granted a famed weaponsmith or a talented healer. That was how he would win a place among these barbarians. He would give them the means to kill more efficiently.

He needed to catch the attention of someone in power, of course, but it seemed like Tolrahk Esal was a city made for displays of power and force. Carver had counted seven arenas and fighting pits in his short walk into the city proper. One of those would give him the opportunity he needed. That the Tolrahkali traded in flesh and that most, though by no means all, of the gladiators who fought in the pits and arenas were slaves would work to his advantage. Showing what his arts could do for a pit fighter would attract all the attention he needed. A sudden transformation in a lowly combatant would be a better demonstration, but no one in power would attend such a display, nor would anyone remember the fighter's previous lack of prowess. No, he would need to purchase a famous slave. Perhaps one who'd been maimed or crippled. His funds were limited, so he'd need to choose his subject carefully—there would be no second chance.

A clear goal in mind, Carver set out to find the highest-profile arena in the city. *A few days to find a likely subject, a few weeks to prepare him for a return to the arena. Two days for the Drokga to invite me into the palace after that.*

As it turned out, only one arena hosted combats between Chosen or magically equipped combatants. It was a small place that only held bouts once every twenty days. Only the richest could afford to attend the exclusive fights.

Carver arrived early to the small arena on fight day. He sacrificed the gold coin to pay the exorbitant entrance charge, eager to start looking over potential subjects. The arena assigned a slave to attend to his needs while he was there. The slave led him to a comfortable seat overlooking the sands. Awnings were stretched over each seat to protect the patrons from the harsh desert sun, as well as to offer some small level of anonymity.

"Would you care for some refreshment, my lord?"

Carver ignored the question. "Who is fighting today? Are any of them famous?"

Apparently well used to ignorant foreigners attending the games, the slave answered without hesitation. "Several popular fighters are taking to the sands today, my lord. Iraxtes, Godchosen of the lady of the thirsting sands, will fight a Godchosen from a rival god, Craltic, champion of the god of storms and skyfire. I have seen both fight in the past; they should provide an impressive show." Carver fought down the urge to berate the slave over the Tolrahkali superstition against naming gods and let him continue.

"The Old Man will also fight at the end of the day. He is the greatest champion this arena has ever known. He has been fighting for seven years and has yet to take a wound. He'll be facing Maran Vras, a champion only slightly less famous than the Old Man himself. Maran is a brute of a man, vicious and bloodthirsty. They will fight to the death today."

Carver was disappointed. It was hardly surprising that a large number of warriors had sworn service to one of the many desert gods in exchange for power in a city like Tolrahk Esal. But Godchosen were of no interest to him. He refused to fight for control over one of his creations with an upstart deity. Since the only other high-profile match was a death match, it likely wouldn't be possible for him to purchase either fighter.

"And the rest of the day?" asked Carver.

"Combatants of varying skill, my lord. Some may be Chosen; others carry objects of power. Many should provide entertainment."

Carver sighed. He would have to watch and hope that one of the lesser fighters would prove adequate. He didn't want to waste nearly another month waiting for the next round of fights. He settled in for an afternoon of violence, measuring each specimen's merits and interrogating the slave about each combatant's popularity and owner.

The Old Man was the oldest champion in Tolrahk Esal, easily thirty years the senior of any other gladiator in the city. And yet, in the seven years since he'd signed himself up to fight as a free man, he had never been defeated. No one had ever drawn blood or landed even the most trivial of blows on him in almost ninety duels. That he was some kind of Chosen was widely accepted, though none could agree whether he was Warchosen or the champion of some obscure god. The champion kept his own counsel. The Old Man was all that he called himself. No one had been able to dig up anything else about him, who he was or where he came from. The mystery only fueled his popularity.

Walking out slowly onto the sands, the Old Man took his place at the center of the arena. If he heard the shouts and cheers of thousands of fans, he made no sign. He just trudged forward, dragging his oversized weapon with him, its design somewhere between a halberd and a falchion. A wide blade extended up the side of the spear shaft with a few handholds cut into it, then extended another arm's length beyond the shaft tip in a curved sweep. The shaft dug a deep furrow into the sands behind the Old Man as he struggled to drag it into place. The champion was not the only gladiator to disdain the use of armor, but few went so far as to fight in a loincloth and sandals as he did. He stood next to his strange weapon, sweat already running freely down his body, a body that would not seem exceptional for any man in his late seventies. His wrinkled skin hung loosely off his skeletal frame. His chest heaved as he fought to catch his breath.

Today's challenger was more what one would expect of a pit fighter. He had Tolrahkali coloring though he was obviously of mixed heritage; his eyes had an odd yellowish hue, and bony plates growing over his skin in patches betrayed deep desert blood. His body had been oiled up before he came out onto the sands to better show off his impressive physique. Tall and lean with tight ropes of muscle bunching under his skin, Maran Vras looked every bit a predator, eager for the kill. He didn't wear much armor, either, though his thick skin made the gesture less significant. He carried a large spiked shield nearly half as tall as he was and wore a heavy, barbed, blackened steel armguard and gauntlet that covered his weapon arm all the way up to his shoulder. His weapon was a crowd-pleaser. A vicious-looking mace with a profusion of sharp barbs and hooks meant to catch and tear skin. A large helm in the shape of a snarling beast finished his look. Maran Vras knew the crowds came to see blood, and he never disappointed them. He was a champion himself in truth, though less storied than the Old Man. This was his chance to become truly famous. The fighter who defeated the Old Man would be talked about for decades.

The crowd's cheers were deafening. The Tolrahkali had squeezed in more spectators than usual that day. The stands were overcrowded. Not a single seat or step was free, and not a single person in the crowd wasn't on their feet cheering at the top of their lungs. Two real champions rarely met on the sands, and almost never in a death match. But the Old Man was adamant. He would not fight a bout where more than one combatant left the sands breathing.

Maran was calm. He was ready. He had seen the Old Man fight several times over the years. His style and technique would not be able to surprise him. Maran was Warchosen himself, though he had decided to emulate the Old Man in his tight-lipped manner and didn't speak of his abilities to those he didn't trust. The Old Man's glaive, as Maran had heard it called, would not be the only enchanted weapon on the sands today. Maran's mace had been prepared for him by a wealthy patron in the Arcanum of Bialta itself. But the mace was not Maran's only advantage. His shield had been with him since his first days in the pits, before he had made a name for himself. Year after year, every copper penny he had been given by his owner went to further enchant the shield. There were so many layers of magic within it, Maran doubted anything could pierce it, not even the Old Man's glaive.

He looked across the sands at the Old Man. The guard pose at the center of the arena was obviously a big part of his fighting style. In every one of his fights it was the same.

The crowd went perfectly silent as the arena master gestured for the signal horn to be blown. Maran charged forward the moment the sound split the air. He knew he was fast. Far faster than any of those he'd seen the Old Man fight, certainly. The old bastard always defended, countering more by placing his weapon in his opponent's way than by attacking himself, tipping the unwieldy glaive into their path as he moved around the weapon that remained set in the sand. They died one and all, splitting themselves open on that incredibly sharp edge.

Maran wouldn't make that mistake. He would batter the champion aside with his shield and crush him when he'd been knocked out of position. As expected, the Old Man dodged to the side around his weapon, the foot of it not moving from its place in the sand. Maran slammed his shield into the glaive, intent on knocking it aside or at least destabilizing his opponent's grip. Nothing. His shield stopped dead the instant it touched the glaive, all momentum lost. Maran was so shocked, he stopped for a moment and almost died as the Old Man shifted his position and brought the head of the glaive slashing down toward him. Maran danced away. *At least the shield held.* The seeming incompetence of the Old Man's previous opponents made more sense now. Maran would have to be extremely careful not to allow his attacks to even brush up against the damned weapon. He hadn't become a champion without facing some unusual opponents though. His brutish exterior hid surprising skill and intelligence. He played up the part of mindless brute both to please the crowd and to throw off his opponents. This time might well be one of those occasions when brutish strength and roaring wouldn't be enough.

When Maran charged in again, his act was gone. He made a series of complex feints and probing attacks, not looking to kill, just seeing what he could sneak past the old bastard's incredible defense. *Nothing. Absolutely fucking nothing.* He cursed in frustration as the spry old fighter danced around his weapon, lowering and raising the blade to block and threaten with incredible speed.

Maran had never faced an opponent like this. He had never faced a real challenge, to tell the truth. His Warchosen talent was considerable. His mind was quick and his training second to none. A little burst of talent was usually all it took. He only ever fought at his full potential in training against stone or wood training dummies. Above all, he was a showman. Making a fight too one-sided didn't attract the fans' attention, nor did it improve his master's betting odds. His attacks now became more complex series of maneuvers, feints, and probes. But, still, each time he tried to land a blow, the damned glaive just barely caught the edge of his mace and stopped his swing dead. And through it all the Old Man stayed impassive, almost distracted, a blank look in his eyes as if breathing and keeping himself moving were the only challenges at hand. But this . . .

this was Maran's chance to show what he could really do. His speed gradually increased beyond what was humanly possible. He didn't waste his efforts on strength. The glaive made any such attempt meaningless. No, he would land a blow on the old fucker if it was the last thing he did. Then it was there. A perfect opportunity. Maran reached around the glaive's blade, while it was turned away from him, in a one-armed hug. He jabbed his barbed mace forward in an attempt to catch the Old Man as he dodged around.

Maran's blow missed, just barely passing between the glaive and the Old Man's stomach. But as he reached farther he stumbled, pulled by his own momentum, and one barb from his armguard raked across the Old Man's chest. Blood dribbled out of the deep scratch. *Success!* He had managed to wound the old bastard at last. It was possible. He would wear him down with little cuts and scratches if he had to, but he would win. Pain flashed in his arm. Maran glanced down quickly and saw the glaive had sliced through his armguard while he was reaching in to land his blow. His bicep was half cut through and he hadn't even felt it happen. He looked up at the Old Man and saw him touching the cut on his chest, then looking at the blood on his fingers.

The Old Man's eyes snapped to Maran's. The disconnected, vacant expression was gone. Hatred and rage boiled in the Old Man's stare. His frail body started to tremble. His muscles clenched. Maran took a step backward, unsure what to expect. The roar of the crowd was gone from his mind for the first time since he had become a gladiator. He watched in confusion while the Old Man rocked back and forth on his feet, before launching himself forward. He propelled himself into the air with the glaive and dragged it after him. He made a perfect somersault in the air, the tip of the glaive only barely brushing the sand before sweeping over him. . . . And then the huge weapon was coming down straight toward Maran with its full weight behind it. Caught flat-footed, Maran had no choice but to raise his shield. It had held against the glaive already. And yet he felt a spark of fear deep within him as he raised the slab of steel above his head and braced for impact.

Time seemed to slow down. The wait for the blow to land was endless, the Old Man seemingly suspended in the air about to smash his weapon down. The glaive hit the shield with the sound of a temple bell, the weight of a world behind it. Maran's arm shattered, as did both his knees, before his own shield collided with his helm and everything went dark. The crowd had gone mad screaming and cheering when the two fighters wounded each other. Then they had surged to their feet in astonishment as the champion had vaulted into the air. To them it seemed like Maran Vras was crushed into the sands like a bug beneath a boot heel.

The Old Man stood panting and shaking uncontrollably. It took him several minutes to get his weapon upright again and to drag it back to set it in the center of the arena. The arena master sent two guards forward to check on Maran. With great difficulty they managed to lift the large shield off him and set it aside.

"He's still breathing!" one of them called. The crowd cheered all the more. The show wasn't over.

The arena master looked down to the Old Man, who shook his head slowly. Then he spoke in a ragged, wheezing voice. "He . . . drew blood . . . let him live." The arena master nodded back and then clapped his hands. Healers and servants swarmed out to attend to the fighters.

High in the stands, Betar smiled. Maran had been a great investment. He had brought Betar a lot of gold over the years. He had always won when Betar demanded it of him, and this time, the time that Betar had bet against his own slave, he had lost. Not that Maran had had any idea of the bet, of course. Or even of the strength-sapping poison Betar had added to his water before the fight. He probably hadn't lasted long enough for it to start taking effect in any case. And now Betar had received another unexpected windfall from the slave gladiator. Moments after the fight ended and Maran was pronounced living, a slave had slipped him a note. It promised a most generous sum of gold for the wounded slave. Nearly as much as Betar had made off the gladiator in the last year, truth be told. And given his current state, even if Maran did survive his wounds, costly magics and alchemies would have to be used to return him to fighting condition. Whoever this Carver was, he was a fool. But Betar had no qualms about taking a fool's money.

The crowd was buzzing as they left, many people talking about the Old Man sparing his opponent for the first time. There was awe in their voices when they spoke of Maran, amazed that he had survived the fight. Betar scoffed. In his opinion, Maran owed his life more to the Old Man's fatigue than to his respect. But he heard the excitement in their voices. Maran's next fights, if he could be put back together properly, might draw a big enough premium to cover the medical expenses. . . . But no. He hadn't become rich by taking unnecessary risks. Sure things and situations that could be rigged to one's advantage were the way to get ahead. Time to cash out of this little game. He'd let this fool Carver take the risks, and Betar would find himself a new game to play.

CHAPTER 3

Salt had no memory of falling asleep again, but he woke to hands shaking him.

"Come on, lad, it's time to get to work." Gurt was standing over him wearing a new-looking set of leather armor. "There's clothes in the trunk at the foot of your bed. Should be a near enough fit. And there's a loaf of bread and a jug of water on the table in the corner. Now get a move on. The rest of the squad is already in the training yard. You may not have taken the oath to become a full member yet, and I know you had a rough night, but I expect you to keep up from now on. Go out the door and down the stairs; you can't miss it." Salt nodded, and Gurt left without another word.

Salt sat up gingerly. His head was spinning, and the cut across his chest was a dull, throbbing pain. All in all, not nearly as bad as he usually felt waking up the morning after putting to shore. He stood up, opened the trunk, and pulled out a city guard tunic and breeches. *What have I gotten myself into?! And, more importantly, how do I get myself out?* He got dressed quickly, all the while looking around at what he guessed was, at least temporarily, home. Eight clean cots were set up in the large room, a large wooden trunk at the foot of every cot. Several tables, chairs, and even a fireplace and two large bookcases were set at the far end of the room. The walls were bare stone, but three large windows were set in the west wall. Looking out at the city, Salt could see that he was in the very heart of the crown district, and a wide wall surrounded the courtyard outside. *I was thinking I needed to find a good place to live for a while. I guess the palace qualifies,* he thought. He opened the door and went out. Three other doors were positioned in the long hallway he found himself in, and he saw a wide staircase at the end. Salt walked out into the training yard. About four-dozen men and women, no two of them alike, were hard at work drilling with swords and shields in the late afternoon sun. Salt was surprised to see people of Keralan or Abolian ancestry. A few even looked to be from Gho or Samora.

Gurt waved everyone to stop when he saw Salt walk into the yard. "Nice of you to join us, lad. You slept later than anyone else here, so I'll expect you to train harder too." Salt looked around, confused as to what he was supposed to do. "Krigare, show the lad the ropes if you will. I'll put him through some drills after you're done."

The man who walked over to Salt barely came up to his chest. His thinning black hair was long and unkempt, trailing down past his waist in a ragged mess. His deep-olive skin hinted at Keralan blood, or possibly even Eastern Borogian. His wide frame and the dark look in his eyes made him as intimidating as a mountain troll. Unlike most of the others Salt had met, Krigare didn't smile. He barely even looked at Salt before throwing him a practice sword and taking a swing at him with his own. Off balance, Salt awkwardly blocked the first swing, only to have his legs swept out from under him. He landed in a heap in the dirt. Clearly unimpressed, Krigare turned his back on Salt and waited for him to get back to his feet. Salt wondered if many of Krigare's trainees were stupid enough to try and attack him from behind. He dragged himself to his feet and held up the wooden blade in an approximation of a guard position. Finally, Krigare turned back to him.

"Coward," he said.

Salt wasn't falling for it. He'd been the new guy on enough ships to know when he was being tested. He stood there with his sword ready to defend himself. Krigare looked around at the other Night Guards training in the yard.

"Okay, who told the new blood what to expect?" He seemed angry. Everyone shouted back a variety of "not me"s as well as some colorful suggestions as to what Krigare should do to himself.

Gurt walked over. "I don't think anyone told him, Krigare. He's just not quite as dumb as he looks." He grinned at Salt.

Krigare squinted at him for a few minutes and nodded. "All right, New Blood. So maybe you're not completely brain-dead. That doesn't mean you don't have a long way to go before you'll be of any use to the Guard. Now defend yourself. I'll go easier on you this time. . . ."

Nearly four hours later, Salt stumbled back up the stairs to the barracks. He was bruised and battered and so utterly exhausted that he could barely walk up the stairs. Krigare had dunked him in a barrel of water before heading off on patrol. *Bastard probably knows I'm too tired to wash. Gods, I think even the stubble on my head is bruised.*

***

Nial walked into the shop in the slums, a tall man floating in the darkness behind her. A gust of wind pushed through the door behind her and blew out the little shop's lone lamp.

"Hello, Mister Skeg," Nial called out brightly as she pushed the door closed.

Skeg focused his power and wove a spark onto the lamp's wick. "Hello, child. Welcome back." Nial was staring at him, eyes wide.

"How did you do that?"

He looked back at her in confusion. "You look at me as if I just performed some kind of divine miracle. It was only a little weave. About all I can manage, truth be told. It's useful enough though."

"What's a weave?" Skeg's skin was covered in a cold sweat. *She must be testing me.* There was no other answer. *This murderous little girl is playing with me. And the two voices . . . could there be two of them in there?*

"Just a way to make our power do other things. Surely you know more about it than I do. The things I've seen you do are far beyond anything I could manage."

"I don't know how to do that fire thing. Will you teach me?" Her voice was every bit the ten-year-old child's asking for a treat.

"I suppose so, child. But wouldn't you prefer to take care of business first?" He gestured toward the man floating off the ground, eyes popping out of his head in terror. "I also have to ask; did anyone see you bring him here? Or even into this area? A lot of trouble could follow if they did."

"We were careful, Mister Skeg. Zuly understands a lot about hiding." Abruptly her mannerisms changed. She stood taller, looked more confident, her bearing more mature.

"I am quite confident we were not seen. I do understand we cannot hope for this arrangement to continue indefinitely without drawing notice. We will think of something. In the meantime, you are right. We should take care of business." Skeg nodded. "We will trade you the flesh of this one in the same manner as the last in exchange for the learning that Nial asked for."

Skeg was torn between confusion and delight. "Of course . . . ladies? There's really nothing to it. That is a most generous offer; I cannot refuse."

The child moved to the back room. Not stopping to ask for a light. *Something else they don't need, I guess.*

When it was over, the girl called out to him. "Mister Skeg? We're all done in here."

There had been no further haggling after that. They fell into a permanent relationship of sorts; the girls would bring in bodies—both men and women—and Skeg would instruct them as best he could in the art of weaving magical spells. They were proving to be talented students. *This can't continue forever. I've already kept the corpse trade going for far longer than is prudent. It's only a matter of time before the Night Guard catch wind and come to investigate me. Besides, it's only been a few weeks and I'm already running out of things to teach them. And what happens to me when I'm of no use to them anymore?* Skeg looked down at the obsidian orb he was carving. It was an exact match to the one the girls used to house the souls they harvested. In truth, they had taught him nearly as much as he them in their sessions, but he still had to question his sanity at voluntarily spending time with what could only be a demon-possessed child.

***

Nial! Stop!

What is it, Zuly? That man is horrible. We have to stop him!

We do, sweet Nial. And nothing would please me more, but I feel something nearby.

"Something?" Nial whispered aloud.

A being from my own world. A demon. And if it is out here and there are no screams and people dying, then someone must be holding its leash. An image of a misshapen thing flashed into Nial's mind. A kind of swollen maggot the size of a dog, with insectlike legs and wings, and overlarge bulbous eyes that twitched above a fang-filled mouth.

Nial looked around the dingy street. They were hiding among the refuse at the mouth of an alleyway, dressed in rags and looking much like any other desperate child. They needed a place to hide, but not in the alley itself. A dead end offered no escape route, and flight was always the best strategy for survival. Over the past months they had learned to draw out their targets, to emulate the poor helpless children who were so often prey in the slums. Their chosen soul this evening was a man in his late forties. He hadn't threatened them. He hadn't spared the lost-looking child a glance. He had dragged an unconscious woman right past them, trusting in the darkness and in people's fear and indifference to hide what he was doing. But there was no hiding from the girls' demonic sight. Since their joining, night had become a world of vivid contrasts and muted colors.

Nial started to follow. *No, Nial! Whoever summoned that demon could be looking for us. We can't afford to do anything until it passes us by.*

"But you said we were strong now. I want to stop that man! Can't we kill the demon if it tries to attack us?"

Of course, my sweet. I have no doubt that we could handle it. Its master is another matter though. Mages are powerful. And they attract powerful friends. If the thing really is hunting for us, then it might mean one of the people we killed had powerful friends, or maybe was powerful themselves. We need to ask Skeg about the city's mages before we destroy any of their servants.

They heard a muffled scream, followed by the unmistakable sound of flesh striking flesh. Again and again the sound came until finally the screams stopped. Nial started to cry silently.

All right, Nial. We will try without using our power. Come on then, find something sharp. . . .

When Nial walked into Skeg's shop, she looked near tears. Her mud-caked clothes were dark and wet with blood. Skeg's heart skipped a beat.

"We're sorry, Mister Skeg," she blurted. "We couldn't bring you the body this time. He was bleeding. There was blood everywhere. It was such a mess!" The tears were coming now, fat drops flowing freely down her dirty cheeks.

"But you weren't seen?"

They shook their head glumly.

Skeg allowed himself to relax as much as he ever did in the girls' presence. "That's all right, child. I was meaning to tell you, I don't think I can sell too many more body parts for a while. It's attracting too much attention."

"So you're not disappointed?" Nial said, sniffling.

"No, child. In truth, I'm relieved. I wasn't sure what to do if you brought me another body so soon."

"But we have nothing to trade for tonight's lesson."

"You've been overpaying me as it is. I'm sure we don't have to worry about another trade for a while."

"Oh, thank you, Mister Skeg!" The bright cheerful child was back as quickly as that. She rushed past him and sat down in her spot inside the ring of wards, not even pausing to clean the blood off herself.

As much as he was growing fond of her, Skeg couldn't help but shudder at Nial's mood shift. *And she's not even the demon.*

"There is another matter we need to speak to you about before we start," said Zuly.

Skeg gestured for her to continue.

"We encountered a leashed demon tonight. We need to know how common such things are in Darien."

"Not common at all," Skeg said immediately. "Even a minor demon would mean Arcanum involvement. No one else would dare send one out in public for fear of attracting their attention."

"This was a flying Karethin demon. They are about this long," she said, holding her hands apart. "They usually feed on the dead."

"A carrion demon, we'd call it then," Skeg said. "Nothing really scary, but the summoner has some power and is definitely connected to be able to send it out into the city." A terrible thought suddenly occurred to Skeg. "You didn't kill it, did you?"

"No, we hid and made our kill tonight without the aid of magic. We were lucky and it moved off before we needed to trap the soul." Skeg let out a breath he didn't know he'd been holding.

"Thank the gods!"

Zuly arched an eyebrow at him.

"Er . . . thank all the . . . something ungodly. . . . If you'd killed it, whether it was out looking for you or not, it would have attracted too much attention. Only a licensed mage of the Arcanum would send a demon out in public and not a weak one at that. If you attract the attention of the Arcanum, you won't last a day in this city."

"What is this Arcanum?" Zuly demanded.

"Are you two going to talk all night? I want to learn more magic!" chimed in Nial's voice. It was saying something that these outbursts didn't even surprise Skeg anymore. It was just like having two people sitting with him but without the need to look between them.

"This will actually make a good start to our lesson for tonight, child. You see, the Arcanum is Bialta's great school of magic. More than a school, really, since most of its members never leave. It is right here in Darien City, and it's the main reason the capital was moved from Korsten. It's also the largest school of magic on the continent; they accept students from every country regardless of political affiliations. But they also put powerful weaves on all their students that make it impossible for them to consciously act against Bialta or the Arcanum. There's all kinds of mages in the world, most of them focusing on one particular aspect of their talent, like the warlocks in the Free Cities and their obsession with fire and war magic. But in Bialta, they try to teach mages a little of everything. They share as much knowledge as they can and encourage their members to innovate and dig deep in any magical skill they please."

Nial sighed loudly.

"Nial, how about I give you something to practice while Zuly and I keep talking for a little while?" She nodded eagerly.

Skeg went back into the shop to find a sheet of paper, a quill, and a small pot of ink, then returned to his usual spot in the circle and drew a fairly complex pattern on the sheet. "We're going to work on doing several things at once now. I know you can move things with your magic easily enough. But if you use a weave, you should be able to move more objects at once and keep them moving separately. Here's the pattern. Try to move these coins around the room." He dumped a handful of copper coins onto the floor between them and stuck the quill into the skin at the back of his head.

"Must you keep that feather there, Mister Skeg?" said Zuly. For some reason, the practice seemed to unnerve her though the myriad other items pushed through his skin didn't seem to bother her. Skeg pulled it out and smiled before pushing it back in over his left ear. Zuly growled at him, showing her teeth. The sound was suddenly cut off by Nial's girlish giggling.

Later that night, Skeg watched Nial and Zuly practice with a sense of pride and wonder. They had taken to the new weave with ease, and then with a fair bit of work from all three of them, they had even figured out how Nial and Zuly could use their power to lift their own body off the ground.

Neither of them could explain it, nor could Skeg understand why it should be so much harder to lift themselves than it was to lift someone else. It was just one more mystery about them that he'd resigned himself to accept. But they had managed it eventually, and Nial's girlish laughter filled the shop as she slowly floated up to the ceiling. He'd never had a family. He'd been a street kid himself who a mage noticed had talent when he was about twelve. The mage had been disappointed though. Skeg had a glimmer of power in him, no more. He reached the First Order and hit a wall. That was as far as his talents could take him. In the Arcanum that meant he was welcome, but he'd never be respected. He'd be an eternal apprentice, an assistant to the more talented mages. Since striking out on his own he'd made himself invaluable to the unlicensed mages of the city as well as to a number of priests and cultists and even a number of Arcanum mages whose research wasn't strictly legal.

But now, his life was becoming increasingly focused on Nial and Zuly, and Skeg had to admit, despite moments of terror when he remembered he was teaching a demon-possessed child, he was actually enjoying himself for the first time in as long as he could remember. Their talents far outshone his, and they thirsted for knowledge, as excited about what they could do as he had been as a youth. He discovered things in himself that he had never expected—a joy in teaching and a feeling of warmth in the company of a child.

Skeg walked over to the counter and pulled out a box of candles. "Let's make things a little more challenging for you ladies. Keep your body moving up and down just like you are now and try to light three candles at once." A frown creased their brow for a moment before all three candles burst into violent flame. Skeg jumped to his feet, but the flames puffed out as quickly as they had appeared. The candles' entire length had been consumed.

"Well . . . that was more than I expected."

"But you said that doing more than one thing at once was harder, so I should feed a little more power to the weaves," Nial said.

"That's true, child. A sliver more in your case. Lighting two candles at once is about all I can do. In my time at the Arcanum, I only barely passed the First Order. What you just did . . . You certainly have power. But my old masters always said control was more important. A mage can always use a magical Source if they need more power, but there is no substitute for control. . . . Now, let's try again." Skeg set out five candles this time.

"Okay, now light three of them—carefully. Remember, it's safer to give it too little power, and try again." Three of the candles immediately flickered to life.

"Perfect," Skeg said, smiling. "Now put them out and light four. . . ."

An hour later Nial and Zuly were surrounded with all the candles Skeg owned—twenty-seven of them. They were all floating up and down at different speeds, the wicks catching fire and puffing out. Nial had a slight frown of concentration marring her little forehead as she slowly rose up toward the ceiling. Skeg sat with his jaw hanging. None of the weaves Nial was making was particularly complex. *But to make so many at once!*

Nial looked at him. "How are we doing, Mister Skeg?"

"Incredibly well," Skeg managed to say. "Isn't it hard to keep all that going?"

"It's a little tricky," Nial answered. "But Zuly just took over to let me take a break."

"Could you do as many again if you both tried?"

"Sure, do you have any more candles?"

Skeg swallowed hard. *This little girl would make an archmage tremble. I don't know what she will one day become, but I thank all the gods that I'm here to see it!*

"That won't be necessary, child. Let's work on something else while Zuly practices that. Now this new weave I'm going to show you is to make light. Light but no heat."

Nial's first light weave nearly blinded Skeg. Clear white light filled the little shop. "Please, child! Put it out!" The light winked out as quickly as it had appeared. The shop seemed dark now even with all the candles still flickering on and off all around them. "Try again, Nial, but look closely at the weave I made. The strands are a lot thinner than the ones we use for fire."

Skeg watched closely as she tried again. She went slower this time, weaving the simple little spell with extreme caution and a look of deep concentration on her face. "It's hard to make the strands that thin." She finished the weave, and a pleasantly bright light filled the room.

"You can just make the weave smaller if you like as well."

Nial's face brightened and, faster than Skeg could follow, she wove four incredibly small light weaves and placed them in the four corners of the room where they combined to make it only slightly brighter than the noonday sun. "I did it!"

"Perfect. Now this next one is very similar." Skeg concentrated for a moment and his eyes glowed briefly and changed color.

"Oh!" exclaimed Nial. "It's like the light weaves. What did you do different?"

"It's a little illusion. Things like glowing eyes are great for putting a little scare into people who don't know you're a mage. All without actually doing much of anything. Now, watch closely while I do it again."

Nial watched raptly. "I think I've got it." She frowned for a second and her eyes blazed with bright light. Skeg was forced to avert his eyes.

Looking at him sheepishly, she said, "But I did exactly what you did."

"With far, far too much power. An illusion is a delicate thing. The light you make has to mirror the light that's already around you or it will glow too brightly. But you can't make this one smaller like you do with the light weaves because they won't cover the area that you're trying to make the illusion on. Though what you just did might have its uses too."

They tried for the better part of the evening, only occasionally stopping as Skeg went to help his infrequent customers. But try as she might, Nial just couldn't produce the delicate strands required of a convincing illusion. Her strands, even her finest ones, were like braided steel cables next to the silken threads she needed.

"Don't feel bad, girls, we'll just keep practicing. And besides, there are worse things than being too strong."

***

For four days, the people of Sacral did their best to spend time with any friends or loved ones who would be sent beyond the Wastes to assist the Abolians. Quartermasters and craftsmen of every description worked day and night to ensure orders were met while soldiers chafed at the waiting, eager to test themselves against the outside world.

When the appointed day finally dawned, the four thousand soldiers selected for the expedition assembled in neat ranks by the West Gate. Warchosen captains stood proudly in front of their companies. The armor and weapons of every soldier had been polished to a mirror sheen for the occasion. The thousands of tradesmen, drovers, and laborers who would accompany them bunched around their wagons waving at the crowd. Children ran and shouted. Musicians played. Brewers had set up stalls and were doing fine trade despite the early hour. The atmosphere was every bit that of a festival day.

Finally, the king appeared on top of the gate tower to address the crowd. "People of Sacral!" he called. His voice magically enhanced to carry over the sounds of merrymaking. "Today we end our self-imposed seclusion. Today we remind the outside world what it means to be a man or woman of Sacral!" The crowd cheered. "We thank you, Captain Jenus, our champion, and each and every one of our brave fighting men and women for your service. We also thank all those who are going with them to ensure their carts are led, their meals cooked, and their swords sharpened. But most of all we thank the priests of the White Mother who will tend to their wounds and safeguard our people's souls while they travel to a strange land. May the White Mother watch over each and every one of you and bring you home safe to us." The king then stood still for a few moments and a whirling rift opened up in the gap of the gate. "I have fashioned a gate to speed you on your way, my brave children. Step through and you will find yourselves but a few short hours from the Abolian city of Sariah where your hunt will begin."

The soldiers all saluted in unison. Jenus then lifted his arm and motioned for the army to move out. Soldiers disappeared into the rift without a sound. In a surprisingly short time, the four thousand soldiers, the thousands of cooks, cartwrights, smiths, and drovers, along with their carts and pack animals, were gone.

The festival air was gone the moment the last cart trundled out of the city. The people looked around and noticed the king had disappeared as well. No one could deny the unexplainable feeling of emptiness. Even the most boisterous of drunks and loudest of children cleaned themselves off as best they could and headed for home. Maura watched the last of the crowd disperse. The sinking feeling she'd had since the day at the arena deepened to dread.

It was a beautiful sunny day. Maura was walking back from the markets with a heavy basket. Several weeks had passed since Jenus and his soldiers had left the city. She had made every attempt to return to her normal life, but the faint feeling of dread never quite left her. She walked up the hill toward her house with playful children dodging around her and a few men and women going about their work.

Somewhere in the distance she heard a shout. It was repeated, this time by more voices. The sound built into a roar of shouts and screams. It was impossible to tell what they were saying. People started running past her. Maura picked up her pace, eager to get home now, regardless of what was happening.

Finally, someone shouted right behind her, "Sacral is under attack!"

Maura felt her stomach clench. Everyone who heard the shout started to run. Panic swept up the street in front of her. More shouts and screams were raised. No more details, only the fact that they were being attacked repeated again and again. Questions boiled inside Maura, but none here would be able to answer nor would anyone even be willing to pause in their flight. She tried to move back up the street toward Beren's shop, but the tide was against her. In moments her basket was knocked from her hands, the vegetables it held trampled by the panicked crowd. As much as it galled her, patience was the answer. She could hear Beren's voice inside her head chiding her and telling her that if she was only a little more patient. . . .

Go home. Wait for someone to bring news and pray that Beren and Gerald are all right.

***

"Look at this, Jerik," Beren said, holding up a sheathed sword. "I've finally gotten somewhere."

Jerik looked up in excitement. "You managed to power more than one rune? Fully?"

"More than that," he said with a smile. "The runes still need to draw power from a living body, of course, and a single body only gives off enough energy to power a single rune. But I've built a matrix linking them together inside the sword that can store some of that energy."

Beren gripped the hilt of the sword, slowly counted to twelve, then drew the blade. It was an ugly construction; by far the ugliest thing Beren had ever made. The whole of the blade was covered in layer upon layer of runes, hundreds of them. It was so overworked it was beyond ludicrous. But Jerik's eyes snapped to the three brightly glowing runes inscribed near the hilt. He let out a deafening cheer of approval.

"You did it! I can't believe it!" Even as the words left his lips, the light faded and went out. He looked back at Beren, who shrugged.

"The period of a rune is still four seconds. Same as if you let go of any rune item. The size or type of the rune itself doesn't seem to matter, nor does how many I link. The three that were powered here are for strength, speed, and healing, and I've managed the same with all kinds of other combinations. But four seconds is something I can't seem to get around, and once the power drops I'm not even getting one to work."

Jerik clapped him on the back. "It's still amazing progress. Will four light up if you hold it longer?"

"Not so far. . . . I'm not quite sure why, either. I would have thought that sixteen seconds would give me four and so on, but it just doesn't seem to work that way. Maybe I've reached the maximum amount of energy the internal matrix can hold. I'll try to tweak it and test it again." Jerik nodded and returned to his own work.

Beren slowly heated up the metal of the sword and channeled his power into the red hot blade, all while taking extreme care not to touch the weapon with his skin. With incredible patience and precision, he coaxed the alchemical mixture into an increasingly complex pattern within the blade. He also made minute changes and adjustments to the structure of the sword as he went. Nothing that could be distinguished with the naked eye, but no flaw could be ignored. The sword might be nothing more than an experiment, but Beren was too much of a perfectionist to craft anything without giving it his all. Then, all of a sudden, a feeling of completion hit him and he knew he would find no more flaws within the metal. The pattern within was somehow *right*.

Out of habit and a lingering doubt about the quality of his work, he continued looking over the steel and the conduit pattern for a long time before he set it aside to cool. After a few hours' rest, he would test the sword again. If the conduits showed the properties he was after, nearly anything would become possible. His work would be sought after by every warrior in the city. Even what he had accomplished so far would be enough to give a warrior a significant advantage in the starting seconds of a duel—not something to be discounted lightly.

Beren looked up from his worktable in surprise as a half-dozen soldiers crowded into the room. One of the soldiers was an officer, a regular customer Beren recognized.

"Captain Harrow? What brings you here?"

"Sorry, Beren. We've all come to get our gear back, finished or not."

"But why would you want it back unfinished? The next games aren't scheduled for another two weeks."

"You haven't heard? We're under attack, man!" one of the other soldiers said, almost yelling.

Harrow silenced him with a look. "The whole city's in an uproar. An army's moving on Sacral. There can be little doubt we'll soon be under attack. I'd expect them to come at us at dawn."

"Of course, of course, just a moment while I find your things." Beren jumped up and fumbled through different pieces of equipment and scraps of paper before giving up and calling for his son. "Gerald! Please come find the armor and weapons belonging to these kind people!"

Gerald stuck his head through the door, looked at the soldiers standing there, and nodded. "Could you follow me, please? All your equipment is in the outer rooms. Captain Harrow, you are fortunate—the work you requested for your shield was completed this morning."

Beren sat back down on his seat and shook his head. War. . . . *For the first time in a thousand years Sacral is at war.*

Gerald walked back into the workroom a few minutes later. His usual frantic, yet efficient movements were gone. He looked lost.

"Father? What do you think will happen?"

"I'm not sure. I've been in here all day. I've only just heard the news. Have you heard who it is by the way? How many they are?"

"It's the Abolians. I've heard all kinds of numbers. Lots, thousands anyway."

"And nearly half our soldiers are away helping them?!" *By the Lady, I wish you'd been wrong, my dear Maura.*

"The White Mother will protect us," replied Gerald with little conviction. "Do you suppose Jenus and the Lightbringer are lost?"

"All we can do is pray they make it back. Jenus and his men are the best Sacral has to offer; they won't let anything stop them." They sat in silence for a time, both lost in morbid thoughts.

Gerald cleared his throat loudly. "Should I get back to work, Father?"

"Yes, Gerald. Let's keep ourselves busy. The streets are a mess at the moment from all accounts. Going home will have to wait. Besides, the army might have need of our services." Gerald nodded and turned to go.

"Gerald, before you get back to it, would you be so kind as to run out back and make sure Jerik knows what's going on?"

"Of course, Father."

Beren sat back down at his worktable and looked at the sword he'd been working on. For the first time he could remember, he had no interest in his work. *Maura was right.* She was rarely wrong, of course; few were as adept at reading people. Still, he had hoped she was wrong this time.

The chaos in the streets continued unabated for hours. People were panicking, but the soldiers were all needed to prepare for the attack that would surely come with the dawn. At dusk, Beren lost patience. He made hasty farewells to Jerik and made Gerald promise to stay inside, then hurried out himself before they could try to stop him. People ran in every direction, some carrying random possessions probably in the hopes of finding safe places to hide them. Others ran around shouting out contradicting news and rumors. Within moments of getting outside, a large man racing down the street slammed into Beren and sent him tumbling into a wall. It took him almost two hours to make what would normally be a fifteen-minute walk.

When he finally arrived at his house, he was bruised and bleeding from a number of small cuts and scrapes. He reached for the door handle just as it flew open. Maura dragged him in by his rumpled coat and slammed the door shut behind him.

"My love! Thank the heavens you're safe!" Then her expression changed to anger in a moment. "But what possessed you to go out in this mess? You should have stayed at the shop!" She led him inside and cleaned his cuts with a damp cloth, never giving him a chance to say a word. Finally, she quieted and looked into his eyes. "Is it true then? Are we being attacked?"

Beren nodded sadly. "The Abolians have come with an army. Captain Harrow tells me they expect the attack to come at dawn."

"I knew those people were up to something!" She shook her head. "How could the king have trusted them?"

"He couldn't very well say no to a request from the temple. Not without a good reason anyway."

"I suppose. But I just can't believe Yeltos Rogayen and the king could be so shortsighted!"

"We should rest while we can love," Beren said, leading her to their bedroom. "We can go see what we can do to help after the streets clear." Maura agreed silently, tears brimming in her eyes.

No one in Sacral slept that night; the tension was palpable. No one needed to be told they didn't have enough soldiers to hold out against what was coming. Some claimed the king would save them. Others mentioned the White Mother. But her priests were conspicuously absent from public places after a rising number of accusations had been heard about them being the reason Jenus and his cohort had been sent away from Sacral.

Shortly after midnight, there was a knock at the door. Their neighbor Karim, a retired soldier himself, had taken it upon himself to organize a militia of sorts to defend the neighborhood should things come to that. "We're putting all our children, and anyone else who doesn't think they can fight, in a few houses and arming ourselves as best we can. If we have time, we'll move some of our valuables in as well, though we're not worrying about that sort of thing just yet. If you'd like to join us, just bring all the food and water you can." He pointed back toward his house. Maura's eyes lit up. *At last! Something to do!* It may not be much but it was better than this horrible waiting.

"I'll come join you and bring what I have. Thanks, Karim. That's a great idea."

Karim just nodded and moved on to the next house on the street.

Beren shook his head. "I don't think I can go. I'll be able to do more good at the shop. Besides, Gerald and Jerik are still there."

Maura's head snapped up. "Don't you dare go anywhere near the fighting, Beren!"

Well used to his wife's protective nature, Beren just continued. "I'm not going anywhere near any fighting; the inner wall is a long walk from my shop, and if I hear things are going bad, I'll come straight home. I promise. They'd have to make it clear through the city to get to my shop from where they are. Besides, I know as well as anyone I'm not going to do anyone any good trying to fight soldiers with a carving tool." He looked at her for a few minutes and watched as the stubborn look left her eyes.

"I'm just so scared."

"I know, love. So am I. But I can't just sit here and do nothing any more than you can." They hugged each other tightly for a time, then reluctantly parted.

The moment she arrived at Karim's house, Maura felt better. Here was a chance to be productive. At first she helped a group of people at the back of the house to organize food stores. Older children were tasked with collecting everything edible from their homes. A few mothers organized simple games to keep the younger children distracted. Everyone else tried as best they could to arm themselves. Maura handed out a number of knives and even a couple of swords her husband had brought home over the years, as well as all the healing runes she had in the house. *Well, Beren, my love, your obsession with rune carving is finally turning out to be useful,* she thought as she went about her work. Most of the others huddled together and did nothing. They were afraid, Maura knew, but she couldn't understand why all they wanted to do was hide. Even some of the larger, stronger men only wanted to sit inside while Karim and others like him took action.

Without quite realizing when she started, Maura started to give the less proactive people work to keep them occupied. Most of them scurried about after that as if completing their assigned task would ensure their survival. She then convinced more of the locals to join Karim's patrols of their neighborhood. They even split the group and organized a second patrol, each team composed of twenty determined men and women armed with whatever weapons they could find. Each time the patrols went out they came back with more people. As they became more numerous and better organized, even the most reluctant started to see the militia as a way to improve their chances of surviving.

Karim's house became too small to accommodate everyone. It became the most central of nine houses the militia organized themselves around. There were still arguments and complaints from some of the new arrivals, many of them wondering why their homes were not being protected as well as some others. But Maura ignored them and gave them tasks to keep their minds and hands busy, leaving the more martial aspects of the patrols and weapons to Karim. It wasn't until three hours past noon that the first news of the war reached them. The Abolians had attacked the outer wall, but the soldiers of Sacral, supported by the magic of their king, had so far held them off despite the enemy's numerical advantage.

The next patrol to return to the militia after that arrived with wounded. The shock of seeing men and women clutching bleeding wounds and crying set off a wave of panic.

"But we only just heard the Abolians were still being held off at the wall!" someone shouted.

Karim sighed. "Well, the bastards who attacked us came from the east, not the west. Looks to me like our whole army is busy on the one side of the city, so the Abolians just sent some men around to cross the wall somewhere else." He sunk down to the floor, clearly exhausted after carrying back one of the wounded men. "We're lucky we didn't lose anyone in that fight. There were only five of them. We hurt a couple, and the rest seemed as eager to get away as we did. They looked lost. They probably got separated from a larger group. There must be more of them around the city. It's a long way to the east wall from here."

"We need to send out more people," Maura said.

Many of the others looked at her as if she were mad. "And have more of our people get hurt for nothing?" someone said.

Maura looked at them all calmly. "I'm not suggesting we go out and hunt them. I'm suggesting we send out small groups, quietly. So we can know if any of them are coming this way; if we have to fight to defend ourselves, then maybe we can be prepared and make sure the Abolians are the only ones who are surprised next time." She looked around the room at all the scared faces that were crowded around the wounded men and women. "We know the city far better than they ever will. I'm sure we can manage to keep an eye on them without them catching us."

Karim grunted his agreement. "Maura's got a good head on her shoulders, people. If we'd been better prepared for that lot we fought with, we may well have been able to take them out and without four of us getting cut up."

"What makes you so sure?" a sour-faced woman Maura didn't know by name demanded.

"Fifteen years in the army makes me sure," Karim said. "That and the fact that we had them outnumbered four to one."

"Thank you, Karim," Maura answered. "I think we should send out people in pairs. I'd be too scared to go out alone, but I want to do my part too."

"Pairs is a great idea," Karim said. "I'll sort out teams of any volunteers. Every team will go out for no more than half an hour at a time so we'll only cover this immediate area. We don't want anyone to get overconfident and move off too far where the rest of us can't help. Just come see me if you want to join in, and we'll work out which area you should cover." Then he turned back to Maura. "But I don't think you should go, Maura.

You're keeping the whole lot of us organized and productive. You're doing too much good here for us to send you off."

Caught between feeling flattered and annoyed, Maura didn't manage to voice an appropriate argument before Karim moved away with the group of would-be scouts.

CHAPTER 4

The Abolian formations were advancing toward the wall. Captain Harrow could see the futility of trying to hold. The enemy had no cavalry. They had obviously come prepared to take a city. Large units of infantry in boiled leather armor, flanking units of skirmishers, and rank upon rank of crossbowmen. This would not be a siege. The enemy would throw themselves at the wall in a flood and pour over the wall to drown the city within. Harrow shook his head. King Ansyl had ordered them to hold the outer wall for as long as possible. But how were they meant to do that? Already the ranks were forming up, preparing to rain death on his men. And they had no way to answer. Never had he expected to face an enemy so cowardly that they would rely on missile weapons. His men would crouch under shields until a lucky bolt found them. They had practiced holding walls, of course, but the sheer length of the outer wall made the task impossible. Harrow set up his men in squads of eight, with a few dozen meters separating each squad from the next. They wouldn't be able to hold the whole wall, but they could make taking it cost the Abolians dearly. *The only thing keeping us in this fight is that they're only attacking in this one spot. If we had to split our forces . . .*

The king's voice sounded in his mind. "Harrow, assemble the Warchosen. Your men will hold the wall as best they can. I will assist you in taking the fight to the enemy."

Harrow turned to his troops and called out to those who were within earshot. "Stay mobile, and don't let them pin you down. Remember the most important thing is not to let them get a foothold on the wall. Now let's show them what the men and women of Sacral can do!"

"Chosen! To me!" he called. And the city's remaining Warchosen moved to join him at his observation point. As soon as they were assembled, the king spoke in his mind again. By the looks on the faces of the others, they could hear him as well.

"Now, you will need to tell me precisely where you want to be at any given time. I am distracted preparing other defensive measures and won't be making any strategic choices for you. Try to stay reasonably close to one another; I will move your group around as required."

"Thank you, Your Majesty. The first target should be the largest unit of crossbows. After that, we'll need to come back and reassess before going out again."

"Understood, Captain. Tell me when you need to get out."

"Get ready, Chosen. We're hitting the crossbows hard and fast. I want a maximum of damage done to that block."

The five Warchosen saluted him and drew their weapons. *Six Warchosen against at least twenty thousand soldiers . . . I can't say I like these odds.*

"Ready, Your Majesty."

There was no transition, no blackness. One instant the six Warchosen were standing atop the parapets, the next they were standing behind their enemy. A lifetime of training took over, and Harrow had buried his sword in the back of the first man before he had fully realized what he was doing. The other Warchosen were half a step behind him, laying in to the Abolians as hard and fast as they could. They tore into the lightly armored men and women like tigers in a henhouse. The crossbowmen were utterly defenseless against the Warchosen. A few tried to defend themselves using their crossbows like awkward clubs, and the smarter ones dropped the cumbersome weapons and drew their shortswords. Neither was very effective. The Sacral soldiers cut clear through the formation.

As they came to the other side, Harrow whispered, "Now, Your Majesty." They stumbled as the world changed around them, and they were once again on the wall. Up and down the line the Sacral troops cheered. Harrow could see the block of crossbowmen falling apart in confusion and fear. Many of the soldiers were fumbling with their weapons, torn between wanting to reload them and pull out their swords to defend themselves. Several had even discharged their quarrels into their companions.

"We will need to hit some of the other ranged units. But I'd like to time it for after they release, just in case."

As he observed the enemy formations, Harrow heard his Warchosen talking behind him. "How many you get, Brek?"

"Twenty-three I'm sure of. You?"

"Eighteen."

"So who's on top?"

"Harrow, of course. I was next to him the whole time. Pretty sure I counted thirty-five."

"I don't doubt it looking at him."

"Bet you fifty I can catch up on the next round. . . ."

Harrow stopped for a second and looked around. The Warchosen were all liberally spattered with blood and worse. When he looked down at himself, he saw scarcely any white at all showing on his tabard or a single patch of metal that wasn't caked in red gore. He shook his head; the games and bets would help keep the troops' minds off how impossible the task was.

"Look sharp, Chosen! We're going for round two. Another bunch of crossbowmen. After that, we're hitting their command. No break this time, and be ready for enemy champions. That bitch Zorat is probably around here somewhere."

"Third crossbow unit on the right, Your Majesty, then ten paces behind their command group on that small rise."

The next wave of bolts crashed into the defenders. Most hit stone or shields, but a few found flesh. Here and there men and women fell out of their defensive lines. Then at some unheard signal, the Abolian infantry surged forward. Each unit carried several tall ladders.

"Change of plans, Your Majesty. Brek, Slogen, and Rikka should stay here and help push back the attackers."

The Warchosen teleported again. Harrow and his three bit deeply into another unit. The other three found themselves jumping between sections of wall as ladders were set in place and Abolians were beginning to pour over onto the ramparts.

Now, Your Majesty, Harrow thought after they had fought their way almost through the unit.

The world changed in a blink. Four men and a woman stood in front of him. All of them wore elaborate armor and were heavily armed. He recognized Zorat immediately. *The nerve of the bitch.* Then he hesitated for a second. The four men snapped out weapons so fast there was no doubt they were all Warchosen as well. Harrow noticed Kabol standing on top of the rise, calmly watching as if he'd expected them to come.

Zorat moved forward, not even bothering to draw her weapons. *I've seen your pride bring you low before.* Harrow and his three charged. Harrow swung his sword at the unarmed woman, but she flowed around his attack and smashed her fist into his face with the force of a battering ram.

Harrow felt the earth jump up to hit him in the back. Then he was lying in the shadow of the wall, a group of healers clustered around him. A worried-looking face moved around above him. Words slowly sunk into his mind. Broken jaw. Teeth gone. Nose smashed. Skull fractured. Then with a sigh he fell asleep, the healer's power dragging him down into a soothing darkness.

It felt like only seconds had passed before a hand was gently shaking him awake. "I'm sorry to disturb you, sir. The priest said not to wake you for at least another hour, but the king is asking for you, sir."

With a guilty pang, Harrow's mind snapped to clarity. He grabbed the soldier's arm. "How are my men?"

The man's eyes widened in surprise. "Fine, all fine. Rikka, Gorsek, and Brek are leading the men atop the wall; I heard Sien boasting she had killed one of the Abolian Chosen. . . ." The man hesitated. "I'm sorry, my lord. Your healing isn't finished. The priests, sir, they are all gone."

Harrow pulled himself to his feet, gingerly testing his body for damage. The splitting headache and a slight fuzziness on the edges of his vision seemed to be his only problems. He climbed the steps back to the top of the wall to assess the situation. The soldiers had done remarkably well in his absence. They had held the entire section, but there were gaps in the line where too many brave men and women had been wounded and killed.

Harrow! came the voice of the king. *Our situation grows desperate. Another army approaches from the east. I have assembled my mages. We will assist each Chosen directly. We need to turn the tide on this front and quickly.*

This time, they hit the enemy lines in a blur of steel. Each of them had only to think of a new place and the king moved them with his power. Brek or Sien moved only when opposition started to build around them, while Rikka and Gorsek seemed to flicker in and out of existence with every other swing of their swords, sowing confusion and death wherever they passed.

The Abolian counterattack was brutally simple. A huge fireball appeared in the sky and swept down toward the wall. But they had once again underestimated King Ansyl. The fireball vanished just before it struck the wall and reappeared over a large unit of Abolians. The soldiers vanished into a swirling mass of ash and charred mud so fast that not one of them had a chance to scream. A flurry of sorcerous attacks flashed down toward the Sacral Chosen, only for each of them to be redirected by the king's power to strike at the Abolians' own forces. None of these attacks had the effect of the fireball. The enemy mages had learned from their mistake, and the spells struck glowing wards or simply winked out of existence before landing. Still, the effect this had on the morale of the Sacral troops was electrifying. Though the Abolians outnumbered them more than four to one, their army was being seriously mauled. The base of the wall looked like a slaughterhouse floor. Blood and fluids painted the stone wet in trails down the basalt where attackers had successfully reached the top before being repelled.

Flights of quarrels started flying toward the tops of the walls again. The Abolians didn't seem to care whether they killed any of their own men so long as they broke in. Harrow shook his head. He couldn't understand how a leader could be so careless with the lives of his followers. And yet, they had the numbers, and the crossbows were slowly whittling down the defenders. The Abolians didn't hesitate. Even as they died, not one soldier shied from attacking.

"Captain Harrow," came the king's voice. "I fear something terrible has happened. The priests do not answer my call. They have all disappeared from my senses, nor can I reach into the temple to speak with Yeltos. We need their healing arts, and, more, we need the power of the Mother herself. I will set you down near the temple. You must find them. I have drawn on my powers too deeply and my strength is failing. Without healing I will soon die. I will hold out here as best I can with your fellow Warchosen. Bring us aid, Captain! Without the goddess we will surely fall."

The now familiar feeling of teleportation followed. Harrow was standing in the middle of a wide avenue that led to the Great Temple. Smoke rose from where looted houses had caught fire. Debris and bodies were scattered around the streets, with the worst of the fighting seeming to have been in the direction of the temple itself. More disturbed by the desperate and confused sound of the king's thoughts, Harrow set off toward the temple at a jog.

***

The following months saw an increase in activity in the Darien slums after nightfall. The city watch patrolled the streets a little more often than usual, the Night Guard stepped up their presence as well, and demons patrolling for their masters in the Arcanum flew overhead at odd intervals. Most of those who disappeared into the slums vanished without leaving a ripple. But now several important, well-connected people had reportedly come to this part of the city for unknown reasons and had never been seen again.

And now this, thought Skeg, reading the message watchman Penn had sent him.

"Hi, Mister Skeg!" Nial called as she and Zuly walked into his shop.

"Hello, girls," he answered, looking up from the note he'd been reading for the fifth time. "Take a seat. I have some bad news."

"What's wrong?"

Skeg hesitated for a moment before telling them. "One of your little burial sites has been found. The Night Guard are out looking for whoever flayed those people and buried them under a hut."

They had gone rigid as soon as he mentioned one of their burial sites, but they relaxed again after he finished. "So they have no idea it's us?"

"No, they seem to think a cabal of some sort is responsible. Probably because you draw your power from so many souls. One of my contacts with the city watch was there and got conscripted into assisting them. A mage named Lera was at the burial site casting divinations and examining the runes you wove into the place. The flavor of your power is confusing them for now, but you really need to be careful for a while. These are not people you want to get on the wrong side of."

Nial nodded as Zuly said, "Thank you. We'll be careful. And we'll think of something else to do with the bodies." Then they went and took their place in the ward circle and looked at him expectantly, ready for their nightly lesson. Skeg sighed and sat down.

Nial and Zuly were so confident in their abilities that Skeg soon let himself relax about the situation. The Night Guard had visited his shop several times over the past weeks but always to follow a lead that led elsewhere or to ask about totally unrelated

matters. Nial had even mentioned that fewer demons were flying about these days. Whether the girls had cut back on their
hunting or had actually found some other way of disposing of
their victims Skeg didn't know.

The next night, an unexpected customer showed up in
his shop. This customer didn't trigger the spells that warned
Skeg when someone was approaching his door. He was simply
standing in front of the counter in a shop that had been empty
a moment earlier, wearing a long gray cloak and a featureless
white mask.

"Good evening, Mister Skeg."

Startled by the sudden appearance, Skeg exclaimed,
"Shade!"

"Indeed," Shade answered in his toneless voice. "I find
myself in need of your services."

Skeg hesitated for a moment. "You know as well as anyone
that I don't provide any services. I only sell materials. And if
you're here for more blood or bones, you'll have to look elsewhere. My stock has dried up for the moment."

"I am not here for anything like that. And I spoke the truth
when I said I was in need of your services. I need you to introduce me to a fascinating young woman whom I believe you are
well acquainted with."

Skeg's palms started to sweat. *He tracked Nial here? And
if Shade has, maybe others are coming.* Keeping his voice even
and calm, he answered, "Sorry, Shade, I don't get out that much.
I certainly don't know any young women who'd be interested
in meeting you."

"Ah, well, I never said she would be. I, however, am most
determined to meet her. And I'm afraid I must insist." He stood
there in silence for a few uncomfortable moments. "I'll trust
you to pass on my request, Mister Skeg. I can be patient, but
don't keep me waiting too long."

Skeg felt like he had eaten bad fish. His stomach was in knots while he waited for Nial to show up. When she finally arrived, he swallowed hard and blurted: "I have a message from someone who wants to meet you, girls."

Nial froze, a faint aura of power enveloping her. "I thought you never told anyone about me, Skeg."

Just like that, I'm not even Mister Skeg anymore. "And I haven't," he said, backing as far away from her as the closed confines of the shop would allow. "We have both learned from each other, and I have no intention of ruining our arrangement or our friendship. But this person is looking for you. He is being most insistent. Unlike any of the others, he has tracked you to this shop. No, I can't tell you how. I only know that he will ruin me if I do not arrange a meeting."

"Ruin you worse than I will if you betrayed us?" Zuly snapped angrily.

"I haven't! I swear it! This man calls himself Shade. He is preeminent among the underground mages of the city. I don't know his real name, or even what he looks like. He is an expert at masking his presence. So I say again—he knows things about you already. He probably even knows what you've been selling me; he did buy a fair portion of what you brought me over the last few months."

"And you didn't think this strange? You didn't think it worth telling us?!"

"All kinds of unsavory characters buy that flesh and blood. Some are not mages themselves but servants or even priests of some of the darker gods. Others are traveling merchants who know of a richer market for such things in another city. And some few are mages from this city—almost all unregistered. A couple are even from the Arcanum but conducting illegal research. . . . Or so I imagine. Demand varies from one group to another as a mage works out some new piece of research or has a weird idea he wants to try, but my best customer in recent months has been Shade. He doesn't announce himself. I've never even seen him enter my shop. He is always cloaked and always hides his features behind a mask."

"How strong is he?" Zuly's voice was devoid of emotion.

Skeg was sweating again. "I'm not sure. I haven't seen him do a lot. The stories are probably exaggerated. I'd say at the very least Third or Fourth Order. He could very well even be an archmage. Shade seems to be more of a title than anything else. Someone has carried it for centuries. I've found references to someone in Bialta calling themselves Shade for a thousand years. I'd be willing to bet, though, that he isn't all that power-ful, just smarter than your average outlaw."

"Did he say where he wanted to meet?"

"No, he only asked that I pass on the request and learn your answer. I'd have to say though, Nial, you've learned all I can teach you myself. If this man needs something from you, he may well be someone who can teach you more."

"Trust a strange man I've never met? One I know to have power?"

"Did you do any less with me? Besides, like me, he can't afford to get noticed. He can't expend too much of his power overtly, and to take you on he'd certainly need to. I've always assumed that's why you felt you could trust me."

Their face shifted from anger to sadness. "No, Mister Skeg," Nial said. "Nothing like that ever occurred to us. We trusted you because you were nice to us. Because you were always fair and never tried to take anything that wasn't offered. Because we like you."

Skeg unexpectedly felt a lump in his throat. "Thank you, Nial, that means more to me than I would have thought pos-sible. But I have to warn you against being so naive ever again. People die around you. That they are not the nicest of people is beside the point. You cannot judge people so quickly and easily. You rarely act on anything you don't see with your own eyes, but with Shade you must. He is a creature of subtlety. Every action of his has unexpected ramifications. He plays a strange game in this city, and none have yet guessed what he wants. I think he will eventually track you down. If he has tracked you this far . . . then he's close. This may be your only chance to meet him on your own terms."

Zuly and Nial looked at him in silence for a moment before Nial nodded. "All right. We will speak with this Shade. But if he threatens us, we will tear him apart and damn the attention that could bring."

"If it comes to that, I will be with you."

"Such sentiment, Skeg; I didn't think you were capable of it," a strangely flat voice said. Zuly hissed and prepared to lash out with her power. Skeg started and embraced his own meager talent.

"Now, now, there is no need for violence," the voice continued. "I will show myself, if and when I am certain you will not attack me."

Zuly considered for a moment. The voice was completely lacking in inflection. She could not decide if it was a man or a woman. "Show yourself then. But do not think I will leave myself defenseless."

"You have since you entered this shop. You cannot defend yourself against me. I have seen you at work several times in the past weeks," the flat voice continued. "I must thank you, Mister Skeg. When I said I was patient, I expected you to wait a few days if not weeks before speaking with the young ladies about me. Now . . . I believe introductions are not necessary. I know a lot about you already, of course, Zulaxrak. I know almost everything there is to know about you and your kind. I was not lying, though. I do not wish you harm. I have a singular problem, and I need a singular tool to deal with it. I want us to become business partners of a sort, much like you and Mister Skeg here."

"What do you want from me?" Zuly demanded. Skeg was not fooled; she was using her anger to mask her fear. Ever since he had met her, Zuly had been obsessed with becoming strong. And now the shield she had built around herself was revealed to be nothing but smoke.

"I need you to broaden the scope of those you deliver your own special brand of justice to. I need you to allow me to suggest some particular individuals who are in need of punishment."

"If I'm so helpless, then why don't you kill these people yourself?!"

"I could, of course. There would be little difficulty in the task. But my methods might be recognized. The flavor of my power—of my presence—might be detected in any number of ways I couldn't foresee. You however, my delightful little hybrid, are a total unknown to those in power who might look into these deaths. You are strong enough to carry out the executions with ease. Your hybrid blood would confuse many of the more common divinations. The removal of their souls contributes significantly to that end as well. In short, you are perfect for the task."

"We only hunt those we decide deserve it—we hunt the hunters."

"Truly? I thought that only an affectation. Or possibly a strategy to kill only those who would not be missed and thereby even gain the support of the common inhabitants of the Muds. But no, I see now. I see Skeg has learned his sentimentality from someone. Fascinating that a human would learn such tenderhearted ways from a demon out hunting for souls. Now I really don't mind so much if you do want to dig into these people's lives a little before you harvest their souls. I have little doubt that you will find them as loathsome as I do and be perfectly willing to take care of them as I suggest."

"And just why should I do anything you ask?"

"Ah, payment, a most mercenary question. I suppose I do need to provide some encouragement. I do need to make these particular souls more valuable to you than your common pedophiles, rapists, and murderers or you would have little reason to range beyond your usual hunting grounds. Very well, I will do as Master Skeg suggested earlier. If you do this thing for me, if you end the lives of these three individuals, I will instruct you in some few things you will find very useful. Agreed?"

"If you're so much stronger than me, why do you fear to show yourself?"

"I did not say any such thing, young Zulaxrak. I suspect your powers are significantly greater than mine, although your friend's account of my abilities may have fallen a little short of the mark. In any case, though, you possess raw power, and I possess knowledge and experience. In a direct confrontation, we would ruffle the feathers of every witch, mage, and priest for miles and you would no doubt defeat me. But you are thinking too simply. Strength, raw power, is not nearly as important as you seem to think in a magical confrontation. Besides, what would be served in me fighting fair? You are unable to detect my presence. I could simply overwhelm you at a moment of weakness." The threat hung in the air. Nial and Zuly stiffened further.

"I will leave some papers with Skeg sometime in the next day or two. The two of you, or should I say the three of you, can peruse them at your leisure and decide who you want to go after first and so on. I would advise, though, that bringing these particular bodies back to Skeg's shop might not be prudent." With that, the voice went silent. Nial and Skeg stood looking around for several minutes before deciding that Shade had gone.

The next evening when the girls walked into Skeg's shop, he could tell that Zuly was in full control. In control, and still furious over being discovered the night before.

"Has he left his list yet?" she snapped.

Skeg put a scroll on his counter. "I found this when I opened my shop an hour ago. None of my wards had been breached as far as I could tell."

The first name on Shade's list was a woman named Banjax. She was the lover and right hand of one of the city's crime lords, a man who called himself the Prince. Shade had given her a detailed list of the hideouts the pair used. All three were in the slums or in the catacombs that lay under the streets of the city.

"People live underground?" Nial exclaimed in surprise.

"Some do," Skeg answered. "Darien City is ancient. There were old burial catacombs and mines under the city before the sewers were built. A lot of the sewers were just built on to tunnels that were already in convenient places. There's a lot of space down there. Smell's not so good, but it gets you out of the rain and snow. Since the Muds have no sewers, the tunnels here are actually a lot cleaner than they are in other parts of the city. It's a maze down there. Crime lords control the upper parts of it, below that the Crawlers."

Nial looked at him in confusion.

"The people who live under the city?" he prompted with a sigh.

"Oh! The Rat people!" Nial exclaimed. "You mean they're real? I always thought they were just a story."

Skeg held out his hands toward her trying to slow the flood of speech he had triggered. *Nial is a sweet girl, but sometimes I wish Zuly was in control more when we have to talk about important things.*

"'Rats' is just a name merchants and nobles use for them. They are people just like everyone else. They call themselves Crawlers. A lot of them never come up to the surface anymore unless they really have to. I think Shade is a Crawler. Don't ask me how I figured that out. It's more of a guess than anything solid. But I think the people he wants killed have made life difficult for the Crawlers in some way. They tend to band together down there. Not that they have much choice. Usually the people who make their way down below are the most desperate, wretched things you'll ever see; it takes a certain amount of fear and desperation to crawl down into a dark hole and think it will be better than where you are. They support one another. They form packs or tribes of sorts and usually survive by stealing. They have to balance on the edge of a blade. Surviving, but not taking so much that the guards take an interest. For the most part, if a real criminal does try to hide down there, they usually kill him and dump the body back up here. Anything to keep the guards out."

Nial's gaze sharpened, and she tilted her head in a way that he'd come to associate with Zuly. "How do you know so much about them?"

Skeg shrugged. "I supply a couple packs of them with bits and pieces. I know of at least two groups down there that are led by talents. Neither are above Second Order, but they need magical supplies to make life better for their pack mates."

"But you said those who end up down there are the dregs of the slums. Even a weak mage can make a living pretty easily up here."

"Magic doesn't make happiness, child. Maybe they lost their families, maybe they had debts or enemies they were running from. . . . Maybe they only discovered their abilities after becoming Crawlers. I've wondered about it myself. But no matter how it happened, their packs earned their loyalty and they haven't abandoned them."

"You sound like you envy them."

"I guess I do, in a way. I was a street kid myself, after all. I know things are far from happy for those people. But they have a place where they belong and where everyone else has their back."

"Are you lonely, Mister Skeg?"

He smiled again. "How could I possibly be lonely with my lovely students visiting me at all hours?" The game of showing up shortly after Skeg went to sleep had become one of Nial's favorites. She grinned at him, and for a moment it was as if Shade hadn't come to interfere with their lives at all. Then the moment passed, and Zuly's sharp look returned.

"Anyway, getting at this woman won't be easy. Taking her soul before getting out of there will be even harder. I wouldn't start with this one. Let's take a look at the other two first." Skeg looked at the next page.

"Hmmm. Sorley. He's a fairly prominent merchant. I've heard his name thrown around quite a few times. Deals in spices and furs for the most part, I think. Looks like his house is on the other end of the merchant district. That'll be a bit of a walk, but it should be an easier target for you. Shade even gave us a list of other merchants Sorley deals with. He must not leave the city very often with a list this long."

"Who's the third?"

"A nobleman," Skeg said with a sigh. "This one is going to be trouble too. A lord named Gunnar Danekor. His manor is near the edge of the noble quarter. The papers here also give us a list of some of his other properties in the city. . . . A few brothels in the slums . . . a few more near the docks . . . more in the merchant quarter . . . and a handful of warehouses. Certainly an obvious preference for what kind of business he likes to get involved in."

"We'll start with the merchant."

"I still don't like any of this, girls. Shade's excuses for not doing these himself don't make sense for anyone but the noble. The criminal? No one would look into that one too much. But why only the woman and not her lover? He's a more likely target." Skeg considered for a moment. "I've heard of him too. He's powerful. He's only been in the city a few months, and the other crime lords are running scared. He might be a mage, or maybe even a Godchosen. He wouldn't be the first to make a pact with a god or a demon lord to gain power."

Nial looked at him, surprised. Skeg nodded at her. "It's not as unusual as you might think. Higher powers use people like people use animals, or pieces on a game board. And they like to give their own pieces an edge over everyone else's. Powers don't play fair if they can avoid it. That's why I steer clear of all the temples, legal or otherwise. We'll ask around a little before you move on this one. Better to get a clear idea what we're getting into."

"We?" Zuly asked, arching an eyebrow.

"Well, I'm not going to go hunting with you, but I'll help with the planning in any way I can."

Though Skeg couldn't be sure, he thought it was Zuly who answered him in an almost inaudible whisper, "Thank you."

CHAPTER 5

It took some time before Salt settled into a rhythm of sorts. He dragged his constantly bruised and aching body out of bed every day, ate the best food he'd ever seen in his life, then endured whatever torture Krigare and Gurt had devised for the day before crawling back to his room sometime after nightfall when the rest of the Night Guard set out, presumably to find more psychotic bitches to burn. Salt had thought a life at sea was hard. That he could handle anything life threw at him, that it had made him tough. But he was so exhausted after his months of training that it was all he could do to keep his eyes open through the evening meal.

Many of the Night Guardsmen were not physically imposing. But Salt had sparred with enough of them to know their thin frames were one and all hiding surprising strength and almost endless endurance. They all trained endlessly with a variety of weapons. Krigare was clearly unequaled by anyone in the Night Guard, and he worked tirelessly to improve the skills of all the others. Many of those Salt had gotten to know had also had their own brush with the kind of dark hungry forces that the Guard was meant to stand against. Seely was the lone survivor after some strange creature destroyed her village. Altog's wife and son had been killed by an insane mage.

The one time Salt had hinted to Gurt about wanting to leave the Night Guard, Gurt had just looked at him sadly and asked if he would be happy to scream for help the next time a crazy something had him tied down to a bed, or if he'd be able to sleep thinking of others in that position instead of him.

Salt had drifted away, his thoughts swirling around and confused. With everything that had changed in his life he had nearly blocked out the experience that had led him here. But after hearing Gurt's words, he remembered the horrible feeling of helplessness. The certainty of his own death at the hands of a smiling maniac.

Salt got up early the next day. Barely an hour past midday, he dressed in the still-dark room and slipped out so as not to wake any of the others. He collected a weighted practice sword from the storeroom and walked out to the training yard. Gurt and a few others were already working up a sweat. Salt owed a lot to Gurt and the others. They had saved his life, his sanity, even his soul. And had taken him in and given him a place where he could make more of himself than he had ever dreamed before. Bailing on them without giving it his all seemed like a piss-poor way to repay them. Now that he thought about it, that was probably why the Guard recruited a lot of their number from victims or their families. *Nothing like a messed-up mix of guilt, desire for vengeance, and gratitude to keep soldiers committed to the cause. Though the food and living conditions don't hurt either.*

Gurt caught Salt's eye and smiled before shifting his attention back to the two Guardsmen who were sparring in front of him. Salt was surprised when he recognized Wheeze, the medic, and Lera, the mage who had helped save him from the bug priestess. He hadn't seen either of them since the night he joined. It was a shock to see them training with sword and shield. Unusual for a medic, and downright strange for a mage of any real ability. In Salt's admittedly limited experience, mages were usually all caught up in looking scary and mysterious. *How can you tell a person is a mage if they don't dress the part?* It looked like both of them really knew what they were doing, too. They were both certainly better with a sword than Salt, though Wheeze sounded like he was going to fall over the entire time. It was a bit of an eye-opener.

Salt decided to warm up with a run, doing laps around the yard. He did drills with sword and shield, then just with a sword, and even worked for a while with a pair of maces that Krigare had started him with the day before. Salt was surprised how natural it was all starting to feel after such a short time. More Guardsmen trickled out and joined them as they got up. Lera and Wheeze had left by the time regular training started at three hours past noon.

The sun was shining down through the dust the Guardsmen were kicking up in the yard. Salt looked at them all and realized that even though he barely had time to talk to any of the Night Guardsmen beyond receiving pointers and exchanging jokes during practice, he already felt a kinship to these crazy bastards who hunted monsters every night. *I guess this place really is home now.*

"So, lad, you think you're ready to go out on patrol?" Gurt asked Salt as they finished their daily training. "I don't usually take new recruits out quite this early, but you seem to be getting the hang of things pretty fast. Besides, Altog and Min got pretty messed up last night, so we're short on numbers."

"What got them? Another shape-shifter?"

"Nothing so scary, lad. Smugglers. Trading in some nasty stuff. There were eight of them, and a couple of them really knew what they were doing. Altog took a sword in the neck, Min a crossbow bolt in the leg. She was lucky; the fool had kept the crossbow strung for too long so it didn't split her open too bad. Should be back on her feet in a couple days."

"What about Altog?"

Gurt laughed. "He's got a devil's own luck. Somehow every time he gets stuck, his armor's more messed up than he is. Wheeze's keeping him out of action for a couple days just to make sure, but it looks like he'll be fine. Best part is he can't talk right now," Gurt added with a grin. He clapped Salt on the shoulder. "So? You up for a romp through the Muds?"

"I'll do my best," Salt answered.

"Wouldn't expect anything less, lad. Make sure you get washed up and fed double time. We're heading out a little early tonight. We have a lot of ground to cover."

That night Salt was so nervous he could barely swallow his food. Roast lamb, steamed greens, fresh brown bread, and cold dark ale. None of his old shipmates would believe he'd hesitate to eat food like this. But all he managed to do was push the food around and drain his single cup of ale far too quickly. His normal mealtime drowsiness was gone.

Gurt came over and sat opposite him. He settled onto the bench and started to heap food onto his plate. "You should try to eat more than that, lad. It's going to be a long night."

Salt made a noncommittal noise and went back to pushing his food around.

"So how do we do this?" he asked. "Do we just wander around the shittier parts of the city looking for trouble?"

"Gods, lad, what do you think this is? The city watch? You're in the Night Guard. We answer only to the king himself. The city watch live in their own homes and eat what they can with the coppers they get paid." He looked down meaningfully at the food on the table. "There are never more than two hundred Night Guardsmen. And in case you didn't notice, we've got mages on our team. Four of them rarely leave the palace. Lera comes out with us now and again though and even conscripts a handful of helpers from the Arcanum if we need them. The ladies do our legwork for us. And, yes, all five of them are women. They do whatever it is they do with their magic and give us a list of places we should look into. I add in a handful of our regular informants or anything else I hear about and split up the list between the squads going out."

"Two hundred? But I've never seen more than a few dozen."

"Bialta's a big place, lad. We send out a few on long patrols or station them in some of the bigger cities."

Salt nodded his understanding. "And we're busy every night?"

"Pretty much."

"How many crazy fuckers can one city hold?"

"You'd be surprised, lad. Big cities are lodestones to trouble. Crowds are the best way for those crazies to get lost. They promise anonymity. Most of the cultists, insane mages, demons, and whatnot find out pretty fast they can't hide in a little town for long. They all prey on other people in one way or another. They get noticed eventually out there unless they keep on the move and that's just as much of a hassle for them as it would be for you or me. On top of that, ports are usually worse with the number of people coming in and out all year, and the Arcanum seems to attract a fair few as well, not that they'd thank you for sharing that fact—that's why almost half the Night Guard are usually stationed in or around the capital."

"But I've never even heard of the Night Guard. And all I've ever heard of these other things are rumors."

"Aye, lad, they are. Because we usually don't spread the stories around too much. That and we do our best to clean up

after a job. We make it so people can live without always looking over their shoulders."

Salt ate a few bites of food, a pensive look on his face. He'd
been through a lot in his life, but stepping out to walk the streets
at night hunting magical threats was a big leap, and he couldn't
help but feel nervous. "So where are we going tonight?"

"Most of our work is in the slums or the dock district. Not
that we don't have to raid the odd mansion or merchant's house
mind you. Tonight is a typical night. We have two stops in the
slums, one an herbalist who sometimes hears things; the other,
a crazy bastard who dabbles in magic and sells arcane supplies.
Then we're going to check out a warehouse near the docks—
Lera says there are some pretty heavy wards on the building.
Might just be expensive cargo, but you never know what you
might find. If we see something we don't like, we call in help."

"So what do we do if we find a crazy-ass mage and Lera's
not with us?"

"We take care of them any way we have to. Even an archmage will die if you stick your sword through them. I dole out
a few enchanted trinkets when a situation calls for them, but
it's best to learn to make do without. Even for us, there's never
enough to go around. I've rejigged the squads, by the way.
Krigare will be leading his own squad now. So that leaves us
with Seely, Greal, Skye, Wheeze, and Brolt, and Min and Altog
once they're back on their feet. Now go get your stuff. We're
heading out in ten minutes."

Salt put on his leather armor and picked up a longsword in a
back harness, a mace, and a couple of daggers from the armory.
Then he went out into the yard to meet the others. Seely was
dressed in plain leather armor like him, an expensive-looking
rapier and parrying dagger tucked into her belt. As always
she looked nervous and didn't look anyone in the eye. Skye
stood next to her. With dark skin and confident bearing, she

provided an almost perfect contrast to Seely. Skye wore a long cloak over her armor, which almost hid the small crossbow that she had strapped to her back. While she waited she took practice swings and stabs with her broad-bladed spear. Greal was even more easily recognizable. The dark leather mask he always wore made his deep-blue eyes stand out strangely. His thick, curly black hair and beard stuck out around it, strands of silver breaking up the blackness. Unlike the others, he wore a heavy suit of blackened steel chain and plate. The huge tulwar he favored was on his back, and a brace of daggers crossed his chest. Brolt disdained armor entirely. He always insisted in training that it slowed him down, but Salt was surprised to see him actually go out on patrol dressed only in nondescript dark clothes. The two thin-bladed sabers he wore at his belt in black-and-silver scabbards would have been enough to draw attention to the man. But his insane collection of symbols tattooed into his skin had most people stopping in the street to stare. Most disconcerting were the quite lifelike eyes tattooed on his eyelids. Filling out the squad were Gurt and Wheeze. Both were dressed in standard leather armor and armed with light wooden shields and shortswords.

Salt's worst fears seemed unfounded as his squad trudged through dark, muddy streets. Most of the people they met scurried off as quickly as they could when they spotted the heavily armed group. It came as a relief when Gurt said they had arrived at their first stop—an herbalist shop owned by a pungent wastrel of a man named Edrel. Edrel's shop was dirty and poorly kept. Boxes and pots of unidentifiable herbs and powders overflowed or cracked and spilled their contents onto the floor. The man himself was little better. He was utterly filthy as only a street urchin had any right being. A ragged fringe of greasy hair hung into his eyes and made him blink with irritating frequency. After a few minutes of listening to

Gurt speak to the man, Salt decided that the stop had been a waste of time. Everything the man spoke of was unnecessarily vague and only included topics that seemed totally unimportant to Salt. Still, the coins Gurt handed him were more than enough to buy a new set of clothes and a year's worth of cheap soap. They moved back out to the street and set off again. The herbalist had seemed to forget they were there as soon as he got his payment.

"So what was all that about?" Salt asked as they moved down the street deeper into the slums.

"Ha! Sounds like nothing but crap I'm payin' good coin for, right?" Salt grunted his agreement.

"Well, most times you'd be right. Some idiot selling tallow for ten times the going price wouldn't mean anything to me. But I have to look into it. It might just be the materials come from somewhere they shouldn't. All the rest of it was pure bullshit, though. Old Edrel likes to pad out the little bits of good stuff. Thinks I pay him more for it. Not that he'd believe me if I told him the truth."

"How often do we have to come see this guy? His store smells worse than a bilge hold on a Keralan merchant ship."

"That it does, lad. . . . We drop in on him as often as Lera puts him on our patrol. She seems to be able to tell when he has something for us. Doesn't happen more than once a month most of the time. But trust me when I say we have to deal with far worse."

"So what's next?"

"We're going to drop in on a guy named Skeg. Nasty piece of work. He's got ties to nearly every mage in the city, legal and otherwise. After that, we're supposed to have a look at a couple of warehouses near the docks. Lera says they're warded but weren't last week. Could just be expensive cargo and the owners are rich enough to hire a mage to make sure it stays safe . . . but we'd best take a look." He turned to the others.

"Brolt and Seely, you go on ahead to the warehouses and take a quiet look. The rest of us will drop in on this tallow merchant on the way to see Skeg and meet you outside the Drunken Horse."

Salt looked mildly surprised. "Aye, lad, we split up sometimes to speed things along. Brolt and Seely are the best scouts we have. Best to let them do their work without us walking on their coattails. Besides, they'll both appreciate not having to see Skeg." The others who hadn't been named all voiced their agreement.

The tallow merchant turned out to be a fraud. The candles the man sold were of poor quality and did not contain any forbidden substances. "You'd be surprised how many freaky people are willing to pay a lot for candles made from human fat," the merchant said in his defense. "I just sort of hinted that my special candles had a special ingredient and charged a lot for them." Gurt just shook his head and said, "Just don't get yourself killed over it."

"Suicidal bastard," he muttered as they left the shop. "As if we don't have enough trouble keeping people alive in this city without idiots like him baiting crazy cultists."

"It might draw some real targets out though," said Salt. Gurt paused for a moment and considered.

"That he might, lad. Might as well make his self-destructive greed work in our favor. I'll ask Lera to keep an eye on the place."

Skye slapped him on the back. "Looks like you'll fit right in, Salty." Unsure whether he was being complimented or made fun of, Salt just grunted and kept walking.

They walked for a while longer until they came to an unmarked door at the end of a long alley. The place stunk even worse than most of the slums. "This is the place," Gurt said as he pushed the door open. He waved to Salt to follow him in. The rest of the squad waited outside. The place was a stark contrast to the other shops they'd visited that night. While the building was as old and sagging as the others, the interior was spotless and well maintained. The dizzying variety of goods that the place contained were all neat and well organized. Salt looked around in wonder until he saw the shopkeeper standing behind a counter at the back of the room. He froze, unsure what to make of the man. His eyes darted between the man's strange tattoos and the chaotic variety of items and tools that had been pushed through the man's skin and flesh. If it weren't for the absence of blood and Gurt's unperturbed expression, Salt would have sworn the shopkeeper had been tortured within an inch of his life.

"Welcome, Night Guardsmen." The man's voice was a gravelly rasp.

"Evening, Skeg," Gurt answered. "Lera said you'd have something for us."

"Of course, she did," Skeg said, a knowing smile on his lips. He pushed a scrap of paper across the counter to Gurt and waited. Salt couldn't make sense of the writing on it. He could read Bialtan after a fashion, but the writing on the paper was totally new to him.

Gurt looked at the paper for a second, then back at Skeg. "This true?"

"So I am told," he answered, shrugging. "Make of it what you will." They looked at each other in silence. There was something really weird about Skeg's unblinking stare, Salt decided. Gurt dropped a handful of coins onto the counter and gestured for Salt to follow him out.

"That guy is seriously fucking creepy," Salt said as they rejoined the others.

Gurt laughed. "As good a description for the old bastard as I've ever heard."

"But he's clean?" Salt asked. "Seems to me he's just the kind of guy we'd be after."

"He's exactly what we're after," said Greal, fingering the hilt of his tulwar. "But he's off-limits."

Salt looked around at the others.

Gurt nodded. "We're sure enough he's involved with things he shouldn't be. But he's also not nearly as bad as he looks. He supplies Lera and her bunch with whatever they need. Not all of which is strictly legal. . . . So long as he gives us information that helps us catch bigger fish, we let it slide."

"But how could he stay in business if he keeps turning in his customers?" Salt asked, confused.

Wheeze looked impressed. "You were right, Gurt, this new guy is sharper than he looks."

Gurt smiled. "To answer your question, he doesn't inform on his customers as far as I know. He gives us news on visitors and newcomers to the city. Half his customers probably feed him info to pass along to us."

"Good arrangement," agreed Salt. "So? He give you something good?"

"Depends what you consider good, lad. It's bigger than whatever might be in the warehouse, anyway. We need to meet up with Brolt and Seely and get on this. Seems we might have a wolf cult in the city."

Wheeze whistled. "Oh, Min is going to be pissed she missed this." Salt looked at him. "Not my story to tell, sorry, Salty. Enough to know Min has a score to settle with the wolf god."

"Amarok cultists have tried to set up in Darien before," explained Skye. "They're never easy to deal with. Worst thing is how generous Amarok is with its power. Near half the cultists are Godchosen to some extent. Makes them more wolflike, on top of being stronger and faster. Probably why there's never any shortage of idiots looking to join."

They met up with Brolt and Seely who reported that there was nothing outwardly suspicious about the warehouses they had been moving to inspect.

"Good enough for me," said Gurt. "We'll take a closer look tomorrow. For now, I want you two taking a look at the house across from the Last Great Inn. Double-time, soldiers. I want you to check things out ahead of us getting there." The two ran off ahead at a jog while Gurt moved the rest of the squad forward at a forced march.

Salt was sweating hard by the time they got to the address Skeg had given them. Though he was thankful for the training he'd gone through the past months, he couldn't believe they expected him to be in fighting form after the day he'd had. Seely met them two streets away from their target.

"Looks to be true. There's a wolf sign on the door, though it's been scuffed and hidden. We haven't seen anyone go in or out since we got here, but there's light inside."

Gurt looked at the others. "You know how fast one of these cults can spread. We're just waiting for Seely and Brolt to catch their breath, then we're hitting them. Take prisoners if you can, but don't expect any of them to surrender." Gurt gave Salt a meaningful look.

Oh shit! This is it! Salt thought. He hefted the mace in his right hand and drew a dagger with his left. It was time to fight. Maybe to die. *Dammit, there's no way I'm going to let one of those freaks kill me on my first night out.* Skye reached over and squeezed his shoulder. Then they were running toward the house. Greal smashed the door in and disappeared from sight. The others charged in after him, Brolt stood watching the street, and Salt was left to go in last. Four men and two women wearing long gray robes stood inside the single-room house. All wore looks of shock and anger. A crude altar had been built on the back wall. A stone chalice rested on it.

Gurt was shouting something about the cultists giving themselves up. But they just looked at one another and smiled. Then all hell broke loose. Three of the cultists changed.

Salt wasn't sure how it happened. One minute they were normal if slightly crazed-looking people. The next, their forms blurred somehow and changed. Two of them had grown taller, had fangs protruding from their mouths and lambent eyes. The third changed more drastically. He grew taller as well, but his head became more wolflike; his body sprouted fur, and his fingers became clawed. The rest of the cultists scrambled to find what weapons they could. Greal didn't hesitate for a moment. He stepped forward as soon as the change started and cut one of the Godchosen in half with his huge tulwar. Skye was only a step behind him, lunging forward to take the wolf-headed man in the stomach with her spear.

A cultist attacked Salt with an old rusty sword, and his attention was drawn away from the others. It only took a moment for Salt to realize his opponent didn't know the first thing about technique. Not that it made him any easier to fight—he was angry and utterly fearless. Salt tried to wound him, intent on taking the man prisoner. But he fought like an animal. A few moments later, Salt was staring down at a corpse. His dagger was protruding from the man's chest. A hand grabbed his shoulder. Salt tensed and raised his mace, only to realize it was Gurt. The fight was over. The Amarok cultists had all been killed. Skye's spear had been snapped into pieces, and Wheeze was leaning over her unconscious form.

"She all right?" Salt asked.

"Got knocked about, but I think she'll be fine," said Gurt.

Salt nodded and walked outside. He nearly tripped over another body. Brolt had apparently seen his share of action outside. Three men lay dead outside the house. All of them showed multiple slash wounds. Brolt himself was standing over them, fastidiously cleaning his sabers with a scrap of cloth. Salt felt nauseated. He managed a few paces before he was noisily sick. Gurt and Brolt came and collected him. Gurt was carefully carrying the stone goblet from the altar.

"We need to get this back to Lera. Blood of the Wolf they call it. Something to do with how they make more Godchosen." Salt nodded dumbly, not fully registering any of the words. "Come on, lad. The others will finish up in there. Let's get you home."

***

Word had gone out about Maran Vras's defeat, and it had been the talk of Tolrahk Esal for a week. But that was nothing compared to the buzz that followed the announcement that Maran had recovered from his terrible wounds and had challenged the Old Man to a rematch. None doubted the result would be the same, yet everyone wanted to be there to witness. Carver looked over his slave and smiled. He had left enough of Maran unchanged so that he might still be recognized, but internally there was little that resembled the former arena champion. He had had to work quickly, too quickly for any finesse. He was sure, though, it would be enough to attract the kind of attention he wanted.

He had carefully observed the Old Man during the fight. The rest of the crowd may not have been able to see it, but Carver knew what the old champion was, and where his strength came from—a fallen Godling inhabited the old fool. It lived off the adulation of the crowds now that its real worshippers were dust. Most of its power was tied up in the glaive, likely the only artifact of its faith left on this world. It used the Old Man as a puppet, reading its opponents' intentions from their minds and reacting to them before they began. He wouldn't stand a chance against the new and improved Maran Vras. Maran's mind, in the truest sense of the word, was gone. Carver had cut off all but the most basic of impulses and reflexes. There would be no reading his intentions this time; Maran Vras might have thoughts, but they would be totally disconnected from the part of his brain that was now controlling his body. Added to that was a reinforced musculature that would not only improve his speed and strength, but his control. Maran could swing a weapon with great strength and stop instantly or even reverse the motion in a way that no natural being could, Warchosen or otherwise. He was now a thing of instinct and reflex incapable of conscious thought. All he could do was follow simple commands given by his master: eat, sleep, kill.

Carver actually felt a sliver of regret when he destroyed the mind of what had been a particularly fine specimen. But a tool was needed to perform a function. Maran had become that tool. If given enough time, he might be able to rebuild the man's mind and make him into something more. If there was anything Carver hated, it was waste.

The arena was crowded beyond capacity. The arena owners had been only too happy to admit everyone who had the coin to pay. Far more people than usual were willing to hand over the arena's exorbitant fees after the hype of the rematch. *Perfect,* thought Carver. *There will surely be a royal or another likely sponsor in the crowd today.*

He had come early. As the owner of one of the famous fighters, the arena owners had shown Carver every courtesy. He had been shown to his previous seat and provided with the same slave to serve his needs. Most of the other seats and awnings were being dismantled to make room for more spectators. Carver had no interest in the fights today. They were of no consequence. The only thing that mattered was finding the right contact in the crowd. He had made no secret of his status as owner of Maran Vras. He had also told the arena owners that he was a mage and had made some significant changes to the champion that would make him far more dangerous. Word would spread.

Carver asked his slave about the identity of the various individuals in the crowd who, like him, were offered full seats to themselves. The slave seemed as well informed about the identity of the patrons as he did about the combatants. *A fine mind in this one,* Carver mused. Then his attention was drawn to a man on the far side of the arena that the slave said was Gruig, eldest son of the Drokga himself. *He will be the one to take me to his father.* The man was a typical Tolrahkali, golden skinned and armed to the teeth. What set him apart were his startling leaf-green eyes and his huge head of scraggly hair twisted into countless small braids. Each braid was ringed with a thick band of gold. *If nothing else, the gold that fool wears in his hair would be enough for me to work for a few weeks.* Carver studied the man through the afternoon as he waited for the champions to clash. Gruig didn't strike him as anything special, but then looks could be deceiving. He would have to be careful how he handled this one. He would not get a second chance.

When Maran Vras finally took to the sands, the crowd went into a frenzy. Carver was pleased to see so many of them pointing to his gladiator and making wild gestures. Indeed, Maran Vras had grown since his last fight. He stood nearly an arm's length taller than he had a month earlier. His muscle mass had increased so much that his skin looked to be straining to contain it. There was no show of being a brute, no pacing and growling like an animal. Maran Vras stood quiet, his customary mace and shield held at the ready. *It will be a short fight.* Carver allowed himself a small smile.

The Old Man dragged himself to his customary place in the center of the sands. Carver was doubly pleased to see that most of the crowd didn't even notice him entering the arena. All eyes were still fixed on Maran. The arena master made some big announcement that Carver paid no attention to. The crowd howled its approval, and, at last, the battle was joined.

Maran Vras moved smoothly toward the Old Man, who seemed to be confused, a clear look of puzzlement on his face. The puzzlement turned to shock when Maran darted in and struck him, the mace crashing against his left hip. Blood flew. The Old Man stumbled. Maran darted in again, this time landing blows on both his opponent's arms. Bones snapped audibly. The Old Man tottered on his feet for a few moments, then slowly his grip on the glaive failed. The weapon fell away from him. A small cry of pain and desperation passed his lips. No one would have heard it at all were the whole of the arena not staring in shocked silence. Maran was without mercy. His next attack broke the Old Man's jaw and opened up gouges across his face. He attacked again and again. Blood spattered and more bones crunched beneath his blows. In another moment it was all over.

Blood soaked the sands. Maran wasn't even breathing hard. He stood impassively over the broken and mangled body of the champion. Carver noticed that the glaive, lying abandoned in the sands, was visibly corroding. It wouldn't last long, nor would the Godling who had inhabited the fallen champion. The uproar in the arena was deafening. Half the spectators were cheering wildly; the others were angry and shouting. Whatever their position, one thing was undeniable. The arena had a new champion. Maran Vras's name would live on for a very long time even if he never fought again.

Carver wondered idly if Maran was taking any satisfaction in his newfound fame and glory, locked away in the back of his own mind as he was. He shrugged and swept those trivial thoughts from his mind. A slave was approaching, fighting his way through the crowd that was moving in the opposite direction toward the exits. *Ah, this is it.*

"Sir? Are you the one they call Carver?" the slave asked with a deep bow.

"I am."

"My master, Gruig Berrahd Tolrahk, asks that you attend him."

Almost too easy. Carver held up his walking stick. "Please inform your master that I will come to him as quickly as I am able." He turned to the slave who had been attending him. "Slave, collect my winnings from the arena master and bring them to me." He shuffled slowly toward Gruig. He could almost smell the man's impatience as he hobbled forward. *Young, impatient, and rich. I couldn't ask for a better target.*

"Greetings, my lord Gruig. How can a twisted thing such as myself serve a great lord of Tolrahk Esal?" Gruig's lips thinned slightly in annoyance at the obvious sarcasm. *Not as stupid as I could have hoped perhaps.*

"I have never seen anything like that." Gruig made a vague gesture toward the sands where Maran Vras was still standing over the Old Man's corpse, waiting for further instructions. Arena slaves were standing a safe distance away, nervously looking at the gladiator. Carver sent a mental command to Maran Vras to meet him outside.

"Thank you, my lord. I do have some rather unique talents when it comes to modifying living creatures. This, I'm sorry to say, is not my best work. I found myself short of funds and was constrained by the arena fight dates."

"I would like to see more of what you can do. Funds are still an issue?"

"Less so than they were, my lord, but mine is an expensive trade."

Well used to being asked for coin, Gruig nodded. "You will come to the palace. I will instruct the guards to expect you. You will be given whatever you need, within reason, but no gold. In two months' time you will show what you can do to the Drokga."

"My lord, it would be a great honor to be your guest in the palace and to put myself in the service of your father." Carver did his best approximation of a bow with his walking stick and twisted back. Gruig stood abruptly and walked away, leaving Carver alone in an almost-empty arena. *No long speeches. The Tolrahkali do have some positive traits after all. And just like that the full resources of the city-state are nearly at my fingertips.*

Carver arrived at the exit in time to see the arena master hand a heavy bag of coins to the slave. Carver took the coins and on a whim asked, "How much for this slave?" He handed over the requested coins and walked out.

"Thank you for purchasing me, master. My name is Roga."

Carver stopped and turned a burning stare on the slave. "You will speak when necessary and never again interrupt my thoughts. Now lead me to the palace by the quickest road." He gestured to the maze of streets that he had only just started to get used to. Roga bowed deeply and walked ahead a few paces.

CHAPTER 6

Beren got to his shop to find it already open. Jerik was already at work making as many weapons as he could in a short time. Gerald was frantically running back and forth ordering and reordering everything in the shop. Neither of them were surprised to see Beren back.

Jerik said, "I've been finishing any weapons I had started. I figure more weapons might be needed so this is the fastest way for me to get anything finished. After that, I guess I can make spear points or something easy."

"That's good thinking. I guess I'll do the same and put simple runes on the weapons you finish. Just pass them out to me as they're ready and I'll do *something* to them," Beren replied.

We're just passing time, and we both know it. If these weapons are really needed, that will mean the soldiers are dead and the city is as good as lost already. Beren started losing himself in his work. Gerald would come into his workroom at odd intervals with food or water. Beren would drink and eat dutifully and continue working almost without noticing the interruptions. He had to admit, the premise of being useful helped.

He had rarely worked so quickly or so well, and it wasn't long before an odd assortment of weapons was piled up next to his worktable, each with a rune of strength or quickness engraved into it. He almost made himself believe, if he could just get enough weapons runed, somehow, everything would be okay.

It was late in the afternoon when Beren got up and stretched. He'd never worked so long in one sitting before. He usually got caught up in a discussion with Jerik or Gerald about some new idea or a particularly exciting match. He realized he hadn't seen either his friend or his son in hours. *Time for a break,* he told himself.

Suddenly he heard a scream from the front room of the shop. A moment later his door was kicked in, and a tall man in unfamiliar leather armor burst in. It never even occurred to Beren to defend himself with his talent. He reached for the nearest thing at hand, one of his carving tools, and threw it at the man. It bounced off his breastplate, and the man only laughed before smashing his fist into Beren's stomach. The edges of his vision started to go black. Beren teetered on his feet for a moment before falling over. The enemy soldier stepped over him and raised his sword, preparing for a killing blow. *A soldier, yes, that's who that is. So the city is already lost. They are inside the walls. And that scream from the front room . . .* Beren was near panicking as his mind connected the events. He reached back and grabbed the first thing he could and swung it at the man's legs. A moment later the Abolian's armored weight crashed down on top of Beren.

Convinced that he would soon be dead, Beren struggled to push his assailant off. Then he noticed the soldier attacking him wasn't moving. He tried to shift the man off him and was surprised when the man rolled off him easily, his body limp. A sword was still buried in the man's leg—the sword he'd been experimenting with for weeks. A small patch of blood was visible where it had slipped through the joint behind the knee and pierced the skin. *Poor workmanship that. Still, not a deep wound, nothing life-threatening certainly,* he thought, before his mind snapped back to the here and now. His eyes went back to the sword. A dozen runes on the blade still shone at full power. Beren reluctantly reached for the hilt. *What have I created?* He pulled the blade out and inspected it carefully, first with his eyes, then with his talent.

The internal network he had traced inside the blade was brimming with power. The almost absurd profusion of runes he had carved into the blade were slowly activating, one after the other. *All of that energy drained from the unfortunate man who let me prick him with it.* He checked the soldier carefully, expecting him to jump up and attack again at any moment. But there was no denying it. Beren's sword had killed the man by barely cutting into the skin of his leg.

By the time he walked out of his workroom, twenty runes had lit up on the sword, various versions of strength, sharpness, speed, and more. All were fully active, as if they were carried by different men, fueled by a life. Three enemy soldiers were busy sacking the front room of his shop when he came into it holding the glowing sword tentatively. The men laughed and shouted something in their own language before one of them lifted his sword and moved forward to kill Beren. He swung his blade in a hard overhand swing, clearly meaning to overpower the bookish man. His eyes widened when Beren's hesitant parry knocked his blow wide. *Twenty-five runes.* Beren tried an attack of his own that neatly took off the enemy soldier's arm. He fell to the ground dead as soon as the sword pierced his skin. More power flowed into the sword. Beren grunted as a strange sensation flowed up his arm. But there was no time to think about it. The other two soldiers were moving toward him with careful steps. Both had their shields raised and were trying to flank him. It did them no good. *Thirty-two runes.* Beren swung the sword at the man on his left, feeling like the soldiers were moving in strange, slow movements. The Abolian didn't have time to react before the blade sliced through his face. The last soldier died with the rune sword through his stomach before the body of his friend had hit the ground, falling across the bloody body of Gerald. *Forty runes.*

"Gerald!" Beren screamed. "What have they done to you?" He tried to drop the sword but it would not leave his hand. With his free hand he reached down and pushed the dead Abolian off his son. The gaping wound in Gerald's chest left no room for chance or hope. *My son is dead, just like that.* Dazed, Beren stepped out of his shop, dimly aware of Jerik emerging from the back room with his largest hammer clutched in his hands like a weapon.

Bands of Abolian soldiers were sweeping through the city, coming from the east. *The east? But the attack was coming from the west!* Beren quickly realized as he walked away from his shop that as the outnumbered Sacral army fought valiantly to stop the Abolians, a second army had moved into the city unopposed from the other side. A passing group of soldiers caught sight of Beren and moved to attack. His sword was glowing brightly now with more active runes than he had ever thought possible. Too many to easily count. With barely any effort he cut them all down. Once he had started, though, it was difficult to stop. More Abolians were moving into the city at every moment. They were around every corner, down every street, all of them he encountered trying to kill him.

Beren wove an erratic path through the city. His strength and speed were always increasing, but it was becoming more and more difficult to control. His sight and mind couldn't keep up with his own body. He tripped over rocks and corpses, stumbled over debris, slipped and fell. But even then he needed only to set his eyes on an enemy with the intent to defend himself before his body surged forward and his blade split their flesh or severed their limbs. He was trapped in a nightmare of death and fear. Only the primal need for self-preservation kept him focused on defending himself from the snarling invaders. More and more soldiers died on his blade, until he lost count. Was it twenty? Fifty? With a shock he realized that the last soldier he had cut down with the cursed sword wore the white tabard of Sacral. A scream welled up in his throat as energy crackled up his arms. When the scream finally tore from his throat, it sent everyone within a hundred paces to their knees, clutching at burst eardrums. Horrified by what he was doing, he pushed himself deeper into enemy lines.

As the sword swelled with energy, it became too much for the internal mechanism to contain. Not that it slowed down its ability to draw in more; it just passed it back to its bearer. Beren became stronger and stronger as the night wore on. His wounds closed faster than they could be inflicted on him. He became greater than any Warchosen. His strength was that of a hundred men, his body near invulnerable. Enemies rose up on all sides, and he cut them down. His movements were too fast to predict. The power continued to build, surging up his arms and across his body. He was its slave. Runes carved to ensure he couldn't be disarmed bound his hand to the hilt as surely as if the sword were a part of his own body.

Then fire erupted around him. The Abolian he was killing burst into flames in front of him. The deepest spark of Beren's mind, the only part that was not lost to the nightmare, screamed. He was dimly aware that a mage of great power was calling fire down onto him. Abolian soldiers were killed by the dozen as he darted around and the pillar of fire tried to track his movements. The flames passed over him several times, but the energy suffusing him protected him from the worst of it. He was not reduced to ash. His hair was burned off, his skin charred to a black ruin, and his eyes burst, sending twin streams of sizzling fluid down his ravaged face. Finally, he crumpled to the ground. The ordeal was finally over.

But the sword was not done with him yet. Mere moments after Beren hit the ground, his eyesight started to return. The pain of his burnt flesh was receding. He realized after a moment that skin was growing back on his arm. He looked up and saw more Abolians closing in on him; the sword's runes still glowed, barely dimmed by regrowing most of his body. *No! Please, not again!* But there was no intelligence within his creation, no mind he could reason with. Nothing but a channel for energies he had foolishly thought he understood and could master. He could not release the sword while the runes still had power. And while there were living enemies around him, the power would not end. As much as he wanted this ordeal to be over, Beren did not want to die. If he could only make it through the enemy army and out into the Wastes. Maybe he could wait it out and return to the city later. He needed to get home. To Maura, to poor Gerald. . . . What would she think of him now with the blood of hundreds staining his hands? So much blood and yet he'd been unable to save their son. Too caught up in his work as always to be of any good to his family.

He suddenly realized what he must be doing to the enemy army. So many men lost. All to some unexplained force. He was certainly doing his share to keep the city and Maura safe. He had failed Gerald. He would not fail Maura. *So be it.* He would be a thorn in the side of the army. He would endure this hell for *her* sake, and pray that it was enough to keep her safe. *However big this army is, if one part of it is focused on killing me, then it isn't attacking the city.* With new resolve he focused his still-healing eyes on the blurry shapes that were only now moving into the area of burning grass and bodies. He darted forward, taking the nearest soldier's head clean from his shoulders. The power started to build again. Clarity returned to his eyes. He wished they were still just indistinct smudges, but he would not stop now. Lightning stabbed the ground around him. A ball of fire flew toward him. But now that he was paying attention, it moved with almost laughable slowness. He moved away from its point of impact, cutting down soldiers like rushes as he went. Flames exploded outward again, incinerating everything in a large area, but he had already moved beyond their reach.

Beren continued his butcher's work, chopping into body after body until he realized the soldiers were running. He pursued a group of fifteen or so and cut them down to a man. The second group he overtook were hindered by a man in dark red robes who seemed unable to walk much less run. *Yes! Run! They are retreating! Just a little more now.* He cut them down like all the others. The man in the red robe offered no greater resistance than any of the rest as Beren continued his clumsy massacre. Finally, there were no more enemies in sight. Nothing but the smoking battlefield and countless corpses.

Beren came to a stop. He looked down at himself and saw that his whole body was drenched in blood. Only the sword was clean. It was still as spotless as it was when he first polished it. He ran his bloody hand down the flat of the blade and watched as the blood dried to a flaky ash and fell away. *I have made a terrible thing,* he thought as he sat down on a rock. *How long will I have to wait before I can let it go? And what in all the hells am I going to do with this thing?* The idea of destroying it occurred to him. He supposed that he should be able to unmake it in any number of ways after the power had all bled out. Destroying it would be the right thing to do. *No man should have this kind of power. It's all the worse that it is not earned. Not worked for. All it takes is picking up a sword. And if I can do this with it, what would a Warchosen like Jenus be able to do? Or worse, Zorat?* She had outfought Jenus himself in the arena. Trained as she was to fight at great speeds, she could crush Sacral by herself. *Yes, I will destroy it.* The sword had absorbed the life energy of hundreds of people. It would take time to burn it off. *But maybe I can speed things up a little.* Beren stood up and started to hack at the stone under his feet. His arm a blur, chunks of stone went flying off in all directions.

***

The merchant Sorley turned out to be every bit as horrible as Shade had suggested.

Nial and Zuly watched from the shadows as he beat employees or other merchants or had others tortured or even killed. He acted more like a demon himself than an overweight middle-aged merchant. What surprised Nial the most was that he made little or no effort to hide what he was doing. The city watch patrolled the streets and yet they never happened to pass down this particular stretch. Those who were killed were dragged out the back of the shop and dumped into a cart and covered with a tarp before being hauled away.

In only three days of watching him intermittently, they had seen the cart leave twice.

Dressed like a street urchin, the girls were all but invisible to the crowds who walked through this part of the city. The merchant's guards had chased them away a couple of times without actually putting any effort into the task. The shop itself was large and ostentatious for this part of the city. The homes and shops in this area were mostly small and cramped, if a little cleaner and better made than those in the slums.

Sorley's shop looked like it had swallowed several of its neighbors. The remnants of old signs had been painted over imperfectly. Still, from what the girls had been able to tell, Sorley still lived in the rooms above his store. It seemed as though the horrid man never left his little kingdom.

Skeg had not been surprised to hear about the man or the seeming indifference of the city watch.

"The city watch are men, same as any others. They make less money than they would like, and in their eyes, changing their patrol route is a small thing for a doubling or tripling of their pay. Even honest men will agree to such things for the good of their own families."

"The other thing I don't like is the carts that come and leave his shop at night. If he's willing to do those horrible things during the day, whatever he wants to hide must be worse," said Nial.

"Now you're thinking clearly, child. If you can find out what he's trading in that makes a man like that ashamed, we may find a clue about why Shade wants him dead."

Zuly looked at him intently. "You really think we can find out who he is?"

"Maybe. Knowing what he cares about can tell us a lot."

The girls returned to spy on the merchant the next afternoon. His mood seemed to have changed. He was almost pleasant to those around him and had those who displeased him only lightly beaten. The cart around back remained empty today. Night brought greater activity than ever before. At least three carts were brought in over the course of the night, the last arriving just a few hours before dawn. Sorley locked up his shop after it arrived. Then he posted twice as many guards outside as he had before.

Time to move, thought Zuly. Four guards, each within easy sight of two others. *We'll go in another way.* Nial nodded and they moved off into the next street. Using their new trick, they lifted themselves up onto the roof of the nearest building. It

was a lot slower than lifting someone else, but Zuly was sure
no one would walk down this little street in the minute or so
that they needed. After they got to the roof, they started moving back toward Sorley's house. They crouched on the edge of
the roof across the street for a long time waiting to see if the
guards had heard them. Zuly jumped off the ledge and used
their power to float over the guards' heads. Nial watched them
a little nervously, but none of the men looked up.

They moved down a little and tried one of the windows
but were brought up short. Nial found she was blocked by an
invisible barrier a finger's breadth from the glass.

*Wards. Strong ones. If we push through these, we'll get
noticed,* Zuly thought. *We'll have to find a different way in.*

"What about just making a hole in the roof?" Nial whispered. *That just might work, my dear Nial.* With demonic
strength the girls pulled up first a few tarred planks, then
mortared stones. No wards blocked their progress. *You are so
smart, my sweet Nial.* Nial grinned as they dropped down into
the darkness within.

They landed without a sound, slowly floating down to the
floor. Their demon sight was more than enough to see in the
dark room. *It's his bedroom,* thought Zuly. A large bed did
dominate the room. There were stains on the sheets, colorless
in the dark, but both the girls could easily imagine what they
might be. Chains hung loose from the bedposts. *This man is
like the others. Tonight we will take his soul.* They opened the
door carefully and crept through the house. The upper floor
was an overly large home for a single man. Several large bed-
rooms furnished like the first filled the extra space. All of them
were empty. A thick door barred the way down to the shop. It
was locked with several well-made steel locks and chains. *We'll
make too much noise opening this.* The girls looked around
again before deciding that the floor would probably offer an

easier way through. Again they tore through the mortar and stone, lifting each stone out of its place and carefully setting it aside. They floated down through the hole they'd opened and into Sorley's shop. Piles of goods were stacked everywhere. Bales of furs and jars of spices and exotic oils. All were neatly organized and ready to be resold.

Still not what we're looking for. There must be a basement. Unless he has a secret way out and we didn't notice him leave. Sure enough, they found another door at the back of the shop that seemed a likely choice. It was as heavily built as the door to the top floor, though most of the locks and chains hadn't been secured. *Just one lock.* Nial bent the metal with her power. Stairs led down. They could see another solid wood door at the end of the staircase. Still not a trace of light. Three steps down and the step buckled under their foot. A line of needles jolted out from the back of the nearest step and punched deeply into their leg. Nial gasped before Zuly could take control and silence their body.

Probably poison. We have to get back to Skeg, thought Zuly. *No,* answered Nial. *We'll never get in the same way again. We'll just have to be strong and finish quick.* Already their leg was starting to feel numb. Zuly floated them over the remaining steps. *Then the time for being quiet is over.* They smashed in the door at the end of the staircase with a burst of their power.

They heard muffled screams and crying as well as a man's voice swearing. Inside the basement torches and lamps blazed. A full dozen cages lined the walls. Nine of them held children. Boys and girls, their ages ranging from six to twelve. Two crates stood in the center of the chamber. Nial recognized them as having been delivered that same day.

Sorley had prepared a cage for his newest pet. He had pried open the front of one crate and was chaining up an unconscious boy of seven.

"What the fuck are you doing in here? Who the fuck let you in?"

Zuly reached out with her power and plucked the man off his feet. "I would have liked to enjoy this more," said Zuly. "But I'm in a bit of a hurry. So you're going to give me your soul and fast."

Sorley's fingers were ripped from his body one at a time. Blood sprayed. Sorley screamed. "Say it! Say you give me your soul!" Five fingers and two minutes was all it took. His soul joined their collection in the obsidian sphere. By then, the tingling feeling had risen to their thigh.

We need to get out of here now! thought Zuly.

"Not yet!" shouted Nial. She reached out and smashed the locks from every cage, from every manacle. "We have to get them out of here."

We can't, sweet Nial. We could die. The best we can do is make sure they have a clear way out. They floated back up the stairs, power lashing out to smash the trap they had triggered. They had been so proud of their floating trick; now it seemed frustratingly slow.

A moment later the front door of the shop exploded in flames. The guards ran forward to see what was happening, only to be plucked off the ground by unseen forces, dragged into the shop, and smashed into walls. The girls left broken bodies and the smoldering remains of the front of the shop behind and floated up into the darkness. Behind them, furtive shapes ran out of the destroyed shop and out into the night. First one alone, then more in small groups. By the time the city watch arrived, no one living remained to answer any questions.

The girls floated into Skeg's shop, their eyes wide with panic. "Mister Skeg! We've been poisoned!" Nial shouted. The cut on their leg had long since stopped bleeding, but the numbness now extended all the way up to their waist.

Skeg ran over to them, not even trying to hide the worry he felt. "I'm no poisoner, but I should be able to help. How did it happen? How do you feel?"

"It was a needle in a trap and now I can't feel my leg!"

"How long ago was that?"

"Just help me!" Nial screamed in panic, tears streaming down her cheeks.

"I need to know, child, or I won't know how to help you. Now how long?"

The crying cut off abruptly. "It has been just over an hour, Mister Skeg," answered a somewhat calmer Zuly. "We couldn't run or even walk so we had to fly, and it's so damned slow! Our foot was numb within seconds of being poisoned, but it's spreading much more slowly now."

"That's good to hear. I'm sure you'll be fine, girls." His trembling hands and the drops of sweat beading on his forehead belied his calm words.

Skeg pulled a small knife out of his arm and passed it through the flame of a candle before quickly cutting open their wounded leg just above the ankle. Blood started to patter onto the floor.

"Don't sit or lie down. Keep floating like that for as long as you can, but let me know if it starts to become difficult to hold yourselves up." Then he tied a thick leather strap around their thigh and massaged their leg, trying to push the poisoned blood down toward the cut. A large puddle was spreading on the floor below them. Skeg looked down at it for a moment. "I don't dare bleed you any more or it will do more harm than good. I'll bandage this up and then you'll need to drink a special tea to cleanse your blood. All we can do after that is wait."

Skeg moved around the shop and quickly assembled a number of ingredients into a small cauldron before hanging it over the fireplace. A few minutes later he ladled some of the mixture into a cup and handed it to them.

Nial wrinkled her nose at the pungent smell when she took the cup from him. "I added some honey to cover the bitterness. It should taste better than it smells." Nial took a sip and nodded.

"Drink as much as you can. Let me know when your cup is empty and I'll get you more."

"I will." She gulped the first two cups down quickly.

"Has the numbness spread anymore?"

"I don't think so, but it hasn't gotten any better, either."

"Give it time. I'll remove the tourniquet in a little while. Sleep should help as well."

Skeg talked to them then about his day, his problems, his customers, anything to distract Nial from the poison. But she wasn't fooled. Every time he thought she wasn't looking, Skeg's eyes darted to their leg.

When Skeg finally removed the tourniquet, Nial gasped in pain. "That's a good sign," said Skeg. "Pain is much better than no feeling at all. Your wound has also mostly healed so it's not slowing down your demonic healing." He looked at her carefully. *Poor girls have been holding themselves up with their power this whole time. Even they must be exhausted.* "I want you to stay with me today, girls. You can have my bed upstairs. I'll sleep on the floor next to you in case you need me."

Nial hesitated for a moment, thinking about home. But her father was still terrified of her and avoided her as much as possible in the close confines of their little house. He certainly wouldn't be bothered if she wasn't there when he woke up in the morning. "Thank you, Mister Skeg. We'd like that," Nial answered in a dull voice.

Skeg got them settled in his little bed and pulled the blankets up over them. They were asleep almost instantly. Skeg just sat on the floor and watched them sleep. As the sun rose from dawn to noon and their breathing was still strong and deep, he finally allowed himself to curl up and doze a little.

CHAPTER 7

It took days for Nial and Zuly to recover from the poison, days where they slept more than they were awake, thrashing about and getting little rest. Skeg watched them as often as he could and would start awake each time they moved. *Hardly surprising that they would have nightmares. Or that Nial would, at least.* To a certain extent, it was reassuring how human the girls were acting through this ordeal. Even during their nightmares, he hadn't once felt threatened by them. On those rare occasions that they woke and were lucid enough to speak, he pretended everything was normal. But there was no hiding his worry from them. He barely left their side and was always there when they opened their eyes. The shop below remained dark and empty, the door barred and every ward raised around it.

On the third night, Skeg finally felt like the worst was over. He left the girls in his bed reading a book and went down to relax in his shop. Skeg settled behind the counter and let his mind wander, the stress of the past days finally starting to fall away. He had been preparing an experiment of his own when the girls had gotten hurt. Now that they were recovering, his thoughts drifted back to his ritual.

Skeg was startled when he heard the signal that meant someone was approaching his door. *Several someones maybe…to think I'd be annoyed at customers coming to my door.*

He grunted with effort and pulled himself to his feet. It was early in the night for any *serious* customers to be around, but after having been closed for the first time since he'd opened the little shop, he really didn't know what to expect.

It turned out to be four members of a small street gang. "You Skeg?" the larger of the young men asked after a few seconds of staring around at the shop in confused wonder. Skeg nodded. "Guy we been working for paid us for our last job with this thing." He held up a delicate-looking wooden carving of strange design. "Told us you'd pay good coin for it."

Skeg held out a hand. The thug hesitated for a second then handed the carving to Skeg. *A spell anchor,* he thought to himself immediately. *And it's active. By the Silent God, if this fool had dropped it, he could have set off the spell it's holding, whatever it may be.* He looked the carving over for a few more moments, noting the breathtaking complexity of the spell, then nodded again. "This guy you did the job for, who was he?"

"No idea. He always wears a mask, but he always pays. So you want the thing or not?"

Skeg pulled out a small coin purse and put it on the counter. The thug eagerly picked it up and looked inside.

His eyes widened seeing gold and silver inside. "Serious?"

"Serious. Now clear out," Skeg snapped, using his talent to make his eyes flare red.

The street thugs rushed out of the room as fast as they could. After they had left, Skeg studied the anchor for a long time, but try as he might, he couldn't make out the individual strands that made up the weave it held. *Hopefully, the girls will have more luck.* Shade had come through on his end of the deal at least. *Smart of him to use it to pay off two debts at once with it too.* Still, the coin he had given the gang members was nothing. A fortune to them maybe, but trivial to Skeg. In his business, knowledge was power, and an active spell anchor was worth many times its weight in gold.

It was several weeks before Skeg showed the spell anchor to Nial and Zuly. They had recovered quickly after the first few stressful days and fell back into their old routine of hunting early in the evening before returning to Skeg's shop to study and practice. They barely ever returned to Nial's father's home anymore and spent most days curled up in a blanket in the back room. The whole incident had left Skeg more shaken than the girls, and he wanted to be absolutely sure they were up to their full strength before they tried to tackle anything so advanced as Shade's spell.

Nial looked at the spell anchor in wonder. The weave it held was much more complex than anything she had seen before. Different strands of varying power were woven together in dizzying patterns.

"What does it do?" she asked.

"I'm sorry, child. This is as far beyond me as making the sun disappear at noon. All I can see is a solid block of energy. I can't even make out a hint of the individual strands."

"Should I take the weave out of the anchor?"

"No!" Skeg said. He stood there for a few moments feeling embarrassed by his outburst. "Sorry, child. We have no idea what it would do. It could blow us up or practically anything else you can think of. Besides, if it's not meant to have a lasting effect, it would vanish and we'd be left with nothing."

"It looks like there are three parts to it," Zuly said.

"That's good. It gives us a place to start. Choose the smallest part and see if you can copy it, very, very carefully—it has to be absolutely perfect."

"Okay, Mister Skeg." A frown marred her little forehead as Zuly and Nial got to work.

Skeg watched Nial in silence, all the while trying to ignore a sick feeling in his stomach. He'd always known Nial and Zuly would surpass him, but watching them try to replicate an unknown spell by themselves was nerve-racking. Skeg could see them working but was unable to understand what they were doing. They turned the spell anchor in their hands slowly, staring at it intently. Power was building in the air above them as their own weave took shape. Skeg toyed with the objects that were currently inserted through his skin, moving and reorganizing them again and again. It seemed like hours before they lifted their head and looked at him.

"I think it's done," Nial said with a grin.

"Are you absolutely sure?"

"Yes. We're sure."

"I'd still like you to check it again, just in case." With a sigh Nial nodded, and they went back to studying the anchor. Skeg jumped to his feet and scrambled around the shop looking for a suitable target for the spell. After considering a number of random items, he finally settled on an old tree stump that he sometimes used as a stool. He grunted as he lifted it and carried it into the back room. Skeg set the stump down carefully in front of them, then waited for them to finish their last check. A moment later Nial looked up.

"You were right, Mister Skeg. One thread was a little out of place." Skeg nodded and tried to look calm.

"Focus your weave on the stump, and let's see if this part does anything on its own."

Nothing happened. Nial jumped to her feet outraged. "It didn't do anything!"

Skeg could see a sheen of magic surrounding the stump that was quickly fading away to nothing but couldn't make out any other effect either. He breathed a sigh of relief.

"I wasn't expecting it to do anything without the other two parts, but then you never know . . . ," Skeg said as he looked over the stump and the air around it carefully. "Now I want you to make the same weave again. Exactly the same as before."

"But why? It doesn't do anything!"

"I know that, Nial. But it's the first real challenge you've had weaving a spell. It took you nearly three hours. I want you to be able to do it in less than half that time before you try the next part."

Nial sighed loudly again. "All right. I think we can do that." She sank back down to her spot on the floor and started working again.

On their second attempt, Nial and Zuly managed to finish the weave in just under an hour. "Can we try the next piece now, please?"

"Go ahead and take a good look at it, child, but only look. You can try to reproduce it tomorrow night. I have work to do, and you need to go home and rest." Nial looked like she was going to argue, but Zuly agreed with a quick nod.

Their skills are improving at a frightening rate, even with these more advanced weaves. Soon I'll be of no use to them at all. The thought made Skeg feel hollow. But it also steeled his resolve to go ahead with his own experiment tonight. Skeg had grown complacent over the years. For too long he'd just sat in his shop and done little more than buy and sell. When he'd first opened the shop, when he'd found ways to become indispensable to so many opposing powers in the city, it had all been to make something more of himself than an apprentice, to prove the Arcanum wrong. Zuly had unwittingly shown him a path if he but dared to walk it. Skeg moved around the shop, slowly tidying up and assembling the tools he'd need for his experiment. It would be a great risk. Possibly the most reckless thing he'd ever tried in his life. *The slow methodical accumulation of resources has done nothing to further my goals. . . . Time for something big.*

He set up in the middle of the circle in his back room, moving a number of small spell anchors into place around himself so they'd be within easy reach when he needed them. Each had cost him a small fortune. Each spell had been prepared by one of his customers in trade for components they had purchased from Skeg. *Not being able to make complex weaves yourself doesn't matter if you can activate them and have enough other mages who owe you.* As far as he knew no one had ever attempted a complex ritual using nothing but third-party anchors. *But there's a first time for everything. I just hope none of them made a mistake.* In the center of the circle, he placed a small crystal carving of a winged demon. It would be the focus of his work tonight. Then he removed the obsidian sphere Nial had helped him prepare and set it down in front of the carving. He walked around his shop making sure his wards were all active and the door secured. Then he drank and ate as much as he could, before coming back to the circle and taking his place within.

Enough preparations, time to do this. Skeg felt a mixture of fear and excitement. He lifted the first anchor and activated the spell within, focusing it on the crystal carving. The carving started to melt as if it were made of wax. The fluid started to smoke and swirl as it resolved itself into the form of a minor demon. An imp. The first spell went off perfectly, binding the

imp and preventing it from moving or even perceiving anything more than it would have when it was stuck within the
carving.

Imps were sometimes bound as messengers or spies. They
were among the least of the demons summoned by men. The
creature was vaguely humanoid, thin to the point of frailty and
stood about knee high to Skeg. It had rough gray skin, and
wide batlike wings protruded from its shoulders.

But I'm not looking for a messenger. Skeg lifted the second
anchor, forcing himself not to hurry, not to make any mistakes.
His heart was hammering inside his chest. The spell activated
and coalesced around the obsidian sphere.

Now the tricky part. Skeg lifted the last two spell anchors
and activated them simultaneously—one in either hand. One
spell targeted the demon while the other he cast on himself,
feeding every ounce of energy he had into it. The imp started to
shriek, keening high-pitched screams that threatened to break
Skeg's concentration. Its flesh started to smoke again, and the
smoke was drawn into the sphere in front of it. Skeg felt a pull
within himself. The strength of the pull grew with the demon's
screams. Before long Skeg's screams joined the demon's as he
fought a desperate tug-of-war with it to save his own soul. *The
pain! Pain of the flesh is nothing compared to this! Gods, what
have I done?! It's tearing my soul apart!* The demon's skin bubbled and boiled. The pain increased beyond all description.
And then suddenly it was gone. The imp puffed into smoke and
was drawn through the orb into Skeg, then the orb exploded,
sending a shower of shards in all directions. Skeg only just had
time to throw his arms up in front of his face.

He barely felt the impact of the shards that shredded his
skin. Hundreds more were driven into the ceiling and walls.
My little talent might have saved my life, he thought ruefully
as he looked down at his arms and chest. Small nicks and cuts

had never hurt him, nor had they ever bled much. *Not that I'll ever react to pain the same way after that ordeal.* It was a moment before the realization hit him. *I did it!* He felt within himself and there it was. A core of power nestled beside his own life flame.

I can't stop now. Skeg took a deep breath and drew the demon's energy into his own. It burned. The wrongness of it, the flavor of its energy, was sickening. But the power was undeniable. His muscles spasmed, became denser; his blood flowed slower and thicker. His whole being was rearranging itself, growing into a shape more befitting the strength and energy it now contained. There was pain, of course—no change could be made without it. But after the soul-tearing agony of the ritual, this was nothing. *Oh, yes, this is almost sweet.* The whole process was over faster than he could have expected. He felt good. Better than ever, in fact. He rushed over to a mirror and inspected himself carefully.

There was little outward sign of what he had done to himself. His skin was a few shades closer to gray, but his face was his own. His body had only become a little leaner and stronger than it had been before. *Much better than I had feared, and not even enough to tip off the Night Guard when they come snooping.* He focused his talent and was overjoyed to feel the wild rush of power, far more than he'd ever had at his disposal before. Picking up a cup to drink, Skeg was surprised when he crushed the clay in his fist. *I guess this will take a little getting used to.* His stomach rumbled. *And I guess with greater strength comes greater hunger,* he thought with a grin. Still, the experiment was a great success. He had taken a demon's ability to steal and consume souls and turned it back on itself—absorbing it into his own soul. *I wonder what would happen if I used this on a demon that had already eaten a soul or two?* . . . Would the soul be freed to the afterlife as it was when the demon was permanently destroyed? Would he consume it himself and so gain even greater strength? Could he use it to steal souls like a true demon? There was great power in a soul, as Nial and Zuly had shown him, and there were certainly souls in this cesspool of a city deserving of being used or even used up. But then the memory of the pain returned. And with it came fear. *No, this ritual won't work a second time. If I want to absorb another demon, I'll have to find a way to do it without using my own soul as a fulcrum. . . .* The thought ended when his stomach growled again.

When the girls arrived back at the shop the next night, they knew something was wrong the moment they stepped through the door. They found Skeg lying on his back in the middle of the shop, his stomach hideously distended. The remains of random foods were scattered around him.

"Mister Skeg, what have you done?" Zuly asked.

He looked up at them with bloodshot eyes. "Something monumentally foolish, I'm starting to think." He gasped and held an arm over his stomach, while his eyes darted around the floor looking for more to eat.

"You are no longer entirely human."

"An experiment I tried last night—" He broke off with another gasp of pain. "I used the orb you made for me to consume a small demon, an imp. . . . I pulled it into myself." He finished with a grimace.

"It's the hunger you're feeling," said Nial. "Every demon feels it, even us. But it has nothing to do with food."

"Then what can I do?" Skeg pleaded. "I'm so hungry I can't stand it."

"It's a hunger for power, not for sustenance," said Zuly. "Though for our kind"—she paused—"the distinction is meaningless. It will never lessen, never ease. You will have to learn to live with it." Skeg's eyes had gone wide. "You can dampen it for a time, but it will not last. The simplest sources of power are blood and flesh. Though that will only satisfy the weakest of demons."

"I ate meat tonight—rabbit, beef, mutton. It doesn't help."

"But you cooked it first, and the animal was probably long dead even then. The life energy would have long since disappeared. An imp or a carrion demon might manage to feed off such food. You are not as weak as that—you have a soul. With greater power comes greater hunger, and the more you feed, the greater your power will become."

"Do you mean I need to eat people? Or hunt for souls?" he asked, aghast.

"Only if you want to, Mister Skeg. Any living animal should suffice. You can kill it before you eat it, or just drain some blood from it. The heart is the seat of the soul and is the choicest meal. We haven't hunted yet tonight. If you like, we can bring our prey here and let you eat your fill once we've finished. Even a cup of fresh blood should make you feel better." If Skeg looked uncomfortable before, he now looked positively horrified listening to Zuly.

"Thank you, girls, but I'd rather avoid that."

"We'll find you an animal before we hunt then. Maybe you'll feel well enough for a lesson when we get back," Nial said.

The promised blood helped. Skeg sipped at it tentatively at first, then drank it down with relish. He was still hungry, but his mind was clearing; he could think past the hunger at least. Then he realized that he hadn't asked where the blood came from before drinking it. *I'm probably better off not knowing.*

After that, their routine changed. Nial and Zuly would turn up a little later in the evening than before, with a large cup of warm blood for Skeg. Animal, they insisted. Skeg would gulp it down, and then they would move on to weaving practice. Skeg's initial excitement over his change faded further when he found that his magical skills had not changed. He certainly had more power to draw on, but he was still maddeningly limited in his ability to manipulate and shape that power.

There was no stopping the girls on the other hand. They had a thirst for knowledge that put Skeg to shame, and the drive to practice for hours on end. It only took them a few days to master all three parts of Shade's weave. Their skills had progressed so far in the past days that it took them no more than thirty minutes now to reproduce the entire weave.

"All right, girls, careful now, let's see what it does. Bind it to the stool." Skeg watched with apprehension and amazement as the stool became indistinct, faded, and vanished from sight.

Nial looked at him in triumph while moving over to sit on the invisible stool. "We did it!"

Skeg smiled. "I knew you could. It's a pretty impressive piece of work." Skeg looked at it and said, as if speaking to himself, "I can't even see it when I'm looking for magic. In all my time at the Arcanum, I never heard of anyone who could do that. Make something hard to see, sure, but vanish completely? All with so little power the weaving of it would pass unnoticed in almost any situation. Whatever complaints we might have about Shade, he's certainly keeping up his side of the deal. I could sell that spell anchor to the Arcanum for my weight in gold. Not that I would, mind you; spreading around a secret like this just makes it more likely that someone else will find a way to counter it." He came back to himself with a start and looked at the girls. "We'll keep the anchor until you're absolutely sure you can do it perfectly without looking at it. Then we'll destroy it." They nodded at him distractedly. "Girls? Are you listening to me?"

Nial looked up at him, gave him a big smile, and vanished. Skeg was dumbstruck. *So fast!* They reappeared a moment later, clearly trying to tiptoe behind him. They seemed unaware that the spell had been broken. Skeg scooped them off the ground and lifted them into his arms. Zuly stiffened instantly and let out a hiss of anger, her eyes glowing red. Then Nial broke into a fit of girlish giggles. *I'll have to remember not to surprise Zuly like that anymore,* thought Skeg, wiping off the cold sweat that had broken out over his brow at her reaction.

"It looks like your new spell won't work if you move. Let's try it again and see if we can figure out its limitations."

"But Shade came into the shop without us seeing him. We didn't even see him open the door!" Nial said.

Skeg smiled. "Shade agreed to teach you useful things. He never said he'd share all his secrets with you. The weave he gave you is amazing. Just think what you could do with it. Besides, he might have something more to show you after you take out the next target."

Nial grinned back at him as she moved to the door. "You're right, Mister Skeg. We're going to go try it out."

"Have fun, girls, and be careful."

Nial just rolled her eyes at him and walked out.

***

Jenus spat out a mouthful of ash and looked around. They had come clear of the damned forests at last. But the fires had spread ahead of them to the grasslands. Ash still swirled in the air and rose up after every step. *I would kill for a good rain.* They had been fighting the Gling'Ar for the better part of a month already. Though chasing was closer to the truth. The savages had set fires to the trees and seemed content to pick off the Sacral soldiers a few at a time in small ambushes. The Sacral army had been choking on the smoke and ashes ever since, and the fodder for their animals was running dangerously low.

As ever, he walked alone at the head of the army. His own men held him in superstitious awe that bordered on reverence. Even the mages and other Warchosen who accompanied him were little better. All of them were exhausted. They had been tested again and again by their enemy, but Jenus himself was the only one who had successfully killed even one of the monsters. They fled from him now. It was, he decided, satisfying to be feared by an enemy. But now his own men would scarcely look him in the eye. The guilt of their own vulnerability and their need for him to bring them to victory were heavy chains.

Jenus, like most of his countrymen, had disbelieved the stories the Abolians told of the savage raiders. Though tales remained, no nonhuman had been seen in Sacral since before their city had been pulled away by the White Mother a thousand years ago. Jenus had expected tall humans in strange garb, little else.

Their first skirmish had taught him the errors of his thinking. The Gling'Ar stood half again as tall as any Sacral man, and they were just as broad. Their eyes were strange, with elongated yellow or orange pupils. Their teeth were longer and sharper than any man's, often protruding from between closed lips. But what truly left the soldiers of Sacral gaping in disbelief was their second pair of arms.

In their first clash, the Gling'Ar had ambushed Jenus's rear guard. Twenty savages had killed sixty-three of his brave soldiers, not to mention three priests of the White Mother, and twelve noncombatants, before being driven off. Only one Gling'Ar was killed in that engagement. Jenus had killed it

himself. The Lightbringer had cut through its bronze shield
and the two arms holding it like a sharp blade through grass.
Its helm had provided no greater protection. Jenus had stood
over the body for a long time, trying to grasp the reality of
the thing he had killed. Many of the soldiers and the work-
ers accompanying them had come for a look at the monstrous
enemy. The Gling'Ar had wielded a huge, oddly shaped two-
handed sword, the hilt sharply bent in the middle, with the two
hands on its right side. The second set of arms had held a large,
sharp-edged shield of polished bronze. Its body was encased
in a heavy suit of bronze scales that it had seemed to wear as
effortlessly as a human might wear silk. A simple open-faced
bronze helm covered its head.

That first night had had a terrible impact on the army's
morale. The soldiers of Sacral were as brave as any in the face
of combat. But they were all shocked by the number of dead.
Barely a handful of the men and women who fell in the ambush
had survived. The strength of the raiders was daunting. Their
strength and skill made the Sacral soldiers feel like children
playing at war, their superior weaponry little better than toys.
What use was a runed shield when the power of the blow it
blocked shattered the arm that held it? What use was a runed
sword when the enemy's reach advantage and speed were so
great that they never had a chance to do anything but attempt
frantic parries?

The Abolians that had guarded the city of Sariah had all
carried heavy metal crossbows. Jenus had sneered at them.
The weapons of cowards. True warriors did not need such
things.... Now he was starting to wonder. He was honor bound
to finish his task, but there was no improvising such weapons
or learning their use on the march. They would have to make
do. Jenus needed to change tactics. All their training involved
fighting other companies from their own city. This enemy was

totally outside that experience. They needed to change or they would be wiped out. Jenus started by reorganizing his troops. He formed as many phalanxes of pikes and shields as he could. They were short on timbers long enough to make the unwieldy weapons, and the constant fires ensured there was no easy way to find more. Every fighter carried the longest spear he could find and tried to make the best of it.

The second skirmish went far better for the humans. They didn't manage to kill any more Gling'Ar outright, but they seriously wounded at least six of them. Jenus lost eight men that night, one of them a priest. Another two dozen were wounded to various degrees. *Not nearly good enough,* thought Jenus. Still, it was an improvement. The static phalanxes had held surprisingly well. But he needed a more mobile force to pin the monsters onto them. *The savages run from me. But I can't hold them against the phalanxes alone. Starting tomorrow, I'll send the Warchosen out. They are wasted inside the formations. They can fight free, and together we can push the giants onto the spears.*

The next attack came four days later. Jenus and his Warchosen were ready. The troops were confident that this newest strategy would get them some Gling'Ar bodies. *Morale is better today. But it's hanging by a thread. If this doesn't work . . .*

An arrow as thick as a spear shaft and nearly as long as a man was tall flew out of the forest and smashed a hole in the Sacral troop formation marching on the left flank. Two men were killed by the same arrow. Then Jenus saw the Gling'Ar; a dozen of them stood on a hill more than two hundred paces away. They clutched huge, thick bows that they wielded with all four hands. Five more arrows flashed into the human ranks. These flew higher and fell among the noncombatants behind the spearmen. Jenus saw a priest impaled by one of the

oversized shafts, his body pinned to a nearby cart. Jenus sig-
naled for his cavalry unit to attack the archers, but after loos-
ing one volley, the giant archers had scattered into the burning
underbrush and were lost.

The phalanxes were ready to repel a charge, but no further attack came. Even with their clear advantage, the Gling'Ar
seemed reluctant to engage with them. They fought furiously
when they were forced, but they seemed content to lead the
Sacral force deeper and deeper into the wilderness. A sudden
thought occurred to Jenus. *What if they are going home? What
if we are being led into an ambush?* The five hundred or so raiders they had counted would prove tough enough opposition if
they managed to close with them. But if there were thousands
more, this hunt would turn into a massacre.

He turned to the nearest soldier. "Call the order to halt and
make camp. I want all the Warchosen, mages, company commanders, and the senior priests in my pavilion within the hour."
The soldier saluted and rushed off to carry out his orders.

If they truly were headed for an ambush, they might have
to resort to sorcery to bring down their targets. As much as the
idea caught in his throat, the idea of dying in defeat was worse.

*We haven't been confronted with any inhuman magics yet.
But something tells me the savages haven't shown us their full
hand yet.* No one could stand undefended against sorcery. The
need to keep his mages fresh and ready to defend the army
was standard practice. Only exceptional arena training had led
the mages to unleash their destructive magics on the soldiers.
This was always counterbalanced with another mage protecting them.

Jenus had never really concerned himself with the business of mages. He had always left them to their own counsel,
assuming they knew their own tasks better than he ever could.
It was time to change that. For the first time he had questions

for them. What were the limits of their abilities? Could they be called on to attack or slow the fleeing enemy so that they could finally close on them? And if so, could they still be counted on to defend them from sorcerous attack should the Gling'Ar prove to have mages among them? His head felt like it was going to split. His responsibilities in the city had not prepared him for the pressures of leading men in the field. The experience was totally new to him and he was all too aware of how ill prepared he was.

An hour later Jenus sat in his tent. His Warchosen and other officers had responded quickly to his summons. They had all arrived before his tent had been erected. The three mages, Nakok, Marean, and Asar, were a little slower to arrive but still early. *And now we wait for the priests.* Though nominally the champion of the White Mother, Jenus was not particularly pious. Truth be told, he rarely visited her temple unless he was accompanying the king. When he did, the priests invariably reproached him and found a variety of ways to punish him for his lack of faith. A favorite tactic of theirs was making him wait, wasting his time. *Well, this is war, I'm not playing their games now.*

"Thank you all for coming so promptly. You do your city honor by taking your duties so seriously in our time of trouble." No one could miss the implied reproach directed at the priests. Traven, his second in command, gave him a wide-eyed look and fidgeted. Most soldiers knew better than to speak out against the priests or their goddess even in jest. It was a foolish man who insulted those who would be treating him should he take a wound. But Jenus was resolved in this. He would not waste a second more than he had to. The Gling'Ar had to be stopped. They may even now be preparing another ambush. His men's lives were worth more than the foolish pride of the clergy.

"All of you must know why you have been called here."
There were nods and gruff sounds of agreement all around.
"The enemy we face is like nothing we have ever seen before.
It is worse by far than any of us could have imagined. Like me,
I'm sure you thought the Abolians weak. Like me, I'm sure
you sneered at the crossbows they use to defend themselves
from the savages." Every pronouncement met general agreement, given in bitterness, for they too were failing. "It is time
to change our tactics. We cannot improvise weapons to fight
our enemy on equal terms. Nor would we have time to train
in their use. I now believe time is against us. The Gling'Ar are
leading us somewhere. They seek only to slow us enough that
we do not follow too closely. But always they show themselves
if we fall too far behind. This latest attack only proves it: they
have been holding back." Jenus could see fear on the faces of
many of his soldiers. *Well, I'm certainly helping the morale
problem along. . . .*

"I believe our only hope of prevailing lies in our mages.
Nakok, Marean, Asar? What say you? Can your talents be used
to neutralize those bows?"

Asar met the eyes of each of his colleagues before answering. "We can take apart their bows. But such a task would be
difficult and time-consuming at the range they shoot from. We
certainly wouldn't be able to stop them shooting a single volley
like they did today. If we are close to the point of attack, we
could likely protect most of our men from the arrows. We will
need time to prepare, though, and there are only three of us.
It is unlikely that we would be where we are needed when the
time comes."

"What about more direct attacks on the savages?" The
silence that met Jenus's words was deafening. One of the most
basic tenets of the Sacral military was that magic was only to
be used in defense. In their contests, it was considered bad

form to attack with magic, similar to using bows or thrown weapons. It simply wasn't done.

"Sir . . . are you certain you wish to pursue this?" asked Traven.

"We have no choice. They use the weapons of cowards and force our hand. We cannot continue to march into the wilds and provide target practice for them!" His words came out somewhat louder than he had intended. And everyone sat staring at him in surprise. Movement at the entrance of the pavilion prevented further comment. Three priests of the White Mother walked in as if they owned the place.

"You haven't waited for us to start? I must say I expected more courtesy from you, Jenus," said Serim, the senior priest accompanying the army. "Although I must say, I also expected our great champion could easily deal with a band of subhuman savages."

Jenus only gritted his teeth as the men worked their way through those present to face him. Somewhat too close for courtesy. Serim stood in silence for several minutes, the other two priests standing a step behind him to either side.

"Another of our brothers lost his life this day, Jenus. What do you intend to do about it?"

"I intend to change our tactics and bring an end to this debacle," he said.

"And you would do this without holy counsel? We have come to guide this army. To provide healing and comfort. You let our defenseless brothers die unprotected and discuss the matter without us present. Your actions come close to blasphemy, Champion. High Priest Yeltos would be shocked to hear of this." His tone made it clear that the high priest would indeed hear all about it, and soon.

"I assure you, I place great value on the lives of every priest, as I do on every Sacral life. We were just discussing possible measures we could take to ensure this situation does not continue."

"None of your ideas have had any lasting effect thus far. You will forgive me if I am not reassured."

"Nevertheless, I am confident that our new tactics will yield greater results."

"Your overconfidence does not become you, Champion," the priest said with a look of disdain. "In the meantime, we demand more significant protection. The soldiers under your command do not seem up to the task. Therefore, all Warchosen, barring yourself, are to be placed under our direct command to act as our bodyguards."

Jenus almost choked at the outrageous demand. "That is simply not possible, Your Eminence. The Warchosen are an integral part of our new strategy. More, they are each responsible for leading their respective companies. Without them we are unlikely to succeed in bringing down these monsters."

"Then rethink your strategy. We will be happy to give counsel on the matter. I am certain that we can find a more effective plan than whatever it is you have thought up this time."

"With all due respect, Your Eminence. You are here to offer spiritual guidance, not dictate military tactics."

The priest's eyes were daggers as he turned wordlessly from the war council and swept out of the tent. The lesser priests rushed to follow him.

Traven smiled at him. "Well, it looks like you took care of that issue. But I wouldn't go looking to get healed anytime soon, Champion." A few people laughed and the tension drained out of the group.

"So we're agreed then? We need to come up with something by tomorrow and be ready for them. I'm counting on the mages to keep them off us. I've also made a decision. Once we have pursued them for another three days, we will turn back.

We will ask the priests to contact His Majesty the king and ask him to bring us home." Jenus held up his hands as his assembled advisers looked at him in confusion. "We have chased the invaders far from the lands of our allies. Our mission was to save them from the inhuman attacks. We have done so and fulfilled our role honorably. We have chased them through the lands the Abolians themselves fear to walk in. We did not swear to hunt them to the ends of the earth and beyond. Nor did we swear to kill them all to the last."

Nakok nodded. "You are wise indeed, Champion. We yoke ourselves with our own unrealistic expectations."

"We are the warriors of Sacral," Jenus said. "We are descendants of heroes one and all. But our city has remained apart from the world for too long. We need to rethink our way of fighting. We need to rethink the ban on missile weapons in particular. We are well trained, but we need to adapt to the realities of the world beyond our borders. Please give the issue some thought, my friends. We will speak again tomorrow."

CHAPTER 8

On the seventh day after his first patrol, Salt got up early, as had become his habit, and went down to the training yard. Krigare had suggested he try a large two-handed mace, and Salt liked the idea enough to try it out and get a feel for it. The weight was daunting. Salt had to adjust his swinging style a lot to avoid being pulled off balance. Seeing the problems he was having, Gurt walked over to give him some pointers.

"Don't fight the momentum, lad, use it. Bring that thing around for another pass in the same direction instead of trying to go back and forth."

Salt nodded and followed the instructions. There was no question that the weapon could do serious damage, even to an armored opponent. But there wasn't much room for finesse or surprise. Still, it made a satisfying crack when he hit a training dummy with it.

Gurt smiled in approval. "That's better, lad. Though you won't often want to carry something that heavy on patrol or you'll be too tired to swing the thing by the time you get into a fight." Salt laughed. His shoulders were already aching from the strain of swinging the mace.

"So what are you up to today?" Gurt asked.

Salt smiled, thinking he was being made fun of. "Same old thing, I guess. Train for a few hours then go out monster hunting."

Gurt smiled back. "You're not on a ship anymore. I know you were drunk the night I explained everything to you, but I would have thought you'd ask about things like this. Anyway, every seventh day after patrolling, Night Guardsmen have a day off. You've been going on patrol for the last six days. It's our squad's day of rest." Salt was stunned, totally at a loss about what to say.

"What we do isn't easy," Gurt continued. "You need some time to yourself to relax and have fun." When Salt didn't say anything, Gurt pressed on. "Now I don't mind you training for another hour or so, but after that I want you to get out of the palace and do some serious thinking—it's time you took the oath and formally joined the Night Guard." He held up a hand to stop Salt from saying anything. "I don't expect an answer yet, but I expect you to have made a decision by the time I wake up tomorrow."

"Where are the others then?" Salt asked.

"Not sure about most of 'em. Brolt will be with his family. He has four kids and a beauty of a wife. Min is probably in the markets. The others . . . getting into whatever trouble they can find likely as not." Gurt shrugged.

After practice, Salt went back to his room to get changed. Sure enough, a set of plain but well-made clothes had been left in his trunk. Dwyn was the last person in the room. He had clearly had a rough night and was moving slower than usual.

"Day off?" he asked Salt.

"Yeah. . . . Not too sure what I'm going to do with myself."

"Hah. I'd kill for a day off right now."

"You have a busy night planned?"

"Not so much busy as frustrating. Lera's got my squad moving from the port to Harold's and then back to the port to check on some new merchant house that set up last week."

"I hate having Harold on my patrol. Never shuts up."

"And Gurt wants me to hear him out, keep him happy. I'll probably be stuck listening to him for half the night."

Salt buckled on his weapon belt as they were talking, strapped a sword to it, then started adding daggers. Dwyn looked at him with wide eyes.

"You planning on starting a war on your day off?"

Salt noticed what he was doing and stopped. "I guess they've just become habit. I'm not sure I want to go out without them after seeing what's out there."

Dwyn laughed. "Well, I can relate to that. But you might want to leave most of the fighting to those of us who are on duty. Here, you can borrow my knives. Strap them to your forearms. You won't attract so much attention, but you'll still have a weapon to hand. It's what I do when I have a day off. I don't think anyone in the Guard would willingly go anywhere unarmed; you just need to be a little more discreet about it."

A short while later, Salt found himself dressed in his new clothes, walking the streets aimlessly. He had a pocket full of coins. He hadn't spent a copper penny from his last sailing job, months past now. Most of the Guardsmen liked to play cards or dice when they got back from patrol. The stakes were always low, but so far Salt had resisted the urge to get involved. So here he was, in one of the biggest port cities in the known world, with full pockets and plenty of free time and yet he was at a loss as to what to do with himself.

Salt tried to have a drink in a nice little tavern he passed near the palace. Nothing ostentatious like the places closer

to Crown Hill where the nobles all built their homes. He just
wanted a nice clean place to get a good meal and a pint or two
while he thought about what he was going to do with himself
for the rest of the day. The serving girls were pretty if more
conservatively dressed than what he was used to. The tables
were straight, and the place actually smelled good. The tavern wasn't crowded this early in the day, so he chose a small
table near the back and made himself comfortable. He asked
the serving girl to bring him a pint of ale. She smiled at him
warmly and brought it right over and asked him for a silver
penny. Salt nearly choked; that was ten times what he'd pay
near the docks. He blushed furiously, excused himself, and left
as quickly as he could, leaving the untouched pint on the table.

He moved on to more familiar areas near the docks after
that and ordered beer and food. But even here he felt uncomfortable. Many of the other patrons were looking at him as if
he didn't belong. He realized it was the clothes. Not one person
in the drinking hole was wearing anything that could be called
new, or might even have been called new when the owner purchased it. For all that his clothes were plain, he stood out like
a noble in all his finery. He sighed and moved on, not bothering to finish the drink or even taste the food. *Gods, how I've
changed in such a short time.* For those watching, his actions
were confirmation enough that he didn't belong. The rest of
the patrons visibly relaxed as he moved toward the door.

As much as anything, Salt missed the company of his fellow Guardsmen. For months now he'd been with them, and the
four months before that he'd spent on a ship. All told, it had
been more than half a year since he had been alone for longer
than he needed to take a piss—it just felt strange. He couldn't
shake the feeling that he was being watched and felt almost
naked without his companions. *And my weapons and armor,
of course.*

Salt wandered through the markets and bought a meat pie from a street vendor. He bit into it and almost spit it out. He very nearly complained to the woman who had sold it to him before noticing that it wasn't really all that bad. *I've just gotten too damned used to the food at the palace. Can't tell a street vendor that her pies are underspiced and that she used cheap mutton.* He handed the rest of the pie to a street urchin who was trying to pick his pocket.

I don't belong anywhere in this city anymore. Thoughts of the dockside brothels kept creeping back into his mind. It had been far too long since he had lain with a woman. But it was a quick way to spend his money, and he didn't have a clear idea how he would get more. Not that he needed coin for his day-to-day living. Despite his convictions, Salt's wandering soon brought him to the docks. He passed in front of several likely-looking brothels, all the while fighting with himself over whether or not to go in. He almost gave in when he noticed a particularly attractive brunette waving to him from a balcony. His blood was hot, and he turned back toward the brothel's entrance. Then memories of his night with the bug priestess flashed before his eyes. He broke out in a cold sweat, and his blood lost its fire.

With a sigh Salt walked resolutely away from the docks and their women. He went east this time, into the slums, and started retracing his patrol route from the night before. *Couple months in a new job and I don't have the first clue what to do without my mates,* Salt berated himself. *And I can't find anywhere better to come to than the worst shithole Darien has to offer.* Refuse and waste squelched under foot. Rats darted between people's shoes. The more desperate inhabitants chased after them, looking for a meal. Salt walked around for hours. The slums were a different place in the daylight. No cleaner, of course, no less run-down, but during the day, these poor streets were packed with people. Even children ran this way and that. Just like in the dockside bar, people here could see him for the outsider he was. Covetous glances toward his pockets were common, and Salt kept a tight grip on his coins.

During the daylight hours, a pretense was made of this only being a poorer quarter of the city. Dirty perhaps, poor definitely, but not a bad place. Certainly not the kind of place where anything worse than pickpocketing would occur. Darkness wiped away that conceit. All but the poorest and most miserable of the slum's inhabitants vanished with the last of the sunlight. Pimps, carash dealers, and worse emerged into the dark streets to do business and look for opportunity. And yet nightfall came as a relief to Salt. It gave him back his anonymity. He was only another man walking the streets in the dark.

The city watch only patrolled these streets occasionally, and then only in numbers. No issue was made of thievery, and anything short of murder was ignored if the culprit was not caught red-handed. Salt couldn't understand how the slums were allowed to remain. *Why don't they just clear out the whole area? Or at least make a proper attempt to take out the gangs and crime lords?* Some of the more unsavory establishments could only attract criminals or encourage budding psychopaths as far as Salt was concerned. And yet the slums had existed, pretty much in their current state, for nearly as long as Darien itself. *At least the Night Guard patrol these streets. And I'm sure the Guard wouldn't stand by and let someone get beaten or killed.*

A commotion was moving up the street. Pimps were herding their dazed-looking women and boys off into the side streets as quickly as they could. Most of the other pedestrians seemed to melt into the shadows. Salt smiled when he saw the reason. A large group of city watchmen was moving toward him. Twelve men strong, the squad all walked with thick truncheons in their hands, pushing or striking out at anyone who didn't move out of their way quickly enough. Salt's smile faltered. He had seen enough men like these to know the type—they moved through the slums like a gang patrolling their turf. Salt stepped out of the way with everyone else, flattening himself against the filthy wall to let the louts pass. One of the watchmen, the largest one of the lot, stopped in front of a man who was standing to Salt's left. The man was obviously a pimp. Salt had seen him herding his girls off the street as he walked up. He seemed to have been slowed in his escape by his last girl who was limping badly.

"Terrel! There you are, you slippery fucking worm." The man Terrel cringed but did not answer. "You've been avoiding me for three nights now. And here I find you hiding almost halfway across the Muds."

Terrel shook his head and forced a smile onto his ugly face. "No, Broten, I would never do that. But business has been slow. So I had to try some different streets. Maybe find some customers haven't tasted my girls' wares yet." The watchman looked back toward his men and nodded at the pimp. One of his men slammed his truncheon into Terrel's stomach.

"You owe me, worm! And you're late!"

Terrel kept his feet with obvious difficulty. He looked up, tears in his eyes. "I'm sorry, Broten, I don't have nothing. Why don't you and your boys take your payment outta my girls?"

"I don't pay for what's already mine," Broten said, a vicious look on his face. He smashed his own truncheon into Terrel's knee. Terrel fell flat on his face in the muck with a high-pitched scream.

"Looks like you don't remember our arrangement, worm. I'm going to have to remind you proper. And then me and my boys are going to take care of your girls since they've been so lonely lately. If you're lucky, some of them might still be worth a copper once we're finished with them." He kicked the pimp a few times to punctuate his words. "Search him, boys. If he was holding anything back, bury him."

Terrel whined a half-intelligible denial. Broten grabbed the whore who'd been standing next to Terrel and dragged her forward. Salt noticed that she was in her late twenties but moved like a woman in her sixties. Her eyes were glazed over and totally without expression. She moved without protest. Broten looked at her in disgust.

"I hope your other girls have more life in them than this old nag—"

His words were cut off by Salt's fist smashing into his jaw. Staggered, Broten took a few steps backward and tripped over the fallen pimp. The rest of the group turned toward Salt, murder in their eyes. Salt calmly drew the two knives Dwyn had given him. After the things he'd seen this past week, a group of thugs held no fear for him. They hesitated for a moment when they saw the shining steel.

"I don't like what your boss is doing. I'm going to have a chat with him." He saw some of them hesitate. "I figure I can kill three or four of you idiots before the rest bring me down with your sticks. So the question really is, how many of you are willing to die for this ugly piece of shit?"

It was a moment before the first man took a step back. A long moment, while Salt's heart was hammering in his chest as he tried to look as threatening as possible. After that first step though, he knew he had won. They all started looking at one another and backed off a few steps before running. Broten screamed threats and abuse after them until Salt kicked him in the stomach to shut him up. The pimp, still pinned under Broten, groaned. *No more than the bastard deserves.*

Salt took the rough cord the pimp had been wearing as a belt and used it to bind Broten's arms behind his back. The man started to thrash around and struggle. Salt punched him twice in the kidneys.

"Keep pushing me and you won't live long enough to wear a noose." Broten twisted to look back at him.

"You have no idea who you're messing with, asshole. The people I work for are going to hunt you down like a rabid dog for messing with me. The Prince always pays back what he's served ten times over."

Two girls dashed over to the unresponsive woman and started to lead her away with obvious concern. Both of them shot backward glances at Salt as they tried to rush their friend away.

Salt gave them a brief nod and returned his attention to his prisoner. "The Prince, huh? And here I thought the city watch worked for the king." Salt dragged him to his feet. "Now move before I decide to poke a few holes in you."

"You don't get it. The Prince can rip a man apart with his bare hands. He's got a demon in him, and he'll kill you and everyone you know!"

"Sounds like just the kind of guy my friends and I hunt down for a living." *If this guy is telling the truth, I should get the Guard on him right away; with a little luck Dwyn will still be at Harold's and I won't have to walk all the way to the castle.*

Salt dragged the man all the way to Harold's apothecary. Dwyn and his squad were still there, most of them standing around making poor attempts not to look bored while Dwyn himself endured one of Harold's infamous monologues. Dwyn looked up at Salt like a drowning man being tossed a rope.

"Salty! What the hell are you doing here? I thought you said you had the night off?"

Broten looked at the group of men and women dressed as Night Guardsmen. "It is, but I ran into—" Salt started to say when his prisoner cut him off. "Help me! This maniac just grabbed me off the street! I'm an officer of the city watch!"

Salt punched him in the kidneys again and dumped him on the floor. "I didn't say you could talk." Dwyn looked at the city watchman with disdain.

"I'm sure he's a piece of crap, Salty, but is he even worth dragging in?"

"I was just going to turn him in quick when he started running his mouth about this guy he works for. Some guy who calls himself the Prince. Sounds like someone we'd want to take a look at."

Broten looked back and forth between Salt and Dwyn.

"You guys are Night Guard, aren't you?" The color had drained from his face.

Harold, calm as ever, looked at Dwyn. "Well, I can see you are otherwise occupied, my friend. We shall have to finish our chat when you are finished with this new acquaintance you have discovered. But pray do tell the commander I miss his visits. Not that you are not a suitable replacement, of course, but one does like to speak to the man in charge when at all possible. I'm sure you understand. . . ." His words continued unabated as he walked from the room.

Dwyn looked down at Broten. "We are. And now you are going to tell us all about this Prince of yours."

It didn't take a lot of convincing. Like most bullies, he crumbled when he saw his situation was hopeless. Broten became a whimpering wreck not so different from the pimp he'd beaten earlier. He babbled about every detail he knew or had heard about the Prince and his operation. Salt wondered if the man would appreciate that all he was buying himself was a blindfold to go with his noose.

"The Prince's not afraid of anyone. He's got this crazy bitch, Banjax, watching his back all the time. She's nearly as bad as he is. I've seen her kill guys twice her size just with a wave of her hand. No one messes with those two. They take everything personal. Three gangs have tried to move in on them since I joined. The Prince wasted them himself and took what he wanted from them."

"You want in on this one, Salty?" Dwyn asked. "I'm going to call in Gurt and some of the others for this. Maybe two, three squads."

"Damned right I'm in. Do you have a weapon I can borrow though? All I came out with are your little pig stickers."

Dwyn smiled. "Glad to have you with us. Ask Urit—he always drags half the armory around with him. He might be willing to part with something a little bigger."

Salt had met the man in passing but hadn't ever spoken to him. He had to smile when he saw Urit though. The man did look like a walking weapons shop. It was a wonder he could move, much less fight, weighed down as he was. He had two sheathed shortswords at his belt, two longswords strapped to his back, an axe in each hand, and more knives and daggers strapped to his body than Salt cared to count.

He parted with one longsword reluctantly when Salt asked. "Thanks, Urit." Salt gestured to his daggers. "All I have with me is these two toothpicks."

Urit nodded in understanding. "Just be sure to get it back to me after, will ya? I feel naked without my whole set. Can't help thinking I'll reach for it when I really need it and it won't be there."

"The minute we're done with this prick, I'll get it right back to you."

Urit eyed him warily as if trying to decide if he was telling the truth or not, then grunted and walked off. *Not many of the*

Night Guard are what I would have called normal, but that guy...

Salt took a few practice swings with his borrowed sword. It was really heavy for his tastes, its blade almost a hand's width wide. *Not too sharp either,* he noticed. *Though I guess smacking someone in the head with a slightly sharpened block of steel should do the trick anyway.*

Dwyn came back into the shop. "Salty, you going to be all right with no armor?"

"I'll make do. Put me in with the mop-up crew. I just don't want to miss all the fun."

"Good man," he answered before raising his voice to address his whole squad. "Gurt's bringing in two more squads for this, and Lera's comin' with him. Grae and Tassos are scouting out the area already. We're heading out as soon as Gurt gets here. After that, it's his show."

Gurt showed up shortly thereafter, Lera on his heels. A large group of Night Guardsmen crowded into the shop after them, most of them more heavily armed than usual. The space was tight for so many armed soldiers, but they all made room for one another without a fuss. Gurt waited for them to quiet down before speaking.

"All right, lads and lasses. Looks like this is a big one. This Prince character is holed up in an old house on the edge of the slums. Lera has detected some serious wards around his place, so this is the real deal. He's got a half-dozen men standing around on the street, couple more at the door. I'd say it's an easy guess that a good few more are inside. Doesn't look like there are any other ways out of the place. We'll cover the street anyway. I'll want eyes on the roof as well. Dwyn? Your squad is on point. Tsoba, the guards outside are yours. After that, make sure no one and nothing gets out. My squad will be second in.

Lera and Salt, you're with me. The Prince is ours. Now let's get this done."

The Guardsmen filed out of the shop and moved off toward the Prince's building. The various squads set themselves up with quiet efficiency. It was late, but no one moved in these streets. Even for the slums it was strange for no one to be around.

Gurt looked over at Lera. "It's your call."

Lera squinted. "The wards are stronger than I thought. Layers of them. Most of them are just to mask power. Probably more inside. Nothing demonic in the wards, but if I push, I might be able to get a peek inside without letting them know we're out here . . ." Her voice trailed off for a moment, then she hissed. "Demon! Definitely something nasty though I'm not sure what exactly it is. I've damaged their defenses. The wards won't keep you out now. Go."

Gurt looked at the other Guardsmen. "You heard the lady. Bring out the good stuff and hit them hard. No quarter till I say otherwise. Crossbows to the front. Tsoba, I want those guards down in thirty heartbeats. Dwyn, on her heels. Get that door open."

The two squads moved forward smoothly. The street guards died almost without a sound. Half were felled by a well-placed volley of crossbow bolts. The last of them died with blades thrust into their lungs before they could call for help. A flurry of bolts flew out of the dark at the ends of the street and took the two men at the door simultaneously. They had barely hit the ground before Dwyn's squad had kicked in the door and moved inside. Gurt motioned his squad to follow and moved in after them. He waved his squad forward and charged down the street with his shield raised. Salt smiled. Gurt always taught by example. You never take chances in a fight. You keep your weapon ready at all times and keep your shield up if you've got one. And if you don't, you hide behind someone who does and bring a shield yourself next time. Salt could hear sounds of fighting deeper in the building. Two of Dwyn's men stumbled out toward them clutching wounds. Gurt motioned for a medic to take care of them and pushed in to join the action.

They arrived just in time to see a group of five rough-looking men and women toss down their weapons and beg for surrender. Dwyn and his squad had them surrounded. At least a half dozen lay dead on the floor already. Gurt nodded to Dwyn, and his men immediately set about tying up the prisoners and making sure they didn't have any concealed weapons on them. Gurt grunted his approval as they moved past. By Salt's count, at least twenty of the Prince's men had died already, and only two Guardsmen had suffered serious wounds.

Gurt moved up to the next door they came through. He kicked it in and dropped to one knee. Two of his men released quarrels over his head into the dark. No sound came from the next room. Nor did any counterattack seem to be coming.

"Lera?"

"There's a residue of magic here but nothing to worry about. Just move up slowly; I'll give us some light."

The room beyond the door gradually lit up, and the Night Guard moved forward cautiously. The room was opulently decorated. Thick mismatched rugs covered the floors, and seemingly random wall hangings and paintings were hung all over the walls. The room was dominated by a large dining table and a dozen thronelike chairs. The table seemed to groan under the weight of the feast that had been laid out upon it. A woman sat with her back to them. A man sat at the far end of the table, apparently asleep. Blood and less identifiable fluids had been splashed around the room liberally. Salt found three corpses in a corner. The bodies were so badly mangled he couldn't tell if they had been men or women. Lera walked over to a green stain on the floor.

"This was the demon I felt from outside. I'm not sure exactly what specific type it was, but it was definitely Algadi, and strong. Whoever summoned this was no dabbler."

Gurt never took his eyes off the sleeping man. He gestured for the other Guardsmen to cover him and moved up next to the table. Walking cautiously, Gurt edged around and held out his sword toward the woman. He needn't have bothered. Her flesh had been peeled back from most of her skull. Her startling blue eyes looked out of her ruined face. She looked to have died no more than minutes before. Her blood was certainly part of what had been spattered around the room.

"Careful, lads," Gurt admonished as his men moved up alongside the unknown man. "That must be the Prince they're all so scared of. Make sure you truss him up good and tight. Consider him Chosen." The men nodded and brought up thick leather straps and ropes. Salt shivered. There was a lot of anger in whoever had been in this room ahead of them. Anger and power if the dead woman was the much feared enforcer they had heard about.

Lera walked up beside Gurt to examine the corpse. "There are traces of demonic power on her. Her and the bodies in the corner. I'd guess the demon I detected earlier did this. The flavor is strange somehow though. I can't quite place what's wrong with it."

"So the Prince guy kills the demon and falls asleep?"

"If he's a mage, then overusing his power could make him pass out. It all looks to me like one or both of these two lost control of a demon summoning."

"Well, we're lucky they cleaned up their own mess before we got here then." Gurt smiled.

Only one door stood on the far side of the dining room. Salt walked over to it and pulled it open. The moment he did, a small thin man threw himself at Salt with a bright-bladed sword in his hand. Salt reacted instinctively. He parried the blow and struck back, driving the man back through the doorway. Not wanting to lose his advantage, he plunged through after him. Then the shining sword burst into vivid green flames. Salt was caught off guard and was almost gutted by the man's next attack. Disgusted with how easily he'd let himself get distracted, Salt pressed his attack. He kicked the man in the stomach and lunged forward with his blade. The thick sword didn't penetrate far into the man's chest, but it was enough. He let out a small gasp and collapsed. The flaming sword hit the ground and went out.

"What is it?" asked Salt as Gurt moved up next to him.

"That, my lad, is a Dreth Firesword if I'm not mistaken."

Salt poked at the sword with his own blade. It looked cool now. The wood floor was unmarked where it lay. It was hard to believe it had been burning with bright-green flames only moments before.

"Go ahead and pick it up, lad. It won't hurt you."

Salt gingerly lifted the saber. The fine blade was long and single edged. Both the blade and the crossguard were engraved with intricate flame patterns. A large green gem was set in the pommel. "It's so light," he marveled.

"And as near to perfection as any smith is likely to ever make according to texts I've read," said Lera.

"I've seen Dreth blades in the market before but nothing like this."

"The swords you've seen are the poorest examples of their craft. They don't sell the good stuff at any price. And the really prize pieces like the Fireswords and Firespears only leave their city in the hands of a royal or one of their bodyguards."

"It's an amazing enchantment," said Salt, taking a few practice swings with it. "Though I prefer to have a little more weight behind my attacks."

"It isn't enchanted though. Not in any conventional way, anyway. Though I'd wager magic has some place in its making. The fire seems to come from the Firestone in its hilt."

"Not the usual contraband you find then, I take it?"

"That's an understatement. I've only ever seen one of these before. More than fifty years ago, a Dreth prince came to discuss trade with King Arlon's father. He carried a sword just like that one. And may I say, Salt, no matter how much you've improved your sword work these past weeks, you're beyond lucky the guy you just fought didn't know how to use it properly." Lera held up a hand to forestall his answer. "One of the king's bodyguards picked a fight with the Dreth and ended up challenging him to a duel. The Dreth cut him in half, warded plate and all, mind you, on the draw."

Salt's eyes widened. "And it's not enchanted? Whatever this fool was trying to sell the sword for, it wasn't enough." He shook his head. "So what do we do with it?"

"The Dreth consider these weapons sacred. . . . I'm sure they'd like it back," Lera answered.

Gurt shrugged. "It's for the king to decide. Now take it and whatever else you think might be of some use here and let's go."

They split up and started to loot the place as quickly as the most experienced team of thieves. Salt looked around in confusion.

"The king likes us to recoup our costs when we can. No sense leaving anything of value for the other thieves to collect." Salt nodded and held out the sword to Gurt.

"Nah, lad, you carry it. You found these guys, after all. Just don't get used to it."

"Oh, and Gurt? There's no point waiting till tomorrow—I've decided my place is here with the Night Guard." Gurt clapped him on the shoulder.

"Glad to hear it, Salt! We'll take care of the formalities as soon as we get back to the palace."

***

Nial and Zuly looked back at the Prince's building. Night Guardsmen were still swarming around the place. The girls had done as Shade asked. Their second target was dead, though it hardly seemed to matter this time. The Night Guard probably would have cleared the whole lot of them out regardless. Still, the woman's soul was a huge source of power. It was the first talented soul the girls had ever taken. It brimmed with energy, easily worth any three normal souls. Banjax had put up quite a fight, weaving a series of powerful spells around herself, and even summoning a fairly strong Algadi demon to help her. Nial was glad the sleeping powder they had poured into the Prince's wine had worked. They wouldn't have wanted to fight the two of them at once. It had been a near thing finishing their work and slipping out before the Night Guard stumbled into the room, but it was done now. The only things Nial and Zuly needed to worry about were the last name on their list and whether Shade would keep his end of the bargain and leave them alone after it was all done.

Zuly didn't think he would. *Power is everything. So long as Shade has a hold on us, he would be a fool not to use us.*

"Mister Skeg will be glad this job is finished. And just wait till we tell him the Night Guard were there!" Nial said with a grin. Zuly smiled in shared amusement as they wandered happily back to Skeg's shop.

***

Three days! For three days Jeb had been waiting for the bastard to die. Jeb's job was simple—cut down the deaders once they'd stopped twitching and roll them into the pit in the corner of the yard.

The well had been dry for decades and was too deep to fill in. Some palace official had then had the bright idea of using it to dispose of the criminals who were executed in the courtyard. The job of dumping them in had fallen to Jeb. Those same officials had never bothered to figure out how much work was involved, so Jeb was usually free to indulge in his two favorite pastimes—drinking, and sleeping it off. He was doubly lucky because those same officials had decided the person tasked with such a distasteful job deserved a very generous salary. Not that there weren't hundreds of people in the city or even in the castle itself doing worse jobs for far less pay. The only time Jeb had gotten in trouble over his work was when he'd left deaders hanging so long they'd run out of space to hang up the new ones and the smells were making some of the servants sick. Jeb had spent a busy afternoon getting caught up. One of the corpses had burst when it hit the ground, spraying maggots, slime, and bits all over. But Jeb was a smart one. He deserved the salary the palace paid him, of that he had no doubt. It only took him an hour of scrabbling around picking up the bits with his hands before he thought to borrow a broom from the stables.

Three days, they told him after that. No exceptions. If he left a body up for more than three days, he would be gone. They'd replace him after the five years of loyal service he'd given them. *But then this skinny bastard comes along and just won't stop twitching.* The birds hadn't even come down to have a nibble. Three days. Jeb had watched them string him up. He couldn't remember what the man's name was or why he was being hanged, but none of that mattered to Jeb. *Leave those details to my betters, I do.* In a rare moment of diligence, Jeb had returned the very next day to cut the man down. But the bastard was still twitching. Still moving and breathing! The next day was the same. Now here he was three days after the hanging. Three days! A drink hadn't passed his lips in the last two. His job was simple. Cut down the deaders. Deaders, not impossibly twitching bastards the crows didn't want.

Maybe he should use his knife and finish the job. Either way the twitcher was going in the hole. But if he cut the guy, he'd have to explain the blood on the ground. *No matter who or what this fucker is, the hole will do for him. . . .* His decision made, Jeb felt the dread and fear of the past days lift from his shoulders. He dragged the old box over to the twitcher and climbed up. He pulled out his worn old belt knife and started sawing at the rope. It took longer than he would have liked. It must be time to sharpen the knife again. There was always a point at which the effort of sawing at rope with a dull blade overcame his laziness about getting out a stone and sharpening it. *Can't have anyone seeing this guy still hanging here. Can't have 'em see me cutting him down with him still twitchin', either.*

The twitcher moved again. A sharp jerk of the shoulders. With a yelp Jeb fell off the box. Any sympathy he might have felt for the bastard evaporated. The man's arms and legs were securely tied with the same thick hemp that had been used to haul him up by the neck. No wonder the city had so many rope makers. Then he noticed the straps. Three thick leather straps binding the man's arms and as many wrapping his legs, all with the ropes tied over top. The king's men weren't taking any chances with this one. *Hardly a surprise. Three days!*

He brushed himself off and climbed back onto the box. He sawed at the rope again until it split and the twitcher hit the ground, still jerking and twitching. Jeb's guts went cold. *The fucker isn't twitching and dying. He's still struggling against his bonds!* The drop into the pit would do for him anyway. Jeb was sure of that. He dragged the twitcher by his noose, not willing to lay a hand on him now that he knew the man wasn't dying. Muffled sounds were coming from the rough sack that was still tied over the man's head. Another strange detail that. Jeb couldn't recall seeing a sack on any of the other deaders. *Though this guy isn't a deader yet, is he? Maybe it's someone else's job to take off the sacks. . . .* He dragged the twitcher to the corner alongside the pit. The bastard's struggles redoubled. *Wonder if he knows what's comin or if it's just the smell?* Jeb shoved the twitcher into the pit with his foot without another thought. He listened for a minute but didn't hear anything. *Well, that's that.* He brushed off his hands on his dirty breeches. *Another job well done.* It was time for a well-deserved drink. The gallows were surprisingly empty at the moment. Jeb wouldn't need to sober up for days.

***

Anger suffused his entire being. Yajel had lost count of the hours he had spent hanging from the gallows. The rope around his neck chafed his skin raw as he continued to struggle against his bonds. Days had passed. He was sure of that. The feeling of the sun warming the thick sack that had been tied over his head was unmistakable. As was the feeling of being watched. It had lessened in the hours following the sentencing, of course. Most observers tired of watching him twitch at the end of a rope after the first hour. He was so tightly bound even his struggles were not obvious enough to make them entertaining for the crowds. But the feeling never faded entirely. The humiliation of it was worse than any pain he felt in his neck and shoulders.

Bastards! As if a rope could be the end of me! I will cut them down one and all. I will hang them by their own entrails. But their king will suffer for judging me, suffer and die before any of the others to make them know failure before their own end. The straps and ropes were slowly giving way. Nothing obvious, of course. Not yet. But utter immobility had given way to the barest hint of movement.

A few more days, maybe. . . . Days hanging with corpses for company and hungry crows impatiently waiting for his last breath. *I was betrayed.* There was no other possibility. His planning was meticulous. His precautions would be thought excessive by even the most paranoid of resin smokers. *Someone drugged me!* For the Night Guard to catch him was unacceptable. That they were able to do so without him being able to fight back was enraging. To fall asleep at night and wake up during his own trial, a noose already around his neck awaiting the verdict. . . . The thought left him so angry he had no words to describe the burning, searing heat of it. It was all impossible. Unless the person closest to him, the only person who knew almost every aspect of his defenses had turned on him. *No. Banjax would never betray me.* But a nagging voice in his head kept asking the question: *Then why is she not wearing a noose next to me?* He had heard the sentencing. Only men were hanged with him.

Lost in a world of betrayal and rage, he didn't notice someone cutting at the rope of his noose until just before it gave way. He fell in a limp heap on the muddy ground, his head spinning from the sudden change in position. *About time they came to cut me down.* His followers were scum one and all. There was no denying that. But he had gotten each and every one of them out of some tight fixes. He had treated them fairly and helped them get rich. *I'll give them shit for making me wait for so long before I reward them for getting me out of this mess. . . .* But the ropes around his arms and legs were not cut. The leather straps were not loosened. Instead he was being pulled across the muddy ground in fits and jerks by the noose that was still tied around his neck. He tried to speak through the gag and sack but could not make himself heard.

What the fuck are they doing?! Then it occurred to him. It wasn't his followers who had cut him down. The king's men had tired of seeing him swing at the end of a rope and decided to finish him off.

The dragging stopped. He waited for the sword to fall. His mind was blank. Robbed of his plans for revenge, there was suddenly nothing left within him.

Then a foot pushed at the side of his chest, and he was falling over a ledge. A surprisingly long fall. He collided with something on the way down that snapped his left shoulder and sent him spinning. His guts clenched as he tumbled through the air. But the bone-crushing impact he had expected at the end of the fall never came. Instead he glanced off several wet, yielding surfaces that bruised every part of his body before landing in a pool of squelching mud. The sack over his face wasn't enough to cover up the stench of putrefying flesh.

Yajel's anger returned stronger than ever. They hadn't even bothered to kill him. They had thrown him out like refuse and left him to die in a pit. His shoulder was swelling, certainly broken. Something sharp was lodged deep into his back near his shoulder blade as well. The pain of it was far worse than his neck. But he was alive. His revenge was not lost to him. They would pay for what they did to him. All of them. He started to struggle against his bonds again and was pleased to notice more movement than before. Another day maybe. At least he was no longer being watched.

When he finally got the ropes and straps loose enough to get an arm out, Yajel was near death. As strong as he was, he could not go without food and water forever. The putrid mud and insects were threatening to drive him insane as well. Things he couldn't identify crawled across his body. Rats occasionally bit him, testing, seeing if he was finished yet so they could start the feast. Thankfully the rough linen sack kept the worst of the creatures away from his face. *I will not die down here!* he swore to himself. His right shoulder was grotesquely swollen after the fall, and his constant struggles had done nothing to improve it. *I will need to find a proper healer to deal with this or I may lose my arm.* He slowly lifted his hands to his neck and removed the rope he had cursed for so long. The sack followed, and he almost regretted removing it.

He was, as he had guessed, in a putrid pool of mud surrounded by decaying bodies, maggots, rats, and insects. A little moisture leaked out of the walls down here. Not enough to be collected by those above, just enough to keep the bottom of the hole wet and muddy. Though by no means squeamish, some part of him wished he only had a human's eyesight and so, blinded by the dark, would have been spared the sight. The stench was indescribable. The sack hadn't blocked all of it, but it had held in the smell of his own unwashed body to compete with the smell of decomposition. He snatched up one of the fat rats and snapped its neck. Then he wiped off his right hand as well as he was able and gouged his finger into the rat's stomach. After he was satisfied he had removed all of the animal's digestive system, he bit deeply into its back. Some part of his mind was disturbed by how wonderful the rat tasted. Its blood, dribbling down his chin, was sweeter than wine to his starved body.

A day, maybe two, eating rats and regaining his strength and he'd try to climb out of the pit. Even with the slick muddy sides he didn't think it was beyond him. His shoulder being the way it was wouldn't make it any easier, but there was no other choice, no other path he could see. At least he had some materials to help him: a dozen leather straps, and several thick lengths of good hemp rope—one on each of the corpses around him. *Their wasteful natures will be the key to my return.*

Yajel frowned. He was as resistant to disease as he was to nearly everything, but several days down here would be difficult to survive even if he wasn't starved and carrying several open wounds and bites. He had to wait, eat, and recover his strength, but if he waited too long, he would never make it out. *And even if I do, there I'll be, covered in shit and worse, with a broken shoulder in the middle of the palace courtyard.* He wound the leather braces around his wounded shoulder and arm, trying to support the limb without losing too much mobility. Then he took the ropes and tore some strips of cloth off the other corpses around them and wound the cloth over every part of his body to protect him from the rats and insects. Finally, with a sigh, he pulled the muddy sack back over his head, propped himself up against a wall, and tried to rest.

Two days and ten rats later, Yajel judged that he was as strong as he was going to get down here. When the sun set, he would either climb to freedom, or fall back down and die. He was no longer starving, but his flesh was hot and flushed. He had woken up sweating in the cold pit. *It must be tonight.*

CHAPTER 9

Waiting for the scouts to return was hard on everyone. The others had realized the truth of Karim's words and they all flocked around Maura asking for advice and looking for purpose. Well accustomed to keeping idle hands busy, she didn't disappoint them, though she was exhausted herself when the scout teams finally started drifting back in. They gave their reports in front of the assembled militia. The news was grim: while the king and all of Sacral's hopelessly outnumbered army were fighting on the western side of the city, a second almost equally large army was attacking from the east. With no one to oppose them, the Abolians were swarming into the city and gradually breaking up into smaller groups as they rampaged through the streets slaughtering and plundering. The tales of burning houses, looting, rape, and murder were repeated by each team that returned.

As fear spread through the city, so too did word of the militia. Scared and desperate people were now flocking to them in hopes of finding safety. Though she had no training or rank, the new arrivals all accepted Maura's leadership role without question. And without quite realizing when she started, she found herself issuing orders and organizing those who wanted to fight back.

With a few well-placed words, Maura quelled their fears and awakened their anger. She looked around at a few hundred would-be fighters. "I know we have no training and few weapons, but every scout we've sent out has agreed. These invaders wander lost in our city. More, they move in small groups. Sacral is our home. Our scouts have proven time and again today that we can move around them without being seen or caught. All we need to do is surprise them. They may outnumber our army, but the people of Sacral, the common people like you and me, outnumber the damned Abolians by far more still. They have forgotten that we are the proud descendants of the legendary army that slew Death. It's time to remind them!" The people roared their approval.

"Now I will hear no more arguments; we need to do something about these dogs who think they can wander into our city and do as they please. Karim, choose fifteen men you think are the best able to handle themselves in a fight, former soldiers like yourself if possible. Make sure you all have some kind of weapon. The rest of you follow more slowly. There will be plenty for everyone, I'm sure. We'll take out a few small groups if we can and pass out weapons to more of our people. Now, let's see what kind of trouble the people of Sacral can cause for these would-be conquerors." The group set out as quietly as they could with a dozen scouts running ahead of them.

The first Abolians they found were just leaving a large house. Their armor was stained with blood and they were weighted down with plunder. Maura held her nervous group back until the Abolians were almost on top of them. The surprise was total. The six red-armored men died almost without putting up a fight. Her mostly unarmed volunteers tore the men limb from limb. Six invaders dead. Only two of her own were wounded, neither seriously. This small victory galvanized the rest of her force. The Abolian soldiers were stripped of their weapons as well as a few pieces of armor. The loot was passed out without a word, and everyone looked at Maura expectantly, eager for the next fight.

Maura shook her head. "Let's not get carried away. Our wounded need to be taken back to the others. More, we need to make sure there are no people in these houses who need our help." *We're going to need a bigger place to keep all the young and the old safe. The houses around Karim's are all filling up, and it's going to get harder and harder to get messages to everyone.* She looked up and saw the great arena in the distance. With a smile she waved her group to come closer and listen.

"We're going to need to get everyone to a safe place and get enough people armed and ready to defend it. I think the arena is our best bet. Anyone we tell about it will be able to find their way there easily too and we won't have to guide each and every person who wants to join us." Eager faces all nodded their approval. "Now, the first thing we need to do is make sure it's safe. Then we get everyone moving from Karim's house over that way in small groups with as many fighters as we can manage."

Karim finished her thought, "Then we'll make sure we spread the word to all the survivors we find to bring all the food and water they can and join us there."

Maura nodded. "All right, people, let's do this again. Same plan. Let's keep moving toward the arena and see how many more swords we can take." The people moved off, with fresh resolve. As they approached the building, they saw signs of fighting. Hundreds of Abolians had been cut down along the main thoroughfare that led from the arena to the west wall.

Her followers gleefully helped themselves to the weapons that were scattered around the dead invaders.

"Every single one is Abolian," her scouts reported. The arena also seemed to be totally deserted.

"One of the Warchosen must have come through here or even the king," Maura answered. "That's good news for us. Make sure you collect as many weapons as you can. Any you can't carry easily, leave in the arena for the others when we get them here. And make sure you explore every part of the building, even the tunnels down below. As soon as we're sure there aren't any Abolians hiding nearby we can start bringing everyone over here and spreading the word."

Two hours later, fresh recruits and people seeking refuge were streaming into the arena, and nearly a thousand proud men and women stood with the militia. Most were assigned the task of guarding the many entrances to the arena while several hundred joined Maura in circling the arena in ever-widening loops, clearing out any invaders they could find. They had developed a system. Scouts would locate enemies, and groups of the better-armed militia would then fan out, encircle, and overwhelm them. Then they would slip into each house as they passed and look for survivors. A handful of people had even taken it upon themselves to pass out water and food to the fighters whenever circumstances permitted.

Everything proceeded smoothly for the better part of the morning. Almost three hundred invaders had fallen to the People's Army, as they were now calling themselves. They fought with barely controlled savagery. No quarter was given to the invaders. Each new survivor was greeted with joy, one more small victory over the Abolians. It was with great excitement that Maura welcomed Jerik to their group early that afternoon. A scout had found him standing guard over a young woman and her three children.

"Jerik! It's so good to see you! Have you seen Beren and Gerald? Are they safe?"

Jerik's smile at seeing her faltered. "I'm so sorry, Maura. Gerald . . . Gerald is dead. I found him in the front of the shop. Beren is gone. I have no idea where. I'm so sorry," he repeated softly.

Maura felt like she'd been punched in the stomach. *My son. My dear Beren.* She started to tremble. Jerik reached out to support her, but she pulled away.

"No, thank—" Her voice broke. She coughed and tried again. "Thank you, Jerik . . . for telling me. I'll have to hope that we can find Beren somewhere in this mess." She shook herself and turned back to Karim.

"Please get everyone moving again. There are still a lot of people in the city we can save." She couldn't stop her hands from shaking, and the pain in her stomach clenched into a tight ball of agony, her mind almost unable to get past the loss of her only child. With incredible determination, Maura pushed the pain deep down and swore to herself she wouldn't give in to her feelings while she still had a chance of saving her husband. *Beren has to be safe. I can't lose them both.*

Karim looked at her sadly and nodded his agreement. "You heard the lady!" he called out. "Let's get moving. Scouts out front." The would-be army moved out. Jerik hefted his hammer and fell in next to Maura.

A boy of about fifteen who had been acting as a scout for the army returned a short time later. "It looks like a group of about twelve hiding in an alley five streets over, ma'am."

It took her a few moments to respond. She rubbed tears out of her eyes angrily before turning her attention to the boy. "Good work. Let's get at least fifty of our own into position around them before we attack. Can you describe the place better to the other scouts?" He nodded emphatically. Maura gave the order to attack, relieved that she had a more immediate worry to occupy her mind. She waited for the sounds of fighting but was surprised moments later by her own fifty returning, leading a group of a dozen Sacral soldiers. Their tabards had been removed, but their armor was certainly recognizable enough.

Their officer stomped to the front of the group. "Who is in charge of this rabble?" he demanded.

"That would be me," answered Maura, stepping out from behind Jerik.

"Common citizens are not to become involved with the war. You will only hamper our own efforts. Now send these good people back to their homes. There is more to war than waving around weapons," he said. He then turned on his heel and started to walk away.

"Unfortunate then that we killed the sixty Abolians that were moving in your direction before you could handle them yourself." The officer paused. He looked at the men and women around him, only now noticing the number of enemy weapons clutched in their hands, the bloodstains, the wounds.

"Perhaps I misjudged you," he said, turning back to Maura. He looked pensive for a moment, then said, "I estimate you have about two hundred with you. That should be enough to help. I want you to march along this avenue. Don't bother trying to be quiet. It's pointless with this many people. My men and I will keep pace one street over in the backstreet. The Abolians will see you coming and my men can flank them when they attack you."

Maura stiffened. "So you misjudged us, but now you think us worthy to throw at the enemy as fodder to save your own skin? Any one of my two *thousand* fighters is worth ten of you." Her pain was turning to anger. It felt good to be angry.

"You'll do as you're told, woman."

"I think not. You can't even be trusted to keep your voice down. How do you expect me to trust you with the lives of these good people?" The man's eyes were pure murder as he reached for his sword. Maura ignored the gesture and continued, "Not one of these people has taken an oath to join the Sacral army. But they have one and all joined with my friends and me—to try and save our homes." The soldier moved to draw his blade but stopped when Jerik lifted his hammer and glared down at him.

"No one is going to draw a weapon on the lady. She saved us, one and all, and we can all see she's our best chance of saving our homes and families."

The officer looked close to bursting with rage. Several of his men reached for their own swords but stopped as dozens of weapons, real and improvised, were leveled at them.

Maura continued, "You and your men are welcome to join us, or you can go back to hiding in your alley. If you come, you could save lives. We don't have many trained fighters."

"My men and I were doing just fine without you. We intend to live through this. Go ahead and get yourselves killed." He stomped away. A few of his men followed, but most just looked at one another and stayed. The officer looked back at them, incredulous. "You're disobeying orders to stay with them?"

A tall soldier of about forty shrugged. "Figure we weren't really doing our duty hiding with you."

The officer's face was beet red. "I'll see the lot of you executed for treason if you survive!"

Maura looked at Jerik and the soldiers who had decided to stay. "We've wasted enough time with that idiot. Let's get back to cleaning up our city. I think you men should be split up. One of you with each of our main fighting groups. You can give tips and guidance as you go that way. Jerik, please make sure they get to where they are needed. Send them with the scouts that are heading back out. We're changing our plan—I want a path cleared to the Great Temple as quickly as possible. The priests might need our help, and we could sure use theirs."

The People's Army next ran into a flood of refugees from the western side of the city. The people had left their homes as quickly as they could. Others seeing the desperate masses pass by their homes had hurried to join them, sure that whatever was chasing them must be close behind. They looked at Maura and her armed mob with a mix of shock and hope.

"People of Sacral!" Maura called as loudly as she could. "We have set up a place of refuge for all who would join us. Come to the arena! Those who would like to join us in taking the fight back to the invaders stay here with us." Slowly the great mass of people started to shift into motion again. A fair number split off from the main group and came to stand with the People's Army with eager looks on their faces. *How fierce we must look to them.*

Maura called out to each group as they passed. "Food, water, and weapons are all you need worry about. Leave everything else."

One of her citizen-soldiers moved toward a heavyset middle-aged man and gestured to an ornate wooden case he held awkwardly in his hands. "Didn't you hear the commander?" he shouted at the man. "No useless junk!"

"But . . . ," the man began to protest, flustered.

The soldier raised his hand to strike him. Jerik, never far from Maura's side, grabbed the soldier's arm before the blow landed. The man grimaced in obvious pain.

"Telling them is enough, soldier. If their things grow too heavy, you can be sure they'll drop whatever they can live without." Turning to look at the man with the case, he continued. "Make sure you keep your pace up. We're not leaving anyone behind, but we can only move as fast as the slowest of us."

"Thank you, good sir," the man stammered. "I understand the need, but this box contains the tools of my art. I thought I might be of some assistance, if I could be allowed to speak with the lady?" He finished in a rush.

Jerik considered for a moment before nodding. "Come with me." He looked back at the soldier he had reprimanded. "Proceed, soldier, but do not forget yourself again."

Jerik waited for Maura to finish speaking with some of the scouts before bringing the man forward. "Maura? This man says he might be able to help us."

"Great lady!" the man said, bowing as well as he was able holding the large case. "Corwin the Magnificent at your service!" Maura's eyebrows rose at that. And Jerik shot her an apologetic look. The man continued his obviously well-prepared speech oblivious to their reactions. "I have been employed by the greatest and brightest minds of our fair city to offer amazing entertainment and delight . . ." His voice drifted off as Maura gestured him to stop, a clear look of annoyance on her face.

"While I appreciate your offer, Mister Corwin, I really don't have time to be entertained just now. Perhaps after we've saved our lives and retaken our city?"

Corwin's face paled. He swallowed hard. "Please, I never meant. . . . I just got carried away. Please let me explain. I am an illusionist. I'm no archmage. But I have a knack for tricking the senses. I know nothing of fighting, but should there be anything I can do for you, please do not hesitate to ask."

Maura's annoyance melted away in the face of the man's discomfort. "I apologize for being short with you, Mister Corwin. I will think about how we can best use your skills. I will have some questions about the scope of your abilities as we travel." She turned to Jerik. "Please find someone to help Mister Corwin with his supplies, and keep him close."

Jerik smiled. "I think I have just the man for the job."

Maura spoke quietly with the man as they waited for the people to be escorted past. "Your group came from the west. Did you happen to pass by the Great Temple?"

Corwin nodded sadly. "We passed by it, my lady. Most of us thought of them when we needed help and refuge. Their doors stayed barred to us no matter how much we begged."

Maura's features hardened. *How dare the priests turn their back on the people in their hour of need!*

"Karim! I'm not waiting any longer. I need to speak to the priests myself. Get twenty volunteers ready and ask the scouts to push out farther that way. Corwin, Jerik, will you come too?"

Maura and her team moved out as quickly and quietly as they could. Most of them were fighting the discomfort of aching muscles and fatigue, but no one complained. Too much was at stake, and each and every one of them was amazed at their role in the defense of their home.

Corwin proved to be far more useful than Maura could have hoped as her team made its way to the temple. He created fantastical illusions that frightened or distracted enemy soldiers or made hidden militia fighters appear to be nothing more than refuse or casks. None of the illusions could stand up to close scrutiny—as Corwin had said, he was no archmage—but the effectiveness of the militia's ambushes grew significantly with his help.

"Corwin, I thank the White Mother you joined us."

Corwin smiled broadly and struggled to catch his breath. His stout frame was poorly suited to running and skulking, and his energy was constantly being drained by his magic. Their scouts reported that the way to the temple was clear but that there were signs of fighting in the area. Several burnt corpses lay on the streets around the great building.

A woman at the back of the group called out, and they turned to see a Sacral captain running up the street toward them. Maura gestured for her people to clear a path for him.

"Have any of you been to the temple?" he asked as soon as he came near enough not to have to shout.

"The priests have barred the door to all those who have come to them for help. I intend to speak with them and demand that they come out and perform their healing duties for our wounded."

The officer looked at Maura. "King Ansyl has sent me here for a similar reason. I am Captain Harrow." Everyone started to whisper to one another, recognizing the name of the temporary commander of the Sacral army.

Maura waved toward the building. "You are most welcome to join us in banging on their door, Captain."

They all turned at a commotion in front of the temple. The doors had been opened, and three priests stepped out, each carrying a long white staff. Shapes burst from shadows and threw themselves at the priests. Maura only just had time to see thin forms wrapped in black leather and armed with daggers before white fire burst from the priests' staffs and engulfed them. Corwin gestured for everyone around him to stay still and wove an illusion of a simple empty street to hide the People's Army from view. Even Captain Harrow stood back and watched, clearly not understanding what he was seeing. Maura saw one of the assassins pull itself back up despite the charred wreckage the priest's flames had reduced its body to. With a start, she saw all the other charred corpses on the street jump back to their feet and join the attack.

"*Undead*," she said.

The undead assassins quickly cut down the priests, but they didn't take any notice of the two dozen men and women holding their breaths behind an imperfect illusion just a few steps away. Then a man wearing the robes of a senior priest threw back the heavy wooden doors of the temple, a look of fury on his face.

"Your kind are not welcome here," he said through clenched teeth. "Those novices were clearly useless. But don't think you'll have such an easy time with me."

He waved his arms, and shadowy tendrils lashed out from the ground and wrapped themselves around the walking corpses, pinning their limbs to their sides. The priest reached inside his robes and brought out a long black dagger. He swung it at the nearest assassin, and a long rope of perfect blackness lashed out and cut him in half from shoulder to hip. Maura felt a chill run down her spine. The white fire the novices had called down on the undead fit well with her idea of the White Mother and her priesthood, but the evil-looking black dagger and the shadowy magic the senior priest called on were at odds with everything she knew of the temple. . . . Maura turned to Captain Harrow and saw her shock mirrored in his eyes.

The priest turned to strike down his next target when a serrated blade erupted from the middle of his chest. Blood sprayed out as he gurgled and collapsed. Another assassin stood behind him. Though shorter than average, his frame was almost impossibly wide. An emblem of a crowned skull marked his chest. Maura caught her breath. Legends and stories were coming to life in front of her.

The assassin turned to the charred undead. "You let a priest get the drop on you? You lot are getting sloppy. You're supposed to be the Crows of the Dead King! Two of you pick up Cyril and get out of here. I'll finish up myself."

The undead assassins gathered up their dismembered companion and vanished back into the shadows beside the temple. Maura felt a lump in her throat as the man turned and looked directly at her.

"You can't hide behind illusions any longer, people of Sacral. The White Bitch is going to pay for her betrayals. Those who stand with her will join her fate."

Harrow drew his sword and moved to stand in front of Maura. The assassin's eyes squinted for a moment. Then faster than Maura could blink, the man shot forward. He grabbed the blade of Harrow's sword in his right hand and slammed the palm of his left into his breastplate. Harrow went flying into the wall in a heap, his sword still in the assassin's hand.

"Find a new god and stay away from this place." His eyes narrowed. "Trust me, you don't want to make me your enemy."

He looked down at the sword in his hand. "This is a fine blade, boy. I'm sure you won't mind if I borrow it. I won't touch those tainted weapons the priests use. You'll find it in the temple when I'm done with it. Look for it in the heart of darkness." He grinned down at Harrow. "You'll be able to tell your little friends Rahz the Insane borrowed your sword to kill a high priest."

Harrow was only just trying to sit up when Rahz took off at speed and vanished into the temple. Harrow's breastplate was bent. The shape of Rahz's palm was pressed into the metal, obliterating the rune that had been set there. He struggled to pull it off.

"Whoever that man is," said Harrow, coughing, "I'd have to agree—we don't want to make him our enemy."

Maura looked at those around her. "Did that make sense to any of you? Could these be undead returned from the days of the founding? That crowned skull emblem that Rahz had on his chest . . ."

"I'm just glad the walking corpses are the temple's problem," said Corwin.

"You would just leave them to face this alone?"

"I don't see that we have much of a choice," he said, helping Harrow to his feet. "If the undead can throw Harrow around like a rag doll, I don't see what good leading the People's Army against them would do."

"As much as I hate to agree with him," said Harrow, "we have big enough problems already. I need to get back to the front." He looked up and said clearly, "Your Majesty, the priests have their own fight on their hands and it is beyond me to help them. More, I have seen them use powers that disturb me greatly. No help will come to us from the temple."

The king's voice drifted into his mind like a weak breeze, the strength and confidence it had always had, gone. *I am sorry, Captain. I have ordered your men to retreat to the inner wall with all haste. Meet them at the West Gate and do what you can for them; they have fought bravely. I am finished. My mages are spent. I fear most of them will follow me into death before the day is out.* The voice faded and was gone.

Harrow looked at Maura and the others. "The king is dead. The outer wall is lost. My surviving soldiers are fleeing to the inner wall."

"King Ansyl is . . . gone?" *Yet another senseless death.* Maura's features hardened and without thinking, she began to call out orders. "Get word to Karim. We need more scouts out on the west side of town. We may have Abolians pushing in from that side now. Try to clear as many people as we can from the houses closest to the wall before they break through."

She turned to Harrow. "Captain, where on the inner wall are your soldiers? Would you like us to send some people to help? We have a nearly a thousand people at the arena who are willing to fight, and probably more have joined since I left."

Harrow looked surprised at the suggestion. Then seeing the flurry of activity that followed Maura's words, he thought for a moment and nodded. "My men are at the West Gate or soon will be. I'll go and see how they are doing and decide from there. I won't ask any of you to join us. Holding a wall and fighting in formation are not things you can improvise. We'll hold out as long as we can to give you time to evacuate the houses and then try to fall back to the arena to support your efforts."

"Thank you, Captain Harrow. I hope to see you there soon." Harrow nodded and took off at a run.

"Corwin and Jerik," Maura continued after Harrow had left. "When Harrow and his soldiers fall back from the wall, they're going to have the whole Abolian army on their heels. We need to prepare a little surprise for the Abolians to make sure our people make it back to us. We need to gather as much wood and lamp oil as we can once we make sure all those houses are empty. . . ."

***

Rahz walked out of the temple a short time later wiping blood off his hands with a scrap torn off a priest's robe. Two undead assassins stepped out of the shadows to meet him. "Report."

"We took care of the lesser priests as they ran out of the other exits. By all estimates we should have gotten nearly all of them. The rest of the murder is doing a sweep of the lesser temples looking for stragglers."

The second assassin added, "A group of Abolian Chosen are moving in this direction. From what they've been saying, we gather their goal is to break any knots of resistance that might be forming in the city. They seem to think the temple would be a focal point for any survivors."

Rahz nodded. "I'm going to go play with the Abolians. Finish the cleanup and let me know if you need me."

They saluted and melted back into the shadows. Rahz pulled out his two favorite daggers, both single edged and heavy bladed, made for slashing more than stabbing. This was a job that required blood and chaos, not quietly bringing down a single target. And if there was anything that Rahz loved, it was chaos. *Time to send a message. Invaders are not welcome here.* The Abolians appeared a few minutes later. They walked in the open, making no effort to hide their presence. *Overconfident bastards. The Sacral grunts must not have put up much of a fight. Or else they're all dead already.* He shrugged, not caring either way. As far as Rahz was concerned they were all trespassing in his city.

The woman in the lead wore intricate metal armor. Every piece of it was lacquered a deep red. The armor as well as the two shortswords she carried held powerful enchantments. *Something nasty by the look of it.* The others had some minor gear between them, but nothing worth thinking about. Rahz burst through them with unstoppable force. He slashed a blade at each of the lead fighters. On his left he took the man in the face, cutting across both his eyes. On the right, the woman pulled back slightly, and he only scored a slash through her cheek. A couple fragments of teeth flew out of the gash, sliced in half by his razor-sharp blade. Before either could fight back, he was past. He smashed an armored elbow into the faceplate of the next man on the left. The metal crumpled with a satisfying crunch. As his momentum slowed, he ducked a clumsy swing and brought his knee up into the last man's midsection. The three Abolians still standing reacted with admirable speed, backing off and fanning out to encircle him. *Two down. Two hurt. Not a bad start.*

Rahz smiled at them. He moved slowly around, keeping them all in sight, shifting his grips on his daggers. They hesitated as they moved forward. None of them had ever seen anything like him before. *That's 'cause there is only one Rahz.* They hesitated and so gave him enough time. Time for the tide of his powers to surge again. The three of them attacked him together. He saw a sword coming at him and chose his target. He rushed toward the attack, guiding the blade past his face with one dagger while he brought his other weapon up under the Warchosen's rib cage. Chain links popped; the tip of the blade pierced a lung. Rahz lifted the man clear off his feet with the blow and threw him into the man behind him. He swept the legs out from under the woman with a kick and slashed her knee open as she flipped away from him. She got up immediately, ignoring the small wounds he had inflicted, but looking at him now with scared eyes. Rahz looked down for a moment and noticed a handle protruding from his chest. *Either she's better than I expected or I'm getting sloppy. Either way this should be more fun than I expected.* He smiled and made to charge them again. The two who were still able fled in panic, leaving their wounded companions to bleed to death on the street.

Rahz let them go. *No fun, after all. But then I guess you can't send a message without a messenger.* He pulled the dagger out of his chest and noticed the thick black paste smeared over the blade. Rahz smiled in genuine amusement and tossed the weapon over his shoulder.

***

The western front collapsed with the death of the king. Thousands of Abolians were dead, but the Sacral army was, for all intents and purposes, destroyed. Red-armored soldiers started to pour over the outer wall as the scattered remnants of Sacral's forces fell back. Barely a thousand soldiers still drew breath, many of them severely wounded. News of the disaster spread fast, and people from all over the city were now converging on the arena. Within the time it took Harrow to run to meet his soldiers, the People's Army under Maura had swelled to more than ten thousand swords, knives, and shovels.

Despite Harrow's instructions, Maura moved up to the West Gate with a large group of volunteers to start evacuating any wounded soldiers who were no longer able to fight. Another team started building barricades in as many of the smaller streets as they could, filling any barrels or wooden boxes they found with anything flammable they could get their hands on. The barricades were then doused in oil and all the boxes and barrels were stacked in the main thoroughfare in precarious stacks on either side of the street.

When Harrow finally called a retreat, Maura had all the barricades fired. The People's Army then guided, and often carried, the Sacral soldiers past the boxes and barrels of oil with the last person passing each stack throwing a torch down.

The fires were far less effective than Maura had hoped, because the oil spread too slowly to do much more than cut off the Abolians' advance. Still, the fires ensured that all the surviving soldiers made it back to the arena safely.

As soon as Harrow was able to get his soldiers settled in the arena, he went to find Maura.

"Thank you for saving my men and ignoring my instructions."

"No need to thank me, Captain Harrow. I'm just doing what I think is right."

"No, Maura. I do need to thank you. What you've done here is beyond anything I could have managed. My soldiers and I were ready to die to make sure you had a chance to evacuate the area. You made those deaths unnecessary. You've given us the chance to fight again, and even the hope that we might live through this war. I've discussed it with my men and we all agree—we'd be honored to join the People's Army."

"I . . . Thank you, Captain Harrow. We will be grateful for your help, but surely it would be better for you to take command?"

Harrow shook his head. "I led a single company and never aspired to more. Jenus and Traven were the leaders. I just kept my company organized and did what I was told. And really, none of us has ever fought anywhere but in the arena before. You have as much experience with real war as any of us and are proving to have more talent for keeping our people alive."

With the addition of over two hundred professional soldiers who were still in fighting condition as well as three Warchosen and two battlemages, the People's Army's attacks became that much more effective. Maura's strategy of using the size and complexity of the city to their advantage continued to show great results as they slowly cut down the Abolian forces.

Captain Harrow ran up to Maura. "Scouts report that the army to the east is retreating. Some serious sorcery is being unleashed out there."

"Could it be the king survived after all?" asked Jerik.

"I hope so," said Maura, not looking convinced. "Anyway, this gives us a chance to focus on the west. Harrow, halve the number of scouts to the east. This is good news, but I still want eyes out there. Now, our first job is clearing out any Abolians who are already in the city. We spread out and catch as many of them as we can while we move outward. Once we're reasonably sure we've cleared most of them out, we can pull some of our people away from guarding the arena and push all the way to the walls."

Captain Harrow nodded and moved off to give the orders.

***

Blades of sunlight cut through the dust cloud. Morning, such as it was, in the Great Desert was well under way. The sands were alive with activity as all the creatures that called this place home ran around frantically making the most of the short window of time while temperatures remained moderate. It would not last. As cold and icy as the nights were, the daylight hours were blisteringly hot. Carver had not been able to determine why. The lands were neither farther north nor south than Bialta and its moderate climate, nor farther from the ocean. The temperatures were only the start of the land's strangeness. Long narrow swaths of scrub grass and narrow rivers cut back and forth across the otherwise featureless expanses of sand and stone. This unusual mingling of desert and grassland had led to the appearance of some of the most surprising creatures Carver had ever encountered in his travels. Indeed, some of the desert predators had evolved to be large enough to prey on the herd animals that wandered the grassy paths. Carver watched in fascination as a huge serpent killed and consumed a large bull ox, much as a more modest snake might swallow a rat. *These serpents must be extremely long lived to reach such a size.* Carver had hoped to study the creature, but even with the considerable resources now at his disposal, the great snake eluded capture.

I will find it eventually, of course. Time is always on my side. In the meantime, he was returning to the palace with a fascinating array of test specimens. The sheer diversity of the creatures that inhabited the desert was like nothing he had ever seen before, an incredible treasure trove of new traits and adaptations.

The desert cat he had captured squirmed as Carver cut into it. It wasn't strictly necessary for him to examine specimens this way anymore. His magic was sufficient to look into their flesh and see far better than he ever could cutting them. But this had been the way he started, back when he took his first faltering steps on this long, long road he still walked. *And really, why change now?*

After he finished up with the cat, Carver wandered through his workrooms to check on his other projects. The space the Drokga had given over to his use was barely adequate, though Carver had made a point of looking impressed and thankful to the lackey who had first shown it to him. Four rooms, all opulently decorated and filled with a ridiculous variety of furnishings, none of which matched, along with a half-dozen old and sickly slaves. Carver knew he was being insulted, but he really didn't care. Space and resources were all he needed. He had had the bulk of the furniture removed and set up a simple workspace as well as cages to house his specimens and projects.

As he wandered, Carver reached out with his magic to look at a few of his favorite pets. Each had inspired him in a meaningful way in the past.

The first was a large snake. It was not the first snake Carver had inspected that could crush the life out of its prey, but it was the first such snake he had ever found that also had a venomous bite and could spit the venom to quite an impressive distance.

The second was a small goat that didn't look particularly impressive in any way. It had intrigued him in its own quiet way though. Carver had found it calmly feeding on the leaves of a tree, while perched in its upper branches.

The third was a new addition to his collection. A Korant ant from the Great Desert. Not one of the Drokga's tame ones, of course. It looked quite similar to a common ant found in every part of the world, though it was far more thickly built and the size of an average dog.

Most of his other favorites had long since died of old age and had been preserved in all manner of ways. They cluttered the remainder of the room's walls and shelves. It was unfortunate that most species' survival strategy seemed to hinge more on reproduction than on longevity.

The innermost room Carver had set aside as his own bedchamber. He parted the layers of wards and stepped around the hulking form of Maran Vras, who stood as a permanent sentinel. Carver's flesh began to rearrange itself. He pulled himself up taller, his back suddenly straight. Each vertebra popped as it returned to its correct position. His stringy, thinning mop of gray hair filled out and grew into a thick glossy mane of perfect black. His preferred form was generally human. An angular, handsome face, dark eyes, perhaps just a little too large to be entirely natural, and a thin, well-muscled body. Reverting to this shape was like coming home. He felt more confident, more aware of his surroundings. It was so very tiring walking around hunched over, his eyes seeing nothing but dusty floors and passing feet. Past experience had taught him the value of appearing to be less than he was—particularly to his employers. The egos that generally went hand in hand with power couldn't imagine that a twisted wreck of a man might seek power for himself.

The single chair in the room was pushed out of the way against the equally useless bed. He had no need of rest. His body was far too advanced for such things. But a true master of the art of deception had once taught Carver that no detail was too trivial, and he had taken the lesson to heart. Night now presented the opportunity for more private research, safe from any prying eyes or perceived accountability to the Drokga. . . .

When the day of his first audience with the Drokga finally arrived, Carver busied himself ensuring that every aspect of his work was ready. He would finally have the chance to show off the creatures he had created in the months since he had taken up residence at the palace. He fully expected the Drokga to be impressed. No other living being on this world could do what Carver could do. He would offer this petty tyrant of a decadent city-state power and the means to intimidate and terrify his enemies, and in exchange Carver would be given resources and the freedom to continue his research. He glanced out the window at the blazing desert sun. It was nearly time. The Drokga would certainly make him wait, but Carver would have to go through the formalities. He would stand by the door of the audience chamber, with his cages and slaves, for as long as he had to, and wait on the pleasure of his new employer.

A squad of the Drokga's personal guard escorted him through the palace's winding hallways while his slaves pushed large wheeled cages behind. It was a long walk and Carver had to struggle to keep up, dragging his misshapen body and breathing hard until they arrived in a stone chamber devoid of any decoration except for a pair of magnificently carved wooden doors. Four of the tallest men Carver had ever seen stood in front of the doors. They wore only simple breeches, leaving their golden-skinned torsos and arms exposed to show off an incredible profusion of scars. Each man held a bare steel saber in each hand.

Carver gasped loudly and mopped sweat off his brow. He made a show of trying to catch his breath and compose himself before his audience. As it turned out, he was only made to wait for a few minutes. *This tyrant might be more considerate than most, or more likely just more impatient.* The great wooden doors opened slowly, pulled by a group of female slaves in various states of undress. The guards motioned for him to step through.

The throne room itself was almost as plain as the ante-chamber. Stone floors and a simple dais a single step off the ground with an unadorned stone throne. Sitting on it was the Drokga himself. Every bit Tolrahkali—golden skin, dark-brown hair, obviously no stranger to the training yard himself, and the piercing leaf-green eyes that marked him as a member of the royal family. Six more slaves shared the room with them. No attendants, no advisers. *Interesting, a ruler who keeps his own counsel.* The Drokga looked at him intently, not saying a word. His strange-colored eyes gave the impression he could see more than other men. *Nice little trick that; probably unnerves most of the fools he receives here.*

"Well, you foolish oaf, my son tells me you have skills that I will find invaluable." The Drokga spoke at last. "Are you going to waste any more of my time? Or do you have something to show me?" His expression said he found the idea extremely unlikely.

"My lord Drokga, if I may ask a question, where is your exalted son? I expected him to be at this audience."

"Did you now? How unfortunate for the both of you. It falls to you to impress me yourself. Show me what you have to offer, mage, or get out. My hospitality does not come for free nor is it without its limits. I hear you have accomplished some feat with a Chosen pit slave. That might impress some, but battlefields are not won by Chosen alone. They are won by the brave fight-ing men and women who dare to fight without the support of magics or the gifts of gods."

Carver bowed awkwardly with one hand on his walking stick. "My apologies, exalted Drokga. My slaves will bring in the first of my creations. It is a construct based on a hound, though the resulting creature is more reptile than anything else. I have taken the liberty of naming it a Tolrahk hound."

As he spoke, a mental order prompted the slaves to bring in the cages. The three slaves Carver employed for this task had been highly modified by his arts themselves. While they had been emaciated and feeble only a few weeks earlier, they were now huge hulking brutes that dwarfed the Drokga's guards. Three large cloth-covered cages were wheeled in. Carver pulled the cloth off the first cage with a showman's flourish that was only slightly hampered by his awkward movements. The thing inside was nothing like a hound, except perhaps for the fact that it was the same size as a very large dog. Its head was flat and wide. Thick scales covered its body, and its long limbs ended with wide, prehensile claws. Its eyes were deeply set in its skull. It growled and paced back and forth inside the cage, moving with sinuous, almost liquid movements.

"These hounds can be produced at a very fast rate. I can build a birthing chamber that would make dozens of these each day. They mature within a few weeks and are perfectly obedient. The cages were simply to avoid unnecessarily frightening your servants." He gestured and one of his slaves pulled the front of the cage off. The Tolrahk hound walked up to the Drokga and became as still as a statue. The Drokga was looking more at the slaves than at the hound.

"I'm sure they are fearsome, but I am more intrigued by what you have done to your slaves."

Carver suppressed a knowing smile. No matter who this man was, he thought as all petty tyrants did. He saw the brutes and imagined himself taller and stronger than any of his subjects. Feigning surprise, Carver explained. "My lord Drokga, they are the very slaves you provided me with when you allowed me to take up residence in your palace. I took the liberty of increasing their size and musculature so that they could better assist me with my work."

"And does this process have any adverse effects? If you can do this with slaves, Tolrahkali soldiers could be fearsome indeed if they were made this large."

"This can be done to any being. I can even produce horses to match this imposing stature. In my slaves, I have modified their minds to ensure their obedience as well. But such a thing is not necessary," he added quickly, seeing the Drokga's features darken. "The only minor side effect of the procedure is that they are unable to breed."

The Drokga's enthusiasm went out like a blown candle. "Then your powers are of little use to me. The tallest man or woman in the city is nothing if they cannot produce children. Your dogs might be of some small use to me in the long run. I will have to see them in action. Perhaps in the arena next week something could be arranged." He made a vague gesture with his hand.

Carver was shocked. *Just like that he's about to have me thrown out.* "My lord, I would be only too pleased to show you what the hounds can do. But I have more specimens to show you. If I may say so, you have yet to see my greatest achievements." Without waiting for an answer, Carver gestured impatiently for his slaves to uncover the next creature. "As I mentioned before, lord, I can make horses to suit the largest of men, but why settle for a horse when you could ride a truly fearsome beast?"

The creature that stood in the next cage was hideous. Its body was a mix of a bull and a horse. But it was thicker and more imposing than any horse, with the long muzzle of a giant wolf. Its gleaming red eyes looked around the room as if trying to decide which of the humans would make the tastiest meal. "As you can see, my lord, I have overcome the difficulty associated with riding a larger-than-horse-sized creature. There is a narrowing of its torso behind its shoulders. I have been assured that it is quite a comfortable ride."

The Drokga's face was impassive. *Damn the man. This place is perfect for me to continue my work. I will stay if I have to kill him to do it.* "I have one more project to show you, sire. One that is sadly unfinished. It has long been my goal to create a flying mount of some sort." At this the Drokga raised a brow in surprise. *He's good, this one. He's got me babbling like a fool trying to defend my work. Damn him.*

The third cage held a large lizard. Despite being in a cage as large as the others, the lizard was only the size of a chicken. It had long wings protruding from its back that dragged behind it. "I have been unsuccessful thus far in making a flying creature with these proportions, but I am confident I will be able to manage it soon. After that, increasing the creature's size is a simple matter."

Still nothing. No answer, no expression.

"All my creations are of course at your disposal, my lord. If you see anything that displeases you, I will be happy to change it. As I mentioned when I first spoke to your servant, I can carve flesh into any shape and purpose given supplies and enough time." *That's it. The inbred whoreson is going to try to have me thrown out and I'm going to have to kill him.*

The Drokga spoke. "Your creatures are only marginally less useless than the slaves you have created. If they cannot breed, then great effort must always be expended to maintain their numbers. You may see it as a way of ensuring your usefulness. I do not." He gave Carver a cold look. "Make me something that will not affect the fertility of my brave fighting men and women. I am the ruler of an ancient people. Our future depends on our children. You have one month." He looked Carver up and down with those strange eyes. "You are not the first mage to enter my service, nor do I imagine you will be the last. There is something you must understand before taking up residence within these walls. I do not tolerate failure. That you are a mage does not excuse you from the consequences of your actions. I could send my warlocks to deal with one such as you, of course, but mage battles cause far too much collateral damage. I far prefer to use weapons to solve my problems. When mages fail me, I have a singular weapon to deal with them. I introduce them to Nasaka Jadoo, my mage hunter."

As if on cue, the doors opened behind Carver and one of the strangest-looking men he had ever seen walked in. Nasaka was tall and lean to the point of gauntness. He walked with a lurching hunched-shoulder gait, his overlong arms hanging below his knees. A crazed profusion of leather straps crisscrossed his body, each holding a different charm or talisman so tightly against his skin it was a wonder his flesh did not split. The straps hung looser around his legs, forming a kind of wide skirt of leather and buckles that just barely cleared the floor as he walked. His hair was waist length and braided into a dozen tight tresses each dyed a different color. He barely glanced at Carver as he walked past him. The Drokga made a slight gesture with his hand, dismissing Carver. Carver backed out of the room slowly, not bothering to conceal the relief he felt. *Let the fool think I am intimidated by his so-called mage hunter.* Carver had come expecting threats.

Killing the Drokga and his hunter would have been a simple thing, he was sure. But Tolrahk Esal was a treasure trove of new materials for him to use. He didn't want to lose the chance to have the whole city at his disposal and have to come back in a generation or two to try again. *Improve his warriors without affecting their fertility. . . . The man is an idiot,* Carver thought angrily. Then an idea hit him and he missed a step, almost losing his balance on the smooth stone floors. *Symbiosis.* Never before had he considered symbiosis. Not on this scale. He often molded two living forms into one. But to leave the process unfinished. . . . To change one and not the other . . . it might be possible. Carver walked back to his rooms as fast as he had come, his mind swirling with ideas, his walking stick snapping loudly every time it hit the floor. His slaves and their cages trailed behind him, forgotten.

CHAPTER 10

A man in an unfamiliar black uniform walked into the training yard. It took Salt several moments before he recognized Gurt. The uniform was obviously tailored to him and made of expensive cloth; a faint outline of an eye over the heart was the only color on him. Salt had never seen anything like it. And was doubly surprised to see anything so fine on his friend.

"Finished gawking, lad? This is a Night Guard dress uniform; there's one waiting for you on your bunk. Get it on double-time. The king wants to hear about how you found the Dreth sword. He's expecting you in twenty minutes."

"Twenty minutes . . . the king?" Salt said dumbly.

"Aye, lad, the king we're all sworn to serve? The guy whose castle you live in? Now go get cleaned up, you scruffy oaf! I'll meet you in the barracks in five and you better look good."

Salt took off at a sprint. *Just when I was starting to get a handle on my life here.* His mind was swimming with rumors he'd heard about the throne room and King Arlon himself. Deciding against a bath, he washed himself off as best he could with a jug of drinking water and, sure enough, found a uniform on his bunk that was an exact copy of Gurt's. He noticed a silver pin of the royal crest was set in the collar as well. He pulled the uniform on and was stunned. It fit perfectly. He'd never worn anything like it, and it felt great. *I could get used to this!* Salt was just pulling on his shiny new black boots when Gurt walked in. He handed Salt a sword belt with a silver-pommeled rapier hanging from it.

"Put this on; it's part of the uniform," he said in answer to Salt's confused look. "Rapiers are the gentlemen's choice for sticking holes in each other. You need to look the part in your parade getup. Anyway, let's go; we have a ways to walk, and we need to pick up the Firesword from Lera's room on the way."

Gurt knocked on the door at the far end of the hall and pulled it open without waiting for an answer.

"Hi, Lera, we're just here to pick up the sword."

"It's right where you left it," she answered distractedly, her eyes never leaving the scrap of paper she was studying.

"The honor's all yours, Salty," Gurt said, gesturing toward the sword lying on a nearby table. "Oh, and make sure you carry it with both hands, lad."

Salt looked over with a rude comeback on the tip of his tongue, but when he saw the look in Gurt's eyes, he just nodded and held it back. Seeing concern and worry in Gurt's eyes took him from nervous to terrified. *Gods! This is a man who's faced down demons without blinking.*

They walked out of the wing of the palace that housed the Night Guard and the Crown Knights, and into wider, more opulent rooms and hallways. Lush carpets covered the floors; vases and paintings decorated every surface. At each set of doors, a pair of Crown Knights in full armor saluted and opened the doors for them without saying a word. The salutes never dropped while they were still in sight.

"There's some real respect for the Night Guard, even with the Knights," Salt remarked.

Gurt just chuckled, a sliver of his normal good humor returning. "As they should. Most of them are hoping to be promoted into the Guard one day." Salt looked at him, incredulous. "It's true," Gurt continued. "Many of our number are attack survivors, and nothing can replace the drive that gives them. But the rest are recruited from the other elite groups within the king's army. Avish was a Crown Knight, Tassos used to be a Pathfinder."

"I had no idea."

"We don't wear the fancy uniforms often 'cause it doesn't serve our purpose to stand out that much, but that pin on your collar marks you as acting with the full authority of King Arlon. Try not to lose it, by the way. . . . Now, we're almost there. Don't worry about formality too much. Bow to the king, of course, and otherwise try to follow my lead. The king knows where most of the Guard come from; he doesn't expect us to act like nobles."

They came at last to a huge set of double doors. Four Crown Knights stood in front of the doors in gleaming silver plate armor. All held heavy halberds at the ready. Like all the Knights before, they saluted and stepped aside. But then a small man in an elaborate uniform stepped out of an alcove and stood in front of them.

"His Royal Majesty is expecting you, my lord Night Commander. Who may I say is accompanying you?"

"The king is expecting us both, Sigmond. Just announce him as Salt of the Night Guard and be done with it."

The royal herald pursed his lips, visibly displeased. "No surname? No rank? No title? You don't give me much to work with, my lord."

"It will have to do. Now be on with it. The king is waiting." Sigmond bowed stiffly and turned to open the doors. The
huge carved wooden doors swung silently inward at his touch.
The throne room was large and opulent, but Salt couldn't help
being disappointed. Rumors he'd heard said that the throne
room had a solid gold floor, that the walls were all polished
gems and silver mirrors, and that the room was so large that
ten thousand people could dance in it without bumping into
one another. *Marble, more paintings, and you might be able
to squeeze three hundred people in here. Not that they'd be
able to breathe much less dance.* The throne itself was an
ancient-looking stone seat, carved out of a single block of gray
rock. Fewer than a dozen people stood in the room, four of
them Crown Knights.

Behind him, Salt heard the herald's surprisingly powerful
voice call out: "Presenting Lord Gurtraven Calmosin, lord of
Easthaven and Teresh, and commander of the Night Guard!"

Salt missed a step when the titles were called out. It had
never occurred to him that Gurt was anything other than the
gruff but good-humored senior Guardsman who gave him
advice. "Also presenting Night Captain Saltig Sodigson of the
Night Guard." At that, Salt stopped dead and looked at Gurt.

Gurt shook his head and smiled. "Damn, Sigmond is too
smart by far. The silver pin on your collar is usually never worn
by anyone below that rank. . . . As for the name, I would guess
he improvised. I assumed your real name was Saltig myself.
Anyway, I hope you like it 'cause he'll never agree to change it
now." He winked and walked on, leaving Salt rushing to catch
up. They stopped a dozen paces away and waited while the
king conversed with a man in elaborate blue robes.

Salt took the chance to get a proper look at the king he had
sworn to serve. His first impression was of a man not entirely
dissimilar to Gurt. King Arlon was in his midforties, tall and

fit. He wore functional clothes and no jewelry. If anything, all the courtiers looked more impressive and more richly dressed than the man sitting on the throne. Still, he spoke and gestured in a way that reminded Salt of particularly capable sea captains; there was no doubt that his wishes would be obeyed without question. When the king finished with his adviser and turned to look at Salt, the impression of an iron-willed captain was reinforced. *Not a man I'd want to cross.* Salt did his best to imitate Gurt's bow.

"So Night Captain Salt, is it now? I was led to believe you were a relatively new recruit."

"Technically he's only been with us less than a year, Your Majesty. I had decided that some sort of promotion was merited given his recent accomplishments. Your herald seems to have decided that a captaincy was in order." Salt couldn't believe the man speaking was gruff old Gurt. He seemed transformed, both his mannerisms and his way of speaking. The king nodded, a faint frown creasing his brow. His eyes flicked to Salt's neck and back to Gurt, who nodded in return.

There's a whole conversation going on here I can't hear or understand. And yet Salt felt like his fate was being decided. *This is a man who really can choose my fate. One word from him and I'm rich or hanging from the gallows.*

Finally, the king said, "He'll do." Then he turned to his blue-robed adviser. "Send for the Dreth ambassador."

The man closed his eyes for a moment, then said, "He is coming, Your Majesty."

All eyes turned to the door, and Gurt gestured for Salt to stand to the king's right with him. Almost immediately the doors swung open again. The man who walked in was the strangest person Salt had ever seen. His clothes were bright with clashing colors. Patterns of greens and reds swirled and overlapped down his long flowing robes. His face was covered with a veil that hung down from his headdress. Only his arms were left exposed. The cloth stopped at his shoulders, leaving his overly thin arms exposed. Bones stood out against his blue-tinged skin. He moved with oddly fluid steps, his body barely moving up and down as he walked into the room.

Again the herald's powerful voice called out, "Presenting His Excellency, Ambassador Nokor Ben Akyum of Dreth."

Salt swallowed hard. *A Dreth here!* His hands were sweating where they clutched the Firesword.

The Dreth stopped about two dozen paces away from the throne and bowed deeply.

"Greetings from Nok Dreth."

"You are most welcome, Ambassador, as are the greetings from Nok Dreth," said the king.

"Your Majesty has anticipated my mission." The Dreth bowed again deeply.

"We know little of your traditions, Ambassador, but we do know how precious these items are to your people. In keeping with what my court mage has told me of these blades, we have allowed no one to touch the sword save the brave man who recovered it."

The king turned to Salt. "Night Captain Saltig, give the Firesword to the ambassador." Salt sprung forward, eager to be rid of it.

But the ambassador was backing away, his hands up to forestall him. "I cannot touch this weapon."

Salt stood confused between the Dreth and the group surrounding the throne before walking back to his place next to Gurt.

"And those who had the Firesword?" asked the ambassador.

"They were criminals. They attacked my Guardsmen. Most were killed in the fight. The others captured in their compound were arrested and interrogated before being sent to the gallows."

"May I inspect the sword?"

"Of course, Ambassador Ben Akyum; please proceed."

The Dreth turned to face Salt, and as if reading the confusion within him, he said, "No need to move."

A few seconds passed in silence before the Dreth spoke again. "The sword is unsullied. Nok Dreth will be grateful. I can offer a generous trade agreement, and a masterwork of Dreth steel, crafted by Thirat Bel Thammar, the personal smith of Nok Dreth. Also a sizable reward in gold for the captain's family."

The king raised an eyebrow questioningly. "I understand the Night captain does not have any surviving family, though I daresay he would appreciate the reward himself."

The Dreth bowed low again. "The Night captain will be honored, and he will be put to death after bringing the sword to Dreth."

An uncomfortable silence dragged on for several minutes. Salt felt his bowels churn.

That's it. I'm dead. I should have known better than to get mixed up with royalty even if I was drunk. . . . Gurt looked to the king before answering the ambassador.

"His Majesty is not in the habit of sacrificing his most valued servants, not even when such generous compensation is offered. There must be some way we can avoid this unpleasantness."

Ben Akyum's tone was icy when he answered. "Nok Dreth does not trade in lives." Then he seemed to regain control of his emotions and continued in a more even tone. "The reward is for the return of the Firesword. But Night Captain Saltig is not of noble blood. We seek to honor his sacrifice."

"And what if we were to inform you that the Night captain is of noble blood? That he holds lands and title?"

"If he were a lord of your people, then his touch would not be unclean. It is unfortunate."

The king nodded. "Ambassador, you must know that we have no intention of offending Nok Dreth. However, we are unwilling under any circumstances to reward one of our most loyal subjects with death for having performed his duties with distinction. Night captain of the Night Guard is one of the most senior appointments that can be achieved in my service. He also bears the silver mark that grants him the right to speak in my name. But as that does not seem to fit with your traditions, I find myself forced to confer a title on this man."

The Dreth cocked his head to the side, clearly confused.

"In front of these witnesses and by my word as king, I hereby grant to Saltig Sodigson the title of Lord of Dustland, with all revenues and rights associated with his new title and lands."

"Gustave, have the proper documents drawn up and make sure Lord Saltig has a signet ring and banner ready for his journey to Dreth." One of the courtiers on the king's left bowed low.

The king then returned his attention to the Dreth ambassador. "Will that satisfy your law? Or do I have to adopt the man into my household to save his life?"

Ben Akyum bowed deeply with his arms held out straight to the sides. "Your Majesty is wise. An elevation is not possible in Dreth; Nok Dreth will be content and grateful for keeping the blood of your servant from his hands." He repeated the bow.

"Excellent. I am glad that we could reach a mutually acceptable agreement, Ambassador Ben Akyum. Lord Saltig will depart for Dreth as soon as arrangements can be made for a suitable escort. Say, seven days?" He looked questioningly at Gurt, who answered with a nod.

The Dreth ambassador bowed again. "I will send word ahead. If you will permit, I will make preparations to accompany the lord to Dreth."

The king waved his assent. The Dreth turned and walked out of the room.

King Arlon sighed loudly. "I will retire as well. Cancel any further audiences. I feel the need for a cup of wine and the company of my family." The king rose and left the room without ceremony. Most of his advisers followed him out.

Salt's legs felt like jelly. Gurt took one look at him and broke out laughing. "Don't get too excited, lad. You may be a lord now, but just wait until you see your fief."

He started to lead Salt out when Gustave stopped them. "A moment please, my lords. There is the matter of the new lord's heraldry." Salt just looked at him, at a loss for anything to say.

Gurt took over. "We'll leave the details to you, Gustave. Try to do something with the Guard colors. A fearsome creature and a weapon of some sort, perhaps a mace or a hammer given the young lord's preference."

Gustave bowed. "Very good, my lord. I will prepare something suitable."

Salt's thoughts were in chaos. Called to see the king, promoted, sentenced to die by a foreign monarch, and made a noble all in the space of an hour. He blurted out, "Just like that he made me a noble."

Gurt laughed again. "It is something of a tradition for Bialta to grant titles as rewards for service. They cost nothing in themselves and yet make the receiver happier than if a pile of gold coins were dropped at their feet." Salt stared at him blankly.

"It may seem like the king is all powerful, especially on a day with a closed court like today. But in reality he would have needed the approval of the council of lords to create a new seat for a noble house. Dustland isn't anything that would concern the council, though, since its revenues amount to nothing." Salt imagined a dusty expanse of land. *Maybe there will be enough scrub to raise goats.*

"Ah, here we are, lad. Why don't you take a look out that next window?" Salt rushed forward and looked out with a mix of fear and excitement. "All I can see is the training yard."

"Yes, Dustland is beautiful this time of year, don't you think?"

Salt started to laugh. Gurt joined in for a time, but when Salt showed no sign of stopping, he put his hand on Salt's shoulder and said, "I'll see you back in the training yard. Don't be too long." Salt stood at the window for a long time after his fit of laughter had died down. He hadn't been through an ordeal this taxing since the night the bug bitch had tried to eat him. *Never a dull day. . . . And I used to think a sailor's life was exciting.*

By the time Salt made it to the training yard, the greater part of the Night Guard was assembled. Several kegs of ale had been rolled out into the yard.

As they got sight of him, shouts were raised. "Lord Salt!" "The Night captain!"

Gurt stood among them, a large wooden mug in his hand.

He smiled and raised his mug. "To the lord of the training yard! And to King Arlon—who watches our backs like we watch his!"

The Guardsmen roared, "To the king!"

Salt had to admit he'd never expected a monarch who would go to such lengths to protect his men. Even supposedly elite troops were often sacrificed in any story he'd ever heard

tell. *Not that there's anything elite about me. Yet.* He burned
with the need to prove himself worthy of saving.

Krigare clapped him on the back and handed him a mug.
"Thanks, Salty. It's been a while since we had a good excuse to
celebrate all together."

The next morning, Salt woke to Gurt shaking him. "All right,
lad, get up and get dressed. I know you probably have the
mother of all headaches after last night, but we have some
things we need to discuss."

Salt groggily pulled himself out of bed and looked around
for something to wear. He felt like he'd swallowed a particularly fetid rat. "Gods, my head is splitting and my mouth feels
like something crawled into it to die. . . ." He shook his head to
clear it. "What's wrong, Gurt? How come the early wake-up?
It's barely past dawn."

"The price of success, I'm afraid. I need to go over a few
things with you before training today so you can take command of your squad tonight."

"Er? What? Command? Gurt, what are you talking about?"

"Remember your promotion last night, lad? Well, if you're
going to get the title, I should at least make you do the work.
I'll be more use here at the palace; besides, I'm getting too old
to be running around every night."

Salt groaned. "But I can't take command. Everyone in the
squad's been there longer than me."

"That's right, lad." He smiled back. "And not a one of them
will begrudge you the extra work. I could offer the job to each
and every one of them and they'd all tell me where I could
shove it. Now, I want you to do the job for a few days to get
used to the idea before I send you off to Dreth next week. You'll
have at least part of your squad to escort you," Gurt explained.
"I can't spare Wheeze or some of the others, but you'll have

Min, Brolt, and Altog to watch your back and make sure you get there safe. Both Min and Brolt have been to Dreth before." Salt looked up, surprised.

Gurt shrugged. "Min's father was a merchant, and Brolt was a caravan guard before he joined up."

With the celebration the Night Guard had had the night before, Salt had somehow managed to forget about his impending journey. Fear gripped his guts, followed by a flood of relief knowing that he wouldn't be facing the trip alone.

"Now, follow me. We need to go to the map room and look over the details of what you'll be doing tonight. I have some tips for you to handle some of the less cooperative contacts you'll be visiting, like Skeg. We also need to talk about Dreth and how we want you to handle yourself while you're there. The king and I know you're not used to court and we don't expect you to learn everything, but you'll need to observe some formalities." Noticing Salt's panicked look, Gurt put a steadying hand on his shoulder. "The worst part is past, lad. They've agreed to let you live, and so far as I know, the Dreth never break their word. You'll just need to learn enough not to embarrass Bialta when you're speaking for us."

As they were walking out of the room, Gurt smiled at Salt. "I've arranged for riding lessons for you before regular training, too, so you'll get to have some fun."

***

"Who is that, Skeg?" demanded Salt. The moment he saw the little girl in her white dress rush into the back room of the shop, his stomach had clenched. He had actually started to warm up to Skeg, but he had seen the uses men and women in this quarter sometimes put children to. If Skeg was trading in child flesh, or had purchased the little doll for his own sick pleasure, Salt would finish him here and now.

"Relax, Salt," Skeg rasped out, raising a hand in alarm at the look on Salt's face. "She's my niece. She has a way of just turning up." Turning toward the back curtain, he said, "Come out here, Nial my dear. The Guardsman is right to be shocked. It's far too late for a child your age to be about this part of town. Even if you are safe in my shop." A little blond-haired girl of about eleven or twelve appeared at the curtain and nodded seriously up at Skeg while he scowled at her. "Now take the safe way home and don't dawdle."

Salt was surprised. Not only was that the longest speech he had ever heard come out of Skeg, but it sounded like genuine concern in his voice. On an impulse Salt offered, "If the child doesn't live too far, my squad can escort her home." He was rewarded by a quickly hidden look of panic washing over Skeg's usually impassive face.

"I wouldn't want to trouble the Night Guard on my family's account. Nial lives but a short distance from here and comes and goes often. I'm sure she will be safe—"

"Skeg," Salt cut him off. "You know as well as I do that the Muds are no place for a kid. Especially not at night. I'll do you this little favor and you can repay me one day."

Skeg looked like a man condemned to the gallows. "Nial, this nice man is going to walk you home. Please behave for him and go straight in."

Nial looked up at Skeg, her eyes shining, and smiled. "Okay, *Uncle* Skeg." Her eyes were laughing, as if what he had said had been a particularly funny joke.

"Come along then, kid. You can show me the way? Even in the dark?"

"Of course," she said. Then she looked pensive for a moment before cocking her head. "Is a way harder to find in the dark?"

Salt groaned. *Why do I always get myself into these situations?*

As the Night Guard moved off with Nial, Skeg sat down in a heap behind the counter. A cold sweat broke out over his body. If the Guard found out what Nial really was, it would be the end of them both. Nial could handle the squad she was with if they turned on her. He was sure of that. But that would draw the full attention of the Night Guard and the Arcanum. At best, they would live long enough to flee from Darien. At worst, they would be dead before morning. Skeg settled in to wait through the longest night of his life.

Nial continued chattering the whole way, bombarding Salt with an endless stream of questions as only a child could. "Why do you carry a sword? How do you catch bad people? What do you do with them when you catch them? Are you a friend of Uncle Skeg's? How come he's never talked about you before? Do you have any kids?"

Salt would start to answer each question only to be interrupted with another. By the time they arrived at a simple but well-kept little house just inside the merchant's district, Salt was only grunting out single-word answers.

"This is my house," the little girl announced proudly. "My dad and me live here. It's only the two of us since my mum died."

"Sorry to hear that, kid. Anyway, you're home safe. We have work to do so we have to go. Take care." Salt spoke as quickly as he could, not wanting to give her a chance to get a word in and start rambling again.

Nial waved happily to them as the squad moved away, led by Salt who was walking quite a bit faster than normal.

Wheeze snorted. "So I take it from your fast march that you won't be quitting the Guard and settling down to father a houseful of those little monsters anytime soon?"

"I think I'd rather spend the rest of my life in the dungeons cleaning out cells with my tongue. Anyway, it was worth it to see Skeg squirm like that. He probably thinks the kid would tell us all his secrets . . . especially since she can't keep quiet for longer than it takes to draw in another breath."

***

The land they were crossing was growing rockier. Jenus looked at the mountains in the distance with apprehension. The Gling'Ar were leading them in a straight line to the pass between the two largest peaks. Thick forests covered the foothills. *They haven't set any more fires. Does that mean we're getting closer to their home?* Jenus asked himself. The thought made him shiver. *Just one more day.* Jenus had become increasingly certain that a trap was about to be sprung and hoped desperately that the jaws wouldn't snap closed before they could return home.

He turned to Traven, who was trudging along beside him. "We'll make camp before we reach that forest. I'm not risking our army in that."

"You know the priests are going to have a problem with that. It was hard enough for you to get them to swallow your idea of turning back. If we stop early on the third day because of a forest, they're never going to let you hear the end of it."

"I can't say I care what they think anymore. The damned priests are out for blood. I caught a couple of them interrogating the scouts. They want to find a Gling'Ar village, make an example of them."

"You know how difficult they can make your life."

"Yeah. But they like to do that anyway. Might as well make it worthwhile and let the men take a little break. Call the halt now."

Traven saluted and moved down the line calling orders to halt and make camp. Jenus took a deep breath and waited. It wouldn't be long now. Sure enough, even before the whole of the line had ground to a halt, Jenus saw a procession moving in his direction. Serim was at the head of the group, his cheeks flushed with anger. It looked like he had grabbed all the priests this time as well as anyone else he could drag along. The group got larger as it came forward, more and more people following along to see what would happen. *Just like Serim to want an audience, probably has some grand speech prepared.* Jenus didn't bother saying anything. He leaned back against the nearest cart and waited for the accusations to start flying.

"What kind of cowardice is this, Jenus?!" Serim demanded. Jenus didn't bother answering. He just looked at the priest evenly and waited to hear the rest. "You disgrace yourself, your noble ancestors, Sacral, and the White Mother herself with your actions! When the king hears of this, he'll have you executed!" Serim's voice rose in pitch as he screamed, droplets of spittle flying from his mouth. "Don't you have anything to say in your defense?!"

Jenus sighed. "I gave you my reasons for turning back. Moving into that forest would only give the Gling'Ar an opportunity to ambush us again."

"And you fear to fight them! So you admit it! You *are* a coward!"

"There is nothing to be gained by fighting them again!" said Jenus, anger creeping into his own voice. "I will not see more of my men die for nothing!"

"You were given a holy task by the White Mother herself! To refuse it is blasphemy as well as cowardice. I formally accuse you of incompetence and cowardice and demand that you step down as commander of this army. If you will not go willingly, I will have you removed." The gathered priests all nodded, mumbling things about the goddess's will and the corruption of the Deceiver.

Jenus shook his head. "Do I have to remind you again, Serim? I lead this army. You have no authority over me or the men and women who follow me."

"Then you leave me no choice. *Jenus*." His name came out with a sneer. "I name you heretic! In the name of the White Mother and Yeltos Rogayen, her most holy servant, I dismiss you from the service of the goddess!"

Jenus was stunned. He'd never expected them to go this far. And yet he was sure they would regret it if they entered the shadows between those trees.

"I have already selected a likely replacement from among the Warchosen. Vegard will lead this army from now on. We will turn back only after our prayers to the White Mother are answered and she deems the Gling'Ar have been sufficiently chastised for their evil."

Vegard walked up to Jenus with a smug look. "Looks like we'll have a new champion soon."

"You raving idiot, Vegard, I'm trying to save us!"

Vegard just sneered at him. "Hand over the Lightbringer. You don't deserve to carry it anymore."

"Forget it. I'll step down and let you get yourselves killed, but King Ansyl entrusted the Lightbringer to me himself, and there is no one here I am willing to surrender it to."

"Are you threatening me, Jenus? I should have you put in chains."

"I'd like to see you try." Jenus stood glaring at the man for a moment while Vegard shot questioning glances toward Serim.

Jenus saw Traven moving up behind the group with a squad of soldiers, weapons in hand. *This is going to get ugly fast.* Traven and the others were ready to shed blood for him. *Sacral blood.*

Jenus looked back at Serim. In a loud voice he called out, "I formally step down as the commander of this expedition. I will go where I am bid and follow any reasonable order I am given that does not countermand my orders from King Ansyl." He swallowed hard. "Captain Vegard is now your commander."

Traven looked at him in shock. Jenus made a slight head movement that he knew Traven would understand to mean "later." Traven nodded back, worry clear on his face. Vegard was glowing with pride. He looked like nothing more than a rooster strutting around in front of a flock of hens.

"This army is now to get moving again," he called out. "Get everyone ready to march again on my order."

Jenus saw with disgust that Vegard looked to the priests for approval after every order he called out. "We will march until after dark tonight to make up for this senseless stop. If that disturbs you, remember you only have your former commander to blame for it."

Jenus ground his teeth and waited for a chance to slip away. But Vegard wasn't about to make things that easy for him. "Jenus! You will be assigned to the last wagon. You are to assist the drovers in any way they deem necessary. You may go now, Jenus. I need to inform the *combatants* of some important changes."

I'm the only one who's managed to kill one of those things and he's making me a drover's assistant? Jenus moved toward the end of the line. If Vegard didn't get them all killed, he was sure the king would sort this mess out. Word of what had happened had already swept through the army. Most of the soldiers Jenus passed saluted him, though a surprising number turned their backs on him as he passed. *Vegard and Serim have been busy. A month ago I would have sworn every one of these people would have followed me against the Deceiver himself.*

The Sacral army reached the edge of the forest shortly before dusk. This forest was nothing like the one they'd crossed on the other side of the grasslands. The first forest had been beautiful and wild. This forest only felt old. The trees, some gnarled variety of oak for the most part, grew incredibly tall and thick. There was no undergrowth here. The ground was nothing but a thick network of knotted roots and dead leaves. No paths were evident, though animals would have little need of them here. *Or Gling'Ar.* But the carts were another matter. Not only would the roots be a problem, but many of the trees grew too close together for a cart to squeeze through. After a long wait, blue-white flashes could be seen among the trees, and the Sacral line slowly started to move again. When it was Jenus's turn to move in among the trees, he saw why. The cart wheels slipped and stuck on the roots. Most of the soldiers had to stow their weapons and help lift and push the carts to keep them moving. The warmages had obviously been at work here. Trees had been felled to clear a path, cut perfectly smoothly and moved out of the way. Jenus shook his head. Vegard had simply had them cut a straight path with no attempt to find an easier way forward, or even to avoid particularly dense knots of trees. *Their talents must be nearly exhausted and all to move us forward a few dozen cart lengths.*

If I do get thrown out of the army, maybe I should consider becoming a drover. I think I could be happy doing simple things and not worrying about idiots making bad choices. Jenus wasn't surprised when the call to halt came a little over an hour later. The army was exhausted. Soldiers and noncombatants alike stood around panting and wiping sweat from their faces. Jenus helped tend to the animals, then spread his blanket on the flat stump of a tree. It must have been ancient to be as big around as Jenus was tall. He thought about the tree for a moment, but in truth he was more thankful for a spot to spread his blanket that wouldn't have him sleeping on twisted roots. He lay down and surprised himself by falling into a deep, dreamless sleep.

Morning came with a slight lessening of the gloom. Jenus was sure the sun was coming up, but very little light found its way to the ground between the huge trees. Even the trees they had cut down did little to thin the thick canopy of branches and leaves above them. Jenus climbed onto the cart bed to look around and froze. Long ranks of Gling'Ar warriors were lined up between the trees on both of their flanks, no more than a hundred paces away. The Gling'Ar had indeed prepared an ambush as he had feared, but this was far worse than anything he had expected. Shouts and calls to arms rose from the camp as others noticed the Gling'Ar. The exhausted Sacral army scrambled to prepare itself for war.

"There must be thousands of them," Jenus heard someone say. *At least four thousand I'd wager.* And if that weren't bad enough, the savages, if savages they really were, had shed their primitive weapons and armor. One and all, they wore spiked iron plate and carried gleaming steel blades and hammers. Worse yet, Jenus saw several hundred of the deadly bows they had faced before. They all stood in ordered ranks, ready to send every last man and woman of Sacral to the afterlife. *There can be no winning this fight. Not with every soldier and mage in Sacral.*

One of the monsters stepped through the ranks on the left flank. Unlike its fellows, this one still had a bestial look to it. It wore leather robes, and its dyed red mane was thickly knotted with charms and fetishes, what looked like shrunken heads among them, their own hair braided with the Gling'Ar's.

"People of Sacral!" it called out in a surprisingly clear voice. "We were content to kill only the priests and those others among you who have allowed themselves to become tainted by their ways. But now you have turned over command of your entire force to a pawn of the White Mother. Moreover, you have drawn too close to our homeland and desecrated a forest where no tree had ever been cut down. Give us the priests. Allow us to purge the unclean from among your ranks and the rest of you will be spared. We can let none of you leave this place, but you do not have to die."

Vegard's voice pealed out in answer. "Mages! Destroy him! Soldiers! Form ranks and prepare to repel charge!"

The Gling'Ar shook his head. "Would you all throw your lives away for this fool? Your mages are no match for me. I have been content to stop you from contacting your home, and your priests from calling to their twisted goddess. But this will not continue if you try my patience."

Blue fire swept out from the Sacral line only to fade away to nothing when it came close to the Gling'Ar. In response, he raised one hand toward the Sacral mages. Dark flames exploded around them. People screamed. A cart caught fire, and the animals that had been tethered to it brayed in panic. Just as easily as that, Mage Asar was reduced to a smoking corpse. Never before had Jenus felt so helpless, so useless. Then he noticed the people around him were looking up at him with hope. Hope that their champion would be able to save them. He jumped off the cart and ran to the head of the column. Vegard was shouting at everyone around him, as was Serim, their orders often contradicting each other.

Serim waved Vegard to silence. "We need to make a charge back out the way we came. The Warchosen can break through!"

Jenus ran straight up to them. "Are you mad? An attack like that would just see the jaws of the trap close on the rest of the army. Even if the Chosen make it out, everyone else here would die."

"Throw down your weapons, men of Sacral. I will not ask again." The Gling'Ar's voice cut through their argument.

Serim looked near panic. "The priesthood must be protected at all costs!" Much to Jenus's surprise, Vegard agreed. "Jenus, we need you for this. Use the Lightbringer. Punch out. The priests will follow in your wake. I'll lead the rest of the Warchosen behind to cover our escape." Serim was nodding his head vigorously in agreement.

"And leave our whole army to be butchered?" Jenus asked, incredulous. Serim threw him a venomous look.

"And what would you have us do? *Champion?* Our mages have been defeated by a single spell. We are cut off from our own powers. We have no other options."

"Then take those who would follow you and try to escape. I will not abandon these people. I will remain with them."

Vergard and Serim looked at each other. "With me, warriors of Sacral!" shouted Vegard, moving back to the end of the line.

Jenus saw that few were those who were joining Vegard. Everyone else looked to Jenus to save them. He took a deep breath and started to walk toward the Gling'Ar mage. He kept his hands out from his sides, his palms up to show he held no weapon. When he was about halfway to the enemy lines, he turned around and addressed his own troops.

"My brave people. Follow my lead this one last time. The Gling'Ar could have destroyed us at any time. They chose not to for a reason. Hold to that, for it is our only hope of survival." He saw the looks many of the soldiers were throwing him. Fear mixed with anger and disbelief.

"Know that none doubt your courage, but throwing your lives away here will avail you nothing. Live!" With those words he unclasped his sword belt and gently placed the sacred blade on the ground, before turning back to the Gling'Ar mage. "Gling'Ar! We surrender!"

Behind him, Jenus heard nothing for a moment. He held his breath hoping that the army would follow him again now that their new leader had abandoned them. A few seconds passed before he heard the clang of a weapon falling against the roots. A moment later another followed. Then many more. Screams broke out briefly to the east. Vegard's retreat was failing as Jenus had expected. Many of the Sacral warriors who were hesitating clutched their weapons tight again, thinking they had been betrayed. Jenus could do nothing but lead by example now. And hope they wouldn't do anything stupid and get themselves killed.

The Gling'Ar clashed with the last of the fleeing priests and their self-appointed guards. The results were much what Jenus had expected. The line of Gling'Ar boxed them in and held fast as the hopelessly outclassed humans slammed into them like an overripe fruit against a stone wall. With primitive armor and equipment, the Gling'Ar had been more than a match for any of the humans. Now, the Sacral soldiers were little more than pests. Only the Warchosen among them seemed to be able to stand toe to toe with one of the giants, but they were badly outnumbered and even they didn't last long. Silence returned to the forest as the last of the priests was cut down. True to form, Serim died cursing everyone around him, calling on his goddess to smite them all, Gling'Ar and human alike. Jenus winced hearing divine wrath being called down so venomously by a senior priest, but no power answered his call.

The Gling'Ar army moved efficiently among the humans, collecting weapons and ensuring that all their captives were disarmed and had their wrists firmly bound behind their backs.

CHAPTER 11

The first day of travel was grueling for Salt. He didn't sleep well the night before; nerves and excitement kept him awake far too late. Not to mention that he had long since become accustomed to working through most of the night and sleeping late into the day. They rose early and set off just before dawn. The Dreth ambassador was waiting for them outside the palace gates. Without a word he moved up to join the group of Bialtans and settled in to a position at the front of the group. Salt wasn't the only Night Guard who stared at the Dreth's mount. The cream-white creature had certainly looked like a horse at first glance, but it was strange in a way that nagged at Salt and kept him staring at the back of the creature. *It has no fur,* he realized. *And its legs are weird.* The Dreth's mount had a thick white hide that was totally hairless. Its legs also ended in long three-toed feet tipped with sharp claws rather than hooves.

It wasn't until they stopped for a midday meal that Salt got a better look at the creature. He walked over to where Ben Akyum was busy sorting through a saddlebag. The creature looked up at Salt with whiteless milky-blue eyes. When he moved closer, it pulled back its lips and showed him a very unhorselike set of teeth that would have put a wolf to shame. Salt stopped and backed up. The ambassador seemed totally unconcerned. He made little or no effort to communicate with the Bialtans. Back on their mounts, Ben Akyum set a punishing pace that none of them could follow. He gradually pulled away from them until he was forced to stop and wait for them with obvious frustration. The pattern was repeated over and over all day, with the Dreth never speaking a word to the Bialtans except to answer a direct question.

After his first day in the saddle, Salt nearly fell off the horse. The crash course in riding he'd received before they set out for Dreth hadn't prepared him for the stiffness and saddle sores.

"Gods, someone just kill me already. I'd rather run the whole way than ride that demon-spawned beast for another minute."

"Don't be so melodramatic, Salty," said Min, shaking her head at him. "The stable master gave you the gentlest mare in the stables. The princess learned to ride on that horse, and she was only seven at the time."

Salt ignored her and walked around with a pained look on his face. "I swear I'll never walk properly again. I may not even be able to father children after another day of this."

"I'm sure you've fathered enough bastards with the dock-front whores already. They'll probably be glad of the change," she said.

"Don't understand why we can't take a ship, anyway. Dreth is close to the coast, isn't it?"

"A ship wouldn't get us all the way there. Dreth doesn't have a port, and there are no safe harbors anywhere close short of sailing all the way around to one of the Free Cities. Besides, there is nothing in this world that could make me get on a leaky pile of wood and leave sight of the shore. You, on the other hand, gave in to riding the whole way pretty fast."

Salt grumbled under his breath but wisely decided not to say anything.

The journey out of Bialta took thirteen days. Thirteen days of pain and stiffness for Salt who practically fell off his horse at the end of every day. They made the best of the various inns and taverns they found along the way. Salt had been entrusted with a pouch of coins to pay for anything they might need on their journey. He was only too happy to spend the king's gold on comfortable beds and hot food. When they finally reached the border, Min and Brolt insisted they buy a couple pack animals and load up on provisions. Brolt pointed into the foothills of the Icespine Mountains: "There's a traders' camp just the other side of the official border. We'll get everything we need at a good price there."

"Most of the caravans from Bialta pass through there," Min said. "It'll take us a few days to cross the hills and then we'll be in the desert. There are a few spots on the way where we'll be able to pick up fresh water and supplies, but we'd best carry as much as we can."

Days later, Salt pulled up his horse and squinted into the blazing sun. The trip wasn't getting any easier. If the pain and frustration of riding all day was lessening, the discomfort and heat caused by the desert more than made up for it. Salt was as badly sunburned as he had ever been in his life. The sun seemed to hammer down on the desert sands like nowhere else

he had ever seen. It was two hours after dawn, and already the
heat was so intense it made his head spin. *And this after nearly
freezing all night. Time to stop for the day.* Salt called to the others to set up camp. The heat would soon be more than any of
them could stand to be out in. Not that it was easier to sleep in
the suffocating tents they had brought along, but at least it got
them out of the sun. He reached up and rubbed his dry, flaking
skin. *I don't think I'll ever get used to not sweating when I'm hot.*
Brolt had warned him to drink a lot even if he didn't notice he
was sweating. The desert would pull the moisture right out of
a man, his sweat drying off into the air before it could wet his
brow. *This place just doesn't make sense. I can see the ocean and
we've crossed two rivers. How can it be that dry?* Neither Min
nor Brolt had an answer for him, and Ben Akyum didn't volunteer any information. Resigned, Salt gave up asking questions.
Everyone's mood was sour after putting up with the desert for
eight days. It wasn't worth pushing to get an answer. The Great
Desert was as it was; why question it? Salt's eyes settled on the
horizon where a dark shadow hinted at an approaching storm.
With my luck it'll probably snow. . . .

On the morning of the ninth day, the sun rose from behind
the walls of the colossal city of Dreth and Salt couldn't tell himself that it was a storm cloud anymore. He sat in his saddle in
slack-jawed awe.

Brolt snickered. "It is a sight to see, isn't it?" His good
humor was restored by the sight. The wall was immense and
stretched across the horizon.

"I-i-it's huge!" Salt stammered.

"Thank you for stating the incredibly obvious, Salty. . . .
I see now why Gurt chose you to lead this expedition. Keen
observational skills and all that," Brolt said.

"Gurt has an eye for talent. What can I say?" Salt said. Brolt
snorted, and Altog laughed his strange laugh.

"Better you than us, anyway. I don't ever want to see what's behind that wall. The Dreth are . . . Well, they're not normal." He said the last in a whisper despite the fact that Ben Akyum had ridden so far ahead that he was barely visible.

"Says the man with the tattooed eyelids," Salt said. The others nodded their agreement.

"Brolt's right, Salty. We'll be waiting outside the city for you. Maybe do a little shopping," said Min. "I've always wanted a real Dreth-forged sword, and they're cheaper to buy directly from the skinny bastards. I never had enough coin to even think about buying one when I was here before."

"With the luck you've been having at dice? I can't imagine you have much left."

"Those coppers I lost? Salty, you hit your head or something? I've got nearly three months' pay here." She shook her pack to emphasize the point. It clinked with the dull sound of gold.

"We get paid?" Salt blurted. His three companions looked at one another and burst out laughing. Salt's horse was surprised by the sudden sound and started tossing about. It took Salt several minutes to calm the beast, which only made the others laugh more.

"Well, you've proved my point that the most important requirement to become an officer is to not have a brain."

"No wonder Gurt likes you, Salty," said Altog.

"Six months. . . . That's got to be a record," said Brolt.

Min nodded. "Most recruits ask within the first month. I asked before I signed up so I guess I'm too smart to ever get promoted."

As their banter went on, they continued to draw closer to the massive wall. They could make out more details of the fortifications now. Tall figures in dark armor walked the tops of the walls or stood on crenellated balconies halfway up. Their tabards and cloaks were as colorful and jarring to the eye as the ambassador's clothes, and each of them carried a long black staff.

"Are those Firespears?" asked Salt.

"So they say. No one's seen them used in ages. But then no one's been stupid enough to test them."

Eventually they were close enough to see the market that had sprung up outside Dreth's main gate. Some of the stands looked permanent, while others were little more than tents or even carts with pieces of canvas draped over them for shade. Ben Akyum seemed to have disappeared into the mass of people.

"Those men over there look Noroshi!" exclaimed Salt. "That's a good four months' sailing. Add that to however long it took them to travel here from the nearest port. . . ."

"There are all sorts here, always are. You might even see the odd bunch come up from the Fingen Islands," said Brolt.

Min chimed in. "Making a run to Dreth can easily make a merchant's fortune. If they can manage the journey and they're lucky enough to bring something the Dreth actually want, that is."

Brolt nodded. "I've seen a fair number of Bialtans here just living off the failures. By the time they make it here, most of those who traveled far are pretty desperate. Desperation always brings out the sharks." He lapsed into silence after that, and the others followed suit. They dismounted and led their horses between the stalls, looking curiously at the strange and exotic wares for sale.

A couple of Dreth walked through the marketplace. The merchants all fawned over them, offering free samples, food, wine, a place to sit, anything to bring the Dreth over to their stalls. Salt even heard one man offering the company of one of his daughters to the strange blue-skinned men. The Dreth themselves seemed well used to the chaos and looked over various stands without paying any visible attention to their owners' prattle.

"They walk out here without guards?" Salt asked, surprised. "This place looks like it could turn ugly fast."

Min nodded. "It can. I've seen it happen a couple times. Most of the merchants out here do their damnedest to help the Dreth when that happens though. Not that they really need the help. They're a lot stronger than they look. I saw one throw a man clear across the road once." Salt looked at her in disbelief.

"It's true!"

"Look, I'm willing to believe they're fast or they have magic or something, but you really expect me to buy that they're as strong as Gling'Ar?"

"Fine. Go see if one of them will arm wrestle you, but don't come whining when he snaps your arm off."

A commotion started to spread out from the city through the market. Everyone who wasn't in the immediate vicinity of a Dreth dropped whatever they were doing and moved to the road to get a better view. Shouts and cheers broke out from various parts of the crowd when they heard a loud booming sound and the giant gates started to open outward.

Brolt looked shocked. "Someone must have made a really big deal with the blueskins. I've never heard of them opening the gates. They always use the smaller door at the base of it."

Ranks of soldiers emerged from the featureless darkness behind the gates. *Crap, that wall must be really thick*, Salt thought. The soldiers were dressed like those patrolling the walls—blackened steel and garish cloth. Each soldier carried a long spear and a teardrop-shaped shield emblazoned with the flame crest of Dreth. As they marched out, the crowd parted in front of them, most falling over one another to get out of the soldiers' way as quickly as they could. Seemingly endless, the troops continued to emerge from the shadows. They marched with perfect precision, twenty ranks wide. Dozens became hundreds, hundreds became thousands. Salt and his companions started to move aside with everyone else, when the procession came to an abrupt stop a few paces away from them.

One man, dressed identically to the others, stepped out of the front rank and turned to address Salt. "Lord Saltig." He gave a salute with his spear. "Nok Dreth welcomes you to our city."

The crowd was instantly buzzing with the news. No outsider had been allowed past the gates in living memory. Everyone was craning their necks looking for who had managed to win the favor of the Dreth monarch. Salt noticed with a grin that they were all looking past him. He looked over at his companions, but the soldier spoke again before he could say anything.

"Your companions must wait. We will provide whatever they require." In perfect unison, the soldiers turned to face outward and took two paces forward, pushing people out of the way where necessary with their shields. And opening a path through the center of their formation.

"Please follow." Salt led his horse after the nameless Dreth.

Hundreds of merchants, their handlers, guards, and families looked at him and pointed. Every one of them trying to decide for themselves what made the scruffy Bialtan so special.

Salt walked as straight as he could, trying to ignore the weight of their stares. They finally walked through the open gate, and he was out of their sight. It was pitch-black inside. Salt kept walking straight for at least fifty paces before he felt a hand on his arm and stopped.

"Apologies, allow me to guide you."

Salt reached out as the guard prompted him to turn. His fingers brushed against the stone wall he had been about to walk into. They walked into a tunnel, and Salt watched the now-distant bright opening of the gate pass from view entirely. Salt had never been afraid of the dark. Not even as a child. But walking through this total darkness, entirely dependent on a stranger, was unnerving. He was further disturbed by the unmistakable feeling of a slow but steady downward incline. Visions of a city built underground in utter blackness filled his mind. Behind him he heard the soldiers reentering the tunnel. The pounding of their boots echoed loudly in the tunnel. Salt tried to start up a conversation with his guide to break the tension.

"Your city has impressive defenses."

"Thank you, Lord Saltig."

He tried again. "Have your fortifications been challenged often?"

An even more uncomfortable silence stretched on until Salt didn't think he was going to get an answer at all. Finally, though, the Dreth spoke hesitantly.

"The last time was one hundred twelve years past. We defended ourselves from your Bialta." Obviously able to see the look of confusion on Salt's face he continued, "Your countrymen fought bravely."

"You speak as if you remember it," said Salt.

"My first day as a Spear Brother. I will not forget." The laughter died in Salt's throat. Gurt warned him that there was more to the Dreth than anyone guessed. Lera and Gurt had told him the Dreth had no mages in the strictest sense, but not to assume they didn't have some kind of power. *I guess I just found the proof of that.*

Salt and his guide walked down for a time until the ground leveled off, then eventually slanted upward again. The nameless soldier guided Salt to the side and opened a door. Salt was stunned. The great wall he'd seen from outside was not the only wall in the city. The city held a complex pattern of similar walls surmounted by soaring towers. The Dreth homes, shops, and other buildings were built in the shadows of the walls in the narrow slivers of space that were open to the air. The homes wouldn't have been out of place in one of Darien's nicer neighborhoods, though not even the street in front of the palace was as immaculately clean as Dreth. A few men and women went about their business in eerie silence. Salt noticed that the bluish skin coloring was far less pronounced in the people around him. They looked far more human than the Dreth ambassador.

"This is the outermost segment on the west side of the city. We will pass through several dozen more segments before we reach the Core."

"Several dozen!" Salt exclaimed. "Just how many walls does this city have?" The guard paused momentarily, his surprise clear.

"The whole city is built this way. It is our last stronghold, and Nok Dreth sits at the center."

At a loss as to what to say, Salt commented on the houses. "The houses here look Bialtan."

"You are kind. I will pass on your words to the architects. The next segment we will pass through is Keralan inspired. After that will be Styrian and then Hollentic. . . ."

Salt blinked. *Styria? Hollent? Where the hell is that?*

"We have prepared a room for you in the ninth northern segment. It too has Bialtan construction. Rest. Nok Dreth will summon you."

***

Salt looked out the window of the room the Dreth had prepared for him and sighed. It was midmorning and still dark outside. Even though the sun was high in the sky, its light did not reach down to the Dreth homes. The room was far nicer than he had expected, nicer than any he'd ever seen, really. A wide selection of foods and wines had even been prepared for him. The building had the look and feel of an inn, but Salt was sure he was the only lodger. The Dreth filling the role of tavern keeper downstairs had welcomed him and offered to prepare anything that Salt required. But the offer had felt forced. The man was cold and distant. The whole city felt claustrophobic and depressingly dark. Salt couldn't bring himself to enjoy the lavish treatment and barely touched the expensive fare that had been laid out for him. Instead, he spent most of his time just staring out the window, trying to make sense of these people who were more different than any he'd ever met, seen, or heard of. He was finally starting to understand Min's and Brolt's comments. Very few people passed by in the street. Salt debated with himself about going out and exploring but finally decided to stay put. The Dreth and their giant city unnerved him in a way he couldn't quite explain.

The Spear Brother who had guided him to the tavern had certainly been more talkative than Ambassador Ben Akyum. Not that that was saying much. But he still wasn't someone Salt would choose to share a few pints with. *They're all just so stiff and serious.* Considering the fuss the Dreth had made about the sword, they didn't seem to be in a hurry to take it from him. Wishing that Nok Dreth would just summon him so he could hand it over and start the trek back home, Salt rummaged through his bags and laid out the ceremonial clothes Gurt had had prepared for his audience with the Dreth ruler. Gray-and-black clothes fit for a noble.

Gods, the guys down at the docks would never let me live it down if they saw me dressed in this. A crest was sewn into the doublet. A stylized hammer and a roaring dragon overlaid the Bialtan royal crest. *Well, at least Gustave didn't give me anything too pretentious.* He found a large gold ring with a matching crest in one of the pockets. Shaking his head, Salt tried on the new clothes. Like everything he'd been given since he took up residence in the palace, they fit perfectly. He looked in a mirror and barely recognized himself.

A loud knock at the door made Salt jump. He felt inexplicably guilty, as if he'd been doing something he shouldn't. He hesitated for a moment, thinking about pulling off the fine clothes, before sighing and opening the door. Eight Dreth soldiers waited in the hall. Not one of them spoke. They just parted to make way for Salt and waited for him to fall in to their formation. The armor they wore was not like that worn by the Spear Brothers who had escorted him into the city. These men and women wore far more elaborate armor, every raised edge lined with silver. The spears they carried had no points. Salt swallowed hard. Firespears. And if he wasn't mistaken, the man at the front of the group wore a Firesword at his belt.

An honor guard capable of leveling a city, if the stories are true. I'm not sure if I should be flattered or disturbed.

Salt mumbled a wordless excuse and ducked back into his room to recover the Firesword. He slung the scabbard across his back and joined the Fire Warriors. They set off at a brisk pace. They kept so close to Salt that he had no difficulty walking through the dark tunnels within the walls. Their silent nearness was unnerving, but Salt was still glad for a guide when they passed into the pitch blackness. They moved through several city segments, each stranger than the last. Salt couldn't begin to guess where the buildings were from. One segment contained a single long sprawling building that left room for no other but looked so awkwardly shaped that he couldn't even imagine what use it could be put to.

Salt didn't need to be told when they finally arrived at the Core. It was awe inspiring, even given the gargantuan city built around it. The titanic tower dwarfed the great walls that radiated out from it like the spokes of a wheel. The segment they had entered held no buildings. Only a small ornamental garden filled the space. It was the only vegetation Salt had seen anywhere in Dreth. The lush greenery and colorful flowers felt out of place in this city in the desert. There were no windows in the side of the Core, just featureless stone and the smallest door Salt had seen since he arrived in the city.

The Fire Warrior at the front of the group walked up to the small door and, without ceremony, pulled it open and ducked inside. The rest of the honor guard took up guard positions on either side of the door.

Salt took one last look up at the huge building. *This one tower is probably twice the size of the king's palace back in Bialta.* He took a deep breath, ducked inside, and was once again swallowed by darkness. The Fire Warrior pulled a long chain out of his cloak. A small bright light shone at the end of it. Then he turned and started walking up a steep flight of stairs. Salt was breathing hard well before he reached the first landing. His guide's steps never faltered. He continued walking resolutely long after Salt had lost count of how many floors they had climbed. The small concession made for their human visitor and his inferior eyesight wasn't very helpful. If anything, the light on the chain made walking up the stairs even more difficult as the shadows jumped and shifted each time the dull light was obscured by the guide's body.

When they finally reached what looked to be the top, the Fire Warrior motioned for Salt to go through a door, then he turned and walked back down the stairs, extinguishing his light as he went. Salt was left alone, forgotten and unannounced, sweating profusely in his finery. As he fought to catch his breath, he rubbed his aching legs with trembling hands. Sweat dripped off his nose onto the floor. Salt trained as hard as anyone in the Night Guard. He was, he well knew, in excellent physical condition. But his Dreth guide had managed to climb up and away from him without the slightest sign of fatigue while fully armed and armored.

Well, no sense in worrying about the clothes now. Salt sat down on the top step with a sigh and tried to recover from his ordeal. He wasn't comfortable in the perfect blackness, but he was tired and light-headed and most certainly didn't feel up to speaking with another Dreth just yet. He had been sitting for quite some time when he noticed that he could see. Not a lot, but he could see a very faint outline of a door not too far away. Presumably the same one that his guide had shown him. The idea of getting back to light, of being able to see again, prompted Salt to get moving. He pushed himself wearily to his feet and went through the door. The faint light that filled the room was almost blinding after the stairway.

The room was nothing like what he might have expected. An oversized forge dominated the center of a huge open space. Chains and pulleys hung from a ceiling lost in darkness. Fragments of armor and half-built weapons and suits of armor were stacked on every available surface, from the heavy stone tables to the numerous wooden chairs. Some effort seemed to have been made to decorate the workshop—a handful of paintings and maps were set into the walls at odd intervals. Above it all hung thick chains supporting shiny black bones. The skull of a giant monster, its mouth filled with teeth as long as his arms, grinned down at Salt. Salt looked at it curiously. *Not sure what it's made of, but if they wanted to convince anyone it's real, they should have at least made the skeleton bone colored. Black just looks weird.* He dropped his eyes and scanned the room for signs of Nok Dreth.

"And just like that you dismiss the greatest treasure this city holds?" Salt turned to see a Dreth in thick leather work clothes standing in the doorway behind him. His head was uncovered, and Salt could finally see what a Dreth really looked like. He had thin white hair and the same bluish skin he'd seen on the ambassador's arms. Otherwise his features were remarkably human, though the proportions were somewhat off in a way he couldn't put his finger on. "That skeleton you so casually dismissed is all that remains of the greatest dragon to visit this continent in untold millennia: Dragonlord Kilmarat himself, my old enemy."

Salt bit back a sarcastic comment about a crown on a scarecrow. "It is impressive."

"You are one of Bialta's new Night Guard, are you not? I understand your king formed the Guard with the express purpose of hunting down magical threats within your country. I'm quite sure I read something about it. That couldn't have been more than thirty years ago or so. Surely your mandate hasn't changed so much in such a short time?"

It suddenly occurred to Salt whom he was talking to so casually. He bowed low. "Your Majesty . . ."

"I am not some human king, Night Captain Saltig. Address me simply as Nok Dreth." Then he held up a placating hand. "No need to continue, Night Captain. I see the intentions of your words in your bearing and posture. You only concern yourself with real threats and you doubt the veracity of the stories you have been told about our race and the stories of dragons most of all."

Salt squirmed uncomfortably. "I'm sorry, Nok Dreth. I didn't mean to offend you."

Nok Dreth waved away his apology. "Of course you didn't. That doesn't keep you from being skeptical. Believe me when I say countless 'truths' that are widely accepted across the world are in fact totally false. Skepticism is a positive trait, particularly in a leader of men or an investigator, of which you are apparently both. In this case, however, your doubts are misplaced.

There is no need to take my word for it, though you will learn that Dreth do not utter falsehoods. Go and pick up that large bone on the table by the wall. Yes, that one."

Salt looked at the huge bone Nok Dreth had indicated. It was taller than he was and nearly as thick around as his thigh. *It must weigh a ton.* He reached under it and pulled. And nearly fell over when the giant bone lifted as if it were no more than a chicken bone. Amazed, Salt turned the bone in his hands and looked back over at Nok Dreth.

"Yes, surprisingly light, isn't it? That's not all. Try to break it. Go on, as hard as you can, smash it into the stone floor or table. Strike it with any of the weapons or tools here; you will not be able to scratch it."

Salt did as he was bid, swinging the thing around and slamming it into the stone floor over and over. Not a chip, not a scratch. Just as Nok Dreth had predicted. *The thing's so light I can't get any power behind my swings. It'll be different with a hammer.* He lifted a heavy-looking smith's hammer that was lying on a table nearby and smashed it down on the narrowest section of the bone. A dull thud and the shock that traveled up his arms from the impact was the only result. Nok Dreth smiled at his look of wonder.

"I see you are starting to accept what I said. That is good. Dragon bones are incredibly strong. They must carry the great weight of the wyrms themselves, and remember that dragons fly. If their bones were as heavy as you'd expect, even their great magics would be taxed by holding them aloft. But we can speak of these things later. For the moment, I understand that you have brought something for me, Night Captain Saltig, Lord of Dustland." He said the last with a small smile.

With another embarrassed look, Salt carefully took the sheathed blade off his back and handed it to the Dreth monarch.

"Here is the Firesword, Nok Dreth. I am happy to return it to its rightful owner."

Nok Dreth took the sword and drew the blade slowly. Then he swirled the blade through a complex series of practice moves almost too fast for Salt to follow. *I need to stop thinking of this guy as old no matter what his age is.*

"Thank you. Captain Saltig. It is good to have my sword back. And you are right. I am its rightful owner. My brother and I made this sword together. The first and greatest of the Fireswords. I feel young again to have it back. But enough. As to your reward . . ."

"No reward is necessary, Nok Dreth. I'm happy to have been given a chance to visit your city and serve both our peoples."

Nok Dreth nodded. "A political answer. Surely one you were instructed to give. Very well, since I cannot ask you what you want, I will decide for myself. I will make for you a weapon from the very dragon bone you were holding."

"You are too kind, Nok Dreth." Salt did his best to bow. Silence followed. Salt cast about for something to talk about. He wasn't ready for the audience to end just yet. He couldn't face going back down those stairs. Then Salt's interest was caught by a painting of a city on a hill by the sea. Something about the coastline was familiar.

Noticing his interest, Nok Dreth explained, "It is indeed your Darien City. It was called by another name in those days. It was beautiful. Our cities had no need of walls in those days."

"Just how big was Dreth back then?"

"That is going back a long, long time. Many thousands of years, to the height of our empire. In the earliest days, Dreth filled what is now the Great Desert. But we were a curious and enterprising people who often longed for more as your kind do. We built great tunnels and roads through the Icespine

Mountains and built some of our greatest cities in what is now your Bialta as well as in Aboleth."

I wish Lera were here. She'd love to be able to ask this guy questions. I'll just have to do it for her and try to remember as much as I can.

"Our arts were unsurpassed. We built ships easily twenty times the size of any seagoing vessel you might see today. We explored the world and traded with the people we met."

A strange look crossed Nok Dreth's face. "Some blame our great curiosity for awakening the anger of the dragons. Some of our most intrepid explorers left on an expedition to cross the Endless Ocean. They did not return. Soon after, the dragons came. Huge monsters who flew across the ocean to bring death and destruction to our lands.

"They were only the first harbingers of the great war. Our ships returned to us in their wake, but their crews had disappeared. Our ships carried monsters. Men and women infected with draconic blood. They fought savagely for their masters and wielded sorceries almost as great as those of the trueborn dragons. Our westernmost cities were caught unaware. Most were destroyed in the first attack, though some exacted a heavy price from the dragon host. We rallied and struck back as they crossed the Icespine Mountains. And still they came. The dragons and their spawn seemed without number, while far too many of our own people were dying, their bodies utterly consumed by dragon fire. Resurrection impossible."

"Resurrection?"

"Has so much of the Dreth been forgotten in the outside world? Has all learning and study ended? Yes, resurrection. The Dreth purebloods can be returned to life if they fall, providing a dozen other purebloods enact the rite."

Salt was amazed. These beings had the power of gods.

"It is one of the reasons we stay in our city now," Nok Dreth continued. "There are so few of us left."

"Few? But Nok Dreth, your city is huge!"

"Huge and mostly empty. What isn't is populated by half bloods. Fewer than two hundred pureblood Dreth remain today, each and every one of us a survivor of the Dragon War."

And I was impressed that the Spear Brother was over a hundred years old? This man must be thousands! Tens of thousands!

"Questions multiply in you, Night Captain. You have a curious mind, a trait the Dreth once valued. It is unfortunate that it has become so rare among our people. I will ask Lamek to tell you some small things about our people's history; he is a bit of an oddity among the Dreth in that he loves to talk. I am sure he will enjoy getting to know you."

Salt bowed. "Thank you for your kindness, Nok Dreth."

"Enjoy your time in my city, Night Captain. Explore as you see fit. Little of what goes on in Dreth is a secret. We simply do not allow many outsiders past our walls. Nor do we venture out ourselves anymore. Even the half bloods have taken to following our ways and rarely venture far unless ordered to do so. We hope to reignite the fire of curiosity among our people someday. . . . But enough of that. Lamek will answer all your questions. I will summon you again when your reward is complete."

Realizing he was being dismissed, Salt bowed again and left through the door he had come in. With a sigh, he closed the door to the workroom and its light and started his slow, careful walk back down the long stairs.

PART II

CHAPTER 12

Dantic was almost giddy as he walked through the long silent halls of the Arcanum toward the council hall. The news had been repeated in every part of the great building that morning—Archmage Tilden had passed away in his sleep during the night. Dantic had never had any use for the conservative fossil. The man's greatest achievement was his longevity—impressive even for a magus of skill. The man had died at three hundred and seventy-eight years of age. *And in all that time the man accomplished nothing. Nothing as a mage of significant power, and nothing as a member of the ruling council of the Arcanum.*

As far as Dantic was concerned the Arcanum was better off without men like Corfon Tilden. But his death was more significant than just the disappearance of a useless individual—it meant there was a seat open on the Closed Council, only the second time such a thing had occurred in the thirty years since Dantic had been initiated into the Arcanum. *I was only an apprentice last time, but now I'm ready.*

Dantic was well recognized within the halls of magic. He was a prodigy the likes of which only came along once every handful of centuries. When he was just a few years out of his apprenticeship, he had passed the trials to achieve the Sixth Order and had received the title of archmage that went with it. At the modest age of forty-three, he had undergone further trials that officially made him the only living mage of the Eighth Order in Bialta. A seat on the Closed Council was the next logical step, and one he'd been looking forward to for years already. *I have ideas for this place. Ideas that will change everything.*

All he needed now was to win a majority vote in the Open Council meeting and he would be setting another record— being the youngest council member since the founding of the institution.

When he arrived in the great council hall, at least a half hour early, he saw that the great room was already nearly full. An election was an event rare enough that even the most reclusive researchers among the Arcanum's ranks had been drawn out of their chambers and laboratories. *Just as I expected.* His arrival after so many of his peers was calculated. *I have to make an entrance if I'm to be noticed.*

He took his time walking down to the very front rows of seats, where a group of the youngest full members of the Arcanum were congregating. They had saved him a seat, of course, as they always did. Dantic was their unofficial leader and something of a hero in their eyes—able to best most of the instructors and so-called experts at their own games, and do it with style.

All any of them had been talking about for years was how the Closed Council needed a younger member, a young voice to inject some fire into the group of ancients who ruled them. "Imagine, someone sitting on the council who hadn't reached their first century of life," he heard someone say as he walked by. All eyes were on him—just as he'd intended. He wore his formal robes, of course, as did every mage in the room. But few were those who had earned the right to wear the black of an archmage. More important, though, was the embroidery woven into the fabric with delicate magic—each rune and color representing a different discipline or skill mastered by the wearer. More runes were added as a mage accumulated skills, and Dantic's robes shimmered more than any in the room, even those of the Closed Council members who were just then filing into their seats from the opposite side of the hall.

Once they were settled, four hundred mages turned their full attention to the eight assembled on the dais. The empty seat near the middle of the row was all the confirmation anyone needed that one of the council members had indeed passed.

Archmage Nesrine called out for order and announced the opening of the council session, taking over the role filled by Tilden for the last hundred and six years. Her voice was thin and barely carried to the back of the room—hardly surprising as she was well over two hundred herself, Dantic thought with disgust.

"We have but one order of business before us today. Tradition dictates that no other decision can be taken by the Arcanum's Closed Council until nine elected members sit at the table. We are here today to address the loss of Archmage Tilden and fill his seat," she said. "Before we hear nominations, the council as a whole feels it is important to remind all mages present that the role of council member is more of an administrative one than a position of power and prestige. First and foremost, our responsibility is to ensure the day-to-day functioning of the Arcanum. Generally, this has far more to do with securing revenue to pay our servants and to buy food and supplies than it does performing great deeds." None could mistake that she looked at Dantic as she spoke, as did most of the other council members. "I ask all mages assembled here today to bear this in mind as well when it comes to casting your vote."

Dantic seethed internally. *That bitch! How dare she try to influence the vote? And so blatantly!* He never let the look of calm confidence slip from his face. He would win despite them, he had no doubt.

"Now . . . Who would you have join the Closed Council of the Arcanum?"

Immediately fifty of Dantic's supporters stood to show their desire to speak, as did a number of other mages scattered through the great hall.

Nesrine called on each mage by name. *Proving she has a good head on her shoulders whatever her other faults.* Only two names were mentioned again and again—Archmage Dantic of the Eighth Order, and Mage Jalim Bagwin of the Fourth Order.

The atmosphere in the hall was tense. Both nominations were controversial. One was fifty years younger than the norm, the other not an archmage. Both defied tradition. *A crafter? There are already two on the council. The other disciplines will never vote for a third. Besides, he's not even close to being archmage material,* Dantic thought with satisfaction.

"Two unusual nominations. Also unusual that we would have so few. But perhaps not given the smaller number of mages to achieve the rank of archmage in recent years," Nesrine pointed out unnecessarily. "We will hear from each candidate briefly before we proceed to the vote."

Dantic had been preparing for this moment for years. He cleared his throat and spoke loudly, his rich voice filling the room. "Brothers and sisters of the Arcanum. I do not have a long speech or an elaborate presentation prepared for you. In most elections, mages vote to support a candidate who will represent their interests, who will ensure the Arcanum provides the support and materials for them to pursue their own chosen form of our arts. In this I believe I am the natural choice. I am a student of every discipline taught within our ancient halls, with the notable exception of combat." He nodded his head toward the group of tough old mages who taught the art of war magic. "An exception I plan to address at the masters' earliest convenience. Indeed, Archmage Hakran himself has himself agreed to take me under his wing and help me address this glaring gap in my knowledge." He made a small bow in the direction of the venerable old warmage before looking out across the Open Council, making sure to make eye contact with the strongest and most influential mages in attendance. "I am uniquely suited to representing the Arcanum as a whole and everything we represent and strive for. I will not disappoint you."

He bowed and returned to his seat, while Jalim Bagwin walked down from the back of the room. The man was nearly bald with no more than graying wisps of hair clinging to his scalp. His deep-blue robes showed a smattering of symbols, nearly all of them related to magical crafting. Dantic knew the man was past a hundred years, though he looked older than Nesrine herself—proof, if any was needed, that his talent was relatively meager.

"Unlike my *young* friend," he started, "I am going to take up a little of your valuable time, for which I hope you will all forgive me. Simply put, I believe I can assist all of you in whatever you are endeavoring to accomplish. Perhaps not by understanding everything you do myself—I cannot imagine how that would be useful, truth be told. No. I will ensure that we all have more of what we need to pursue our own brand of knowledge by removing the financial constraints the Arcanum has been working under for so long. What I propose to do will have nobles and merchants—not only of Bialta but of the known world—lining up to fill our coffers.

"Ladies and gentlemen of the council," Bagwin called out with a broad smile, "it is my great pleasure to show you the results of my team's efforts over the past months—the Silver Servant." At his words a gleaming metallic being walked up to stand next to Bagwin. It was perhaps the height of a child of twelve, finely built and reminiscent of a fine suit of armor.

"As you all know," Bagwin continued after a moment, "the Arcanum has, on occasion, managed to impart the semblance of life to inanimate objects. The process is usually time-consuming and expensive, and the resulting constructs usually require both physical and magical maintenance. The greater the complexity of their quasi minds, the greater the difficulty in completing the weaves. Though the Arcanum has had some success in this area in the past, the efforts were made to match or understand stories of great war golems built in ages past." He shook himself as if remembering where he was. "The Arcanum's need for gold is endless. All of us have projects we are working on that require great sums of coin. What I propose, ladies and gentlemen, is not to build great golems capable of mighty tasks, but Silver Servants to delight the nobility and merchants. Which one of them will balk at paying a hefty price for an unsleeping servant who literally cannot tell their secrets?" There were noises of interest and approval from everywhere in the crowd now. "Once they are seen, we expect requests for them to come in quite quickly."

A few sounds of dissent cut through the general approval and Bagwin didn't fail to notice. He held up a hand. "Ladies and gentlemen of the Arcanum, if you will permit me a few final words to address the entirely justified concerns some of you may have before ceding the floor. We know that there are those who might turn nearly any tool they are handed to unsavory purposes. To avoid this, the Silver Servants will be granted a quasi mind that is only capable of general domestic tasks.

They will also be only as strong as a human of comparable size, though they will not tire. The face of each servant will be customized for the individual client, and house crests can also be added. At the time of sale, the servant will be imprinted with one or several masters, a simple matter I assure you, and one that will keep our customers returning to us for generations to come as Silver Servants are sold or inherited."

Bagwin bowed low in a sweeping gesture that somehow included all the mages arrayed around him. "My team will require help in this endeavor, of course, but not so much as when the Arcanum is forced to send some of our number away to act as advisers. The Silver Servant is but the first in a series of initiatives I have planned that will keep us all comfortably funded for the foreseeable future. And so it is with the hope that many of you will take some small time away from your own projects to assist us that I cede the floor."

The applause was thundering. Dantic sat at the back of the room seething. Bagwin was a middling mage at best, more of a merchant than a true mage. *But right now, he has a better chance of getting the seat.*

Archmage Nesrine raised a hand, and the room settled back into silence. "We have heard from both our candidates and must now proceed to a vote. Would the mages casting their votes for Archmage Dantic please stand."

A reassuring number of the attending mages stood up immediately. *A little less than half. . . . With the normal group of abstainers, I should have my win.*

"And those casting their votes for Mage Bagwin?"

A very similar number of mages stood silently and waited to be acknowledged. Dantic sat in stunned silence. He had secured two hundred and ten votes to Bagwin's two hundred and six. Not nearly enough of a majority to be granted the seat.

Whispers started throughout the council chamber and gradually rose in volume as the assembled mages discussed the implications of the deadlock.

Archmage Nesrine called for silence. "The Closed Council will need to consider the implications of this unprecedented situation. Those few of our fellows who were not able to attend our meeting today would not be a sufficient number to sway the vote either way, though we may need to hear their voices before we reach a decision. The Open Council will reconvene in exactly twenty days, whereupon all votes will be recast. We leave it to the candidates to attempt to sway the opinions of their peers. In the meantime, the Closed Council requests special dispensation from the Open Council to go about its usual business with but eight members until the matter is resolved."

Dantic was the first on his feet to indicate his approval of the new motion, quickly followed by most of the younger mages in the room . . . and, slowly, nearly all the Arcanum members in attendance. *When the election comes around again, it won't even be close—I'll crush him.* Dantic bit down on his pride and joined the group of mages working their way down to the floor to offer their help. *If you can't beat them, join them. Besides, this way I'll be able to improve on their work and come out on top.*

A few of those moving down looked at Dantic with looks of mild surprise. He'd never been a team player. *And as soon as I don't need to be anymore, I'll stop.* His face hurt as he forced a smile onto his lips and stepped forward to speak with Bagwin.

"Archmage," Bagwin said. "I must say it's a pleasure to see you offer your time to assist with one of my 'menial projects' as you called them the last time we spoke."

"Well, you certainly proved me wrong this time, Bagwin." *Never have words tasted so bitter.* "I'm looking forward to joining the team."

"We are blessed indeed," Bagwin said, smiling. "But I'm sure you have more important things to do. These are, after all, rather simple tasks better suited to lower-ranking mages. There is no need for an archmage such as yourself to neglect the great things you must be working on to assist me." He gestured toward the crowd of mages clustering around them. "As you can see, I have plenty of help."

Dantic bit the inside of his mouth and somehow managed to keep his smile as he nodded politely and walked out of the council room.

***

The following days in Sacral saw a slow whittling away of the invading forces. The Abolians would push into the city and the People's Army would cut them down. The People's Army fared poorly in a few pitched battles, but the remaining Abolian soldiers were low on supplies and starving. They eventually surrendered. Conspicuous in their absence were all the surviving enemy Warchosen and their commander, Kabol. By Harrow's count, at least five Warchosen were left unaccounted for, including Zorat. When they finally finished their sweep of the city and moved out to the western fields, Maura's army were shocked by what they saw. Thousands of bodies were scattered around the fields amid squawking flocks of carrion birds. Ragged burn marks scarred the earth where sorcery had been unleashed.

"Maura," said Jerik, "they're all Abolian. Every single one."

Maura looked around at her circle of advisers and officers. "What or who could have done such a thing? Could it really be the king? Or Jenus returned to us maybe?"

Harrow shook his head. "Jenus is beyond the rest of us, but even with the Lightbringer he could not have done all this.

Maybe a full hundred Warchosen with the king protecting and helping them as he did on the western front."

Sevren, one of her battlemages, nodded. "Most of the wounds we've seen appear to have been inflicted with a blade, not magic. Whatever talents our king might have hidden from us, I would guess swordplay was not one of them."

Karim nodded his agreement. "I can't imagine an army that could do this without suffering a single casualty. These Abolians know how to fight."

"Could those who did this have cleared away their dead and wounded already?"

"I don't think so, Commander," answered Harrow. "There doesn't seem to be any blood pools that don't belong to the bodies that are still here."

"Captain, broaden the search. See if you can get a better idea of what happened here. If we have unexpected allies, I want to meet them. If the Abolians had been reinforced from this side of the city, we may well have lost the fight."

"Yes, Commander." He saluted and moved off to make the arrangements.

As she continued her slow patrol of the outer fields, Maura was shocked anew by the scale of the slaughter. Abolian bodies were strewn around in zigzagging patterns.

"By the heavens, there are thousands of them," she mumbled to herself.

Scouts reported back every half hour. Captain Harrow was both meticulous and organized. *He's got a good head on his shoulders.*

"Commander," said Sevren, "I can try a spell to shed some light on all this. Life leaves a kind of echo behind. Especially at times when life burns the brightest, such as in combat. If you are willing to wait a few moments, I can weave the spell in our immediate area."

"That is an excellent idea. Thank you, Sevren."

Maura watched in fascination as Sevren wove his magic. She had never before had the opportunity to observe a mage this closely while he performed a spell. She was rather disappointed that there was so little to see. There was little outward sign of him doing anything beyond an intent look of concentration. Ghostly shapes began to form around them. Maura could just barely see the outlines of people marching in formation. Then a blinding white shape dashed through the area of the spell. It moved with incredible speed, and everywhere it passed the ghostly shapes of soldiers winked out.

"Sevren . . . What is that?"

"I have no idea, Commander. It blazes with life energy."

"Could it be a goddess? The White Mother herself come to save us?"

"I cannot say for sure, but I get the distinct impression that this being is a male. I also think it tripped and fell twice in the short space of time we observed it."

"The wide world has come back into our lives. Our home is now the playing field for a game we don't understand. Our first priority has to be finding out who the players are."

"Yes, Commander."

They continued walking in silence for a time. When Maura spoke again, her voice was uncharacteristically hesitant.

"Sevren . . . I should probably not ask you this." She would not meet his eye.

"No, my lady. Ask anything you wish. It will be my pleasure to help you in any way I can."

"It's my husband, Beren. He disappeared during the invasion. I haven't seen his name on the list of fallen. Is there any way you could find out if he's still alive? Or where he is?" She seemed to regret her words as soon as she finished speaking.

The lives of everyone in the whole city are at stake. I can't place my own needs ahead of everyone else's.

"There may be some things I can attempt, Commander. Though none of them are foolproof. Would you like me to proceed?"

"No! No . . . Thank you, Sevren. Please forget I asked. Too many people are looking for lost loved ones, and your talents are too valuable to waste on my worries. All I can do is pray he is still all right and deal with what is in front of me."

"Of course, Commander. If that is your wish."

Sevren considered the woman who had gone from being a housewife to being the commander of a city-state's armies in the space of a day. Unlike many of those who had responsibilities and power handed to them, she struggled to be just, to do the right thing, not just when it suited her but always. As kind and thoughtful as she had shown herself to be with others, she would not allow herself to stray from the path that she had chosen for a single moment.

Well, Lady Maura, in gratitude for what you have done for us all, I will ignore your last command.

It was a simple weaving. Much simpler than the last, and it did not require him to pause as they walked through the killing fields. It would allow Sevren to see her life flame. A lifetime spent with her husband, and genuine love and affection, would have linked their flames. Sure enough, her flame leaned slightly. It pointed west through the fields of slaughter. He could tell nothing about distance. Only that the man's own flame still burned and lay in that direction.

Perhaps the invaders took him. He was an exceptionally talented runesmith, after all. Perhaps not the best theory to share with the commander just yet.

"Commander? I sense something living in that direction," Sevren said, pointing. "Perhaps we could focus our efforts that way for the time being."

"Of course, Sevren. Thank you."

As they drew farther away from the inner wall, the signs of sorcery and the scale of the slaughter increased. Whole swaths of pastureland were charred and blackened by destructive magics.

"Sevren, the scale of destruction out here is beyond anything I've seen in the arena. Who among our people could do this?"

"Only the king, my lady. And even he could not do all this alone. I would guess there were at least three archmages out here, or one archmage with seven lesser mages assisting him."

"We found their supply train, Commander," said a scout running up to Maura.

"I'm surprised it's still here. I would have thought they would have pulled out by now."

They walked for a time until the wagons came into sight. Dozens of large wagons were pulled up into neat rows. "But why are they all empty?"

Harrow shook his head. "Looks like the animals used to pull them were all slaughtered too."

He pointed to large fire pits that were dug past the wagons with large bones stacked around them.

"They didn't prepare for a return journey," Maura said in shock. "There was no way back through the Wastes for any of them unless they took our city."

Complete confidence, as if they could not conceive of defeat. They offered their soldiers only one way home, and that was through victory. The willingness to gamble with the lives of so many was appalling.

"These Abolians are monsters," she said.

As they drew closer, they found bodies lying under each of the carts. Nearly naked, they were chained by the ankle and seemed to have died of thirst. *Slaves.* The barbarity of their attackers was incomprehensible to Maura.

Forcing her mind back to the task at hand, Maura asked, "Is there anything useful at all out here? Anything we can use?"

Harrow called over the scouts and sent more runners out. "It looks like we've got a fair stock of ammunition for the cross-bows we captured, as well as a small supply of materials for maintaining them and some weapons and armor. The carts themselves will be useful for our cleanup crews."

"Let's get some horses and oxen and get the carts into the city as soon as possible. But keep the scouts out and as large a force as we can nearby. If any survivors are left out here, they may be desperate enough to try something."

"Commander!" A scout ran toward them.

"Commander! We've found him!" He stopped in front of her gasping for breath. ". . . Your husband!"

Maura's knees almost gave out beneath her. She tried to blink back the tears that suddenly filled her eyes and failed. The scout's smile only broadened when he saw her relief. "He's unconscious, but he doesn't look hurt. They are carrying him back now."

The scout's smile vanished in confusion as she threw herself on him and hugged him so hard his ribs creaked. "Thank you," she said. "Which way?"

"Please follow me, Commander." Out of breath as he was, the scout had a hard time keeping up with Maura as she jogged forward.

Beren was still unconscious when she reached him. The soldiers carrying him set him down gently and moved a discreet distance away at a gesture from Captain Harrow. She touched Beren carefully, looking for wounds, and was relieved when all she found were a few bruises. He looked terribly thin. *He must have been out here for days.* His hands were clutched tightly around a twisted piece of metal that may once have been a sword. She tried to take his hands off it, but he held on with desperate strength.

Captain Harrow stepped up beside her. "He's holding on to that twisted thing for dear life. The scouts didn't want to hurt him, so they let him keep it. A healer is already on the way."

Sevren looked down at Beren. "He must have been captured. Whatever was killing the Abolians must have given him a chance to escape."

Maura couldn't even answer him. Tears were falling as she held on to her husband's hands and thanked all the gods that he was all right. She had kept herself from feeling anything since the invasion began, but now the floodgates were open, and she was overcome by the pain and sadness from the loss of her son, worry for her husband, and relief for his return. She wept openly and unashamedly as she walked next to the stretcher that carried Beren back to Sacral. Harrow took over the People's Army's efforts, determined that no one would intrude on her grief.

Back at her makeshift quarters in the arena, Maura sat next to Beren, holding a healing rune to his forehead with one hand while she clutched his arm tight with the other. She wouldn't leave his side for a moment or trust anyone else to care for him in her place. She couldn't begin to guess what he'd gone through, but she was determined to be right there next to him when he finally woke up.

At some point in the night, she must have dozed off because she was startled when Beren's ruined sword hit the floor next to the bed a moment before he wrapped his arms around her and pulled her into a desperate hug.

"Maura, I'm so sorry. Gerald . . ." They clung to each other for most of the night, sharing their grief and the relief at finding each other alive.

The reconstruction efforts were progressing slowly. Maura had assumed overall command of Sacral's military, but more and more palace officials were sending her missives asking for direction. King Ansyl had died with no heir, and they seemed unable or unwilling to make decisions on their own. Worse still was the void left by the disappearance of the priesthood. They had occupied so many important roles within the government in addition to holding a jealous ownership of the city's healing magics. Cuts and bruises could be mended in short order by anyone holding a healing rune, but the number of people who were seriously wounded, not to mention those who had fallen ill, were testing the makeshift medical stations Maura had set up around the city.

Maura accepted the extra responsibilities eagerly, desperate to keep her mind occupied. She put people with good judgment in charge of many tasks and trusted them to see it through. Harrow had agreed, reluctantly, to oversee the repairs of the walls. Corwin was organizing the medical stations. Karim was taking charge of the corpse detail and the removal of rubble. Beren worked tirelessly to help in any way he could, rarely straying far from Maura's side except to carve more healing runes while she slept, though he still refused to share what he'd been through during the attack.

The city had lost over thirty thousand people to the attack. Many of the farmers had been lost because their homes were often located among their fields, and they were the first overrun on both fronts. Maura found volunteers to help tend crops and clear debris. Sacral's dead were carried into the crypts below the city by volunteers from the People's Army and interred with their ancestors. Many of the bodies couldn't be identified, but places were found for all of them. The invaders were dragged to mass graves outside of the city walls.

The whole of the People's Army was put to work. They were split into thirds and rotated between working the fields, repairs or their own trades, and weapon training. Led by Captain Harrow, the new soldiers were organized into cohorts and trained in the use of the weapons they carried. The vast majority of the city's arms supply was weapons and armor looted from fallen enemies.

Maura had ordered the surviving Sacral soldiers and weaponsmiths to study the crossbows the enemy had used and to train their own people in their use. They had recovered thousands of the weapons and she did not intend to let them go to waste. They were heavy, cumbersome things and they seemed slow to reload, but Maura couldn't imagine a more effective defensive weapon to be used from atop the walls.

"Commander, we've had a look through the outer rooms of the temple. It appears that the priests did not flee the city, after all. It looks like they barricaded themselves inside. Whatever broke in made short work of them. It's not pretty in there." Maura nodded at the man giving her the report. It was no more than she expected. That undead thing had been terrifying. Still, she couldn't help but feel responsible. She hadn't tried to help them. *There was nothing any of us could have done to help.*

"I need to see it for myself," she said. She started walking in the direction of the temple, and Jerik fell into step next to her. The messenger kept pace a step behind.

"I wouldn't recommend this, Commander. Most of those who went in were being sick outside when I came to find you." Maura held up a hand.

"None of that matters. Besides, after the last few days, I am no stranger to death. I have to see it. I have to understand, *really* understand, what we are fighting against." They walked the rest of the way in silence. Soldiers standing by the huge doors parted when she approached. The messenger who had accompanied her to the temple made some excuse and left her before going in. Maura scarcely noticed.

The smell hit her like a wall. The thick metallic smell of blood was almost enough to cover the stench of excrement, loosed bladders, and exposed entrails. Steeling her nerves, she stepped inside. The accounts of the slaughter had not been exaggerated. Worse, the strange chill that always pervaded the temple had somehow slowed or stopped the decomposition of the dead priests and their servants. Everything looked fresh, as if the slaughter had only just ended a moment ago. Blood and gore were splattered across the floors and up the walls. Bloody trails ended in bodies with twisted looks of fear and agony on their faces. Not one of the temple residents had died quickly or easily.

The temple was lavish by Sacral's standards. Thick carpets covered the floors, and ornate statues of the White Mother stood nearly as high as the vaulted ceilings. Colorful murals covered every wall showing scenes from the White Mother's teachings as well as the lives of her more famous priests and champions. As always, Maura felt a little overwhelmed by the place. A soft light always infused the temple. It was Sourceless, lighting everything perfectly and allowing no shadows to form. Today it allowed for no detail of the massacre to be missed. No flies buzzed around. No birds fought over scraps of meat. It was so fresh, as if Maura was walking in the wake of the killer. Her mind screamed at her that he must be just up ahead. Surely these people could not have died more than a few minutes ago.

Jerik had stepped into the temple behind her, and Maura could hear him being sick. Fighting out in the open—killing enemies in a fight or even seeing friends fight and die—was one thing, but this one-sided massacre where dozens of unarmed men had been torn apart was different.

"Jerik! Karim!" she called out, surprised herself at how strong her voice sounded. "Get some stretchers in here and find some volunteers to start carrying out the bodies. We need to get this place cleared out."

After waiting to make sure they got started, Maura walked on ahead of the corpse detail. As disturbed as she was by the sight of the dead, she felt compelled to see all there was to see. To witness the end of these men who were sworn to a peaceful goddess. The undead killer—the one who called himself Rahz the Insane—had spoken of the White Mother and her priests as if they were worse than monsters. Maura desperately wanted to believe he was lying despite the feeling that he had spoken only the truth. And so she explored alone, stepping carefully over dead men or their body parts and continuing deeper and deeper into the giant building that sat at Sacral's heart. Very soon she passed out of areas she had been in before and into parts of the temple that were reserved for the priests and their servants. The killings in this part of the building were even more gruesome if such a thing were possible, and she considered turning back several times.

But something was different about this part of the temple. The paintings and statues in this area did not depict the White Mother as the radiant saintly woman that one usually saw around the city. Here the images were all rather suggestive, if not obviously sexual. Robes were parted to show the swell of breasts or a length of bare leg underneath. Faces were inviting or teasing, but most certainly not motherly or compassionate. Five doors lined each wall of the hall Maura was in. The doors were open and a dead priest lay within each cell. She looked inside as she passed and was shocked to see the walls of the sleeping cells filled with wantonly sexual paintings of a white-skinned seductress.

Deeply disturbed, Maura walked on. She passed many similar rooms. Apparently such cells were where most of the priests had slept. Finally, she came to a room that could only be described as a throne room. After all the overly decorated rooms and hallways of the temple, this starkly empty chamber was almost more shocking than the paintings. The bare black stone floors and the massive throne looked to have all been carved out of the same block of basalt. Covering the back wall, though, was the largest, most intricate statue Maura had ever seen. Hundreds of naked humans, their faces hidden behind featureless masks, crawled over one another and reached out toward the empty throne.

Almost more disturbing still was the fact that the entire room was bare, unadorned black stone. No attempt had been made to lighten the walls or hide the unlucky color. A flight of wide stone steps led down into darkness on the right side of the room. Four more men had died in this room. These four looked to have fought back. Each of them wore a long black robe that was shredded by blade slashes. Blood soaked their robes and had sprayed out in every direction. Each man had wielded a long jagged dagger. *Weapons inside the temple. . . . It's almost as bad as the paintings. They all died trying to stop the assassin getting down those stairs.*

Maura was shaking now. She had never been particularly devout, but to think the temple and maybe even the goddess herself were so base and twisted was hard to accept. These priests had helped the king govern the city; they had tended to the wounded and the sick. *And everything anyone ever thought they knew about them was a lie.*

Thinking about the assassin's last words to her, Maura realized she'd been looking for Harrow's sword since she entered the temple. The assassin said he would leave it in the heart of darkness within the temple. . . . That meant down the stairs, in the dark. She was sure of it. She backtracked into one of the previous rooms, and with an intense feeling of guilt that she couldn't quite shake off, she took a thick candle from one of the altars and went back to the throne room.

"Come on, Maura. You can do this," she whispered. She took a deep breath and stepped down into darkness. The steps were broad and even. They had been cut into the rock that lay under the temple itself. The candle she carried did little to illuminate the stairwell, but the little spark of light gave her the courage to continue. At first she counted the steps, but her mind soon wandered and she lost count. She tried several more times, but eventually the fear and the shocks the day had brought pushed back into her mind and chased the numbers away. When her foot finally met flat ground, she stumbled and almost dropped her candle. A hallway led off into the darkness.

Maura hesitated. She had no idea how long she'd been gone, but surely she'd be missed by now. Her legs ached from the stairs. Jerik must be close behind her. If not Jerik, then one of the others. She started walking again. The hallway wasn't long. After a hundred paces, it ended in a small room of bare stone. An altar dominated the far wall. Dried bloodstains covered everything. The smell of rot and corruption was thick in the closed air. *The temple's preserving magic doesn't seem to reach down here.* A body lay wrapped in a black robe on the altar, its face bloated and unrecognizable, a familiar blade driven through its chest. She reached for the sword, meaning to pull it out and take it back up for Harrow. But as she stepped closer, her candlelight brought out more detail on the altar, and the symbols carved into the wall behind it. Maura recognized it instantly. They were all taught that symbol in their first visits to the temple. It was the main component of every cautionary tale the priests ever told. The symbol of the Deceiver.

What did it all mean? Had the Deceiver corrupted the cult of the White Mother? Had he defeated her? Or more terrible still, was the White Mother the Deceiver? Could every part of their religion be a lie? Could the Deceiver have lived up to its name and misled all of Sacral for more than fifty generations? She knew then who the wrapped corpse must be. Yeltos Rogayen, high priest of the White Mother. The assassin had spoken the truth. He had left his sword in the heart of the darkness. With numb fingers, she reached for the sword and tried to pull it out of the dead priest. But it would not move. It had been driven clear through his body and deep into the stone beneath.

Holding her candle tightly in her hand, Maura walked back the way she had come. She walked all the way back to the temple entrance in a daze. It wasn't until she stepped outside and a cool breeze hit her that she returned to herself fully. Several of her people were standing around her, concern evident on their faces. Dozens of bodies had been carried out of the temple and had been lain out in neat rows, each one wrapped in thick white cloth leaving only the face exposed. People walked down the rows in small knots hoping and dreading to see a friend or a loved one.

All around the temple entrance were statues and murals of the White Mother. Seeing them made Maura feel sick. But everywhere she looked there were more. It made her want to scream. She only managed to hold herself together for the benefit of those watching. She stood for hours outside the temple, a silent witness to the continuing task of clearing out the dead. The faces of the men and women on corpse detail were increasingly troubled as they came out with bodies from deeper and deeper parts of the building. As they assembled more and more pieces of the puzzle they looked to Maura for understanding and guidance. A look from Maura was all they needed. Each would look into her eyes, nod, and walk back in to continue their work. No one spoke now. The lives of the people of Sacral had been supported by unshakable sureties. They all knew their places in the city and in the universe. Little or nothing had changed in Sacral in living memory. All that had been swept away. They were floating lost now. Each of them clinging mentally to Maura for support and for purpose.

Maura felt the weight of their expectations, their needs, heavily. She didn't buckle under the weight. In that dependency she found her own purpose, her own escape from despair. By morning, stories and rumors of what was in the temple were running through the streets. Many of them were horribly exaggerated. But the doors to the temple were not barred. Hundreds of curious citizens braved the building to see for themselves if the stories were true. No one could fail to remember that the king had sent Jenus and a third of their fighters away on the word of Yeltos Rogayen. It was enough to change the despair and shock of the past days into hate.

Images of the White Mother were being vandalized across the city. Maura witnessed people who had remained calm and composed during the battle scream like animals while they smeared excrement on paintings or threw holy relics into bonfires. Maura tried to stop them. She hated seeing her people reduced to this. But Harrow stopped her. He put a hand on her shoulder, the only time he had made physical contact with her.

"This is an enemy they can strike against. This is a battle they can win without losses. I'll send out enough dependable people to watch and make sure they don't get too carried away."

Maura looked at him for a moment, searching his eyes. She nodded once and he was gone. And so the wave of destruction swept across the city. Only days after the invasion, the people of Sacral did more damage than the attacking army had. But Maura could see the wisdom of Harrow's words. The riot was a cleansing of sorts. The people woke ashamed, but feeling more in control of their lives. The reconstruction efforts were redoubled. Though the Great Temple resisted every attempt at destruction, it was looted thoroughly and every burnable scrap that could be found within was fed to the flames. Materials were pillaged from shrines and lesser temples and were put to use repairing homes and shops.

Though repairs were still her priority, Maura decided she needed to show her people some support. She detailed one of her work teams to start removing every trace of the goddess from the city. Anything that could not be reused was thrown into the open fault that served as the city's refuse pit. The Deceiver's cracked altar joined the rest in the pit, as did the bodies of all the priests who had been found in the temple. People who had been proud of their family members' calling were busy trying to disassociate themselves from them now.

Maura had to put her foot down when a group came forward asking to purge the catacombs of every past priest and champion. "We don't know for sure what happened to our priesthood or how far back their perversions reach. I will not allow the bones of the dead to be disturbed." They reluctantly agreed, and the subject was never broached again. No one in the city was willing to speak out against Maura. Her supporters were too numerous and zealous. Some people had been heard calling her their champion. Others were calling for her to take the crown of Sacral and become queen. The question came up the next morning when she was speaking to her group of advisers.

"It's not such an outrageous suggestion," said Jerik. "You already rule the city in fact if not in name."

Maura blushed. "I'm not a queen. I'm just doing what needs to be done."

"Sounds to me that would make you the best ruler we've ever had," he answered. There was a chorus of agreements from around the room.

Only Beren stayed quiet, as he so often did these days. Maura was worried about him. He didn't speak much, and his attention often drifted off. *He still blames himself for Gerald's death.* She shook herself and pulled her mind away from Gerald. Though she thought of little else during the night when she lay in the dark and cried, she couldn't allow herself to think of him during the day. She wouldn't allow herself to. She had to be strong and make sure the people who had killed him didn't win.

Beren had come through his ordeal a changed man. He didn't shy away from plying his trade per se. He worked like a man possessed, but he refused to carve runes into either weapons or armor. Instead he carved them into shovels, into picks and plows. He also created dozens of small objects with healing runes carved into them every day. Healing runes were in high demand with the disappearance of the priesthood. The city's herbalists did what they could, but some things simply could not be done without magic. The runes themselves were a poor substitute, but they helped. When Maura had asked him about his ordeal or his insistence in working himself so hard, he just answered that the city had enough weapons already, that he wanted to help with the rebuilding.

Many of the city's mages had come forward to offer what help they could for the sick and wounded. But they were working in the dark. The secrets of the healing arts had been jealously guarded by the priests. It occurred to Maura that the priests must have kept some tomes on the subject. But the idea came too late—anything that might reasonably be made to catch fire in the temple had long since been destroyed.

She realized that Corwin had been speaking. "I'm sorry, Corwin. I missed what you were saying. I'm not feeling well this morning."

Corwin gave her a half bow with a sad look on his face.

"Of course, Commander. I was just saying that taking the crown might be a good idea. The people need stability, and you don't actually have an official position within the city. Besides, I've heard people are worrying about who will take the crown if you don't. . . ."

CHAPTER 13

The Gling'Ar mage took a firm hold of Jenus and guided him through the forest, often holding him up as he lost his footing on the thick roots.

"You are a victim of your own success, human. Had you failed in protecting the priests days ago, my hunting party would have simply melted away into the trees and you would have been left to return to your homes. Even then we were prepared to wait a little longer. Had you not attacked the trees . . ."

"Why would you care about the priests? I can't say I think too highly of the lot of them myself, but they do no real harm. Certainly they've never done anything that could affect your people."

The Gling'Ar looked down at him impassively, ignoring his questions. The weight of his failure settled onto Jenus's shoulders. He had led his people into their first real confrontation with the outside world in a thousand years. His leadership had only brought his proud people to shame and death. Dejected, lost, they walked with heads bowed, humiliated at having been taken without a fight.

At least they're alive. He had followed the only course open to him from the start. There had been no chance of success on this mission; from the very beginning he had been doomed to fail. But he couldn't silence a voice in the back of his head that still blamed him for everything, that said that *he* was the leader. It was *his* responsibility to find a way to win, or at least to return. If he hadn't seen it and couldn't imagine it even now, then he really wasn't deserving of the position he'd been given. Though he couldn't see them from where he walked at the front of the procession, Jenus suspected the noncombatants among his army were having an even harder time. Many of them hadn't volunteered for a life of danger. Most had simply been chosen to accompany the army.

The forest was vast and ancient, but the Gling'Ar walked through the shadowy woods as if born to them. Which they likely were, Jenus realized. Despite their insistence on disarming and binding the arms of all the humans, the Gling'Ar were not cruel captors. Each prisoner had one of the four armed giants walking at their side, keeping them from falling and making sure they did not stray. Jenus even saw several giants pick up and carry soldiers who were wounded or were unable to continue walking on their own. They made much better time moving through the forests than they had with the carts. Jenus idly wondered what had become of the pack animals that pulled them and decided he'd rather not know. The idea of the mild-tempered oxen he'd been tending ending up as a meal made him feel inexplicably sad in a way the loss of the priests and their supporters among his men hadn't. They arrived at the first Gling'Ar village after several hours of walking. The mage urged him along.

"We'll stop here for the night; some of your people are having difficulties keeping up."

Jenus nodded glumly. A thick wooden palisade was set around what turned out to be a surprisingly large village. It meandered in an odd way as the houses and the outer wall itself were all set so as to accommodate the great trees. *They brought the wood for the construction from elsewhere.* The thick canopy extended unbroken over the village. *They must not like light too much either.* The prisoners were settled on the ground around the village. About two hundred Gling'Ar seemed to live there. Jenus was stunned to see four-armed children playing and laughing, then shying away as they caught sight of the humans. The houses were very well built, clean, and well kept. Every villager wore well-made clothing in a variety of muted shades that was at least the equal of what was worn on the streets of Sacral—there was nothing savage about these people at all. So far only the mage who walked beside him looked the part.

"Just wait till you reach the capital and meet the king," the mage said, as if reading Jenus' thoughts.

The humans were given food and water, a thick soup that was mostly green vegetables and fresh baked bread. As he sat and ate in silence, Jenus watched the Gling'Ar in fascination. Each dwelling seemed to house a family of at least four children and their parents. Either the male or the female of each family wore heavy armor and weapons. The other seemed to be tasked with the upkeep of the house and tending to the family. Jenus watched one huge Gling'Ar male gently cradle a sleeping child in one set of arms while it made repairs to its family's home with its free hands.

Days passed and each night they stopped at another village. *How many thousands of these creatures live in this forest?* Jenus had thought his army was the greatest the world had ever seen. He'd been raised to *know* it was the best. But he shuddered to think what would happen if these so-called savages ever attacked his homeland. *Better the king think us lost. Better that he renew the great wards and keep Sacral apart from the world for all time.*

Jenus wasn't sure when they started to climb. He'd been too lost in self-loathing to notice much since the first day of the forced march. Since then he'd been moving without any real awareness of what he did or where he was.

The captive army was led into the foothills of a mountain range where the great trees finally started to thin. Jenus caught sight of snowy peaks through the thinning canopy. The sight of an open sky was a welcome one. All the Sacral prisoners recovered some semblance of hope.

"You return to us," said the mage still walking at his side. Jenus didn't bother answering. "If the sight of the sky is what has made the difference, then hold to its memory, human. Soon we will enter the caves."

Jenus shuddered at the thought. *Caves.* As if the endless dark forest hadn't been enough. The mage led them to an opening in the rock face at the foot of a stone cliff. The Gling'Ar picked up glass lamps that had been left inside the cave mouth and led the prisoners inside. Jenus knew every one of his people was experiencing the fear he felt at leaving the bright sunlight behind. He had noticed them starting to talk to one another during the last day. They whispered before sleeping or talked of simple things as they walked. Their captors didn't seem to mind. He would have liked to call out encouragement to them before they left the light, but that part of his life was done. He was a failure. He had led his people to their doom. They would not welcome his words. All he could do was face his own end with as much dignity as he could. They walked into the cave and Jenus felt like he was being swallowed up by a great beast. The strange lamps the Gling'Ar carried did little to lessen his discomfort. They gleamed with such a cold light that the caves and those passing through them took on a ghostly appearance. All talking among the captives stopped. Whenever words had to be exchanged, voices were never raised above the faintest of whispers, while the Gling'Ar themselves seemed content to travel in silence.

The tunnel they walked through split again and again. Each time they encountered only darkness and stone, but the mage guided them through the maze with easy confidence. Jenus thought that hours had passed already, though it was hard to tell underground. A rumble started growing in the distance and Jenus could hear strange echoes bouncing off the walls around him. They were blinded when they stepped out of the tunnel onto a wide stone shelf that overlooked a vast, brightly lit cavern. The prisoners cried out in surprise and wonder as their eyes started to adjust. A great city, one easily the equal of Sacral itself, filled the cavern.

Jenus couldn't believe what he was seeing. The city mirrored his home in many ways. The pattern of the streets, the style of the buildings. Only the color of the stone was different here—gray granite instead of black basalt, all of it left bare. The prisoners were led down large avenues toward the heart of the city. *Toward where the Great Temple sits in Sacral if I'm not mistaken.* Gling'Ar of every age moved around the streets shopping or going about their business. Jenus noticed a few humans moving among the Gling'Ar. Not only moving among them, he noticed, but doing most of the menial tasks. Many were dressed identically in long gray robes and featureless iron masks. *Slaves,* thought Jenus. *So this is to be our lot.* Jenus caught sight of the temple and for a moment hope filled him. He'd never been overly fond of the priesthood he supposedly championed, but the temple was identical to the one at the heart of Sacral. *This must be a temple to the White Mother.*

We'll sort out this whole mess soon and be on our way home.
Cheerful thoughts, but not ones that Jenus could make himself believe. Soon his people were settled onto the ground in
the square. The Gling'Ar rounded up the officers and surviving
mages and led them into the building.

What little hope he'd been able to build up within himself
faded when they stepped through the great doors. The familiar
fresh feeling and Sourceless light filled the temple, but there
were no devotional images or statues here. Nothing to suggest
the cult of the White Mother held sway here at all. Only simple carvings adorned the walls, simple reliefs carved delicately
into the stone of the walls themselves. Outlines of men and
women wearing featureless masks, and above them, the shape
of a person neither man nor woman whose mouth was sewn
shut. They were led into a large empty room. Platters of food
and jugs of water had been left on the floor. The mage gestured
toward the food.

"Eat and rest. Your people will be cared for until you return
to them." Then the door was pulled shut and the humans were
left alone. Traven ignored the food. He walked over to Jenus.

"Jenus?" he asked in a hushed voice, as if fearing being
overheard. "The others are wondering what the plan is and why
you're waiting so long to get us out?"

"Waiting so long . . . ," Jenus answered, confused. Did his
men really think he could save them from this hopeless situation? *Actually, it was hopeless when they first took us; now that
we're in their capital we've reached a whole new level of shit.*

"I've told them you're waiting to learn more about the four-
arms so we can report back to King Ansyl. . . . But when, sir?
We've watched you walking next to that savage mage day after
day, not giving an inch. Refusing to answer any of his questions, refusing to ask for help. But please, Jenus, we're not as
strong as you."

Jenus felt like a fraud. They had taken his fugue as stubborn resistance. He fought with himself for a moment, trying to decide whether or not to tell Traven the truth. But no. He couldn't bring himself to extinguish this last spark of hope in his friend. "Be strong, Traven. We can't give in. Not now, not ever. We've seen things we thought only existed in storybooks. We are the best Sacral has to offer and we *will* be up to the task. Just tell the others to be strong and follow my lead. I'll move as soon as I can."

"Thank you, sir. I'll tell the others."

The mix of fear and genuine gratitude in Traven's voice was as disturbing as anything to Jenus. Even Traven, one of his closest friends, had no idea what or who Jenus really was. *He even called me sir in a private conversation.*

A few hours later, the Gling'Ar returned for the prisoners. Their hands were not bound this time. Jenus found it inexplicably insulting that they should consider the threat posed by Sacral's Warchosen and mages so minimal that they made no effort at all to limit their movements. They walked deeper into the strange temple and were shown to what must be a throne room. The room took the carving motif further. Every wall, every pillar, even the three empty thrones that stood at the far side of the room were shaped like the naked bodies of many different races, males and females both, like statues twisted together into the desired shapes, each bearing the same featureless oval mask that totally obscured their faces. The wall behind the thrones was a roiling mass of more of the same statues, each one with a hand outstretched, as if in desperate plea, toward the central throne.

The Gling'Ar dropped to their knees, except for the mage, who bowed deeply. The Sacral prisoners stood in confusion as two people walked into the room from a side door and took their places on the thrones. The first was, hardly surprising, a

Gling'Ar. He wore the heaviest suit of blackened metal armor Jenus had ever seen. If any proof of the Gling'Ar's strength was needed, the simple fact of being able to walk in such heavy plate was ample proof. He carried an axe in two of his hands that was large even by Gling'Ar standards. Its reddish-hued blade hurt Jenus's eyes to look at, and he was forced to turn away.

The second man who came in was human. He wore a long dark-gray robe, and his skin was so pale he almost looked like a skeleton in the depths of his hood, but there was no doubt he was human. Jenus felt a sliver of hope return at the sight of him. The strange man took his place on the central throne and Jenus was sure he was looking at the ruler of the underground realm. *And he's not a Gling'Ar!*

The third throne remained empty. The mage turned to the humans and hissed. "Bow if you value your lives. Bow before the Dead King and Warchief Sonum!"

The Dead King?! Fear and confusion filled Jenus. The man in front of him was a children's story brought to life. *It can't be.* The king threw back his head and laughed at the humans' reactions.

"Now, now, Masul, you know I don't care about the formalities—I never have. Stand, all of you, please." He looked over the humans and his eyes latched onto Jenus.

"So who is it that leads an army to attack my people unprovoked?" The Dead King's voice had lost its warmth, its humanity. It was as cold as a grave, and hearing it, part of Jenus started to believe. He swallowed hard, not fully trusting his voice.

"I am Jenus Chenton. I lead the people of Sacral."

The Dead King's tone was accusatory. "You have come far from your home, human. You have come far to make war on innocent people. The Gling'Ar have done nothing but defend themselves against the constant encroachments of the Abolians and you would give them aid? You would kill in the name of those bloodthirsty fools and that traitorous White Bitch you serve? *Champion?*"

Jenus clenched his jaw. Pride and anger won out over fear, at least for now. "My people do not kill the innocent. We were too trusting of the emissaries sent to us and we were misled. The Abolians saw us as an easy way to ensure their city was not attacked for a time, and to do so without wasting a single man of their own. And to answer your question, no, I am no longer champion of the White Mother. I have been cast out of the temple's service. Though that does not end my responsibility to my people here."

The Dead King stared at him for a moment, then an aura of powerful magic enveloped him. "I hadn't expected her champion to be such an impious son of a bitch. But I guess it's fitting, since I don't think she ever believed in anything but herself," the king said, as if to himself. "I like you more already, *Champion.*" He stood up and started to pace back and forth in front of the thrones. "Your people really are innocent and overly trusting, Jenus. You were misled and not only by the Abolians who are even now laying siege to Sacral, but by the twisted whore you thought to serve."

Sacral under attack? How could I not have seen it before? We sent away a full third of the army and even the Lightbringer!

Jenus dropped to one knee. "Your Majesty, if what you say is true, then we have a common enemy. Please allow us to return to Sacral and try to save our homeland."

"You still aren't thinking clearly, human. It would take you months to get back to Sacral, and by then the issue will have been decided long since. For all my vaunted power, I was never able to master Ansyl's trick of bending space. . . . In any case, you are right when you say we have a common enemy, but the Abolians are not it. They are irritating, I admit, but their obsession with expansion gives all the other kingdoms of the North pause when they think about conquest. None dare weaken themselves too much with the Abolians around. They've been trying to make gains against the Gling'Ar for years, but they know every soldier they send out into the woods doesn't come back. They just fed you some story to get you to rush out here to their rescue and destroy a good portion of Sacral's army without losing a single man of their own. A weak ploy, I must say, and one that shouldn't have worked had another not been using the Abolians and their predictable behavior for their own purposes." He paced back and forth in silence, then turned back to look at Jenus. "No, human, you haven't been listening. Your enemy is your very own goddess."

Jenus was so tense he thought it a wonder his shoulders didn't split.

"I know you're dying to run off and help, young warrior, even if it means months of walking. But trust me when I say there is nothing you can do. The enemy you face is hiding among your own people. Possibly even some of the survivors we brought here today, though we will fix that soon enough."

"You will not lay a hand on any of my people!" Jenus shouted, surging toward the Dead King with his fists raised. He didn't get far. He had barely made a step when he was brought up short by a huge hand closing around his throat and lifting him off the ground. The armored Gling'Ar had acted so quickly Jenus hadn't even seen him move. *He's a Chosen! A Gling'Ar Chosen!* Jenus thought in despair as he fought to draw breath. He had barely managed fighting against regular Gling'Ar warriors, even when wielding the Lightbringer. *This warchief is more terrifying than any child's story.*

"It's all right, Sonum. You can put him down. Jenus is no threat to us."

The warchief looked at the Dead King and nodded before dropping Jenus in a heap on the floor. He did not return to his seat, though; he stood over Jenus with his axe at the ready.

"Jenus, you are in no position to make any threats. This is my city, and I have welcomed you here as an alternative to killing all of you—a choice I can reverse at any time. But don't think I'm not sympathetic to your situation. As you can see by the vacant seat here, one of my colleagues is away. Away in Sacral to be precise. I sent Rahz and his Crows to take care of our mutual problem. He will cut out the heart of the perverse religion you Sacral sheep have followed for so long, and if I'm not mistaken, he will also help with your Abolian problem. Rahz has a soft heart deep down, you see, and I'm sure he won't be able to pass up the chance to help those in need. Or he won't be able to pass up the chance to test himself against the Abolians and show off a little." He waved his hand. "Either way, the result should work to Sacral's advantage."

The Dead King closed his eyes for a moment. "From what I've been able to see, your countrymen have acquitted themselves admirably so far. Your king did not survive the first day of fighting. Not that I could have let him live, you understand. He was as much under the influence of the Bitch as any of the priests, though he may not have known it himself. Still, he died bravely giving every last sliver of his strength to hold off the attackers. I had expected Rahz to take care of him, but that happily proved to be unnecessary. I have yet to decide if I'm going to get involved further. I built Sacral, after all." He stopped and looked at Jenus for a moment before continuing. "Yes, that much of your legends is true. It is my magic that keeps the water rising from the depths in that desolate place, my magic that hardened the stone of the houses and walls so that they stand as if new after all these centuries. The valley you call home was every bit as barren as the rest of the Wastes before I took up residence there. Retaking Sacral is something I've thought about a lot over the centuries, but now that the time is here, I find myself unsure. Revealing myself to the world would create a whole host of new complications for my friends and me. I also find myself enjoying living in relative anonymity underground. There are those who suspect I'm still around, of course, but to give them proof? And as much as I wouldn't want to see Sacral fall into Abolian hands, I'm not sure I want to support the decedents of the very people who took it from me in the first place."

The Dead King looked around at the prisoners from Sacral. "The other problem we have is that the existence of this city and the true nature of the Gling'Ar tribes are very closely guarded secrets. Secrets that many thousands of lives depend upon." Jenus opened his mouth to speak, but a raised hand by the Dead King forestalled him. "I might be inclined to trust the word of an honorable man such as yourself, Jenus. But I simply cannot extend that trust to several thousand unknown individuals. The fact that all of you were sworn to uphold and defend my greatest enemy just reinforces that argument."

"So we are prisoners?" growled Jenus.

"Think of yourselves as involuntary guests. You will not be locked up, but you will not be permitted to bear arms or to pass beyond the city limits. You will all be provided with houses. We have space in abundance in Ischia. If your people have a craft other than that of war, they will be welcome to practice it. The mages who accompany you will have their talents shackled but will not be treated any differently than the others."

Jenus tried to protest again, knowing full well how devastating it was for mages to be parted from their natural ability.

"I am sorry, Jenus. I learned my lesson a thousand years ago when I was betrayed by the very goddess who now claims the first city I built. As Rahz would say—never trust the living."

"But you'll leave us free to wander the streets?"

The Dead King nodded. "I cannot trust you all to keep quiet about what you have seen, but I don't hold any ill will toward you. Nor is having you in my city the danger you perceive. Believe me when I say you cannot hope to harm us here. My guards do not sleep or tire, my own Chosen are far beyond you, though you do have a fair measure of potential. Nor, as I said, will any of you be permitted to carry weapons. Your sword will also be taken."

"The Lightbringer was entrusted to me by my king!"

"Lightbringer? Hah! As good a name as any it has borne over the ages." He waved away Jenus's protest. "The sword was never your king's to give away, or the Bitch's, either, for that matter."

Jenus gritted his teeth to keep his temper under control. There was little doubt that the Dead King was keeping a lot of the details to himself, but his words rang true. Jenus had already realized that his own abilities were undiminished though his goddess's influence had been severed days earlier. The priests had all found themselves powerless in the end, their link to the goddess cut off by Gling'Ar magics. But Jenus . . . Jenus was unchanged. He had always been a reluctant champion, despite the priesthood's insistence that he should be grateful. The only explanation was that his abilities had always been his own, not the gift of some motherly deity. He had been chosen to serve her not as a reward or because of some vague destiny, but because he offered an opportunity for the ancient woman to create a powerful champion without expending any of her own strength. It was what he would expect of someone who would pull herself to godhood over the corpses of her companions. The fact that some of those corpses still walked around changed little.

Before he knew it, Jenus and his surviving officers were led to an empty street not far from the temple/palace and released. Their bonds were simply cut and the Gling'Ar waved toward the large houses lining the street. "Choose your new homes, humans." Then they walked off without another word.

A head appeared at an upstairs window, and a Sacral soldier cried out in greeting. Men and women Jenus recognized streamed out of houses and rushed to welcome him and the officers. Any semblance of military order was gone. While some of these people were soldiers, far more were drovers, craftsmen, cooks, and laborers. They were scared and confused, and not one of them was prepared to answer Jenus's questions before they got some answers themselves. It took time before everyone was settled down and Jenus was able to make sense of what he was being told. While he and the officers were meeting the Dead King, the rest of the Sacral army had been marched to this empty section of the city and settled into homes. Shortly thereafter, iron-masked slaves marched through the street stacking food and supplies at the door of each occupied home.

They really mean to keep us here, Jenus thought numbly. Home felt so very far away. He was helpless in front of the Dead King and his men. He shook his head—there was no choice. He rounded up his officers and tried to ensure some sort of order was maintained and that all his people were settled and comfortable.

"We're going to be here for a while. The Dead King and the Gling'Ar don't mean us harm, but they aren't going to let us go either." There were cries at those words that were quickly hushed by others eager to hear the rest. "In the meantime, we are guests—not prisoners. We have been promised accommodation and supplies, which I am glad to see have already been given. We have been offered the chance to work our crafts and take part in the markets of the city. In exchange, we have been asked not to bear arms or disturb the peace of Ischia."

He was interrupted by more grumbling, from the soldiers this time. "The warriors among us will continue to train and prepare for the day we are to leave and return home. I will lead the training myself each day. For the rest of you—make the most of your time here. I beg you all to abide by the Dead King's rules for as long as we reside here."

"But how long are we going to be here?" came a cry. "My husband and my children are back in Sacral!" came another.

Jenus held up his hands and silence gradually returned. "I am no happier than the rest of you. My place is in Sacral just as much as yours is. But we are alive. And we are being given the opportunity to prove ourselves to those we wronged. Yes, we did wrong them! Though we didn't know it at the time. In the meantime, we are being given more freedom than I ever could have hoped for. So again I ask—please make the best of your time here."

The crowd slowly dispersed until Jenus was left alone with Traven. "You really think the Dead King will let us go?"

"I do, my friend. I have to believe it. That belief is the only thing keeping me standing right now."

Though never bright, the huge cave that housed Ischia gradually grew darker as hours passed. Jenus guessed that night must be falling in the world outside and the cave's magical lighting must be mirroring it. *At least there's some way of keeping track down here.* He settled into the surprisingly large and comfortable home that he'd chosen for himself. The solitude and quiet were welcome. Many of his countrymen had decided to share homes, despite the abundance of space available to them. They needed the support and proximity of their friends. But Jenus couldn't wait to get away from them and their hopeful looks.

Jenus rose early the next morning, or at least he guessed it was early. The pale light of the city was only just starting to rise to the levels he'd first seen the day before. *Now to find somewhere to train my men and keep them from thinking too much about where they are.* He opened his door and saw a procession of the iron-masked slaves walking through the street, placing heaving bundles of foodstuffs on the ground outside each home. They moved in eerie silence, never complaining, never speaking with one another. And this despite the fact that no guards accompanied them.

A bundle was placed next to his own door as the gray-robed men and women filed by pulling large carts. Jenus nodded his thanks but got no response. He reached down to pick up the bundle and was surprised by how heavy it was. Nearly the whole bale was filled with grains and dried beans. *And they are offloading them as if they were nothing. Not a groan, not a complaint, not one of them out of breath dragging carts full of such bales. . . . Not one out of breath . . . or even breathing,* he realized in shock. Menial labor in Ischia wasn't done by slaves but by the dead. Jenus shuddered. This was another of the terrible evils the priesthood had taught them about for his entire life. Necromancy, and it was placed in the service of everyone in this city—of all things delivering food to its living inhabitants.

Jenus shook himself. *I'm not doing any good just standing here, and if I know my soldiers, they'll need to be kept busy.* He found a clear space halfway down the street that had been turned over to the refugees, a nice wide square of well-cobbled stone with only a well breaking its clean emptiness. *Yes, this will do.* He returned to his temporary home and brought back an empty barrel. He pulled the iron bands off and split the staves apart. *And so I return to childhood. A grown soldier swinging around a barrel stave like I did as a boy, dreaming it was a sword. I wonder if the others will come.* He started going through training sequences, the movements as familiar to him as breathing.

It wasn't long before his countrymen started to rise and step out of their homes. Traven was the first to join him. His old friend walked up and picked up a stave from the pile before falling into step with Jenus. One after another, the other soldiers joined them. Many of the noncombatants crowded around to watch for a time as hundreds of their countrymen silently moved through sequences of moves. There was no sound but the message was being screamed as loudly as the prisoners could manage it—*We are together and we will not give up.*

***

That morning, as she lay down to sleep, Zuly felt herself fall. Her mind and Nial's fell far beyond the normal realms of sleep. They fell into a deep, perfect darkness. . . . And something was waiting for them there. They couldn't see anything, but they could feel it. Something vast and hungry had pulled them down to this place, and now it searched for them in the blackness. They could feel its immense hunger like the breath of a great beast. They woke screaming. Even Zuly had been deeply affected by the nightmare.

"What was that, Zuly?" Nial asked, half remembering the nightmares they had had when they were poisoned and feverish.

"I don't know, my sweet Nial. Just a dream." She was trying to sound unconcerned, but Nial could sense the worry in her. "Just a bad dream. Nothing to worry about. . . ."

But the dream returned the following night, and again the night after that. Each time the thing that hunted them in the dark seemed closer—more terrible in its fury and power. Nial asked Skeg about the dreams when they got to his shop but he seemed unsurprised.

"You girls have been through so much these past months. You've seen some of the worst things that humans can do to one another. Let's continue with your studies and try to take your minds off the bad dreams. Shade has left you another gift." He held up a thick leather-bound tome. "I found this book on the counter when I came down to the shop today."

Interested despite herself, Nial looked up. "Is it something good?"

Skeg smiled. "The details are a little beyond me, but this is a tome of pattern carving."

"What's that, Uncle?" Nial asked.

"Kind of what you did with the obsidian globes."

"You mean we can do other things that way?"

Skeg was once again at a loss for words. It was so hard to believe that the girls' perfect mastery over the complex carving and enchanting process had been nothing more than the imitation of something Zuly had witnessed. "All kinds of things are possible with this skill," he said. "Making a simple pattern object will help it to weave energy for you so you only need to focus your power through it to get the same effect each time. That's how I do most of my magic, I use pattern items that others have made. Other pattern objects can be used to store energy. They're usually called Sources. Greater pattern items have their own power and continually produce their effect. I'm sure you've heard stories about magic swords and such. They are extremely hard to make and the materials are very expensive. But it's a very useful skill for a mage with the knack." Skeg looked down at his hands. "I even used pattern items and spell anchors I traded for to do my little imp-eating ritual."

Nial's eyes lit up. "Maybe we can make some for you then."

"That would be wonderful, girls. But don't waste too much time on me. You have another tough target to take care of before we're rid of Shade."

The girls took the book from him and ran off to their usual spot in the ward circle to read.

Days passed, but as interesting as the new book was, the girls' nightmares continued to get worse. They were starting to feel the strain. They drew more and more power from the souls they had captured, trying to avoid sleep as much as possible. The timing couldn't have been any worse. They had heard Shade's target would be taking ship to Noros soon, which would put him beyond their reach for months.

That night, when the girls closed their eyes, *it* was waiting for them. Zuly's mind was pulled down into the blackness and Nial's went with it. This time was different. This time was much, much worse. The thing that stalked them in the darkness had caught them at last. It clutched Zuly's mind and touched her with its thoughts. It was too much, too vast, too dark to comprehend. The brush of its consciousness threatened to shatter their sanity. Foreign knowledge swirled into her thoughts. And all the while, she was aware of its hunger. Tightly controlled, but infinite in its depth. A hunger that wanted to consume her utterly. They woke screaming and did not stop until their throat was raw.

The girls dressed quickly and set out for Skeg's shop. It was barely midmorning. They had only slept a couple hours, but they couldn't risk lying down again. They knew the thing waited for them. It was Zuly who finally figured out what it was. The echoing pain the thing had subjected them to held a message—a message in the tongue of the Karethin demons. They ran as fast as they could, desperate to speak with Skeg. He woke when they arrived. His eyes were red and swollen from lack of sleep.

"Girls, you just barely left—" He stopped abruptly when he noticed the look on Nial's face, then asked, "What's wrong?"

"The dreams won't go away, Uncle Skeg. We need to stay awake all the time now. . . . We can't let him touch our mind again." Tears were welling up in her eyes. "H-h-he wants Zuly to go back home," Nial stammered. Her lower lip trembled.

"Who? Home?" Skeg asked.

"The demon lord Amon Kareth," Nial answered as their tears started to fall.

Skeg watched her cry in silence for a time, desperately trying to think of something, anything, to do to help. "I don't know what old Amon wants you girls for, but do you think you could reason with him? Is there any reasoning with a thing like that? Could you offer him souls? I really don't know the first thing about demon lords but they sound a lot like gods, just a little nastier than most."

"You may have a point, Mister Skeg. Souls are all the lord ever really wants. But to give them to him, I'd still have to return, and Nial with me."

Skeg was chilled. He couldn't begin to imagine the realities of a demon world, and for a mortal girl to set foot on one . . .

"We'll have to think of something. For now, why don't you go sit in the ward circle? The mages who carved it for me said it would keep out an angry god. We'll have to see if it will hold out a demon lord." The girls sat down in the circle. Despite their fear and desperation, exhaustion pulled them down into a deep sleep. Skeg hesitated to wake them up. He watched for a time, but when their sleep seemed untroubled, he left them to get some much needed rest and went out to his shop to pore through a few relevant tomes and try to think of a solution to their new problem. *As if we needed another one!* Skeg went up to his room and brought back a stack of blankets. He'd make the girls as comfortable as he could. Until they found a solution, the girls would stay with him. Besides, Nial's father would probably be relieved she was gone. As Skeg moved about the room he noticed the wards around the circle were glowing faintly, but getting brighter. He froze, his nerves on edge. Something was trying to get in, and it was very, very strong. He thought about waking the girls up. But then the glow of the wards slowly dimmed again and went out. Skeg breathed a sigh of relief.

So the wards held. . . . For today at least.

The girls slept through the day and well into the night. Skeg was pacing with impatience while he waited. He hadn't slept a wink himself. The worry that the demon lord would return kept him close to Nial and Zuly the whole time. When they finally woke up, he rushed to their side.

"You're finally awake! I hope you feel better, because I don't think we have a lot of time."

The girls sat up looking a little guilty. "Thank you for letting us sleep here, Uncle Skeg." Nial looked at him quizzically. "You look terrible."

"That's because I had to watch the wards all day while Amon Kareth tried to batter his way through them. I can't say how lucky we are he's in a whole different realm. The power he's using . . ." His voice trailed off when he saw Nial's face blanch.

"You are safe for now. You can sleep here from now on, and I'll watch and wake you up if the wards get too hot."

Zuly looked at him. "But we cannot continue this way for-ever. We will have to find a way to go back."

Skeg nodded glumly. "Only if we can't find another way. I've sent out messages to some of my contacts. I'll try to find someone who can build stronger wards, or . . . or something," he said, frustrated. Nial walked into the shop.

"We'll help look. There might be something in one of your books."

"That might be true, but I think our best bet would be to find a book of Sorenak lore," Skeg said, following her out of the back room. "A few thousand years ago, some fool who called himself an emperor of a little island on the South Sea got his whole little empire eaten by demons. The Sorenak demonolo-gists were the ruling caste. Gates and demon wards have been used often enough before. But this was a whole empire devoted to demonology. If you can call a little island with a handful of cities on it an empire. The power-crazed idiots even used demons as familiars. Made them powerful, there's no doubt about that. But every time one of their mages died, its famil-iar would eat their soul and go insane. Wasn't long before the place tore itself apart, and that was the end of Sorenak." Nial was looking tired and resigned.

"My point is, girls," he said, "that I learned about all that at the Arcanum. Some of the Sorenak tomes must have survived. If anyone had the ability to stop an angry demon lord, it was them."

"But, Uncle Skeg, we've seen demons moving around the city before. The knowledge can't be that rare."

"You saw some very minor demons under Arcanum con-trol. So tightly controlled that the summoners probably have to petition the Closed Council every time they want to assign the creature a new task. The Arcanum mages don't encourage any of their students to practice demonology. They tolerate small uses because of its obvious advantages, but playing with wards that would affect a greater demon is a far cry from summoning an imp."

Skeg looked at his nieces with concern. "This won't be a quick process, girls. If I ask questions too directly, the Night Guard will be at my shop before I can blow out a candle. They give me some leeway, but the weaves we're looking for are way past what they'd turn a blind eye to. Even if we get what we're looking for, we'll have to figure out how to do it ourselves. Gunnar Danekor will have to wait." The girls agreed glumly.

"Now, you go ahead and read through the books in the shop. I need to get a few hours of sleep myself or I won't be able to stay awake when you need to sleep in the morning. Just wake me if any customers come in."

The girls looked through book after book with little luck. They stopped now and then to help the odd customer who wandered into the shop. Enough of Skeg's regulars had caught a glimpse of Nial in the past that no one questioned where Skeg had gone to. When dawn was finally near, Zuly and Nial walked back to the ward circle and made themselves comfortable.

"What are we here for, Zuly? We can't sleep yet. We need to wait for Uncle Skeg to come down."

"We need to make ourselves stronger before Amon gets his hands on us, Nial. We need to feed, deeply."

"But I thought you said that feeding would make us go crazy?"

"Only if we consume the souls completely. But we can drink more than we have been."

She started to siphon power from the souls they had captured. It was sweet beyond description, pleasure beyond reason. The very memory of their hunger was swept away like a leaf in the wind. Nial trembled and gasped with pleasure. The feeling went on and on until she could barely remember a time before it. Then slowly, it started to ebb.

"More! I want more!" Nial screamed. Zuly was almost as lost in the moment as Nial, but the memory of their night-mares kept her focused.

"We can't. If we do, we will consume the souls themselves. Better to wait and feed again tomorrow." Reluctantly, Nial agreed. They slowly became aware of their surroundings again.

Skeg came into the back room to see what the shouting had been about. He flushed and looked away as soon as he saw them. "I'm . . . I'm sorry, girls. I'll be . . . right back. I need to find you something to wear."

Nial looked after him in confusion. The euphoria slowly fading, she looked down at herself and gasped. Feeding so deeply had changed her. She jumped to her feet and tottered unsteadily. She was taller than before, her limbs longer, her body less childlike. Her little dress no longer covered her body properly. Only then did she understand Skeg's discomfort. She blushed furiously and tried to cover herself as best she could while she waited for him to return.

CHAPTER 14

The Korant ant thrashed around as Carver's magic peeled the chitin off its body. There was a kind of poetry to using the Tolrahkali's insect servants to build their suits of armor. The realization that the ants were a perfect source of raw materials had struck Carver the moment he had walked back into his rooms and looked at his captive ant. The Korants had impressive strength and endurance. Their musculature was far more efficacious than standard mammalian muscles. Their outer chitin was also surprisingly strong and light. Though the final form still eluded him, Carver had a vision of chitin-armored Tolrahkali soldiers who would be stronger and faster than normal humanoids. He immersed the plates of chitin and loose strands of muscle in a vat of alchemical fluids he had prepared. With time and a little creative use of his magic, he would mold the fragments into a shape that could fit over a person's body. The question remained of how to keep the armor alive once it was taken out of the nutritive solution.

Symbiosis in nature usually involves one of the organisms feeding the other. . . . No reason to change something that works.

The soldiers themselves would have to feed the new armor they would be wearing. Carver briefly considered adding in a digestive pouch that the soldiers would need to fill with food of some sort, before dismissing the idea. Nutrients would need to be transferred directly by blood. For the armor's muscle structure to augment and work with the wearer's own, the armor would need to be linked directly to the wearer's nervous system as well. Unsure how the Drokga would react to such an invasive solution, Carver shrugged. The avenue of experimentation was worth pursuing either way. He would need to make a very basic armor plate with a few functioning muscles and try to link it to a slave. The formation of a full suit would wait until he had worked out the details.

The first four attempts to bind chitin breastplates to slaves ended in failure. The bonding process worked quickly, and the test subjects were able to control the extra muscle he had provided, but in only a matter of days, the slaves weakened and died. *I expected the trauma of the binding to be a problem, but all of them live long enough for that not to be an issue. . . .* All four slaves had followed the same progression—successful bonding and early signs of increased strength and faster recovery, black spots then developed on their hands and feet within a couple of days, followed by debilitating pain and bleeding from various orifices, and finally death.

Carver looked at his slave assistant, Roga, in frustration. The living suits of armor he had developed were genius itself, far more impressive than anything he had ever created before. The bonding to humans was a complex process. It required the armor to burrow tendrils into the host to link with its nervous system as well as to draw nutrients. The armor even left the reproductive faculties of the host unharmed since no magical fleshcarving was performed directly on the host. It was frustrating to say the least, and time was fast running out. He'd done the impossible and developed his first prototype in a matter of days, and yet here he was almost two weeks later without a living host to show for his efforts.

"If only I were free to change the hosts' bodies to accept the new additions instead of rejecting them," Carver said.

"Or change the armor so the host bodies wouldn't know it wasn't part of them," Roga said.

Carver looked around, startled. "What did you say?"

"Nothing, Master!" his assistant pleaded. "I only meant to agree with you."

Carver waved his whining aside, and Roga's mouth snapped shut. "You may not have intended it as such, but you have just handed me the solution to the problem. We will mix the intended host's essence with the armor they will receive. It will take longer to grow each suit and the hosts will need to be chosen before the work begins . . . but . . . an elegant solution. You have served me well this day, Roga."

Roga bowed deeply, unsure how to respond to the unexpected compliment.

Carver had left the door to his rooms open, waiting for the Drokga to answer his invitation. Unsure when and if the tyrant would answer such a summons, Carver busied himself with his work. It was one day short of the deadline the Drokga had set him. If he was not pleased with the results, Carver would have no choice but to kill him and take his place, or at least replace him with a tame look-alike. Here, in his heavily warded rooms, he had the greatest chance of pulling off the coup without anyone else knowing about it.

The Drokga stormed into the room, his son Gruig on his heels.

"My lord Drokga," said Carver, bowing as low as he was able. "If you please, I have prepared a first demonstration of my newest creation. I dare say, I think you will be pleased."

"Get on with it, Carver, I have other matters to attend to."

Two slaves were chained to wooden posts in the center of the workshop. One wore a full set of Bialtan-made plate armor, the other wore an evil-looking suit of deep-russet chitin. Four soldiers with light crossbows stood in front of the two.

"Proceed," said Carver.

Crossbows bucked and two bolts found each target. One glanced off the Bialtan armor, the second found a weak point in the shoulder joint and punched deeply into his flesh. The slave screamed in pain. Both bolts aimed at the chitin armor punched into the slave's chest. He grunted with the impact but did not otherwise react.

The Drokga looked at Carver with an air of impatience. "Well? Get to the point!"

Carver nodded to the soldiers. They ran forward and wrenched the bolts out of the slaves. Both were untied and dragged over to stand in front of the Drokga. The slave wearing the Bialtan plate left a trail of blood on the ground and collapsed before he reached the monarch. Though pale, the second slave walked on his own, looking nervous, but no more so than most slaves did in the presence of the tyrant. The holes in the armor were already closing over. Though the bolts that had been pulled out of him were stained red, the slave had not lost a significant amount of blood.

"Intriguing, Carver," the Drokga said. "Does he feel pain?"

"He does, Your Majesty. That is, he is aware of it, but he is not slowed by it. The wounds themselves are not as deep as that suffered by the other slave. The carapace is compensating, using its own muscle structures to supplement the slave's torn ones. It will also speed up the healing. There should be little trace of the wounds within a few days. Within a week he will have only the barest of scars. Were I to give him full control over the carapace, his strength and speed would be significantly improved as well."

"And the price he pays for this?"

This man is too smart by half. "The carapace cannot be removed, ever. Or the host will die. Only the helm is removable but cannot be left off for too long lest it wither. It depends on its link with the carapace for nourishment. The host also requires more than twice the usual amount of food for a man his size, three times more when recovering from a wound. His reproductive capabilities are not impaired, however, as you requested."

"How long does it take to construct one of these things?"

"With my current workspace and staff working on the project, I can produce as many as two dozen each week, though the first dozen will likely take longer. I would also need to take blood from each soldier. A carapace needs to be grown and fused with the living matter of its host for the bonding to be successful. I am also working on a new type of chitin weapon to complement the carapace armor. I do not have a suitable demonstration prepared, unfortunately."

The Drokga nodded, considering. "You have not disappointed me, Carver. I wish to know how this creation of yours fares in real combat. Have this slave trained in weapon use for three days. He will face hardened gladiators with standard equipment. If he survives three rounds, he will be given his freedom and a place among my troops. And I will offer your carapaces to the greatest of my warriors."

Three rounds! Still, so long as he isn't facing a champion it should be possible. I may have to add on one of the weapons I've been working on as well. . . . But, no, he said standard weapons. . . . Damn him!

"What is your name, slave?" Carver asked the test subject after the Drokga had left.

"Sigian, my lord Carver."

"You understand the opportunity the Drokga is offering you?" The man swallowed hard.

"I do, Lord Carver, but there is little point. I know nothing of fighting."

"You will learn, Sigian. You will learn. I will give you full control over the carapace armor. You will need some time to adjust. Then tomorrow you will start your training at dawn. You will not disappoint me, understood?" The man was shaking with fear. During his time in the workshop, he'd seen what Carver did to those who displeased him. The Drokga himself didn't terrify him half so much.

**

Sigian rolled around in the dark, grunts and groans escaping from his ragged throat as he struggled to endure the full bonding with the carapace armor. When Carver had put the shell on him, it had been a harrowing experience that dragged on for a week. He thought that had hurt, but the carapace digging into every part of his body to bond with his nerves in a single night made the kiss of a whip as insignificant as a scratch. There were times he didn't think he would make it . . . but that promise the Drokga made not only of freedom but of a place among his soldiers! He clung to it like a drowning man to a scrap of floating driftwood. Clung to it and survived.

When morning came, Sigian hadn't slept. His lips were cracked and his throat raw from screaming. He hesitated a moment before pulling himself to his feet . . . and did so with ease. He stood and marveled at the simple feeling of moving. Had lifting his arm been an effort before? It felt like it had been compared to how he felt now. He looked around the room and noticed scraps of food and broken plates. The simple furnishings the room had contained had been crushed to pieces. A vague recollection of eating returned to him, but he couldn't quite hold on to it. *It doesn't matter anyway. This thing they put on me really works! I've never felt so good in my life! Strong, confident... like a warrior!* He punched the wall of his cell with a satisfying crunch. The chitin gauntlet left a deep indentation in the plaster.

The gate of his cell opened and Carver's assistant, Roga, walked in with an unfamiliar Tolrahkali warrior, a woman who carried two practice swords but also wore a heavy-looking sword strapped to her back.

"Sigian, this is Alyre Manek. She is one of the greatest Warchosen Tolrahk Esal has ever seen and would not normally waste time on a slave. Lord Gruig Berrahd Tolrahk himself has asked her to train you. Be sure not to disappoint her or Lord Carver."

Alyre gestured to the gate with her chin and walked out without a word. Sigian rushed to follow her.

Alyre was becoming increasingly frustrated by him. He could tell. For all that the carapace armor made him stronger and faster, Sigian was still a twenty-seven-year-old man who had never held a blade in his life. After the first day, Alyre hadn't bothered with the practice swords. They now used steel—sharp steel—and she'd given him a heavy wooden shield to hide behind. He'd taken half a hundred minor hits from Alyre, and only a few had pierced deeply enough to touch him through the chitin. *But if she keeps hacking up my armor, won't it stop working? What if it gives out while I'm in the arena?*

He just couldn't manage to wield the blade properly. At least half his swings and parries used the flat of the blade. He'd even snapped one sword off at the hilt ineptly trying to block a particularly savage attack.

Eventually she brought him a large club. The thing was so massive he doubted he'd even have been able to lift it off the ground one-handed before being given the armor. From there the training went somewhat better. Alyre was still thrashing him soundly, but at least the more straightforward combat style of the club meant he felt like less of a fool trying to swing his own weapon around.

Sigian ate like a king before and after each session with Alyre and slept the sleep of the totally exhausted as his carapace worked to heal itself from the damage she inflicted on it during each session. Sigian had awkwardly attempted to thank the laconic Warchosen for her training at the end of their last session, but true to form, she turned and left without a word. *I'm still a slave and unworthy of her attention. But that will soon change. Next time we meet, Alyre, I will be one of the Drokga's soldiers!* There was nothing romantic in his dream of acknowledgment. To one born a slave, being worthy of a nod of recognition from so lofty a figure was a far greater dream than that of any physical intimacy.

Morning saw him fed a huge breakfast and led out onto the sands.

***

Roga watched the slave move out onto the sands and take his mark with only minimal hesitation. The man had courage. Even professional fighters would never agree to more than one fight in a day. Three opponents and no magical healing was a death sentence for even the most talented; it was usually a fate reserved for criminals or escaped slaves. Though to be fair, *only* three rounds were never specified for them.

The arena master called for the first opponent to be brought out. Roga didn't bother listening to the details. A lean wiry slave fighter strutted out onto the sands. He was armed with a standard sword and shield in the Bialtan fashion. Not crowd-pleasers, but smart and effective.

The arena master called for the fight to begin and the two moved cautiously toward each other. Sigian blocked the man's first attack and swung his club in a horizontal arc. The man was sent tumbling from the force of the blow. Sigian pressed his advantage but was brought up short when his opponent rolled nimbly to his feet and lunged forward with a two-handed grip on his blade. The sword pierced Sigian's stomach, tearing its way through the chitin and into his flesh beneath. The fighter looked up at Sigian with a dark grin. Until he noticed that Sigian wasn't falling. Then the club collided with the slave's skull with a wet crunch and he collapsed to the sands. Not taking any chances, Sigian hit the man a few more times, splattering himself liberally in his blood.

The crowd roared and Roga gritted his teeth. *The fool hasn't learned much. He has already taken a deep wound in his first moments on the sands. . . .*

The second duel was also short and brutal. It ended with the unnamed man's brains soaking into the sands and with a blade protruding from Sigian's back. The crowd was ecstatic.

The arena master's voice rose above the crowd's cheers again. "A slave who doesn't bleed but bathes in the blood of his enemies!" The master looked around and paused. "Shall we see if Sigian the Bloodless can handle another opponent? This time another fighter who has earned himself a name on the sands—Liat! The Butcher of Urom Anata!"

Earning a name in the arena was no mean feat. A slave who managed had to be exceptional enough to earn one, and live long enough for anyone to remember it. The fact that Sigian had earned such an accolade after only two battles spoke volumes to his crowd appeal. . . . *But the first two fights count for nothing,* Roga reminded himself. He knew more about the carapace armor than any save Carver himself and it could not compensate for such wounds indefinitely. Sigian would need extensive rest and copious amounts of food if he was to live to see another sunrise . . . and he had yet to face his toughest opponent. Had the approval of the Drokga not hinged on this single battle, Roga—and no doubt Carver—would have viewed the test a great success. *And yet it will all be for nothing if the fool doesn't manage to pull himself together and keep from getting himself killed.*

Sigian had been told that he would only be facing normal, nonaugmented pit fighters. No Warchosen, no Godchosen, no runes or magic weapons . . . and yet there had to be something magical in the way Liat moved and fought. Sigian had an unfair advantage in his carapace—he was faster and stronger than any normal man had a right to be—but not one of his attacks came close to landing. The Butcher of Urom Anata deftly dodged each and every attack before slashing Sigian with one of his twin meat cleavers. None of the blows came even close to penetrating the thick armor, but the damage was starting to add up, with flakes and slivers of chitin flying off in every direction. The fight drew on and on, Sigian flailing and his armor becoming further and further mauled. *He's going to peel my carapace off me piece by piece and then cut me to shreds.* Sigian was near panic. As fear overwhelmed him, he forgot Alyre's lessons and stopped paying attention to his footing. His foot came down in a wet patch left by one of his previous opponents, and all of a sudden he was slipping. He tried to catch his balance; his club fell from his clutching fingers. As he fell he felt an impact against the rim of his shield moments before he hit the ground. He lay in the sand for a second and then another, waiting for the killing blow to land. Nothing. Then the sound of jeers and booing from the crowd penetrated the fog in his mind. He pulled himself back to his feet and saw that Liat had collapsed to his knees in the sand. There was a large dent in the front of his helm where Sigian's shield had struck it. Blood leaked across Liat's face. The master shouted at arena attendants to get the wounded slave to a healer.

Hardly an elegant victory, thought Roga. *But Lord Carver will be pleased to hear of the outcome.* He rushed off to share the news with his master.

That's it! The third opponent is down! I'm free! And I didn't have to kill him! Sigian looked back up at the stands almost overcome with relief and saw Roga moving toward the exit.

The arena master looked to Roga for instructions, but finding him gone, he shrugged and announced, "And now Sigian the Bloodless will face a captive slave from the deep deserts!"

"No, that's not right! They said three rounds!" Sigian shouted.

But the gate opposite him slowly opened and an eager desert warrior with a tulwar and a dagger clutched in her hands ran out to face him.

"But they said three rounds!" Sigian glanced back toward the stands, but Roga was gone and with him, freedom.

***

Carver hobbled down the long winding hallways that led to the Drokga's throne room. It was always tempting at times like these when he was alone and frustrated by the hardships of his assumed form to cast aside the disguise and walk upright, but he never gave in to the temptation. For a disguise to work, it had to be perfect. Carver had to live his new form. Besides, it seemed to amuse the Drokga to force his crippled mage to limp back and forth across the palace. *At least I know it's for a good reason this time.* Roga had informed Carver before he left that the slave Sigian had indeed survived three rounds in the arena. Not only survived, but defeated all three of his opponents decisively. *Now that bastard Drokga will finally give me everything I need to work. . . .*

A shadow cut across the hall in front of him and pulled him out of his reverie. Carver cursed himself for his weakness. He didn't fear any potential assassins, but there was no sense in letting anyone know that. Nor would he want an assailant to escape after daring to lay a hand on him. Carver stopped, leaned heavily on his walking stick, and pushed his scraggly hair out of his face. *Unexpected.* The Drokga's mage killer stood a few paces away, leaning casually against the wall with his arms crossed. They looked at each other in silence for a moment, Carver squinting up at the tall assassin.

"To what do I owe this dubious pleasure, Nasaka? Has the Drokga tired of me already?"

"I am not here at my master's bidding." The man's voice was soft and smooth as silk, like a soft wind blowing through grass.

"Well, since you haven't tried to kill me yet, I imagine you aren't going to. So you have succeeded in doing something that happens too rarely these days—you have made me curious, mage killer."

Nasaka nodded. "I have seen your work these past months. I want to know what you can do for me."

Carver was caught off balance. He had expected contempt, perhaps veiled insults or threats from a competitor for the Drokga's favor. *But this . . . is as welcome as it is unexpected.* By all accounts Nasaka was more formidable even than Maran Vras. And to have a warrior as feared as the mage hunter as an ally in the Drokga's court would scare off many of those who saw him as a threat they could act against.

"You are welcome in my workshop, Nasaka. Come to me tonight. I don't expect my audience with the Drokga to last past sunset."

Nasaka gave another nod. "Until then, Carver." Then he reached out a window, pulled himself out, and was gone. Carver shook his head and resumed his painfully slow walk to the throne room. *I waste far too much of my time wandering back and forth in this damned building. I may have to devote some effort to creating something to carry me that won't shit on the floor.*

The Drokga made Carver wait longer than usual that day. He also had far more questions about small details and the workings of the carapace armor than before. *There's something else on his mind. Something he's not quite ready to spit out.*

"I am pleased by the work you have done with the armor for my warriors. Your mounts are also of some interest to me, though I want them able to breed as well. It would not do for my people to become less than they were because of the disappearance of a single mage."

"I thank my lord Drokga for the compliment, and for the concern for my well-being. I am ever your servant."

The Drokga sneered at him. "Drop the false servility, Carver. You and I both know it's nothing but an act." With obvious difficulty, he reined himself in. "I did not summon you here for you to scrape and bow for me, though making you do it does provide me with a sliver of amusement. I called you here to discuss a new project."

Carver's interest was piqued. "A new project, Lord? Of course. What is your wish?"

"I want you to make something for me. Me personally. I want to walk into battle beside my men and inspire fear in both them and the enemy."

"A larger version of the carapace armor, Lord?"

"Something like that possibly, but I want you to find a way to make it removable. I don't care how difficult it is. So don't give me your excuses as to why it won't work. Being locked away in a suit of chitin is fine for my warriors, but it is not acceptable for me!"

Carver reluctantly agreed and left to begin his work. The Drokga had a knack for pushing Carver in directions he wouldn't normally consider. His demands were selfish, but the tyrant's quick mind and vision never failed to spark new ideas. *A truly responsive carapace that was removable? Is that even remotely possible?* To avoid the brain, the carapace would need to respond to the movements of the host. Or possibly be controlled by less central nerves. Possibly the Drokga would consent to some small neural modifications and some new orifices for the links . . . concealed with scar tissue, of course; he had enough children so he might not be too concerned with his own reproductive faculties. *And Nasaka will stop killing and become a poet.*

Then an idea hit him. It just might be possible. But if he were to make that much of the carapace external, it would be much bulkier. The weight would then be a problem. *So maybe this suit should include larger muscle fibers. Hmmm. . . . It would be quite large. Possibly twice the size of a man. But why stop there? Impossible egos demand impossible constructs. I could make it colossal. The host temporarily transformed into a titan! But how to feed such a huge construct? There is no way an unaltered body could sustain it. . . . But maybe if I add in its own stomach. And at least one mouth! That will make it more fearsome and give it more weapons besides. Yes, oh yes, this could be quite good indeed.* The new project occupied Carver's thoughts almost completely while he made his slow way back to his rooms.

He found the door open. Power surged into him. A variety of spells to inflict death and pain sprang to his mind. *Someone has defeated my wards!* It was unthinkable. No mage in Tolrahk Esal was his match. None of them would have been able to crack his defenses without him knowing. Then a worse thought occurred to him. If his outer wards had been breached, it was possible that whoever had broken in had made it into his inner rooms. He pushed the door wide, his power coiled into a weave of devastating power ready to destroy the intruder.

Nasaka sat on a heavy-looking wood chair that he must have brought with him. His long legs were propped up on one of Carver's worktables. He looked up at Carver with irritated boredom.

"You're late, Carver. I'm not used to being kept waiting."

A quick look toward his inner rooms was enough for Carver to confirm that his inner wards had not been disturbed. His jaw unclenched a fraction. *Mage hunter indeed,* he thought, grudgingly impressed.

Nasaka saw his glance, and a slow smile touched his lips. "Don't worry, Carver. Whatever sick secrets you keep locked in there are safe from me. I only availed myself of your hospitality, minimal as it is, to pass the time while I waited." He lowered his feet to the ground and sat up straighter. "I have asked you to perform a service for me, Carver. I do not want to make us enemies."

"It would seem your reputation is well earned." It took great effort for Carver to keep his temper under control. He wanted desperately to torture the man into a broken husk to find out how he had managed to break in. But Nasaka was about to put himself willingly into Carver's hands. There would be time to slowly make some adjustments to the man's mind and find out what he wanted to know.

"Know, Carver, that there is nothing I would not do, nothing I would not risk, for power. I've seen what you can do, and I am willing to pay the price for it."

"I do not recall demanding payment."

"And yet we both know that anything you do for me will not be without cost. Once I put myself in your hands I will be practically defenseless. No doubt you can extract information from me or even bend me to your will in countless ways. The lesson of Maran Vras was not lost on me. I can posture and make threats, or promise revenge by my cadre of apprentices. . . . Such things are beneath us."

And yet you voice them anyway.

"I'm willing to hazard that my value to you as a willing subject and ally in court will outweigh your anger at me coming into your rooms uninvited."

"Just how willing are you then, Nasaka? You have seen only a small fraction of what I can do."

"Simply put, do with me what you will." He got to his feet, the motion strangely fluid. "My name is already feared across half the continent. My skills are without equal, and I have access to funds and mages who are only too happy to create whatever tools or enchanted weapons I might desire. My own apprentices whisper my name in fear to each other from their pallets in the dark of night. But it is not enough! I want archmages to quake in fear at the thought of me. I want the terror my name inspires to reverberate through the ages and never be forgotten!"

Carver watched him for a time through the veil of his own greasy hair.

"I believe we can work together then, Nasaka. If you do not fear risks or balk at consequences, I can indeed do many things to your flesh to make you more formidable. You understand, though, that the most basic price you will have to pay is the loss of your ability to sire children?"

Nasaka shrugged. "I have half a hundred already, some of them with enough promise to train as apprentices. I do not need more. I intend for my deeds to be my legacy, not the mewlings of children."

"Well then, Nasaka. Let me reset the wards on the door. There is no better time to begin than now."

"What is it you can do for me then?"

Carver gestured for the mage hunter to follow him into the next workroom.

"The possibilities are endless, Nasaka. Take this subject, for example. I have modified the structure of his nerves to improve his reaction speed as well as his ability to learn." He gestured to the slave who jumped to his feet and started to perform an intricate series of practice moves with a wooden sword. Without warning, Nasaka lunged past Carver and buried a dagger in the slave's eye. Carver looked at him in shock.

"Can't say I'm impressed so far." Nasaka pulled his dagger out and let the slave's body collapse. *Days of work wasted. A promising specimen and willing servant killed.* Carver's temper snapped. His body exploded into a mass of tentacles and grasping limbs that reached for Nasaka. The mage hunter vaulted over the grasping appendages and swept his dagger through several tentacles as he passed over them.

But the thing that was Carver was changing at a horrific rate. Nasaka was neatly plucked out of the air before he could gain his feet and smashed into the wall. Shelves and jars were crushed as the man collided with them. Carver lifted the battered man again, but Nasaka struck back. The palm of his left hand came down on one of Carver's limbs. The blow felt like a shard of ice cutting through Carver's soul. He howled wordlessly and flung Nasaka away from him. The mage hunter hit the far wall hard enough to send plaster raining down from the ceiling. Nasaka pulled himself to his feet slowly, his eyes following Carver's every movement. He was covered in small cuts, the left side of his face was swelling quickly, and his left leg was badly broken, a shard of bone protruding from his calf. Carver slowly returned to his normal crippled form, and the two men looked at each other with newfound respect.

Nasaka spit out a mouthful of phlegm and blood. "I have to admit I hadn't counted on such efficacy from a twisted old mage."

Carver shrugged. "A body is nothing more than a tool. I too am surprised by your abilities, Nasaka. Your blow hurt me in a way I have never felt before. That you were able to cause me pain at all has reawakened my curiosity. That you survived what I just did to you . . . increases my interest."

Nasaka nodded. "Then we have an understanding. I will show your work greater respect in the future."

Carver returned the nod. "My slaves and I will be busy this evening cleaning up the workshop. Return tomorrow night, Nasaka Jadoo, and we will begin our work." Carver smiled. It was satisfying to be the one to send a limping wreck of a man to walk across the palace for a change. While directing his slaves to repair the damage the brief confrontation had caused, Carver noticed something amiss with one of his pets.

"Roga! What is the meaning of this? My serpent eats live food, not eggs!"

"I beg your forgiveness, Master. They are not food. I watched the snake lay the eggs itself not two hours ago."

"Do you take me for a fool, worm? She has never been bred. You will suffer for your mistake and doubly so for lying to me!" Roga backed away from his master until he bumped into the wall with a start. His eyes were brimming with tears.

"I swear, my lord! I would never lie. Not to you, sir!" Then he dissolved into a weeping mess on the floor. Carver looked down at him distastefully. His power engulfed Roga, and a moment later the weeping changed to piercing screams as long bony spines grew from inside Roga's body, shredding his skin. Carver turned away from his assistant and moved back to inspect his favorite snake. He reached out with his magic to look over the animal and check for any signs of mistreatment. There were none. His pet was extremely well cared for.

On a whim he turned his senses to the eggs. A momentary glance turned into a detailed magical inspection. Slowly he turned back to the serpent.

"What secrets are you hiding, my pet?"

An hour later he had his answer. The great snake had the ability to breed itself when deprived of the company of its own kind for too long, all without losing the ability for sexual reproduction in the future.

"Fascinating." Carver chuckled softly. "Life is really a wondrous thing, is it not, Roga? Even after all these years I never would have imagined this was possible." Only then did he seem to hear Roga's continuing whimpers. He moved back to his assistant, who was lying in a slowly spreading puddle of blood. "It seems I was hasty in punishing you, Roga. You were honest with me, and even had the foresight not to dispose of the eggs. Those are rare traits that I value highly in my assistants." Roga gave no indication that he had heard Carver speak.

"We will put our new knowledge to good use. But first, I do believe I should undo your punishment, and a reward may even be in order." The spines melted back into Roga's body. His skin closed up over the wounds, and he sprang back to his feet, pulled by Carver's magic. Roga looked down at his blood-soaked clothes, an expression of mixed relief and confusion on his face.

"There you are, my loyal servant. The damage has been reversed. Now for your reward. . . ." The look of fear reappeared on Roga's face a moment before his body started to spasm and his screams started anew.

***

It took Salt the better part of the day to make his way down the dark staircase. He stumbled often and had to sit and rest. *Damned Dreth. If I have to come back here, I'm damned well bringing my own lamp.* The city was dark when he emerged hungry, thirsty, and bone weary. Few if any lights showed in any of the buildings. His escort of Fire Warriors was still waiting at the entrance of the tower as if they hadn't moved. *Maybe they haven't.* The thought was disturbing. Salt was too tired to even attempt to talk to the closemouthed Warriors. He let them guide him back to his room. Dignity barely kept him on his feet for the entire walk. There was no word for the relief he felt when he finally pushed the door open to his room and stumbled inside. He poured himself a generous cup of wine and dropped down on the bed with a sigh. Sleep came quickly but was interrupted by a sharp pain in his side.

Salt woke up with a start. He'd left three lamps burning when he went to sleep, beyond sick of the dark for one day. But when he opened his eyes, the room was pitch-black. He also noticed a strong smell that made him think of both flowers and something rotten. He fumbled around in the dark until he got a lamp lit. His eyes went wide when he saw what was standing in front of him—a shambling mass of flesh, lumpy and twisted like no living thing should be, wrapped in what looked like a very expensive silk dress.

"You look surprised to see me, lover."

Salt was stunned. There was no mistaking her voice. It was *her*. The filthy bug-ridden priestess who had tried to eat him almost a year earlier. He forced his voice to a semblance of control, not willing to let her have the satisfaction of having rattled him.

"I did kind of think Gurt and Lera had burned you to shit. . . . But I guess that was just wishful thinking."

The priestess ignored his last comment. "Oh, they burned most of me. They cost me a lot, and it's taken me all this time to pull myself back into a human form. I won't be snaring new prey quite so easily now. . . . Still, it was lucky for me they didn't check you too closely."

Salt's mind raced, trying to think of a way out of his situation. *I'm not tied down this time, bitch, and I've learned a thing or two since we last met.*

"One blood mite dug into the cut on your chest. . . . That's all that was left of me. You could have ended my existence by squashing me with your finger. It was a stretch even for me to pull myself back together after that." Salt couldn't help but look down at his chest. The scar she'd given him that night stood out clearly. He rubbed it as if it were dirty.

"It was difficult to escape from your body and find a safe place to recover my strength. I've been living in the sewers below your palace for months regrowing my body. She Who Feeds was generous and gifted me with thousands of her children to meld into my own flesh."

"Do you like the new me?" She posed for him as if she were a young beauty still and not a half-rotted monstrosity. Salt's stomach heaved.

"Now, my dear Salt, I believe we have some unfinished business, don't you?"

I need to keep her talking, he thought desperately. "You're right, I almost didn't recognize you. But then I really didn't ever expect to see you again. I'm surprised you managed to find me all the way out here."

"Oh, that wasn't so hard. I always know where you are, my lover. I chose you for my mate and you gave yourself to me willingly. She Who Feeds sanctified our union. There is nowhere in all the worlds you could go that I would not be able to find you. I must admit, I am surprised by how far you've come since last we met. No longer a simple sailor, are you? That is why I chose you. I saw the potential in you before you could even dream it was there yourself." She smiled down at him, the smile twisting her already misshapen face into something horrific.

"I've done well, I guess," Salt agreed. "And in a strange way, maybe I owe that success to you. . . ." Then he smiled back at her. "Or maybe I owe it more to the crusty old bastard who was stomping on you that night." Her smile was gone.

"Do not mock me, meat sack! You are mine, body and soul, to do with as I please! I can make my meal last a long time. I can savor the taste of your pain as I slowly eat you over the course of months." As she talked, Salt slowly moved his hand toward his sword. Her eyes widened as she noticed, and her grin returned.

"Do you really think you can hurt me with your puny sword? You've seen me hit with a bolt, shattered with sorcery, crushed, and burned. And yet here I stand. Could you really be so foolish? Perhaps I missed a mind flaw when I looked you over at our first meeting." Virulent green energy played around her gnarled fingers as she spoke.

"You will sire a clutch for me before I consume you, but you don't need your limbs or even most of your face to do it."

Salt jumped to his feet, sweeping his blade after him. The priestess's condescending look changed to surprise as the sword swept the bedclothes up and flicked them over her head. During the brief moment she was distracted, he grabbed the lamp from next to his bed and threw it at her feet before throwing his sword through the window and jumping out after it. He saw flames engulf her as he crashed through the remaining glass. Salt hit the ground like a sack of bricks, only narrowly avoiding falling on his own sword. A blast of energy blew out the side of the inn where his room used to be. He groaned, more hurt by the fall than he had expected. His head was spinning with pain and shock, his left leg was badly hurt, possibly broken, and all he could think of was—*Shit, now I made her mad.* Salt crawled as close to the inn's wall as he could, trying to keep in cover.

"You can't escape me, Salt!" the priestess shrieked.

Magic pounded down against the cobblestone street. The stones dissolved where the priestess's spell struck them, leaving a fetid bubbling mess in ragged slashes across the street. Somewhere in the distance a bell rang and was answered by another fainter one, then another. An idea struck Salt. *If what Nok Dreth said was true, this place was built to fight off dragons.*

"Okay! Okay, I'll do whatever you want! Just stop, please!"

A billowing mass of insects and crawling *things* swarmed out of the broken wall and down to the street in front of Salt. He couldn't see how it happened, but the mass of wriggling bugs contracted and suddenly the twisted woman was standing in front of him again, a wicked grin on her face.

"It was foolish of you to come to this place, Salt. Your friends are far away, and I sense no magic at all in this place, no priests, no mages, no one to save you. I'm surprised I never came here before, such a ripe city waiting to be devoured—"

A beam of shockingly bright green fire slashed down from atop one of the city walls. Faster than a lightning strike, it hit the priestess full in the back. Salt saw the look of agony on her face the moment before she shifted back into her swarm shape. But the Dreth fire would not be denied. Each and every insect seemed to carry a spark of the green fire within it. The cloud burst into flame and crumbled to black ash. The flames spread through them all as if hungry, then winked out. Salt blinked repeatedly to clear his eyesight. The glowing wreckage of the front of the inn gave him enough light to see the scattered husks of burnt bugs scattered around the street.

"Knew you'd be too damned stupid not to come out and gloat," he said to the remains. He looked up at the top of the wall where the Dreth Fire Warrior stood with his Firespear. "Thanks for the save!" There was a good reason why Dreth wasn't a target for supernatural things. The Dreth were not ones to relax their vigil, and they were armed to deal with anything.

The innkeeper came out a moment later and picked Salt up as if he were no more than a child and carried him back into the building. The man moved him to a new room without comment, not looking the least bit surprised to see him out in the street naked and wounded. The innkeeper put him down on the bed, then brought over all Salt's surviving belongings. By the looks of it, nothing had been lost except his fancy new clothes. Salt couldn't help smiling when he imagined what Gurt would have to say.

"I may need a healer," he said to the innkeeper. The man nodded and left. Salt was surprised the man didn't have a thing to say about the damage done to his property. Not that there were any other guests. And if Salt was the first outsider invited into the city in generations, they probably didn't have much use for inns anyway.

Salt drifted in and out of sleep, jolting himself awake every time he moved his leg. He wasn't sure how much time passed before a new Dreth dressed in the now familiar clashing colors, headdress, and veil came into his room.

"Welcome to our city, Night Captain. I am Lamek Bal Jasak. Nok Dreth asked me to show our great city to you and teach you something of our past. First, let me apologize for not coming to you earlier. We are aware of the attack that took place last night, and we know you were hurt. Unfortunately, we could not decide on a course of action to assist you. None of us has any real understanding of the medical needs of a human. We have therefore arranged for the services of a healer from the camp outside. He will be here shortly."

"You let in another outsider? I'm surprised but grateful."

"Well, this healer has done nothing to earn this honor; he will be returned outside the moment he has completed your treatment. Most outsiders think us secretive—this is not true. We are more what I would call overly cautious. The attacker who followed you here is a good example of why we try to keep the outside world and all the threats that come with it at arm's length."

Salt mulled over what the Dreth had said. "Thank you for telling me that. There really are many things that I don't understand about your people. I guess I didn't know what an honor your people were showing me till now."

"The most important difference between us, Night Captain, is that there are no empty words or actions among the Dreth. Every action has meaning; every word is said for a reason. I'm sure you have noticed the lack of small talk among our people."

"I have. It's not an easy thing to get used to. Even Ambassador Ben Akyum . . ."

"Nokor Ben Akyum is much the typical Dreth in that respect. He generally isn't happy about leaving the city either, but as the youngest living Dreth, the risk of traveling beyond our walls falls to him. But there's no need to hesitate with me. I spend a lot of my time outside in the market camp. I find I can learn so much from those visiting. I enjoy speaking at length with as many different people as I can. Nok Dreth can be something of an oddity in that respect as well, when the mood takes him. He reads extensively and is particularly curious about you humans and every aspect of your civilization."

As promised, the healer was shown in a short time later. Salt couldn't identify his clothes or understand a word the man said. Lamek translated for him. Whoever the healer was, he knew his craft. Salt was stunned when he was able to stand up with no trace of pain after only a few minutes. Lamek thanked the strange healer again, and the Spear Brothers returned to guide him out.

"Now, Night Captain—"

"Please, just call me Salt. There's no need for titles."

Lamek nodded. "Thank you, Salt. Please call me Lamek. As I was saying, I would like to take you to the libraries to start. They are the foundation of Dreth in more ways than one. They, almost as much as the remaining purebloods, are what these great walls were built to protect."

"Of course, Lamek. I would be happy to see them." Salt groaned inwardly. *If I'd known I'd be stuck in a library looking at books, I would have insisted Lera pick up the Firesword when we found it.*

"Are the libraries near the Core then?"

"Oh, Dreth no. I would not ask you to walk so far so soon after being healed. The libraries are located under the city's inner walls. The nearest entrance is just over this way."

Lamek led Salt into one of the inner segment tunnels, but instead of a fairly direct route that would lead them out into the next segment, they made a series of sharp turns in the dark before opening a heavy wood and steel door. Faint light filled the vast room beyond. Salt was once again astounded by the number of secrets the Dreth city held. Thousands upon thousands of tomes and scrolls were arrayed on long shelves and racks that extended until they faded from sight in the distance. Hundreds of scribes moved silently around the room endlessly copying and recopying the books lest they be lost to age.

Even Salt, who was less than enamored of reading, was stunned by the sight. "I never knew so many books existed in the whole world."

"There are indeed many. We purchase some new tomes from merchants at times if we think they are worth adding to our store of knowledge. But, more importantly, our own history is kept in these libraries. The history of our city and of every living Dreth. This particular library holds the tomes that record my own life, among many other things, of course."

"Why would you need to record your life? I understood from Nok Dreth that even if you die, you can be brought back."

"That is true. But the return to life is neither easy nor without its price. Every time we are forced to return to our bodies, something is lost. Memories fade over time, of course; in that respect we are no different from you humans. But the resurrection costs us far more of our memories. What is lost can't be predicted. We record everything so that we might learn who we were and what we did when we return from the great darkness."

Salt was quiet for a moment. The word *forced* had not been lost on him. *There are no empty words among the Dreth.*

"If you don't mind telling me, Lamek, why are so few Dreth left then? If you can't die . . . Hasn't it been ages and ages since your empire fell and you locked yourselves in your city?"

Lamek bowed his head. "It is our hope to one day multiply as we once did. That avenue is closed to us for the moment. We try, of course—Children are born to the purebloods often. At least one child every decade or so. The problem lies with the aftermath of the Great War. Our children are different. They are not quite Dreth. . . . Not anymore."

"Are those the people you call half bloods then?"

"No. The half bloods are born of the union between a Dreth and a human. Many of the humans who joined us in those early days were from the area that is now Bialta. More are brought in every few hundred years as fertility rates among the half bloods are particularly poor." Lamek hesitated for a moment, then moved to a nearby shelf and lifted a heavy leather-bound book. "But look here. This tome is an account of the coming of the dragons and the final victory we won here in our last city."

Salt took the hint and let him change the subject. "Nok Dreth told me a little about that. The dragon armies swept through most of your empire and finally attacked you here."

"And then Nok Dreth saved us. He gave us hope again by creating the first Firesword. The very sword you returned to him yesterday. Fueled by the willing sacrifice of his own brother, Nok Dreth used the great weapon to slay three true-born wyrms. The dragon's sorceries were no defense against the Firesword. More of the weapons were then made, as were the Firespears."

"The willing sacrifice?"

"The weapons that protect us, that ensure the safety of Dreth against the return of the dragons, are fueled by the will and the souls of our people. Each gemstone that powers the swords and spears is made from the life of a pureblood. Such was the resolve of all the Dreth that many volunteered their lives to power the gems and destroy the enemies of their people.

"We gained the advantage in the war. Still, the price was too high. Our last ships set sail with fully half of the great weapons to take the war to the dragons' homeland. None ever returned, but the dragon host received no further reinforcements.

"The war continued for nearly another century. Though the dragon armies were much reduced, we were more so. Their sorcery and fires clashed with our own arts. The end came here, in the one city we had built from the ground up to defend us against dragons. Wide swaths of land were laid waste. The very soul of the land was damaged. The Great Desert was once green hills, fertile farmland, and gentle forests. Now it is a breeding ground for monsters."

"Monsters?" asked Salt. "I crossed the edge of the desert and didn't see anything all that unusual out there."

Lamek shook his head. "There is no shortage of dangerous creatures in this world. But I have yet to hear of another place where serpents breed so large they can swallow men or even larger prey whole. We have even seen man-shaped creatures with the skin of snakes walking the sands armed with rudimentary weapons. At first, we took them to be some form of remnant of the dragon host. But after capturing and examining a few, we found they were just a bastardized form of you humans. Probably changed by the lingering powers that destroyed the lands they live on. We have since forbidden our people from traveling into the sands lest the corruption left by our enemies twist our own bodies. It is part of the reason we do not often leave our home anymore. It is a sad thing indeed to see our great civilization reduced to what it is now. Our empire was not like one of your human kingdoms or empires. We did not remove or conquer the people who lived near our lands. We built our own cities where we would and left the primitive tribes of early humans to hunt or build their crude dwellings in the shadows of our great towers. We built ships such as you cannot imagine and explored the seas and their hidden treasures. We greeted all who came to us in peace, though on occasion we had to defend ourselves. It was our golden age, before the dragons came. . . ." His voice drifted off, lost in thought.

CHAPTER 15

"A trader is here to see you, sir. He insists that he has a creature worthy of your time." Roga bowed deeply. Carver hid his annoyance at the interruption. Roga was, after all, only following instructions, and this merchant may well have found an interesting specimen. When Carver entered the main workshop, the fat merchant was grinning ear to ear. Without waiting for an introduction, he pulled the tarp off a large wooden cage that he had had brought into the room.

Carver stopped dead, his mouth gaping. The merchant's grin widened when he saw Carver's reaction. Inside the cage was a large lizard, perhaps as long as Carver's arm. It had birdlike feathers covering most of its back as well as a pair of ungainly wings that were fixed to its forelimbs.

A reptile with the instinct for flight! This could be the key! Carver was so excited he barely noticed the merchant and the look of obvious greed that was spreading across his face. *If a reputation for paying well can get me this kind of specimen, I'll have to live up to it. For a while at least.* He motioned to one of his assistants to bring him some gold, then tossed the whole bag to the merchant when it arrived.

"Now get him out of here so I can get to work." Guards walked the merchant out, who still hadn't had a chance to speak a word. He moved as if in a daze, his every greedy dream having been exceeded.

"Bring this creature to my chambers at once!" Carver shouted at his slaves. "The new specimen takes precedence over all other experiments."

Carver had long harbored a secret: the ultimate goal of his research. In his search for a solution to the great problems that were society, decadence, and indolence, he had come to the conclusion that rulership was at the root of the problem. Gods were too remote, too self-serving. Mortals were flawed, corruptible, and too short-lived to offer society any kind of stability. Even the so-called long-lived races among them could not hope to see more than a few centuries pass by. Mages were occasionally longer lived. Some few, like Carver himself, had overcome death. But he knew that any mage who was willing to pursue the studies of power and magic as long as he had would have no real interest in ruling or the constant interruptions such a station would bring. The answer was simple. It had always been in the fairy tales he had heard as a child—dragons. They were the perfect choice. If they did not exist, and Carver had found no trace of them in his thousand years of searching, then he would create dragons that embodied the best of every legend and eventually place them in their rightful role ruling the world. It was the only way he could see to stop the madness of divisiveness and turmoil that he had observed over and over again. It was true his own creations had caused deaths. His weapons and creatures helped petty despots to become conquering warlords. But none of these things had any importance. It was all so transient. Nothing would matter until he had made things as they should be. Order and peace would exist for all when he was done.

His former master had had a similar dream, though his vision had been imperfect. Worse, his master had lacked the vision even to extend his flawed vision of peace to the world and had kept it to himself and his favored few. Carver would not be so restrained. He intended to transform the world. Dragons were said to be supremely intelligent. The life of a single dragon would be longer than dozens if not hundreds of human generations, even if the stories about their lives were grossly exaggerated. These things Carver could accomplish already. Flight had been the most recent barrier to his efforts. No matter how hard he had tried, he had been unable to create a flying reptile. *And here one just falls into my lap.*

The project advanced even faster than Carver had initially hoped. In just a few weeks he was looking at his newest creation with pride. The original creature had been more suited to gliding than true flight. He suspected that it had lived in a heavily forested area where it could glide between the boles of trees. Its claws and body shape, well adapted to climbing, supported his theory. The new creation could do better. Its wings were independent appendages, not just leathery skin anchored to its limbs. And though it sometimes struggled to gain altitude, especially when taking off, it could actually fly! He'd already given it the parthenogenetic ability to self-reproduce he'd learned from his pet snake. But more changes were necessary before he started a full-scale breeding program. Feathers were not part of his final design, nor were the hollow bones or overall fragility the creature displayed. A few unexpected changes had followed his modifications as well. The creature's plumage was somewhat longer and the colors had changed from dark greens to vibrant whites and reds.

Anything unexpected was a mixed blessing, of course. It implied there was something new to learn, some new connection or trait he hadn't known about or had previously misunderstood. But it also meant delays. The Drokga would not be pleased with delays. Carver's promise of flying mounts for his carapace warriors to ride into battle had not been forgotten, despite the weak show of interest he'd received when he first spoke of it. He would have to push ahead and deal with any problems as they arose.

He had originally wanted to give the mounts thick scales like true dragons, but the weight of any significant scale armor would be a very large problem when it came to maintaining flight. The chitin he'd been working on in most of his new creations would be far more effective. Far easier to work with as well given his abundant sources and recent chitin-molding experience. The resulting creature wouldn't, strictly speaking, be a dragon. But it would be a large step in the right direction, not to mention an interesting experiment and one that would give the Tolrahkali forces a certain elegant uniformity. *The Drokga might even appreciate that.* An addition of chitinous plates to the bull-like mounts might also be a good idea. As would parthenogenesis if he could manage to impart the trait to a warm-blooded creature. *Maybe if I maintain the link to egg laying. . . . It would certainly facilitate the breeding program.* Carver had never had so many exciting projects. He spent his days working on the Drokga's projects and his nights working on Nasaka. Both days and nights went by too quickly. It was always with mixed feelings that he set aside one project to move on to the next.

Though less relevant to his plans, Carver relished the chance to work with the mage hunter. Never before had he had a subject resilient enough for him to really push the boundaries of what fleshcarving could accomplish, all without allowing for lengthy recovery periods. He sculpted and molded the man's flesh until no one who knew him could possibly recognize him. Those few times that he stopped and asked if he should proceed, the answer was always the same: "Power is worth any price."

They had started slowly. A few changes, a few modifications of existing structures within the body each night, such as nerve and reaction time improvements, then they had moved on to more comprehensive alterations.

As was often the case, Carver was irritated by the amount of space the digestive system occupied in a normal body. Not only was it cumbersome, it was almost unavoidably a vulnerability. In his own body he had reduced the need for nutrients so sufficiently that he had also reduced the size of his digestive system. But Nasaka was a killer, a man who thrived in the thick of battle, who lived for combat. No weakness could be left. With barely a shrug, Carver ripped the whole thing out of the man. External feedings would be necessary. Immersion in a vat of nutritive liquids would provide all that was needed. If he fine-tuned the body enough, Nasaka would only need to be fed in such a way once every few weeks. No need for a carapace this time, though. As much as Carver had learned with the external creations, it was liberating to be able to work with no restrictions.

Nasaka Jadoo's bones had also been made thicker and heavier. They were then reinforced with a mixture of minerals that made them nearly as hard as steel. His overlong arms had been further extended, as had his long legs. His muscle fibers were replaced with stronger, thinner versions that made room for Carver to double or even triple their number. He had also added a second, smaller heart linked to a fully separate secondary circulatory system. Not enough to provide full functionality but certainly enough to keep Nasaka alive through even the most severe of wounds. His skin was thickened and made into a supple variant of a carapace. Not as strong as the thick chitin perhaps, but far better than a leather vest and less restrictive of movement. Besides, standard armor could still be worn over the new skin. With a glance at one of his favorite lizards, Carver modified the structure of the skin further. Once Nasaka learned to control it, he should be able to achieve limited color changes.

Carver looked over the once-human mage hunter with pride. A feeding would be needed before the work resumed the next night. He summoned four slaves and had them bring one of the nutrient vats from the main workshop up to his rooms. He wrapped the mage hunter in a broad weave and lifted him into the dark liquid. Nasaka only woke for a moment. Red eyes flashed in the depths of the vat before they slid closed. *A few more days and he'll never have to sleep again.*

Carver had learned much from working on the assassin. Not least of which was how far he could push the body of a Warchosen without breaking it. *I may even apply some of what I've learned to Maran Vras if I find the time.*

Carver had also been fascinated to learn that the whole basis of Nasaka's quasi-religious sect of mage hunters was the crystal Nasaka always had strapped to his left palm. He had found it as a child and had learned to use its unique properties to dismantle weaves. As his Warchosen abilities had grown, so had his magic-negating skills, to the point that he'd even managed to teach the ability to his apprentices in a limited fashion. *It's a shame I can't isolate the trait that allows him to make use of the trinket, but the ability certainly makes him a more useful tool for as long as he lasts. . . . In any case, the hardest part is done. Tonight it will be time to fine-tune his new body and maybe think of some new and creative ways for him to kill people. Perhaps even add something in the vein of the Drokga's own titan carapace? Not as large, of course. Perhaps only half again the height of a man. . . . . The whole process would be so much easier given the modifications I've already made to Nasaka. I'm sure the Drokga would approve of his favorite killer having more of a presence on the front lines so long as it's that much less impressive than his own. Certainly a possibility worth exploring. In the meantime, my latest clutch of winged lizards should be grown enough to fly.*

Carver stood on his balcony and watched his newest batch of constructs with a critical eye as they flew around above him. The creatures were impressive in their own right, he supposed. But dragons were supposed to fly majestically through the air! To soar! They could get airborne and could cover vast distances faster than any land animal. But his specimens moved with all the grace and majesty of a chicken trying to take flight. The beasts, still conservative in size compared to his final designs, were just too large and heavy; the loss of the feathers had also had a significant impact. He would have to sacrifice combat effectiveness to improve their flight, and that was just unthinkable.

They should still be enough to impress the Drokga. . . . One would hope. They will undoubtedly be effective for his small-minded purposes. The dragonids' nervous systems had been prepared very carefully—when a carapace-equipped rider mounted one, a temporary link would form between the carapace and the mount, giving the rider access to the mount's senses as well as granting almost perfect control of the creature.

His creations were still missing one of the most obvious aspects of dragonkind, of course—magic. Humanoids would need to be included in the mix—*talented* humanoids.

Harnessing their power could provide the dragons with improved flight, possibly even the fire breath every legend agreed they had. The larger body would, in turn, provide greater fuel for the talent. *Perhaps modifying the powers of a Warchosen would be easier . . . at least initially.*

The Drokga wasn't likely to hand over any of his mages or Chosen for him to experiment on, not even for the promise of dragons to accompany his armies into war. *I may be able to convince him to hand over interesting prisoners though. But no,* he quickly realized. *It's extremely unlikely that any really interesting specimens would be taken in any kind of useful condition.*

Then it hit him. *Children might be the answer.* The difficulty would be in selecting probable talents. The next logical step was to find a pool of suitable talents and start a breeding program. No one had ever proved that magical talent was hereditary, but there were enough indications that some sort of link to parentage existed. If nothing else, the breeding program would help him learn just how likely a talent was to be passed on.

Come to think of it, I don't even need whole people to start, just a few of their more relevant parts. Those parts could be kept working for quite a long time and provide more than enough new breeding and test subjects. *Freshness will be vitally important, of course.* With all the new weapons and creatures Carver was handing to the Drokga, it was only a matter of time before temptation became too strong and he marched to war to try out his new toys. Carver would have to send out the majority of his assistants in the hopes that they would be on hand to collect what he needed should a suitable specimen—from either side—fall. *I can get samples from Maran Vras and Nasaka Jadoo quite easily. It's unfortunate that I didn't think of this before I modified them and made them unable to breed with other humans.*

With a smile, Carver started to prepare new birthing chambers. No matter the results, this would be one of his more interesting experiments.

"Master Carver? If I may interrupt your thoughts for a moment?" asked Roga. Carver's reward had transformed the slave—he was both taller and more muscular than he had been before. He also didn't tire as easily and barely slept. But as much as his confidence had increased to match his new stature, his fear of Carver was undiminished.

"What is it, Roga?"

Roga swallowed hard, clearly struggling to keep hold of his courage. "I had an idea, Master, for the army's supply problem. And uh . . ."

"Well? Spit it out!"

Roga was too flustered. He stood there with his mouth flapping and no recognizable sounds coming out. Carver's anger was close to the surface. His eyes held Roga's death.

"If you waste another moment of my time, boy. . . ."

"The mounts!" Roga managed to say. "Couldn't we change the link so the mounts transfer nutrients to the riders?"

Carver's anger vanished in an instant. He looked at Roga with newfound respect. "An excellent idea. If we can manage that, then a few extra hours grazing would feed a sizable part of our army. The mounted troops will have to move more slowly than they could otherwise, but then we wouldn't want them to outdistance the foot troops anyway. The same could be done for the dragonids as well." He continued thinking aloud. "Yes, consuming flesh would be ideal for such an exchange." He looked up and saw Roga still standing expectantly beside him. "Yes, you've done very well, Roga. I shall have to think of a suitable reward for you. It's a pity you don't have a stronger talent yourself or you would have made an excellent apprentice. Still, you may be able to learn some small things of fleshcarving and become an exceptional assistant."

"Thank you, Master," Roga said, falling to his knees.

***

For six days, they continued to search and exploit every resource Skeg had access to. For six days, Zuly and Nial continued to feed deeply. They had only left the shop once and had been frustrated by the changes in Nial. They could no longer pass unnoticed in the slums.

Though Nial was not yet twelve, her shared body now looked like a woman's. More, she was attractive, healthy, and obviously well fed. Eyes now followed Nial wherever she went, when before she had been all but invisible. The girls soon gave up trying to hunt, and went back to the shop to return to their reading.

An hour later Zuly threw their book aside. "This is pointless. It cannot be done."

Skeg looked up in surprise. "We can't give up, Zuly." He was determined to save the girls even though he now knew the link that existed between Amon Kareth and each and every Karethin demon was all but unbreakable. No matter what they did, he would always be able to find Zuly. No matter how strong the wards they built up around her, he would eventually batter them down.

"I don't mean to give up. I mean to do as he commands and return to the Karethin realm before we are dragged back and our minds destroyed in the process. We found a way to build a portal days ago. Let's do it and stop wasting our time. The lord will get what he wants from us eventually. We can only hope that the souls we've harvested will be enough to bargain for our freedom."

Skeg grudgingly agreed. "I suppose it is time. I set aside the materials we'll need for a gate. We'll have to build it inside the ward circle to stop anything else coming out."

"I think we'll be able to seal it from the other side, at least temporarily. But the wards would be a good idea."

The construction of the gate was surprisingly simple. They needed to shape an arch out of blackwood. The springy branches had to be woven into a pattern that Nial and Zuly were easily able to manage with their talent. After that, it was just a matter of enchanting the arch. It took the girls the better part of two days to create the necessary weaves and set them into the branches with rare paints and exotic minerals.

When it was finally done, Nial and Zuly both checked it over carefully, searching for any mistakes.

"Ready, Uncle?" Nial asked, doing her best to sound cheerful.

Skeg nodded, his hands clenched into fists at his sides. Nial looked at the arch and activated the spell.

The portal swirled in front of them. Nial looked over their shoulder and saw the naked fear on Skeg's face. He had tried to hide his feelings during the gate's construction, though the girls had felt it on more than one occasion, but there was no hiding it now that the gate was open. They couldn't blame him, really. They were afraid of the gate as well. Well, not so much the gate as what lay on the other side waiting for them.

Faces started to form in the mists. Demons, braver than most, testing the gate, pushing against the barrier the girls had woven into it.

Nial stood in front of the swirling rift. The girls both knew what lay beyond it. Zuly had come to Nial and they had built a life for themselves in her world. Neither of them had ever expected to return to the realm where Zuly was spawned. No sane mortal would dare set foot there. Nial's soul would be the object of desire of every demon in the realm.

But we are not mortal anymore, Nial, not entirely anyway, and fighting demons is nothing new to us.

Nial nodded, still trying to find the courage to step onto another world with no clear idea of when or if they would make it back. *We have no choice, my dear Nial. We can't stay awake forever.*

Some part of Zuly was eager to return. She knew many of the denizens of Karethin would test them, but she relished the chance to prove herself among those who had once hunted her, to destroy them at a whim. If the demon lord himself hadn't summoned them, she might even enjoy the prospect of returning home.

"It will be fine, Uncle," Nial whispered, not trusting herself to speak any louder. She stepped through and the mists dispersed. Skeg was left looking at the twisted archway they had carved. He slumped to the ground, unable to tear his eyes from that empty space. Nial and Zuly were gone and he doubted he would ever see them again.

Nial stepped through the gate into darkness. Something large moved in front of them. Nial only saw faint light from the dispersing gate reflect off long fangs right in front of their face. Zuly reacted instinctively. She grabbed the thing by the muzzle and held it back. They felt the thing's hot, fetid breath as it grunted and pushed to free itself from their grasp.

They blinked, and their vison adapted. Nial recognized the world she had seen in Zuly's memories. This was a world of eternal darkness. The sky was the yellow-gray color of a week-old bruise. Dark clouds swirled around in the upper air, torn apart by violent air currents showing glimpses of a black sun. And riding those currents were swarms of nightmarish creatures. Carrion demons and imps banded together in swarms to hunt and for the dubious protection of others of their kind.

The demon they held was a head taller than they were. Its skin was pasty white and wrinkly topped by a slick wolflike head complete with a slavering maw and finger-length fangs. Zuly held its slavering mouth back with one hand. Then she calmly reached up and grasped the demon's lower jaw with their other hand. Its teeth pierced their skin but they barely noticed. With a growl of her own, Zuly pulled. The demon squealed for a moment before its lower jaw came away with a wet popping sound. She threw the jaw aside before taking a firm hold of the thing and tossing its imposing frame to the ground where it was instantly swarmed by a multitude of smaller demons that fought and struggled over the sudden bounty.

The land around them was barren of all plant life. Rust-colored stones and dust dotted with patches of fungus were all that made up the plain as far as the eye could see. Small animalistic demons moved around in packs attacking each other or fleeing from stronger foes. Larger demons, like the one Zuly had just destroyed, hunted alone, battling groups of smaller demons or fighting each other. The demons of this world took a thousand different forms, but one and all, they fed on one another. There was no rest, no respite, and no mercy. Demons did not sleep. They hunted, especially at night, and this world was an endless night of strife and death.

Nial watched a large demon, which looked vaguely like a cross between a crab and a bear, tear through a pack of a dozen six-legged monkey-rat things only to be killed itself by a horrific beast that seemed to be nothing but tentacles. Through all the mayhem, carrion demons and imps swooped down to carry off forgotten parts of carcasses. When a swarm of carrion demons flew down toward Nial, she set the air around them on fire. Zuly sent a surge of power at them and scattered the burning demons across the plain.

That should be enough of a show of force for now. None of the smaller ones should bother us for a while. They started to walk. Zuly was certain she knew where the demon lord wanted to meet them. It was next to the pool where Zuly had been spawned. When a demoness was ready, the new demons were spawned into a pool of water like those that dotted the plain and then forgotten. Demons of every type bore spawn. The spawn fought to survive and grow like any other demon—by feeding off each other. Once they got big enough, they left the pool and moved onto the plain in search of bigger prey. Though that didn't stop the odd larger demon from feasting in the pools from time to time.

The pool turned out to be a fairly large lake of muddy, brown water. Eddies and splashes appeared randomly across the water, as the half-glimpsed forms of the demon spawn fought beneath the surface. Fins and less recognizable appendages flashed above the waves.

They stood by the pool for a time and watched as demons caught their scent or saw them and rushed toward them. A few fire spells were enough to kill a few and scare the rest away. There were no truly formidable demons in the area, at least for the time being.

Zuly felt something then and looked up at the sky. "Hide yourself, Nial! The demon lord comes! If he sees even a hint of you within—"

"But, Zuly," Nial interrupted, her voice exasperated, "we've come so far this last year. Surely one demon isn't enough to scare you now. We've defeated more than a few already."

As if in answer to her question, a dark shape resolved itself against the sky.

"Quiet! He comes!"

The obvious terror in Zuly's voice silenced any further protests. Nial pulled herself to the deepest part of their shared minds, daring only to watch in horror and fascination as Amon Kareth, demon lord of the Karethin realm, came closer, blotting out first the clouds, then the sky itself.

If common demons spawned in forms that terrified mortals, that embodied their nightmares, then Amon Kareth was the worst nightmare of gods and dragons. His form was vaguely draconian, but bulkier, lacking any of the terrible grace and beauty of the eldest race. The monstrosity was large enough to grasp the greatest of dragons in one hand. Four massive batlike wings extended from its back, beating in slow, lazy movements that cast the surrounding lands into deeper shadow. The creature's head was squat and devoid of a neck, reminiscent of a short-nosed crocodile with disproportionately large teeth. Its skin pulsated, as if even this massive shape strained to contain the power within. As terrifying as the sight of the demon lord was, it was the demon's eyes that sent Nial screaming to find new depths within herself to hide in. Eyes that swallowed all light like holes in the fabric of existence. Eyes that held a hunger so deep, so insatiable, that all the souls in existence could not satisfy it.

Zuly stood in shadow, buffeted by the wind the giant wings created, trembling in fear, unable to move. Never before had she attracted her lord's attention. Never before had she laid eyes on him, even from a distance. Few were those who did and survived. Zuly was a smart demon, and smart demons knew to run for their lives when they felt their master approaching. She felt fear in the demons around her. Even the smallest of them was running. The spawn moved like a tide to the edge of the stagnant pool. Like the parting of a monstrous sea, the demons fled from their lord's path.

In fits and jerks the demon lord started to draw its body in on itself. An amorphous mass slowly floated down as it continued to shrink. Finally, a bubbling, wriggling ball of dark flesh and scales touched the ground a few paces from Zuly. She took a step back, unable to control herself. After an interminable wait, the shape of a man started to resolve itself. It drew itself upright and the demon lord stood before her on two legs.

"We can speak more easily this way," he said. His voice was as deep as the abyss. Zuly had to strain to make out the words, even as she fought every instinct that told her to run for her life. Still, she had to admit, it was certainly more pleasant than when the lord had spoken to her mind directly.

In the guise of a man, Amon Kareth looked like a knight of legend hopelessly corrupted. He stood half again as tall as any human. His skin was a charcoal gray that constantly shifted and twitched. His long black hair melted into serpentine tentacles that thrashed around behind him before falling back into hair. As if to complete the image, he was dressed in plate armor that looked to be forged of shiny black metal. But like every part of him, it was not still. Veins pulsed and rose from every plate at odd intervals. He exuded power. The aura of great weight had not left despite his smaller form. Stones cracked and broke under his feet as he walked forward. Nor had his eyes changed. Though they were smaller, being this close to that hunger was even worse. Zuly could not bring herself to raise her eyes to look at him more closely.

He reached out and touched Zuly's shoulder. She screamed and collapsed, her body shuddering and trembling uncontrollably. A thin claw had extended from the end of his finger. A single drop of her blood beaded on the tip. He brought the drop to his mouth. A long black tongue lashed out from behind sharp teeth to taste it.

"You have joined with this mortal in a way I have never seen before. Your essences have truly become one."

The sound of his voice was making her head spin. Blood was dribbling out of her ears. Her stomach heaved at the wrongness of his presence.

"How many souls have you harvested for me, little Zulaxrak? And how did you avoid the madness?"

Struggling to move, Zuly reached down and drew out the obsidian orb. "Almost two hundred, Lord," she squeaked, holding up the orb full of dancing sparks.

"Ingenious. How did you come to learn of this thing? Those few who know the secrets of its making do not share easily." He grasped the orb between his thumb and forefinger before lifting it to his face. The long black tongue licked out again, passing through the volcanic glass as if it were smoke. The orb was empty and shattered when Amon Kareth let it fall to the ground.

Zuly squirmed where she lay, blood flowing more freely from her ears now, her head spinning from the onslaught of his voice. Amon Kareth looked down at the pathetic thing writhing in pain at his feet, awaiting an answer. "No matter, you represent a unique opportunity for me. Never before has a mortal body been able to cling to life in my presence, even for a moment." His gaze sharpened. "I shall use you."

He bent down and pressed his finger into her abdomen. Zuly struggled faintly as blood welled up from the wound. His finger dug deep into her, coiling and bending like an oversized worm. Zuly tried to scream, but it only came out as a wet gurgle. Bitter fluids were boiling up her throat from her stomach. All she could think of was wanting him out, of getting him off her. The feeling of being sullied, of being violated not only in body but down to the very core of her being was far worse than the pain. She lost control of herself; her arms and legs thrashed around on their own. After what felt like an eternity, Amon Kareth pulled his finger out of her stomach and stepped back.

"I am curious to see what you will become. You and the spawn you now carry. I would not see you weakened for too long; therefore, I gift you a trinket made by another ingenious demoness of a past age." He dropped something beside her. "I'll be watching you, Zulaxrak." And with those last words his body surged up into the sky, bursting out in every direction until the titanic dragon blocked out the sky once again. It flapped its giant wings and slowly moved off in the direction it had come from. Zuly lay on the ground, unable to move or control her shivering body until long after the dragon had faded from sight. Her hand moved slowly to her stomach. A trickle of blood and thick black liquid still dribbled out of her wound. She could already feel a faint lifespark growing within her. She rubbed herself, everywhere she could reach in her weakened state, desperate to feel clean again, to rub away the memory of his presence, of his touch. She rolled over and vomited up blood and bile. *What am I going to tell Nial?* For the first time in her existence, Zulaxrak, demoness of the Karethin realm, wept. She sobbed uncontrollably and shivered in the mud, feeling broken.

It was hours before any demons dared to come near the place where their lord had landed. But, as always, hunger pressed them and a braver or perhaps less intelligent carrion demon dared the wrath of Amon Kareth to approach the demoness who seemed weakened and vulnerable. Zuly struck out with an instinctive lash of power. The demon was neatly slashed in half. With a grunt of pain, she pulled herself to her feet. Nial hadn't returned from her fugue, and Zuly was grateful. She didn't want Nial to see what she was about to do. Numbly she reached down and picked up Amon Kareth's gift and stuffed it into her belt. She didn't want anything from him but couldn't risk insulting the lord or passing up something that might help her recover some of what had been taken. She felt hollow without her captive souls. For the first time since she and Nial had captured their first soul, she felt the hunger rising and had no immediate way to feed.

Clutching her still tender stomach, Zuly started to walk back to the portal site. The smell of her blood and the sight of her limping triggered a feeding frenzy among the demons of the plain. They attacked in droves, hoping for a mouthful, the merest taste of her power. With all the rage and hate she felt for the master of this realm, she lashed out at his servants. Fires burned so hot that stone glowed red, vast nets of energy trapping those that tried to flee. The larger creatures, she tore limb from limb with her bare hands. Zuly was without mercy. For hours she rampaged across the plains killing everything that came against her. Though hunger gnawed at her more and more, she did not taste the flesh of her victims. She had savored the sweet power of a mortal soul and would not return to the cannibalistic ways of the weaker demons.

It wasn't until every surviving demon had fled well beyond the reach of her magic, and she stood panting and exhausted that she decided to open the portal and leave. Images of Amon Kareth and what he had done to her flashed before her mind's eye and the rage returned. She could barely stand to be in her own flesh with the *thing* inside her. With a desperate wail she called Nial back and then fled consciousness herself.

Nial stood blinking in confusion, looking at the charred devastation that surrounded her. She felt ill used. Her whole body ached, and she was feeling the hunger worse than ever before. She realized with a sinking feeling that the orb that had contained all the souls they had harvested was gone. Still, Zuly had done it. They had survived the meeting with Amon Kareth and they could go home. A couple hundred souls were a small price to pay. There were always more monsters roaming the streets of Darien. Nial started to weave the complex spell that would open the gate again. She was surprised by how hard it was. Her wellspring of power was nearly exhausted. They would need to make a new orb quickly and go hunting.

Skeg had been growing more and more agitated as he waited in front of the gate. Hours had passed without any sign of change. If the girls didn't return, or if something else tried to get through, he would have to destroy the arch. He had already waited longer than he should have. If all had gone well, the girls should have been back within a few hours. Now the sun had risen and night was falling again outside. There could be no other explanation: Nial and Zuly had been killed by the demon lord and would not be returning. Skeg had told himself the same thing over and over again and knew it to be true; knew destroying the gate was the only safe thing to do, not only for himself but for Bialta, maybe even the world. *Just a few more minutes, then I'll destroy it.* When he saw a stirring in the mists of the gate, Skeg couldn't believe his eyes. Was it his imagination? *No. Something is coming through!* Skeg jumped to his feet and prepared to smash the delicate gate while he silently prayed that he hadn't waited too long. Then the girls' arm pushed through the mists as if reaching out for help. Skeg jumped up and grasped their hand. With a grunt of effort, he dragged them back into the world. Nial nearly collapsed at his feet.

She looked battered and bruised. There was blood and less easily identified fluids spattered all over her. Nial's clothes were torn and burned. His heart thumping in his chest, Skeg reached out and snapped one of the branches that made up the gate, and the swirling mists simply winked out of existence. Then he scooped up his tottering niece and carried Nial and

Zuly up to his room. *This is becoming a habit. I should build the girls a room of their own.* He brought a basin of fresh water for Nial to wash and pulled out spare clothes of his own for her to change into. They were poor things and too large by far, but anything was better than the soiled rags she was wearing now.

"The hunger," Nial moaned.

Skeg felt a chill run down his back. They were starving. They had lost their souls and for the first time, Skeg would need to go out and find food for them. *A cup of blood, a fresh heart. Maybe I can find a stray cat or a dog.* No, it was getting dark, but the markets might still be open in the merchant quarter. He would buy a couple small animals and bring them home. *It's normal. People buy rabbits or chickens to kill and eat every day.* He'd been hiding in the Muds for so long he felt exposed leaving the filthy streets. It wasn't just the attention his appearance attracted—plenty of strange people and stranger sights were seen in a city the size of Darien—it was just being outside his shop. *I haven't left the dump in months, and it's been a lot longer than that since I went farther than the end of the street.* But today there was no choice; Nial and Zuly were not going to bring him his hot cup of blood to curb the hunger pains. *I'm part demon now. I need to accept that and start doing something about taking care of my needs instead of being so dependent on the girls. They have more than enough to worry about without having to find dinner for me.*

Skeg made it back less than an hour later with two plump rabbits struggling in a sack slung over his shoulder. He climbed the stairs up to his room and held one of the rabbits up by the ears. The girls' eyes opened and Skeg took a step back. The bestial side of his nieces was nearly out of control. Nial grabbed the rabbit out of his hand, snapped its neck, and ripped its chest open before sinking her teeth into its still beating heart. Skeg's head was spinning. He felt sick from what he'd just seen, but he couldn't deny that his mouth was watering at the same time. He wandered back downstairs and sat staring at the sack where his own rabbit still lay.

Nial came down a few minutes later. "Thank you, Uncle. That helped, but I really need to go out and hunt." Skeg recognized the hollow look in her eyes. The rabbit had gotten Nial back on her feet, but the girls' need to feed was far stronger than his. A rabbit wouldn't be enough.

Nial raced outside. *Zuly?* she called for the hundredth time, but still there was no answer. She could feel Zuly hiding, unwilling to speak or hear anything. Nial didn't understand. She needed Zuly. She'd never felt the hunger like this, and it was hard to think. People were looking at her as she rushed through the muddy streets. She put a hand in her pocket and felt the strange glassy blade she'd found in her things when she came back. It was made of obsidian she thought. It was a little bit different color from their orb, more green than red brown. *It must be something like our old orb. That's why Zuly brought it back.* It was carved into a viscous blade with nowhere safe to hold it. *I'll find someone and try the old way.*

She rushed through the streets heedless of the looks she was attracting. From the look on her face and her shaking hands, most likely assumed she was an addict of some sort, desperate for a fix. And she was becoming desperate. The hunger was so strong Nial didn't know if she cared who she killed.

It wasn't her usual way of looking for a target, but it worked. A desperate beauty walking the streets of the slums after dark was a prime target for the city's predators. Nial was walking fast and was brought up short when two men blocked her path. They were typical Muds residents, with shabby clothes, greasy hair, and rotten teeth. They both smiled widely when she looked up in surprise. Their smiles broadened further when she looked around quickly and saw that the muddy little street they were on was deserted. Before she even knew what she was doing herself, Nial had stabbed the glass blade into one of the men's stomachs. Her own hand was cut deeply, and she felt a tearing feeling inside her. Her scream mingled with the would-be rapist's. She snatched her hand away. The cuts were not deep, and the pain winked out the second she let go of the blade. The man whose stomach it was buried in wasn't so lucky. His scream rose in pitch for several seconds while his shocked friend looked on, unable to do anything. He fell to the ground a moment later, stone dead.

Nial snatched the blade out of him with her power and stabbed it into the second man, ramming it up under his chin and into his brain. There were no screams this time. His life winked out like a candle flame. Nial was confused and starting to panic. *I have to get out of here. Those screams will attract attention even here.* Worse, she had killed two men with the strange weapon and hadn't had a chance to capture their souls. The still warm bodies were almost too tempting to pass up. *No! I have to get away. If they find me eating a body, the city Night Guard will come hunting for me.*

She pulled the blade out of the corpse's head and used her power to float up onto a nearby roof. There was something strange about the blade now. It felt warm to her somehow. She cleaned the blood off against her shift and was startled to see two little fireflies of light dancing inside the volcanic glass. *It took their souls! Just like that!* With a sigh of contentment, she drank deeply.

As the days passed, Nial recovered her strength and slowly tried to coax Zuly back to her. All she was able to get were vague images or ideas. Zuly was adamant in her desire for solitude.

The Soul Knife, as Zuly thought of it, was making a huge difference in Nial's hunting. There was little or no need to hide bodies now. A knife wound wasn't anything unusual. Men and women both were found with a stab wound or a cut throat in these streets. Nial would just hide in a likely place, hidden by her magic, and wait. Once she had chosen, the Soul Knife would flash down from a rooftop and one or more souls would be added to her store of power. Her only source of frustration lay in the knife's weight. It felt heavier the more souls it held. Not really heavy, of course, but harder to move through the air with her power. So long as it was strapped to her arm it didn't impede her movements at all. But now that a dozen little sparks danced inside it, she felt like she was pushing it through water when she moved it with magic.

She looked down at the strange blade. She had taken three more souls tonight. How long would it be before it became too hard to move? Or too slow to use as a weapon without holding the target in place? The limitations of the thing were frustrating.

Nial occasionally got little flashes of thought from Zuly, especially when she was hunting or feeding, but so far it was little she could understand. *My poor Zuly. I can't imagine what you had to go through for us, but please come back to me. You said yourself we're strong when we're together.* An image floated up into her mind, an image of a swollen stomach. Nial was shocked. She reached down and put a hand on her belly and knew it was true—she was pregnant. It made her feel scared in a strange sort of way, a very human way. The fear of a young girl with only the most basic idea of what was happening inside her body.

Zuly had spared her the memories of being violated by an archdemon but had been deeply wounded by the experience herself. Nial reached back out to Zuly with all her fear and love and felt her respond faintly in kind.

I'll take care of Shade's last target. After that, we can tell Uncle Skeg and figure out what to do.

CHAPTER 16

"My lord Drokga, the mounts you requested are ready. If you would permit me to show you, they await us outside in the courtyard." As the hunchbacked mage led the Drokga and his retinue out into the sunlight, he heard the murmurs and exclamations of shock as they caught sight of his creations. *A far more suitable reaction than what I got from the Drokga himself when I first showed him my work.*

Two large creatures stood as still as statues outside the stables. The first looked to be somewhere between a bull and a large horse, though covered with thick plates of the chitin. Its legs ended in three-toed claws, and long, sharp horns extended from its head. The second was chitin plated as well, but it was more reminiscent of an insect and a lizard. It also had large leathery wings folded on its back.

The Drokga and his generals stood at a cautious distance as Carver limped forward with his walking stick. "First let me describe the beast that will replace all other mounts for our city. Indeed, it may replace most beasts of burden. I made this from the first mount that I showed you when I arrived in the city, my lord Drokga. This is the mastikide. The creature was created from a large bull. It has innate combat reflexes that I have enhanced. The horns are extremely strong and are edged like a blade in addition to having a sharp point. They are similar to the weapons your soldiers now use and, like those weapons, can grow back if damaged or broken. They will bite enemies as well as gore and kick them. If the rider wears a carapace, it can link directly to this mount to give him instinctive control over its actions."

There were appreciative murmurs from some of the generals. Carver continued, "The gait of one of these creatures is not as smooth as a well-trained horse, but they are nearly as fast and can move at full speed for much longer stretches. I've also changed their digestive systems. They can eat nearly anything—grass, leaves, carrion, even wood. They can also drink water that would poison any other animal. My assistant, Roga, contributed his own sliver of genius to this creature as well. The link between the mount and a carapace user can be used to transfer nutrients and water."

"So if my soldiers are riding these beasts, they need not worry about carrying food?"

"Indeed, my lord Drokga. They need only let the animals graze. It will not fill their stomachs or remove the feeling of hunger, but they will not suffer otherwise. The females have also been developed with our army's greater need for food in mind. They are just as large as the males but totally nonaggressive and make ideal pack animals. They also lay a large egg every day. This gives us a simple way to breed more as well as create an exceptional food source while traveling."

Carver hobbled over to the second creature. "This, my lord Drokga, is the first dragonid. It can carry an armed warrior at speeds beyond anything possible before now. With this mount, my lord, your men can fly. Unlike the mastikide, the males and females are nearly identical. They are bred for combat and offer the same advantages to a carapace rider as the land mount."

The Drokga nodded. "You have done well, Carver. The world will tremble at the coming of the Tolrahkali."

Carver bowed and stood by as the assembled generals admired his creations and discussed possible uses for the new creatures. He had seen it all before. It wouldn't be long now before the fools decided to try out their new weapons and attack some other country or city. The logical target was Bialta, though they likely hadn't thought of it themselves yet. Really it was the only possible target of consequence given the Tolrahkali's lack of a significant naval force. The coming battles would provide plenty of opportunities to test his creations and resources in the form of captured enemies. But if the Drokga bit off more than he could chew, everything Carver had built could fall apart. *Best to arrange for a contingency plan.* Noblemen and wealthy merchants visiting from virtually every nation on the continent were common in Tolrahk Esal. Such people invariably came to taste the city's forbidden pleasures. *And people who are slaves to their appetites are both predictable and easy to manipulate. All I need to do is find a likely candidate and awaken a little extra ambition. I should speak with Nasaka Jadoo about getting a few of his apprentices involved as well.*

New flying units were formed within days and were coming along extremely well. The link the carapace warriors shared with the dragonids had worked wonders and helped the desert warriors with overcoming their initial fear of taking to the skies. Carver had armed them with living bows as well as chitin arrows and javelins. Growing the ammunition had resulted in lighter, stronger, and more consistent weapons. The riders could either fire directly at individual targets or drop bundles of arrows from overhead. The effects of wind were unpredictable, but the riders were training hard, and accuracy was improving quickly. As pleased as the Drokga was with the progress, nothing could sway him from his demand that he be temporarily transformed to a stature worthy of leading this monstrous new army he was building. If anything, it became more and more important. *Perhaps he needs to assert his ascendancy over his people. These Tolrahkali do act like dogs much of the time, posturing and playing dominance games. Lucky for him it's finally ready.*

Carver dispatched a slave to tell the Drokga that the titan carapace was complete, asking him to come to the workshop at his earliest convenience. It didn't take long. The door to the workshop crashed open and the Drokga walked in followed by two of his guards.

"Is it finished?" asked the Drokga, walking around the raw slabs of flesh Carver was working on.

"Nearly, my lord, nearly. I just have a few minor adjustments to make," came the wheezing reply from somewhere behind the fleshy mess.

The disconcerting tingle the Drokga felt told him sorcery was being used nearby. He waited, one minute, then another, his anger and impatience starting to brim.

"I believe we are ready now, my lord. Please take your place on the central slab. I will summon my assistant as well as slaves to attend to Your Majesty."

"It's about time, Carver. You promised me something truly incredible, but then you made me wait for weeks longer than expected. I do not like delays."

"I know, my lord, I know. I have done it though. Done the impossible. Though I must caution you again about testing this newest creation on your own august personage. Initial trials with the smaller version on Nasaka are promising, but let us use a slave or even one of your sons if you do not wish to sully the creation."

"Are you really so ignorant of the minds of men after spending so long rummaging around in their innards? I cannot place such a weapon in the hands of a slave. Should it choose, it could lay waste to my palace. And one of my sons? They are ambitious, as they should be. Handing them this weapon would be my death. Now hurry up and get it moving."

Carver bowed as low as his twisted back would allow. *I can unmake my creations with little more than a thought. There is no need to fear their misuse, but then you probably wouldn't want to hear that, my dear Drokga.* Carver smiled in amusement. The slaves moved forward and reverently disrobed the Drokga before helping him to lie back on the cold stone.

"Now bear with me, my lord; this first melding will take some time. It will be much faster in the future once we have attuned the construct to you."

"Just get on with it! Why must all my servants always waste my time!?"

"Of course, my lord, of course." Carver slipped a circlet over the Drokga's head. *A simple rune of sensing to allow him to see outside his living armor. Another trick learned from my former master.* "Bring forward the stomachs and the shells!" Assistants and slaves pushed and dragged massive wheeled tanks of murky green liquid. Unrecognizable dark shapes floated and twitched within.

Carver reached out and stroked the nearer slabs of muscle. They began to convulse and twitch. Great bloodless masses of flesh rose up and plunged into the organ tanks at his direction. Every part of the construct was becoming more defined as its component parts came together and Carver's power melded them according to his plan. Long tendrils of muscle extended between the tanks and started to pull the various pieces together. A massive chitin-armored arm emerged from the mess, a fang-filled mouth in its palm, and grabbed hold of the nearest slave. The man gave a gurgling scream and went limp, the huge hand wrapped entirely around his emaciated body. A few gouts of blood sprayed out between the fingers as the hand crushed the slave's torso into the slavering mouth. The body was flung aside, the strangely hollowed-out corpse crashing into the far wall like a rag doll.

Carver glanced down at the Drokga and was grudgingly impressed. The man had courage to match his ego it seemed. He lay impassive and unmoving, though he lay naked at the center of the bloody spectacle. The only hint of emotion he betrayed at the slave's death was impatience.

Slowly, carefully, Carver guided the segments of the great body toward his lord. With small fleshy tentacles reaching out around the Drokga and linking with one another, the four limbs and their attached sections of torso were fully defined now and were closing in around the stone slab.

"The link must now be made. It will be painful, my lord. It is, as I said, regretfully unavoidable."

"Dammit, I know that! Just do it! I am no stranger to pain!"

Carver chuckled inwardly. *No stranger to pain, are you? Well, let's see how you feel with a whole raw, quartered body joining itself to your nervous system. Don't say I didn't warn you.* White tendrils extended out of the masses of flesh and struck like vipers, sinking into the Drokga's arms and legs.

The Drokga grunted, then grimaced. The tendrils dug deeper and then the screams started. *Oh, yes, he's going to be angry after this. But it can't be helped.* The screams were cut short as the construct took over Drokga's breathing and air supply. His eyes were darting around in shock. *Hmmm. I guess*

I forgot to warn him about that part. But I did tell him I got the idea from examining the breathing of embryos before they are born.

The sections started to close. The tentacles and muscles pulled the chitin plates over them and sealed the wounds between. *Yes, the carapace healing works even on this larger scale. Everything is a success so far.*

Finally, the last piece of the puzzle was dragged out of a large stone tub. The massive head of the colossus, carefully carved in the likeness of the Drokga himself. *Never before have I seen a man so proud of his own face. I guess being recognized helps when there is so much fear and awe associated with who you are.* The giant shuddered and started to rise to its feet. Fully three and a half times the height of a tall man, armored in spiked, steel-hard chitin a hand's width thick. Clawed fingers curled around the fang-filled mouths set in each hand. And above it all the unmistakable face of the Drokga, complete with a chitin likeness of the iron crown that nearly reached the vaulted ceiling overhead. *Oh yes, I think he will be pleased after his temper cools. . . .*

***

Dantic seethed as he returned to his rooms in the Arcanum. There had to be a way. He could outweave any of the fools in either council. He wouldn't let an upstart Fourth Order outdo him. *I'll just have to beat him at his own game whether he lets me join or not. It can't be that hard to make a magical servant if that idiot could figure it out.* He summoned an apprentice and instructed him to return with a number of relevant tomes. Then, as an afterthought, he summoned another apprentice and sent him out into the city with a list of items he would need to purchase. He would need to choose a better medium than the shinning steel Mage Bagwin's team was using, of course. If Dantic was going to dispense with costly alchemical reagents, he'd need to use something that was easier to enchant. The essence of magic was life, so enchanting something that had once been living would be far easier. Besides, he couldn't afford that much steel, much less the fee a smith would charge him. Bone would be ideal though the result might be . . . unsettling for some. *All those prohibitions against necromancy and such would probably get raised.* He would have to settle for wood. It was by far the cheapest choice and the most readily available, and a large marionette such as he had seen in the markets as a child would save him the trouble of shaping the thing.

He settled down to study and figure out just how he was going to manage the weave. He scarcely noticed when the apprentices came and went, leaving stacks of books and materials around his rooms.

Less than a week, he thought with pride. Less than a week and Dantic had figured out how to make a magical servant. And not only figured it out but improved on the idea in a number of subtle ways. He could create a magical servant for a fraction of the price that it was costing Bagwin's team. His own version of the enchantment even allowed for the automaton to use simple voice responses—something that had been remarkably simple to add to the weave. His innovations also allowed the construct to anticipate regular requests and perform the tasks without being asked. Both were additions he was sure rich nobles and merchants would desperately want. They would ask him for the trick of it he was sure. And he'd be generous with his knowledge . . . as a Closed Council member was expected to be.

The core enchantment would be a challenge of course. He'd have to make do with no rare metals or expensive catalysts, or even spell anchors to hold the weave in place and allow for breaks. But the Arcanum wasn't about to offer him funds to mess with what looked to be their most profitable project in centuries. Not to mention that what he was planning was reckless to attempt alone at best, extremely dangerous at worst. He would succeed despite them. When he walked through the halls of the Arcanum with his new servant, the council wouldn't be able to ignore his brilliance.

Dantic examined the notes he had spread out across the floor and let out a slow breath. The rest of the Arcanum would call him foolish or worse if they knew what he was attempting to do alone. The sheer amount of energy he would be working with could easily get out of control. But he was determined to prove he didn't need help to best Bagwin. His door was locked and warded. He had eaten as much as he could force down his throat. *Time to get to work.* By his best estimates the spell would take at least eight hours to complete. He raised his arms, and glowing threads of power stretched out around him, knotting themselves into increasingly complex patterns and shapes around the marionette.

A drop of sweat rolled down his forehead into his left eye. As he blinked it away in annoyance he vaguely noticed the sun was setting outside. At least ten hours had already passed and he was nowhere near finished. His stomach rumbled. His mistake had been in not anticipating the slippage on the outer edges of the weave. The enchantment as a whole was fraying as the pressures in the center mounted. Dantic had to devote most of his efforts to holding the weave together while desperately trying to widen and mold the pattern.

By the time it was fully dark in the room, his back was aching and his arms were starting to spasm from being held up for so long. He felt his bladder release an hour later, the warm wet spreading down his robes before slowly cooling. He did his best to block out the sensation and the feelings of shame that went with it. Three hours later, his mouth felt like sandpaper. Drops of sweat rolled into his eyes one after the other and he couldn't even afford to blink to alleviate the burning sensation. *I'm so close, dammit!*

He briefly considered calling for help. With the assistance of even a middling apprentice the weave would have been completed hours ago. Any help at all would allow him to finish in moments at this point instead of the excruciating hours he guessed were still ahead of him. But the thought of anyone seeing him in this state, soiled and helpless, was unthinkable.

It was too late to backtrack now, anyway. If he released the weave entirely, the energy he'd been feeding into it for the past however many hours would likely destroy several floors of the Arcanum. *Which may be what the rule against undertaking major rituals alone is intended to avoid.*

His progress had slowed to a crawl. Nearly all his efforts were consumed by holding the whole together. *I'm so close, damn it all!* But his body was failing him. The trembling was getting so bad he could barely stand. His vision was so blurred he realized he'd been working more by instinct than sight for at least the past hour. Black spots swam in front of his eyes. Failure was not an option. With a final surge of will he completed the weave only to feel it jolt out of his mental grasp and start to fray again even as he released it into the puppet. He had a split second of utter panic before everything went black.

***

The assembled armies of Tolrahk Esal were turned out in the desert outside the city. Never before had the entire force of the Tolrahkali been fielded together. Throngs of the city's mercenaries and merchants crowded around the edge of the buildings to watch, none of them daring to move beyond the perceived safety of the city limits. The Drokga stood in front of his assembled soldiers wearing his titan carapace. He raised his arms above his head and roared. The soldiers responded in kind with a mix of wordless shouts and war cries. The army looked more like a force of monsters or demons, their king the largest and most formidable beast of them all.

Their military was composed of excellent individual fighters. They were feared among the Free Cities, whom they occasionally skirmished with or raided, and they were popular bodyguards in Keral. But they had never been the victors in a large-scale war. There simply weren't enough of them, and their focus on individual prowess and recognition made them poor formation fighters. Only the presence of the many foreign and local mercenary companies in their city had dissuaded their neighbors from attempting to conquer Tolrahk Esal.

But today was the day. Today they would prove themselves to the outside world. The other Free Cities were too small to satisfy the Drokga's ego, and Dreth was more trouble than it was worth. They would sweep out and attack the greatest power on the continent and then, yes, then, the rulers of every nation would shake and tremble at the coming of the Tolrahkali.

Carver stood unnoticed in the shadows of a building and smiled. The coming war would prove to the Drokga how valuable he and his constructs were. He would be given yet more workspace and resources. Prisoners taken in battle would be especially useful—prime specimens trained for combat were expensive and always in short supply.

The Tolrahkali army would be split into three parts. A small force consisting almost exclusively of carapace-wearing foot troops would cross the Bialtan border first. The Drokga was insistent that he should be involved in this first battle. A second, larger force would follow with a number of the new cavalry and flying units and pull the bulk of the Bialtan units out of their regular places and far to the south. The last group would strike deep while the eyes of the army and the Arcanum were turned south and assault Darien directly, a final attack that was meant to coincide with a little surprise Carver had cooked up with the help of Nasaka.

The Drokga's force would fall back after the first battle and remain with Carver near the border. It would be ready to march in and secure the capital should his plan work, or ready to fall back and prepare for counterattack should it fail. *A bold plan. And yet one that places the Drokga himself at risk only in the easiest and least important confrontations.*

At worst, the Bialtans would manage to defeat his distraction force, and his men would have to flee back to the border where they would reorganize and begin a more conventional war. The Bialtans would have no way of anticipating the greatly improved speed and endurance of his carapace soldiers. They would be able to fall back without significant losses.

This would be a new kind of war, fought as much in the minds of their enemies as on the battlefield as the Tolrahkali brought a new level of savagery and fear to break the Bialtans' morale.

Magic is the only complication. Carver had insisted the Drokga's famed warlocks should concentrate exclusively on trying to obscure the troops' locations and to counter magic attacks until the mage hunters could neutralize the threat, but there was no telling just how many mages the Bialtans would be able to conscript from the Arcanum. The mage hunters were a central part of the Tolrahkali strategy. The new and improved Nasaka Jadoo would be in the thick of things along with a dozen of his most promising apprentices. Nasaka would remain immersed in a tank of nutritive solution until they reached Bialta. The large tank of dark liquid sat on a cart pulled by two female mastikides. Only a vaguely humanoid form was visible within the murky depths along with the occasional flash of deep-red eyes.

***

Salt was surprised that he was given total freedom to roam the library, indeed all the libraries of the city, at his leisure. There wasn't much for him to do, and no one but Lamek would talk to him, so he was grateful for the distraction. *If Lera could see this, she'd never want to leave.* But the books held only passing interest for Salt. It was the maps that fascinated him and kept him coming back again and again. He took a blank page off a nearby table and started to try to copy what he could. More than a few of the maps he'd seen before had wide blank spaces while this one even showed a network of rivers and lakes at the heart of the great desert! *I'm sure Lera and Gurt will be interested in seeing this.* It took him a few attempts but he finally managed to make a reproduction of a map of the continent surrounding Bialta. Far from impeding his efforts, the silent scribes of the library brought him ink and paper and even offered wordless assistance by pointing out mistakes or showing him how to improve. What had started out in part as a time-wasting exercise was quickly becoming an enjoyable activity. The greatest difficulty lay in deciding which map to trust since so many were different. The map he finally completed after days of work was perhaps simple compared to the painted masterpieces that were held in some of the cabinets or frames between the bookshelves, but he felt that the simplicity of ink on paper made the map clearer than many of the others. *It's also nice to know exactly where I am in the world for a change and just how far from home I am.*

"Ah, there you are, Salt," called Lamek, walking up to him. "I see your interest in our maps is undiminished. There are more in the fifty-third southern library that may be of particular note. They show the continents across the Black Sea. The Endless Ocean unfortunately was never completely mapped. We started, mind you, and have some beautiful charts of the small islands we encountered—they are in the twenty-third northern library by the way—but the only expeditions we're sure of that reached the other side came just before the Dragon War and their charts were all lost."

Salt looked at him with wide eyes. "I would very much like to see them."

"Any in particular? I seem to recall there are quite a number."

"I haven't got a clue, Lamek. Until you just told me, I didn't even know there were lands across the Black Sea or the ocean."

"No? Oh, well then. Maybe it's not my place to show them to you. I do tend to overestimate just how far you humans have come in your short time on this world. You must ask Nok Dreth if he will allow you to see the charts. Perhaps he'd even let you keep a set of copies. Which reminds me—he is waiting for you. That is why I've come to find you."

"Oh . . . thank you, Lamek. Do you think I could borrow a lamp from here? The stairs up to Nok Dreth's rooms are a bit challenging for me in the dark."

"Of course, please go ahead and take one," he said, waving vaguely around the library. "They are here to be used. Just be sure to bring it back when you are finished."

"Of course. And thanks again."

Salt found the climb back up to Nok Dreth's room far less strenuous with a lamp, but he still stood panting at the top of the stairs for quite some time before he felt ready to speak to the Dreth ruler. *Maybe I'll finally be able to leave,* he thought hopefully. *If I can take back some of those maps, I'm sure it would make Gurt and the king happy too.*

"Ah, welcome," Nok Dreth called when Salt pushed the door open. "You are just in time. I only just finished the last touches." He gestured to a steaming trough of water. "It should have cooled enough to handle." He reached into the water and pulled out the ugliest weapon Salt had ever seen.

It was essentially an overlarge black hammer made out of a twisted mass of the black bone he'd been shown at their first meeting. As if hundreds of pieces had been twisted together and imperfectly fused into a whole.

Nok Dreth read his reaction easily. "It is not a thing of beauty. The dragon bone resists shaping. But this is not a weapon of subtlety. Nor is it a thing to inspire and enrapture. It is a weapon of war and a tool for killing, and it will serve in both capacities exceptionally well." He moved the weapon from side to side as if looking for imperfections. *The whole thing looks like one big imperfection.*

"The lightness of the dragonbone is a flaw for most weapons, of course. I have only made two bows from it before, as well as my own suit of armor, which is as yet unfinished." He gestured to a suit of scale armor that was hanging from a rack at the back of the room. One half was exquisitely finished gleaming black scales while the other half was a twisted mess, much like the hammer he now held. "The black bone resists being shaped, and bending it fully to my will requires significant effort. I have been working on my own armor for many of your human lifetimes, and it is, at best, half-done." He made a dismissive gesture as if to say it was of little importance. "I'm sure you can appreciate the benefits the lightness and strength of the bone would have for armor. But for your own weapon, a certain amount of weight was required. I built this great hammer around a core of Dreth blood steel that I had Thirat Bel

Thammar forge for me. At first I thought this would suffice. The result would have been fearsome enough certainly, but I wanted this gift to be more a weapon of Dreth than the echo of a dragon lord's power. And so I encased a full dozen drained power crystals within the head of the hammer. The fires of the gems have died, but the memory of what they were remains. Sorcery will not easily deny this great hammer, my friend."

He's serious. He wants me to have this thing. . . . And he called me friend.

"I see your surprise that I would name you thus. You begin to understand the importance of spoken words among the Dreth. You are learning. Some words can be a greater gift even than a legendary weapon. So, as I was saying, you have done my people and me a great service by recovering the First Sword. More, you have reawakened in some of us the pleasure to be taken in the company of others and the desire to create. I have not spoken so much in decades, nor have I sought to make something truly new. I have made for you a weapon befitting your stature and your status as a hero among my people. That you are human allowed me rather more creative freedom than I would have had rewarding those of my own race. I present to you Bretuul the Demon Hammer. Take this, my greatest creation, and may your enemies fear your coming."

"I'm honored beyond words, Nok Dreth, both for the Hammer and that you would call me friend, but I can't accept this. I'm not much more than a common sailor who fell into a better job."

"No need for modesty here, Salt. I know you for what you are, perhaps better than you do yourself. The truest measure of a man's greatness is the quality of his enemies, and you, my friend, have gathered some rather impressive enemies in your short years."

Salt was silent. There was more being said here than he understood. Nok's thoughts were so far beyond him sometimes that he didn't think he could ever come to understand the Dreth. Then it occurred to him that the man standing in front of him had warred with dragons, and not only warred with them but had slain the greatest of their kind. Salt accepted the ugly weapon from the Dreth ruler. It felt strange in his hands. Both light and heavy at the same time. Surprisingly well balanced, too, given its misshapen appearance.

"I don't know what to say, Nok Dreth. I hope I prove worthy of your gift."

Nok Dreth waved his words away again. "You are fond of wasting words, Night Captain. I can clearly see the desire to prove yourself in your every move and breath. I have no doubt you will succeed. Now, as much as I have enjoyed your visit, I expect you are eager to return to your home."

"I—" Salt started, then stopped with a wry smile and nodded. "Nok Dreth. If I may ask one more favor before I leave. Lamek spoke to me of maps that I might see or maybe even obtain copies of, maps of the lands on and beyond the Endless Ocean and the Black Sea."

Nok Dreth looked at Salt like a father looking at a bright if misguided child. "No, Salt. Your kind are not ready to go so far beyond your shores. There are many lands you have not seen or heard of, thousands of creatures that we met during our travels. Many of those would snuff out your human race like a hurricane blowing out a single candle."

He walked around the workroom pointing at odd items that were mounted on the walls. "These things we brought back are just a handful of the artifacts we collected during our wanderings. We traveled as merchants, as peaceful explorers. But many times we were not accepted as such. Miscommunications, cultural differences, or simply violent tendencies led to more wars and battles than our entire race can now accurately recall." He looked around the room sadly. "We have tried to record all our history in the library, but we are in a battle with time to accurately set everything down before it is forgotten forever. We are so very long-lived. . . . Can you imagine trying to write down everything you have learned in your life, Salt? Can you imagine then living a hundred lifetimes? A thousand? Ten thousand? Some of those we encountered were nearly a match for the Dreth at the height of our power.

"Your little human race that prides itself on its divided control of two small continents and a few hundred islands is little more than an infantile race in a forgotten corner of the world." Nok looked up pensively for a moment. "Of course, some of those we met must have fallen in the meantime, either to each other or simply to the passage of time. It matters not. Those who remain and have the means to cross the great oceans have not done so for one reason and one reason alone. And trust me, it has little to do with fear of Bialta's armies."

Salt couldn't help bristling at the comment. "You're saying we owe our continued existence to you? That all those scary fuckers you Dreth fought thousands of years ago are still running scared and avoiding our lands because of it?"

"That is precisely what I am saying, Salt. The time frame involved may seem ludicrous to you, but the Dreth are not the only long-lived race in the world. Some races do not forget and, to be blunt, we Dreth did not leave much room for doubt when another race chose to attack us. We struck them back hard and fast enough to make sure they would never attempt it again. We never gave any of them a chance to make a second attempt. Though we decided some were not even worth the bother of fighting. The Palic, for example, are a strange race that more closely resemble trees than sentient beings. They grow in groups of four and attain mobility after a few centuries or so of life. Their magics would rival even the great sorceries of the dragons, but they seem incapable of crossing saltwater and are unwilling or uninterested in anything beyond the shores of their tiny island home. From what little we were able to learn about them, they never die. They simply get older and grow larger. Some of the tallest ones could very well be the first of their race. Magics such as your entire Arcanum could not begin to comprehend, and they are far from the worst."

"Tell me then. Who are the worst?"

Nok shook his head. "You disappoint me, Salt. You have heard more about us than any human scholar has ever hoped to learn and you ask me that?"

"The dragons," Salt said.

"The dragons! Yes, the dragons! What other race was able to cast down the Dreth Empire? To reduce us to a single city? What other race was able to push us to the very brink of defeat?" Nok was shouting by the time he finished, his face deepening to a darker shade of blue. "You Bialtans are the young race we feel the greatest kinship with. Your capital is built on the site of our last free city. Our own half bloods share your bloodlines. Moreover, you follow in our footsteps in spirit. You travel far and wide to explore and learn, to trade and meet new people. Through just such a spirit of wonder the Dreth achieved greatness. But do not overreach or think yourselves beyond harm as we did. There are powers on this world beyond your understanding. But the Dreth know. We know because we are one such power. All that you have, all that you have seen has been built on the bones of the past. *Our* past."

Salt bowed as low as he could in front of the enraged Dreth. He did not waste words. He regretted bringing up the maps entirely. *Stupid of me to ask for more right after he gives me something he's so proud of.* Nok Dreth was silent for a time and Salt didn't dare look up. "It seems patience is something I need to rediscover as well, Night Captain. I apologize for the harshness of my words, though not for the words themselves. Go in peace, Saltig Sodigson, and know that you are always welcome among the Dreth."

"You have taught me a lot, Nok Dreth. I will not forget." Salt bowed again and left, more eager than ever to leave the fortress city and find himself back in familiar company.

At the base of the stairs, he found Lamek and a guard detail of Fire Warriors waiting. One of the Fire Warriors was carrying Salt's pack. *They must be as eager to see me go as I am to leave.* Lamek gave Salt a small nod. "I am very sorry to see you go so soon, Salt. It was a true pleasure to entertain you."

"Thank you, Lamek. I've enjoyed my time here. It's been a real eye-opener."

"Now, if you will follow us, we will guide you back to the gate. Your horse should be saddled and ready when we get there. Your companions have also been alerted to your imminent departure and have been given fresh supplies for the journey back to Bialta." As tired as he was from going up and down the long stairs, Salt didn't argue. He would camp with the other Night Guardsmen once they were out of sight of the city. The great gates were opened for the second time in living memory, and Salt was shown out. He handed the library lamp to Lamek as they parted.

"I hope we meet again, Lamek."

"As do I, Salt. Farewell."

The other Guardsmen clustered around him, hundreds of questions in their eyes. Min saw something in him and stopped the others from coming too close. "When we're alone," she insisted. The others nodded and stepped back. The rest of the marketplace was watching them like hawks as they walked away from the slowly closing gates, Lamek and the honor guard disappearing back inside.

"All right, guys, let's get out of here. I need to see the sun rise tomorrow without a giant ugly wall blocking it and with a good old hangover making me wish my skull was cracked." They rode in silence until the marketplace was out of sight and the city was nothing more than a shadow on the horizon.

"This will do," Salt said, climbing off his horse. "Now please tell me we have something to drink, 'cause I'm not answering any questions without it."

Min laughed. "Glad to hear it, Salty. We have some prime stuff for you. The Dreth didn't stint with the provisions they gave us." She was as excited as a child with a new toy. He raised an eyebrow and she laughed.

"It wasn't just supplies they gave us." She drew her sword in a fluid motion. "Dreth steel! We each got to pick one. For free!" She gave Salt a tight hug and moved away, suddenly embarrassed.

Altog smiled. "I think the girl's grateful you chose to bring her along. As are we all, I think. Hope you don't mind if I don't hug you though."

Brolt laughed. "Holding out for a kiss, are ya?"

Suddenly Salt felt like everything was back to normal. He started to set up camp and just let the others' banter wash over him.

"Salt, what is that monstrosity you have strapped to your horse?" Altog asked, pointing to Salt's new hammer.

"This is Bretuul the Demon Hammer," Salt said with a smirk, as he brought the weapon over to show the others.

Altog burst out laughing. "Pretty freaking grand name for an ugly piece of crap." He turned to Min. "Guess we were the lucky ones." Brolt and Min weren't laughing. They were staring at the Hammer with looks of mixed dread and awe.

"Salty, that thing reeks of power," Min said, looking at it intently but not moving any closer.

Brolt nodded. "And 'reeks' isn't a strong enough word. But it's weird. I couldn't feel it until you were holding it."

"Nok Dreth made it for me. That's why we had to wait so long."

"I can't wait to see you use it, Salty," said Min. "But Gurt is going to have a fit when you bring that into the castle. It's anything but discreet." Then her eyes went strangely blank.

Salt reached out, but she came back to herself before he touched her. "That was Lera. She said the Tolrahkali have attacked a Bialtan trade caravan near Dreth and they have an army moving toward the border just north of here. Gurt wants us back yesterday."

Salt sighed. "No fucking rest for the wicked. I'll have to drink as we ride." He made a face as he pulled himself back up onto his horse. "So much for setting up camp. Let's get a few more hours in tonight."

The others were ready only moments later, and they set out with a new urgency, as if an invading army were on their heels.

CHAPTER 17

The sun was beaming down on the white city. Sacral in the full of summer was a place of great beauty. The wide, tree-lined streets were filled with people going about their business. Maura noticed an eagerness in the crowds that hadn't been there just the day before. With spring over and the city and its lands lush with new life and crops, people were finally waking up from the daze that had held them since the Abolian invasion.

Maura could almost ignore the burnt-out ruins of destroyed houses and shops that dotted nearly every neighborhood. Repair efforts continued, of course, but Maura had insisted that the walls and fields take precedence. Enough people had been lost—often entire families—that there was more than enough space to house those who had lost their homes. Thankfully all the buildings in Sacral were made mostly of stone, so the fires hadn't spread far. The biggest problem was deciding how the newly vacant homes should be handed out. Families often took exception to others being placed in the houses of their dead relatives. In the meantime, some families had been settled in the Black.

The Black was the closest thing Sacral had to a slum. The buildings were bare stone—the black basalt left uncovered. The poorest segment of the population lived here. The homes were as well built as any in the city since they all dated back to the founding, but it was considered unlucky to live in a home that didn't have white walls, so most of the buildings were left to gather dust. The histories showed that the Black had shrunk over the years as Sacral's population had increased and more and more homes were occupied and painted. Now only a narrow strip of the Black remained, but Maura doubted it would ever disappear. Those few undesirables the city held had made their homes here and seemed unwilling or unable to even paint the walls. Bars and gambling dens were the only businesses in the area. All of them clustered around the building that was Maura's destination—Sacral's prison.

Only a few dozen prisoners had been locked up in the huge building before the invasion. Now, it held almost fifteen hundred men and women, all of them Abolian. They were the few who had been lucky enough to escape the backlash from the crowds when Sacral had gained the advantage in the battle. The city was using considerable resources to ensure the prisoners both survived and did not escape, which was Maura's primary reason for coming to this unsavory part of town.

She didn't have a clue what to do with them. Most of the prisoners didn't even speak a language she understood. Still, she couldn't decide their fate until she had attempted to speak to as many of the Abolians as she could. Beren had insisted that the safest course of action was to keep them locked up for the time being, that their nation would surely ask for them back and they could be ransomed for supplies and construction materials. Harrow wanted them put to work repairing the damage they had caused. Corwin had insisted that they could not be trusted not to attack them again either way and that a few drops of spider venom in their evening meal would be the kindest solution. Maura shuddered just thinking about it. The generally jovial man had shocked her deeply with his pragmatic suggestion.

Maura had killed more than one Abolian during the battle and had ordered the death of many others, but this was not war. There was no struggle happening here. She couldn't order a single person murdered much less a thousand. As much as anyone in Sacral, Maura wanted a return to stability, to safety. The presence of so many of their enemies here in the city made that impossible. She almost hoped that the prisoners would be vile and disgusting individuals, that their evil would be obvious in their faces and words, that Corwin's solution might yet be justified. That she could look at them and see the source of all her pain and rage at the senseless loss of her son. Such people could be put to death without remorse. *Maybe . . .*

The Black had hardly been disturbed by the attack or the goddess riots. Looting Abolians had moved away from the poor or sparsely populated areas looking for richer spoils, and the rioters had had no need to disturb the area either as no statues or paintings of the White Mother had ever existed here.

Ten soldiers walked with Maura under the command of Squad Leader Molt. Captain Harrow had tried to insist on accompanying her himself, but she would have none of it. He was needed elsewhere and she couldn't allow him to waste his time following her around. But after their discoveries in the temple, Harrow saw dangers and traitors everywhere, and he would simply not let her leave the palace unprotected. They passed a few people on the street who made Maura shiver. She'd never been to the Black before. There was nothing wrong with the people who lived there per se. It was just the way they looked at her that made her thankful that she had relented and allowed Harrow to assemble this small honor guard.

Maura noticed the prison long before they came to the building itself. It was far larger than she had expected, a giant stone block nearly a match in size to the White Mother's temple. And yet if anyone actually lived inside the giant building, there was no sign. No windows or openings of any kind marred the featureless black walls. *I guess it would have to be big for over fifteen hundred prisoners to be locked up in it, not to mention the guards.*

"It must be worse than living in a cave," she said.

"It's actually not unpleasant inside, Commander," said one of her bodyguards. She looked over at him questioningly. "I had to bring prisoners here a couple times before, but getting stationed here permanently is one of the biggest punishments the army has. No one wants to be a Sword Brother."

"And why is that, soldier?"

He shrugged uncomfortably. "They're a strange lot. Locked up in that box with the prisoners all the time."

They came around the front of the building. Huge iron doors blocked the only entrance. "I'll have to remember this place if we're ever attacked again. It's the most defensible building in the city, though I don't like the idea of only one entrance."

Her bodyguard pounded on the door. It opened smoothly. Two armed guards stood in the doorway wearing white robes embroidered with the sword of justice over their leather armor. One of the Sword Brothers looked Maura up and down, then turned to the nearest of her bodyguards. "Pretty heavy escort for one woman. What did she do?" His voice was gravelly and cracked with disuse.

Molt flushed and shot an apologetic look at Maura before glaring at the Sword Brother and answering. "This is High

Commander Maura of the People's Army! Savior of Sacral! Show some respect!"

Unperturbed, the Sword Brother looked back to Maura for a moment and mumbled, "Thought you'd be taller." Then he paused long enough to make her bodyguards bristle before adding, "My lady commander." Then he moved out of the way and waved them inside.

The inside of the building strongly reminded Maura of the White Mother's temple. The same soft Sourceless light lit the inside of the bright and surprisingly airy interior. Although plain and suitably austere, the long empty hallways didn't feel foreboding or confining.

They didn't have far to walk before coming to the cells. Hundreds of small single enclosures lined one side of the hallway that seemed to wind around endlessly within the huge building. Each cell had three stone walls so that the prisoners were unable to see each other. Thick iron bars sealed them in. Each cell had a stone shelf for sleeping with several blankets piled atop it, jugs for water and pots for waste, as well as enough room to comfortably walk in a circle, albeit a small one, should they feel the need to move around. Maura was surprised again by the airiness of the place. With so many bodies confined in a tight place, the smells should be strong in here, and yet she realized she couldn't smell anything at all in this strange place. Not even the smell of her own clothes when she raised them to her face. The Sword Brother called out and all the prisoners stood at attention next to their bunks. Despite the disorganized rabble these people had devolved into during the sacking of the city, they had obviously received military training and were accustomed to taking orders. Maura briefly wondered how the Sword Brothers were able to enforce this level of obedience in the prisoners, then pushed the thought from her mind. She had enough to think about already. The prisoners were clean and looked to be well cared for. That was enough for now.

Maura walked down the long hallway with the same two Sword Brothers leading the way and her bodyguards behind her. Maura barely noticed them. Her attention was focused on these men and women whose fates she needed to decide. Some of them returned her stare with defiance in their eyes, while others bowed their heads meekly or in fear. Not one of them inspired the immediate sense of loathing she had almost hoped for. Choosing their fates was all the more daunting now that the prisoners were not faceless numbers anymore, but real flesh and blood men and women who were locked up in cages. Maura stopped so suddenly that her bodyguards almost tripped over her. The man in the cell she had been passing had turned away as she approached, but not before she had seen his face. Impossibly, she knew the man.

"Sword Brother," she called out to the prison guard who was still walking away down the length of the hall ahead of her. "I need to see this man more closely." The Sword Brother shrugged and unlocked the cell door with a heavy key. The prisoner moaned and curled up in the corner.

Maura's bodyguards moved in to bring the man out of his cell. When they touched him, he started to struggle violently. Molt looked at her apologetically before punching the man in the stomach twice. Then they dragged him out and forced him to his knees in front of Maura. The blood had drained from his face and he was trembling. Maura had no doubt she knew who he was. His reaction to her presence, so different from all the other Abolians, had confirmed it.

"Sword Brothers, I need this man taken somewhere private where I can speak with him." The two guards nodded and gestured for the bodyguards to follow them. Whispers and shouts were rising from all the cells now. Prisoners wondering if their time had come to an end, wondering if they would be dragged away next. Maura could feel the tension building. She looked back at the prison guard.

"Sword Brother? Why was this acolyte of the temple locked up with the Abolians?"

The guard's bored façade cracked for a moment as he looked at the prisoner in confusion. "A what? But he couldn't be. He speaks Abolian same as all the others. How could he be a priest?"

"That's exactly what I intend to find out. There can be no mistake. This man presided over my son's name day when he came of age just last year." Maura made sure her voice carried, despite the renewed surge of pain the happy memory awoke in her. Most of the Abolians may not be able to understand her, but she figured enough would for word to spread. She hoped to avoid creating any ill feelings over the incident. There was no sense in making the prisoners hate her and her people. Particularly since she might yet be releasing them.

The prisoner was taken to an empty room. A chair was brought in for him, and Molt started asking him questions: "Why were you pretending to be Abolian? Who are you really?"

Despite his obvious terror, the man wouldn't answer the most basic questions. As time dragged on, Maura's men became more frustrated and rougher in their treatment of the priest.

They are letting their anger and the White Mother's betrayal show, and they're taking it out on this man. The worst thing is, I can't blame them. "That will do for now, Molt. Sword Brothers, have this man put in a cell away from the other prisoners. Treat him fairly, but send word if he decides to speak. I need to return to the council."

"So there's a priest hiding with the prisoners?" said Sevren, leaning forward at the council table. "Do you think he hid in there to avoid the purge?"

"Not possible," replied Harrow. "The prisoners were all locked up well before the purge started. The only way it would be possible is if the Sword Brothers had turned, and if that were the case, they surely wouldn't have led you past the man in the first place. There are more than enough Abolian prisoners in that building to satisfy even the most curious of inspections."

"Whatever the reason, he speaks their tongue as if born to it," said Maura.

"This strikes me as something long prepared then. Certainly not a way to hide. Even using magical learning, picking up a language is not something that can be done in a day," added Corwin. "It seems to me we need to find out why he's there, and soon. The priesthood's plans concern us all directly." His comment met with nods and words of agreement from around the table.

"How hard was he pressed during his interrogation, my lady?" asked Harrow.

"Hard enough to be bruised. I stopped Molt from going any further. We are not savages."

"I'm sorry, my lady, but I think that was a mistake. Our enemies have no qualms about using any and all means at their disposal to hurt us. That one of those enemies seems to be our patron goddess makes this all the more critical."

"You would torture the man then?"

"I would, my lady. If doing so would save the life of even one of our people."

Maura was shocked. She never would have guessed any of her councillors were so cold. Then she remembered Corwin's comment about spider venom from that morning. *Maybe I'm the one who's too soft for all this.* She looked around the council.

One by one her councillors all nodded, though Jerik looked as if he might be sick as he did so. Feeling almost as if someone else were speaking through her lips, Maura said, "Do it."

Harrow returned early the next day to report his findings. Maura hadn't slept at all. She'd barely left the council chamber. She couldn't let go of the image of the priest, whom she'd first met at such a happy occasion, suffering at her command.

"What did you learn, Captain?"

"Not as much as I would have liked," he said, not taking his eyes off the floor. "But he has admitted to being a priest of the White Mother . . . and the Deceiver. Those little truths came out not long after he admitted to speaking our tongue. He spoke quite calmly most of the time but would then rave and scream with no warning. I believe he is insane, as is the goddess he serves."

Maura's eyes widened in shock.

"He spoke of Sacral being a grand sacrifice to the goddess. The people's weakening faith was weakening her in turn. So the priests were tasked with consecrating every part of our city in her name. They made every building and street into an altar upon which the dying would be a sacrifice to her, then invited the wolves in to slaughter us. The Abolians were simply the first to arrive and offered a convenient way for the temple to get a large part of our army out. I believe they may even have intended to use Jenus and his army further, possibly in an attempt to retake the city, but I haven't been able to confirm that." He lowered his eyes and let out a slow breath before continuing. "The priests were to remain in hiding. They used the White Mother's magic to learn the Abolian tongue and customs before Kabol and Zorat even arrived at our door. Some were to infiltrate the Abolian army and spread the Mother's cult to their lands. Others were to wait and come out to rule over any who might survive after the army had finished sacking the city. The priest swore he didn't know how many others were among the Abolian survivors. I do not believe him."

"I'm worried. What am I to tell the people? They already feel betrayed and lost. I've heard many of them speak of leaving Sacral and traveling to Bialta or Keral. How will they feel when they hear that not only were they abandoned and betrayed, but we were all to die, sacrificed to that bloodthirsty monster?"

"The important thing is they failed. Who knows what would have happened if we hadn't gone to explore the temple when we did? Or if that minion of the Dead King hadn't killed the priests for us?"

For the first time since he arrived, Harrow met her eye so she could see what the torture was costing him. "I intend to continue the interrogation. In truth, I only came to give you an update. And to . . . breathe. But I have to push him. I need to know more. I need to know if we can trust the prisoners not to be harboring another priest."

Maura's gaze was far away. "We were nothing more than cattle to her. Swelling in numbers for all these centuries until she was ready to have us slaughtered and glut herself on our blood and souls. And now even one of the happiest memories I had of my son is tainted by the presence of one of her priests."

"I'm sorry, Lady Maura," said Harrow softly, calling her back to the here and now. "I'm sorry that you have been saddled with this decision. But what must I do with the priest after I am through? I do not think he can ever be freed, nor should any others we find among the Abolians."

"You are right, my friend. We can't let him go. Nor can we trust him not to spread *her* influence over the other prisoners or even the guards." She took a deep breath. "His place is in the pit with the other priests." A tear ran down her cheek. *What would Beren think of me if he knew I'd done this?*

Harrow saluted and moved to leave when Maura stopped him. "Harrow? When you do it, please make it quick."

He nodded without looking back at her and left in silence. *Just like that I ordered a man to be murdered. A man who likely did little if anything wrong himself beyond taking vows to serve the same deity we all followed blindly for generations.* Maura felt dirty—dirty and confused and miserable. Prayer had always helped calm her before . . . but now? She didn't think she could ever trust another god or priest. She was denied her usual support, now while hundreds of thousands of people in the city were placing their hopes and trust in her. So many responsibilities, all of them heavier than she could have ever imagined, and no one to lean on. *Not even Beren.*

While Beren was rarely out of earshot during the day, he spent long hours locked up in his shop at night. There was something fragile about him that prevented her from sharing her burdens with him. She missed the comfort of being with him. The simple nearness and easy understanding. Maura felt like they were miles apart. Beren worked himself into exhaustion, carving runes into every conceivable object or tool that he thought would help anyone. Maura could see the pain in his eyes. *He must blame himself for Gerald's death. As if there was anything he could have done. If only he would talk to me.* She stared off into space and let out a slow breath.

I guess we've both made our choice. We've both put the good of the city and its people ahead of our own needs. Perhaps one day they would both be able to step back from a city at peace with itself and help each other heal. But today was not that day. Today was the day Maura expected to order several more priests to be put to death.

***

Beren looked down at the plow blade he was working on. His supplies were running out and this might be the last rune he could carve unless he started charging for his services again. Since the invasion he'd been desperate to work, to help in any way he could, if only to silence his thoughts for a few precious moments. *They were attacking me!* he told himself again and again. *They murdered Gerald!* But the guilt of what he had done, the weight of all those lives he'd taken almost by accident, the fact that he'd done so too late to save his son, just kept gnawing at him. *No, it wasn't an accident. I chose to pick up the sword. I chose to step outside. I chose to take the fight to the Abolians.* He shook his head in frustration.

One final adjustment and the rune was complete. One more farmer would have an easier time plowing his fields. *And now I have nothing left.* His workshop was nearly empty. He'd had every single sword, axe, and shield taken out of the place, finished or not. The only weapon left was the very one that still haunted his dreams—the twisted piece of metal that was all that was left of the sword.

Beren had originally intended to unmake it completely, not trusting that beating the blade out of shape would be enough. But he just couldn't bring himself to do it. It was, in every possible way, the culmination of his life's work. *And what if it's needed again? What if I need to use it to save Maura?* He found himself holding it often. Turning it over and inspecting it with his talent.

Without quite realizing when he started, he found himself working his magic on the twisted blade. He started to smooth out the damage and imperfections. Under normal circumstances, Jerik would have reforged a weapon before Beren would have tried to fix a shattered rune or finesse a sharper edge onto it. He would have found doing all of it magically tedious and painfully slow . . . but not anymore. At least not with this sword. There was no doubt and no hesitation in his actions. The shape of the sword, as it had been, was seared into his memory—both the internal matrix and the profusion of runes on the surface. *I'll leave it incomplete. Just the smallest of segments left out in the internal pattern of the weave. Just in case . . .*

***

"I don't like this, Nial. This is a nobleman's house you're talking about attacking. You just can't do something like that and not attract the full attention of the Arcanum *and* the Night Guard. This guy has friends among the city's mages, too. I asked around a little, discreetly, and heard he entertains mages at his home fairly often. Zuly? What do you think?"

"Zuly doesn't want to talk since we went to Karethin. It's like she's asleep all the time."

"All the more reason not to go!"

"I'm sure I can get into the house. He won't want to have all those guards with him all night. We need to finish Shade's list. Danekor only just got back from Noros, and I want to make sure we get him before he leaves again."

Skeg sighed. "You're probably right. But there's got to be a better way. Maybe you can get a job there as a servant? You're a pretty young woman. I'm sure they would hire you. I might even be able to pull some strings."

"No, Uncle. It would take too long. I'm going tonight. But I'll see if I can borrow a servant's clothes; it might help in case someone sees me."

"I just don't understand why you're in such a hurry. We planned more carefully for the other two, and they were easier."

"I . . . I'll explain when I get back. I'm sorry, Uncle. I just have to get free of Shade. I can't wait any longer. Gunnar Danekor has to die tonight."

Skeg nodded glumly and watched her go.

Getting into the nobleman's house was more difficult than Nial had expected. Guards patrolled every part of the grounds. Thick walls and complex wards covered every approach, including the sky. But Skeg was right—servants moved through the great house easily. It only took a little while to find one who was being sent on an errand to the markets. A young girl, attractive, as all the servants seemed to be. Nial followed the girl at a distance and waited for her chance. An hour later she was walking back to the estate carrying the spices the serving girl had been sent to fetch, wearing her uniform. *She'll have a sore head when she wakes up, but she'll probably be glad she was far away when she hears what happened in her master's home.*

No sooner had Nial slipped through the door than an officious-looking man in an overly elaborate uniform set her to work preparing for the evening's festivities. She joined the army of identically dressed girls who were setting up elaborate tables in a dining hall several times bigger than her father's entire home.

"By all the Gods, girl! Who taught you to fold napkins?! Every place setting you've prepared is wrong!"

Nial did her best to look contrite and stammered apologies until the man ordered her to make herself useful elsewhere. Nial dissolved into tears, as if upset by the idiot's disapproval, and then ran, slipping behind one of the heavy wooden doors that was sitting open. A quick weave and she was invisible and free to watch the proceedings in peace. *We'll watch him for a while. When all his guests have left, he will be tired and alone....*

For the most part the evening passed as the girls expected. About forty guests came to Lord Danekor's home that night. They were all dressed in expensive silks and glittered with gems and gold. Three of the guests caught Nial's attention by their comparative lack of ornamentation. All three were men, and they wore simple robes of black and green. *Mages! And they haven't seen us. Uncle Skeg was right. This weave Shade gave us is wonderful.* Still, she couldn't help glancing back at the three every so often, just to be sure they didn't suspect anything.

The tables in the ballroom had been set up to one side as if leaving space for a show, though no entertainment was provided during the meal. Servants came and went with more food and drink than Nial's family would have eaten in a year. Most of the guests didn't even finish what they took, though they all called for more and more. Through it all Gunnar Danekor sat like a king. He spoke with each and every one of his guests, always calling them by name and asking after a relative or a business partner. They all fawned over him and visibly competed for his attention.

When the meal was finally over, the plates and platters were all cleared and, to Nial's surprise, the heavy wooden doors were closed and barred. One of the mages even traced a ward onto the thick oaken wood. Only a select few of the servants had been allowed to remain in the room to pour brandies and refill wineglasses. *Something strange is going on.*

Lord Danekor stood up and raised one hand for silence. His guests all stopped talking immediately and looked at him in rapt attention. "Welcome again, my friends. I hope you have enjoyed your meal. We will now move on to the entertainment. You all know my good friends Devin Teps, mage of the Third Order; Elias Holen, mage of the Fourth Order; and our most recent addition—Nolan Terillion, mage of the Fourth Order." The three stood and bowed as they were named, the rest of the guests clapping politely. "I believe that Mage Elias and Mage Nolan have each prepared something special for us this evening, and I will be giving a prize of a hundred gold crowns to whichever of the two provides the very finest show." The crowd clapped, and Lord Danekor returned to his seat.

Elias Holen moved over to the clear half of the ballroom. He motioned to a servant who set a fire in the great fireplace despite the fact that it was late spring and quite warm. "I like to call this little trick the Curse of Flame." He waved his hands dramatically and a woman shuffled out of the back room flanked by two of Lord Danekor's house guards. She was wearing heavy furs and had blankets wrapped around her thin frame. The audience clapped appreciatively. "Ah, I see many of you anticipate me here—a female wrapped in winter rags is hardly worth applauding, even in this weather. The curse I spoke to you of is a little spell of my own devising—it pulls the heat from her body. Useful to anyone on a particularly hot day of course"—he paused as the audience tittered at his joke—"but this is a stronger version of the spell than any of us would want to use on ourselves. She simply cannot get warm now, no matter how hard she tries. The effects on her behavior have been growing along with her need for heat. I believe this evening we will have a singular show for you all. This woman will soon burn herself, without any compulsion. She will likely even burn herself to death."

The audience applauded. The mage bowed deeply. "Now, before we begin, my lords and ladies, I have a wager for you all. I wager this tramp will not only set herself on fire, but she will do so with a smile on her face!" The assembled men and women laughed louder this time. The mage made another extravagant bow and stepped back, waving at the guards to release the woman. Like a moth to a flame she moved to the great fireplace, reaching out with desperation toward the flickering flames that somehow could not warm her flesh. The applause was much louder this time. Men and women both, calling out bets to each other over how long it would be before the woman killed herself.

Nial couldn't believe the fancy-looking people were all gathered around and watching this. They were more twisted than most of those she'd harvested in the slums. Shade was right. These people were deserving of her own particular brand of justice. Nial looked around the room and thought about the best way to stop them. She missed Zuly's help more than ever. Since their visit to the demon world, Zuly had only returned to her in moments of violence, unwilling to speak with Uncle Skeg or even answer any of Nial's questions.

Nolan Terillion took his turn at the front of the room. "While this one goes about her business, let us see if we can't keep you all entertained with her sister. Yes, yes, I assure you. These two . . . *ladies* we picked up for our night's entertainment are indeed sisters. One must wonder if such behavior runs in the family." The guests laughed again. The mage used his power and another woman moved into the room. Completely naked, her thin half-starved frame was a pitiful sight. She walked in strange fits and jerks as the mage moved her like an oversized marionette. Her hand slapped down on a table and lifted a large carving knife the mage had obviously prepared for the occasion. The woman's eyes were wide with terror. He trotted her around the room doing pirouettes and bringing the blade closer and closer to her skin. The audience jeered and clapped.

Without thinking about the consequences, Nial reached out with her own power to stop the woman's movements. The mage's eyes bulged. A frown appeared on his face, and beads of sweat broke out on his brow.

Nial's rage was incandescent, a pure unwavering hatred like only a child can muster. *These people deserve to die. Not just Danekor—all of them.* The mage looked around in panic, trying to find who was opposing him. Nial stepped out from her spell of invisibility.

"What are you doing, you foul little creature?" he screamed at her.

Nial wove fire into his robe while Zuly awoke and used her power to throw him halfway across the room. He landed on a table and crashed to the floor. *Zuly! You're back!* The only response she got was the impression of a cruel smile. They struck out with their magic and sent the other two mages flying. Then Nial plucked the poor woman back from the fire she had been about to jump into.

By this time, the crowd's applause had turned to screams. Some were beating at the doors, others were drawing weapons and shouting at each other. Almost fifty people—the girls had never killed more than a couple at a time. But there was no choice. No room for hesitation. These people had clapped while the mages hurt people—they had to die.

Nial and Zuly cut through the assembled men and women like a scythe through wheat. They crushed them to the floor or smashed them against a wall before stabbing them with the Soul Knife. The blade glowed brightly as it tore soul after soul from the defenseless bodies. Guards rushed at her with swords drawn and fared little better. The sick cowards who had but moments before been enjoying the spectacle of the women being tortured with magic blubbered and begged for their lives. Some promised Nial wealth, others demanded to know what they had done to deserve their punishment. The girls spared none of them.

The mage who had been presiding over the sick show recovered enough from his initial attack to try to hold them with sorcery. They smashed him flat against a wall. The other two tried to bind them with a weave of glowing energy. They ripped it aside almost without seeing it and pulled them forward to meet the Soul Knife.

Gunnar Danekor they kept for last. Nial's power held him immobile, even holding his eyelids open so that he would miss no detail of what they did to those assembled. When they had finished off everyone else in the room, they walked back to him. Tears streamed down his cheeks. Zuly wove fire into his limbs and watched as he tried to scream though her power held his mouth closed.

"Now you have some idea what it's like to be helpless." Nial was surprised how hard it was to speak. Her jaw ached from clenching it in her fury.

"Know before you die that your soul and those of all your friends will feed our hunger for eternity," Zuly said, enjoying the man's fear and pain. The Soul Knife flashed as she took his soul before they let the smoldering corpse fall to the floor.

Looking around at the chaos she had wrought, Nial thought, *We can't leave things like this.* Zuly started to make a huge fire weave, pouring more power into it than they had ever used before, until the massive glowing weave filled the room. Nial reached out and ripped the last traces of the spells off the sisters they had saved. They walked out of the room carrying the dazed women with their power as Zuly unleashed the flames.

"Uncle. It's done. They're all dead," Nial announced as she stepped back into the shop.

Skeg didn't miss the choice of words. "All? Girls? What did you do?"

"What we had to. All the people in that house were . . .
twisted. They won't hurt anyone anymore."

Skeg was dizzied by the implications. The unexplainable
death of one nobleman would be a shocking event in Darien.
But if that wasn't enough to draw excessive attention down
on them, then the death of everyone attending his little celebration certainly would be. There must have been dozens of
nobles in attendance, not to mention several wealthy and influential merchants and even mages from the Arcanum.

"What did you do to them? Did anyone see you?"

"No, Uncle. We didn't leave anyone behind who'd seen
us. Only two girls made it out of the ballroom alive and they
won't remember anything, their minds were wrapped in so
many layers of weaves. I don't think either of them has a clue
what happened to them. I left them in one of the huts I warded
for hunting months ago with a handful of gold I took from
Gunnar's house. Besides, the estate is probably nothing but
ashes by now."

"I hope you're right, Nial. For all our sakes."

CHAPTER 18

Urotan Oskmen Tolrahk, supreme commander of the Tolrahkali army, looked over the battlefield he had chosen for their first confrontation with the Bialtans. Outwardly, Commander Oskmen looked no different from any of his soldiers, if a little shorter than average. His bearing alone set him apart. He wore the same featureless dark chitin armor. A heavy-bladed longsword hung at his side. He had fought too many battles with his trusted sword to turn it in for one of Carver's chitin things despite their advantages. He didn't need such advantages. He spoke with such iron command in his voice that men jumped to obey before their minds fully comprehended what they were being asked to do.

The Bialtans knew where to find them and would be unable to resist the temptation of the advantage that Urotan was dangling in front of them. As overconfident as the Bialtans were in their martial superiority, he had no doubt they would take the bait.

***

The Bialtan Eastern Army stood in perfect ranks, their bright armor gleaming in the afternoon sun. General Solten looked out over the valley where the battle would take place. The Tolrahkali had not challenged his control of the high ground. Their own ranks were maybe a little less perfect, their strange insectoid armor more barbaric, and they had perhaps half as many troops, which was a surprise. He had expected them to have more men. Solten couldn't understand why the enemy would give up such a significant advantage. It was almost as though marching up here ahead of their enemies was beneath them.

"It all looks too straightforward to me, General," said Neskin, his second, stepping up behind him.

"It does. And that makes me nervous. Surely they need every advantage they can get. We have greater numbers, and our longbows will cut them apart from this height. That ridge on the right is so perfect I would almost believe they want me to send the bowmen there."

Neskin considered for a second and nodded. "The range looks about right for them to hit the Tolrahkali right where they are assembled, and that mess of loose rocks will keep them as safe as any wall. I daresay you've overestimated this rabble's commander. We'll be on the road back home by morning."

"The Drokga wouldn't trust his newly formed army to a fool. If the Tolrahkali know anything, it's fighting. Has Mage Lasven looked over the battlefield?"

"He has, Commander. Nothing untoward that he can detect. The camp is obscured, of course, but there is no trace of power on the ridge."

Solten stood for a few more moments staring out at the valley. "We can't ignore the advantage he's handing us here. But we have the numbers to take a few precautions. Send two units of heavy sword and shield to stand with the longbows.

The rest of the army is to advance in a standard attack column. Cavalry on the right and prepare to flank their main force or cut off their cavalry if they show any. I want a defensive line two hundred paces from them. I want the archers to hit them until they have no choice but to retreat or charge uphill at us. Also, inform Mage Lasven that I would be grateful if he could keep an eye on the ridge." Neskin saluted with a fist to his heart and moved off to see to the disposition of the troops.

General Solten waited while his men prepared to advance. *What surprise do you have for me, Tolrahkali?* His eyes moved to the large, well-ordered black tents behind the Tolrahkali soldiers. Could they have hidden catapults inside the tents? Ballistae? *No, the range is too great for any kind of accuracy. Their losses would far outnumber our own with such an exchange. The Tolrahkali cannot afford to waste their men.*

The Bialtan army moved out with admirable discipline, each unit moving forward in precise formations. The long-bowmen and their escorts took up position above the ridge. Each soldier pushed a half-dozen arrows into the soil in front of them.

***

Near the back of the Tolrahkali lines, Supreme Commander Oskmen watched the brightly armored ranks move down toward him. "Inform the Drokga that the Bialtan are deploying as expected." One of a dozen runners standing behind him ran off. "First horn!" Urotan bellowed as the Bialtan neared charging distance. Deep horns sounded up and down the line followed by squad leaders shouting, "Ready shields!"

Urotan smiled to himself. Now was the time to spring their trap. "I wish I could see that pretentious Bialtan bastard's face," he said.

There was risk to his plan, of course. Standing around while the enemy fired arrows at you was rarely a sound strategy. But Urotan was not afraid to take risks, and those bows had to be taken out of the equation. Carver had changed the face of war, and soon Bialta would know how outmatched they really were.

"Second horn!" he shouted. The horns sounded just as the Bialtan longbowmen loosed their first volley. The Tolrahkali troops stowed their weapons and lifted massive, thick shields above their heads. Each shield took two men to lift, but the neat formations were suddenly hidden beneath a hand's width of heavy wood. The flight of arrows fell right on target. The sharp steel arrowheads bit deeply into the shields. A few even found flesh as careless soldiers allowed the shields to drift apart.

Their reputation is well earned, Urotan thought to himself with grudging respect. *But today your famed bows will not save you. Carver's pets will be your undoing.*

"Third horn!" Again the horns sounded up and down the line. But this time they were answered with a chorus of high-pitched squeals and howls. Four-legged shapes burst out of the black tents and streaked around the Tolrahkali lines. Wider than they were high, the Tolrahk hounds were vaguely dog shaped, with thick limbs splayed out to the sides, flattened oversized heads, and thick scales. They ran straight for the Bialtan archers, covering ground faster than any horse. A second volley of arrows was already arcing toward the Tolrahkali shields.

And now it is too late, thought Urotan.

The beasts flowed over the jagged rocks and up the near-vertical side of the ridge as if it were open ground—their long prehensile claws finding ample purchase. The infantry-men reacted quickly and moved in front of the bowmen, but the creatures were inhumanly fast and did not seem to feel pain or fear dying. Long claws gripped the sides of shields, or curled around sword blades. Hundreds of the beasts were killed, but the infantrymen were sorely outnumbered. The bowmen tried to help, but their shortswords and light armor were of little use. It was not long before the bowmen and their protectors vanished under a howling pile of scaled black bodies.

"Drop shields!" Urotan called. The order was repeated up and down the line. Soldiers dropped the thick wood and prepared for battle.

Now, my Bialtan friend, will you gamble and charge down toward us with the beasts loose at your back? Or will you try to withdraw?

Suddenly bright-orange flames erupted among the beasts. Their flesh ignited and burned with unnatural speed. A portion of the Bialtan rear guard armed with spears broke away to deal with the few that remained.

Urotan felt like he had swallowed a stone. That the spell had been completed showed that his own mages were outclassed, unable to block the power or skill of the Bialtan mages. *That worm of a warlock swore to me that he and the Bialtan mages were evenly matched. His damned pride is costing me men. I will make sure Carver himself teaches him the consequences.* He had to work fast—his men would not last long. They were all but fearless in battle, but what man could stand in the face of magic? Magic was incredibly destructive, but it was indiscriminate and extremely difficult to control on a large scale.

"Sound the charge!" he shouted. "We have to get close so they can't unleash those flames on us! And get Nasaka Jadoo out here. I want those Bialtan mages taken care of!" Urotan ground his teeth. Magic was forcing him to do what arrows could not—forcing him to play to the Bialtans' tune. *So be it. We will still crush you.*

The Bialtans countercharged when they were but a few dozen strides from their lines.

The two armies crashed into each other. The Bialtans'
momentum and the weight of their armor as they came down
the hill pushed the Tolrahkali back. Soldiers fell on both sides as
the pressure mounted and the tight formations ground against
each other. But the living weapons Carver had created made a
mockery of the Bialtans and their bright steel. In the tight press
of bodies, moving was difficult, skillful fighting near impossible. The living armor flexed or retracted to help the Tolrahkali
move. It closed over wounds and cuts, stopped bleeding, while
the living weapons twisted and reached for the enemy's flesh.
Urotan stayed as far back as he dared, not wanting to lose his
view of the battle, but mindful of a new magical attack.

Ten Bialtans fell for every Tolrahkali lost. *Better than I had
hoped.* Though he well knew the value of Carver's creations,
seeing them used so successfully in the field against seasoned
troops was satisfying. This field test was going more smoothly
than he could have hoped. The Drokga would be pleased.

Fire erupted among the Tolrahkali tents. *That damned
mage!* Most of the tents were now empty, of course, but many
still hid reserves of hounds as well as a full unit of mastikide
cavalry, and the Drokga himself, ready to step out onto the
field in his titan carapace the moment the magical threat was
neutralized.

There! Urotan could see a Bialtan formation buckling.
A single warrior on the Tolrahkali side was cutting his way
through them as if they were straw practice dummies. *Nasaka
at last.* The mage hunter cut his way through the remainder
of the soldiers who opposed him, then vaulted over the group
who were coming to support them and plunged in among the
rear ranks of the Bialtan lines. The fires in the Tolrahkali camp
winked out in an instant, leaving nothing but smoldering wisps
of smoke. *And so their magical advantage dies.*

"Inform the Drokga that the magical threat has been dealt with," he shouted to one of his runners.

Moments later one of the largest tents was torn apart from the inside, and the titan carapace strode onto the battlefield, a pack of Tolrahk hounds two hundred strong streaming around his feet. Its effect on the Bialtans was dramatic. The soldiers shied away from the monstrous construct. The Drokga roared as he plunged into the thick of the fighting, and the hounds flowed across the battlefield, pulling down helpless Bialtan soldiers left and right. Soldiers were crushed, dismembered, and devoured. The Drokga laughed and roared as he killed. With his coming, the slow, grinding defeat of the Bialtans turned into a slaughter. Discipline started to fray, then shattered entirely as soldiers threw down their weapons and ran for the hills; the heavy cavalry units withdrew in disarray, their mounts panicking as the hounds dodged around them, the Drokga's roars of triumph echoing after them.

Some Tolrahkali started to press forward, but Urotan stopped them. "Let them flee. The survival of broken men is nothing to us. They will spread the stories of our might, and fear will sweep across Bialta ahead of us!"

***

The ride back to Darien made the first half of the trip feel like a picnic. Salt was lost in a blur of days spent enduring the pain of riding his hated horse, and far too few breaks when he would fall to the ground, immediately asleep. It felt like only minutes had passed before Min was shaking him awake, telling him it was time to move on. As often as not they had to walk the horses while they made their way out of the desert, but once they reached the border camp, Min insisted they step up the pace. They changed mounts several times; Salt felt a momentary pang when his horse was led away. His loathing of all things equine had softened a little during their shared ordeal. It didn't last, of course. His hatred for his new mount grew to new heights and set the idea that all such animals were secretly evil and intent on killing him when it tried to scrape him off on a low-hanging branch while he dozed in the saddle. As luck would have it, he didn't have to put up with the animal for long. Early the next morning Min found them another set of fresh horses in a village they were passing through.

"We can move faster now that we're in more civilized lands."

"Faster? How in all the hells can we move faster?"

"Easy, Salty—we start pushing the horses more. We can get fresh animals every few hours from here to Darien. We should be able to make it back in just a couple more days if we really push ourselves."

Cursing loudly the entire time, Salt managed to hold on to his horse for almost ten minutes as the group frantically galloped up the road. Then, he slipped out of the saddle and only barely managed to avoid falling headfirst and being trampled by his own mount.

"You guys go on ahead of me," he said, gasping for breath. "You all ride a hell of a lot better than I do. I'll be along in . . . oh, a month or so. I'll get moving again just as soon as I kill and eat every last scrap of this damned animal."

Min laughed. "Can't do it, Salty. Gurt wants us back, but he wants you more. Needs to ask you all kinds of questions about the Dreth. The Eastern Army is on its way to deal with the Tolrahkali already, so we'll be missing out on that bit of fun anyway."

"War is fun?"

"It is when you're on the side that outnumbers the other four to one."

Salt groaned loudly. "All right, so no more galloping, but push the hell-spawned animals as hard as you like otherwise and I'll do my damnedest to hold on."

The four Night Guardsmen were a sorry sight when they made it back to the capital. Never ones to primp or worry overmuch about their appearances, they were dirty and disheveled. They dragged themselves into the palace grounds with jeers from the gate guards ringing in their ears.

"Damned nice to be home," Salt grumbled as they walked into the training yard and stopped dead. Though it was late afternoon, the yard was filled with ranks of soldiers not outfitted for training, but in full armor and carrying real weapons.

The whole of the Night Guard was being mobilized. Salt couldn't imagine what could prompt something like this. They had dealt with things already that he had considered scary, but they'd always managed it with a few squads at most. A feeling of nervousness permeated the air as he watched the last stragglers stowing their training gear and strapping on the real thing.

Gurt walked up in front of the assembled squads. "Night Guard, I know this is unusual, but the king himself has asked that the Guard help take care of a little problem for him. As some of you may know, the Tolrahkali have been attacking our trade caravans on their way to Dreth and the Free Cities. Some of you may also know that the king sent the Eastern Army to deal with the problem. What none of you know is that they failed. They were slaughtered. Survivors, including the two apprentices of the warmage who was providing magical support for the brigade, have been streaming across the border in a panic. The Tolrahkali are apparently using strange weaponry—the survivors swear it was alive. Both their weapons and armor twisted and moved to suit their needs. The Tolrahkali are a lot stronger and faster using this new gear. They had beasts of some sort fighting for them as well, and it all proved more than a match for our people—particularly after one of their infamous mage hunters managed to sniff out and kill our warmage.

"This is where we come in. The king has ordered a much larger force to mobilize and deal with this threat. The Northern Army, small as it is, is moving down to provide support. We're also using the bigger part of both the Western and Southern Armies with nearly every scout in Bialta fanning out to make sure we don't get flanked. The Night Guard is going to lend a hand with the weird things, and do a little additional scouting and intelligence gathering. We're moving out ahead of the army. We can move faster than they can. Our goal is to find some of these beasts and figure out where they come from and form a strategy to deal with them. King Arlon has pulled out all the stops on this one. I'll be handing out a fair bit of the sweet stuff for the more experienced Guardsmen to use. Lera will also be coming with us. Inksharud is here from Korsten. He, Krigare, and the ladies will stay and keep a skeleton crew of Guardsmen working along with some conscripted Crown Knights. This is it, boys and girls; this is the biggest job we've ever had. We move out in three hours. Make me proud."

The Night Guard made ragged salutes and moved off to get ready. Gurt turned to the returning group. "Fine time you lot chose to show up. I meant to put you to work on the Tolrahkali situation but since everything turned to shit on that front this morning, I'm taking care of it myself and taking near everyone with me. I'm not going to make you get ready and come with us after making you rush back for no reason. You can rest up tomorrow and join the crew who are staying here to keep an eye on the city."

"I think we'd rather come along, Gurt. We've pushed as hard as we could to get here and we wouldn't want to miss all the fun." Min, Altog, and Brolt all nodded emphatically.

Lera moved up to stand next to Gurt with an odd look. "Salt, what the hell do you think you are doing bringing that thing into the castle?!" she practically screamed at him. Gurt's eyes widened at the uncharacteristic outburst.

Salt just shrugged as he looked down at the weapon in his hand. "It was a gift from Nok Dreth. I couldn't very well refuse it. He practically forced the ugly thing on me."

"Forced," she repeated, shaking her head. She turned to Gurt. "We'll have to lock it up in the vault. That weapon is more dangerous than everything else we have down there put together!"

"There's no need, Lera, really," argued Salt, but she wasn't even looking at him. She was focused solely on Gurt while trying to keep as much space as possible between herself and Salt.

Salt lifted the hammer up and dropped it on the ground with a dull thud. Lera's eyes darted to the fallen weapon, then back to Salt with a look of confusion. "If you would just let me say something . . ." Salt tried again. "Min, Brolt, and I already figured out it doesn't seem to do anything at all if I'm not holding it. Nok Dreth wasn't kidding when he said he made it for me."

She relaxed. "I'm not sure how he managed that. It is a relief, but you'll still need to leave it in the castle. Pulling that out each time you get into a fight is more than a little excessive."

"How about if I just keep it as a backup? It stays in its harness and I use my sword unless I absolutely need it. Good enough? Besides, it might be useful. Nok said sorcery wouldn't stop it, and we are going up against Tolrahk war-locks, aren't we?"

Gurt shrugged. "If you're all so eager, fine. You can march out with the troops. They'll be leaving in three weeks. Salt, you'll take command of whatever Guardsmen Inksharud man-ages to pull in from other cities and thinks he can spare. And keep what Lera said in mind about that new toy of yours—don't use it unless you absolutely have to. At least until she and the ladies have had a good chance to look it over. Until then, you lot take orders from Inky. He's acting commander while I'm gone. Oh, and make sure you don't get yourselves killed doing anything stupid. Lera and I have a whole lot of questions we want to ask you about the Blueskins. . . . Now go get cleaned up, the lot of you. You're stinking up my training yard."

Salt and the others gratefully returned to their rooms to rest after a welcome visit to the baths. *It was all rather anticli-mactic,* Salt thought. He had trouble settling. *All this effort to race back to the capital to be left here for weeks.*

Salt slept late the next day. It was midafternoon when he finally made it down to the training yard. Min was already there, as were Krigare and a half-dozen others Salt didn't recognize. The man sparring with Krigare was nearly as tall as Salt. A thick mane of deep-red bristles covered his head and spread down his back. There was something odd about the man's body. His limbs were too thick, too heavy somehow, and that wasn't including the huge muscles that stood out on his large frame.

Min came over and nudged him. "Never seen a Dolbari before?"

"A what?" he said.

"A Dolbari—Inksharud's the only one in the Night Guard. They come from someplace in the far south, I forget where. He's been running the show in Korsten for a couple years now.

He and a couple of his men are here to take over while we're gone. Remember?"

"He's Inksharud? People have been talking about him since I joined up. I just never expected him to be so . . ."

"Different? Well, you haven't seen anything yet, Salty. Wait till you see him fight. He can give Krigare a run for his money."

Salt moved out into the practice yard and tried to concentrate on his usual training, but his eyes kept straying back to the Dolbari. When he finally caught a look at the man's face, he missed a parry and Min smacked him with her training sword. The Dolbari had no nose, or nostrils even. His eyes were large and set deep under a thick brow. His jaw was square and oversized with overlarge, even teeth that his lips didn't seem able to cover.

Min smacked him again. "Stop staring! And get back to work. You look like a farmer who's never seen anyone different from him. I thought you sailed to half the known world?"

Salt had the good grace to blush. "I did. And I've seen some strange sights and stranger people. But I've never served with a nonhuman. Never even got a chance to speak to one, to tell the truth—the captain and first mate would always handle that part of things. He looks like a mean bastard though."

"Well, this nonhuman, as you put it, is on your team now, and he's your new commander, so get used to it." She punctuated her words with a vicious swing of her practice sword. "And if any of the others hear you call him that, they'll kick your ass worse than I'm about to."

For the next half hour Salt had to defend himself desperately against Min's attacks. Despite his efforts, a fair number of hits were sneaking their way through, and he was getting battered and bruised. Finally, Min lunged at Salt, smashed his nose with the tip of her wooden blade, and knocked him to the sand.

Salt shook his head to clear it and looked up at her with blood pouring down his face. "What the fuck are you so mad about?"

"I just thought that you had seen enough in your time with us to know that appearance doesn't count for shit." She threw the practice sword at his feet and walked out of the yard.

Krigare walked over as Salt dragged himself to his feet. "What did you do to piss Min off like that? I've never seen her lose her temper before. Not ever."

Salt couldn't meet the weapon master's eye. "I guess I said the wrong thing."

"I wouldn't have expected this from you, Salt. But if you did anything to hurt her, I'll beat you to death myself. We protect our own. Always. Don't ever forget that again. Now, you're going to train with me and Inksharud today." Salt nodded glumly and stoically accepted the punishment. He knew he wouldn't be able to move by the time training was finished, but he'd be expected to go on patrol anyway.

With their smaller numbers, the Night Guardsmen were spread thin. They only checked on the most pressing, most dangerous leads the ladies were able to dig up for them. The days following Gurt's departure were rough on those who stayed. In the space of two days, Salt and his squad, which now included three Crown Knights, had to face a group of slavers and a mage who had clearly lost track of reality, and now he was stuck investigating a magical attack that killed dozens of people, including three Arcanum mages in the home of a prominent nobleman no less. Unfortunately for Salt, that also meant he was left dealing with Holit Nobesid, a "special investigator" from the Arcanum, instead of Lera.

"Everything is confused here, Night Captain."

"Can you tell me anything? Was this a magical attack? A mage duel? A spell gone horribly wrong?"

"The power unleashed here was . . . disturbing. Archmage Lera and I have conferred magically at length, and I tend to agree with her that this was done by the same cabal of mages who left that little gravesite you uncovered in the slums." He walked around the site poking his staff into mounds of ash. "These mages are either very powerful or very numerous and well organized. I'm not sure which possibility disturbs me more. That a group of such individuals could operate in the city for such an extended period of time without our knowledge . . ."

"Just how many are we talking about here?"

"That is hard to say for certain, Night Captain; there are far too many variables. Though I'm quite sure of at least a dozen significant contributors." He wandered around and kicked through a pile of ash. "We know for certain that three fully trained members of the Arcanum were present at this . . . gathering. One of them was a junior member and not very strong in his art, but the other two were quite talented mages. Young and prone to showing off, of course, but such things can be forgiven."

"So at least two of the mages here were young guys showing off for the nobles. Not something that shocks me any. Are you sure this mess wasn't any of their doing?"

"I do not like your implications, Night Captain. Arcanum mages would never do such a thing. Besides, while there are light traces of their magics here, I cannot detect any attached to the destructive magic. I can tell you for certain that neither of them was involved with the fire." He turned back to his examination.

"What about the other one?"

Holit Nobesid paused. "I cannot be certain. His relatively meager talents would be difficult to pick out amid the other flavors. Besides which, I am quite certain all three of them were killed here. I cannot be perfectly sure, mind you, not with this level of destruction, but I am relatively sure that Devin Teps is part of that ash pile there. Elias Holen is at the end of the hall, and Nolan Terillion is near the remains of the outer wall."

"Who would know how to do this?"

"That is part of the problem, Night Captain. Any apprentice knows this weave. It is one of the first every mage learns. It is used for lighting candles and nonmagical lamps. It's a simple, if not particularly efficient, way to start a fire. To see it brought up to this scale . . . to see such a simple little weave cause this kind of devastation is appalling. If the Arcanum had not intervened, the fires would still be burning and probably would not have stopped for a good many days if not weeks. As it was, thirty of us were needed to funnel the great energy out of the spell . . ." His voice trailed off for a moment. "I'm sorry, Night Captain. A most disturbing thought just occurred to me." He held up a placating hand as Salt moved to speak. "No, nothing I'd care to share just yet. I need to speak with some of my colleagues as quickly as possible. If you will excuse me?"

Salt split up his squad and sent each team to take a look at the homes and families of the victims. *There must have been a reason for the attack. It couldn't have been random.* All the Night Guard came up with was a long list of battered servants and abused family members. Salt himself spoke to the orphaned son of a couple who burned to death in the fire. The boy, who couldn't have been older than fourteen, had been busy shouting at servants to clear his parents' "crap" out of the master suite to make room for his own things. *No tears for lost family here.* Salt compared findings with his squad and went back to the palace to report.

Though he had gotten used to the Dolbari, Salt was still a little nervous when he went into Gurt's map room to report to the acting commander of the Night Guard. The man's brutish appearance was misleading. Salt had already come to understand that a shrewd mind hid behind the square jaw. But he was still constantly thrown off balance by Inksharud's soft, melodious voice. It just didn't seem to fit the man's form.

"There isn't much left of the house. The fire was burning so hot the stones started to melt. Even the best of the Arcanum's investigators aren't going to find much in all that. All we know is the fire started in the ballroom. Most of the servants had been sent out after the guests finished their dinner. Some kind of entertainment was prepared that they weren't good enough to watch apparently. Only Danekor's favorites were allowed to stay and they all died with him."

Salt thought for a second and added, "Couldn't it be warlocks? I've heard they do fire like no one else, and with the troubles we're already having with the Tolrahkali . . ."

Inksharud grunted a laugh. "I had the same thought, Salt, but the ladies don't think so. They said warlocks think of themselves as artists of destruction. You'd never get one to do anything so base, especially not a whole group of them. They compared it to getting a dozen of the best silk weavers in Keral and asking them to make sailcloth for a year."

"From what we learned from their servants and families, I think Bialta's better off without the people who died in that house."

"Not for us to decide, Salt. But I think you're on to something. If those who died were all as unpleasant as you suspect, that could be why they were killed. I won't miss them, but I can't have some crazed bunch of mages running around the city meting out their own justice. Lera thinks maybe they're

Arcanum themselves, cleaning house. Though with what you've told me I think they might be former victims of any of these people. We know a fair number of unregistered mages are spread out through the poorer segments of the city."

"So they're a powerful bunch without the training? Holit Nobesid seemed to think the use of such a simple spell was a message of some sort, or a strategy for not tipping off anything about their style or training."

"Holit may think that, but he's a very smart, very educated man. Tends to think everyone is as educated as he is, surrounded by Arcanum people all the time. I think it's just anger, lots of power, and too little training."

"Scary mix. Maybe worse than an organized bunch even. Gods only know what the bastards will do next."

"Whoever did it, they sure pissed the Arcanum off. Their team of special investigators has been assigned to help us with this case until further notice. Normally we have to get the king to order them to give us one or two extra mages for a few hours.... The council has pulled out all the stops on this one too. They've approved the use of summons for the investigators."

"Summon*s*, as in more than one?" Salt was horrified.

Inksharud nodded. "Expect to see quite a few moving around the city for the next while. In the meantime, I got a tip for you to check out in the Muds before you do the rest of your patrol tonight."

The six of them tore through the moldering furniture and trappings that had been left in the shack without success.

"Well, I'm not sure about you lot," said Wheeze, "but I'm satisfied the tip was bad or whatever it was is already gone." The others nodded their agreement.

"I'm going to take one more look through the place," said Salt. "Altog, you're with me. The rest of you finish your sweep of the docks and we'll meet you before we head to the temple district."

As it happened, Salt was right. Altog was poking at the walls and Salt was digging little holes in the dirt floor, when his foot sunk in, ever so slightly. The grime covering the floor was perfectly uniform, there wasn't so much as a hint that the dirt had been disturbed since the shack had been built decades ago. Salt used his knife to dig around the spot and was ecstatic when the blade hit something hard. He pulled out a long bundle wrapped in oiled cloth. He sat down on the bed and unwrapped it eagerly.

He lifted out a familiar-looking sword. The pommel and guard were nearly identical to the Dreth Firesword, but already he could tell this blade lacked its balance and artistry. He started to draw it slowly out of its sheath and noticed the familiar flame motif carved down the blade. Then the blade burst into bright-orange flames.

"Shit!" he shouted, jumping to his feet and nearly dropping the sword.

Altog was wheezing he was laughing so hard. "You should have seen the look on your face, Salt. Damn near crapped yourself, didn't you?"

"Just lucky I didn't burn my balls off." Nothing was even singed. The first time he'd seen a Firesword, the heat coming off it was like standing near a volcano. Salt touched the tip of the sword to the bed.

"Salt! I know you're pissed, but there's no need to burn down half the Muds over it."

"I won't burn down anything. Just look at the bed." Sure enough, not a plume of smoke rose up from where the orange flames touched the soiled blanket. Salt touched the corner of the blanket. Not even warm. *Now for the big test.* He slowly moved a finger toward the blade. Gritting his teeth and expecting the worst, he jabbed his finger down . . . onto cold steel.

"Ha! I knew it! An illusion!"

"Well, I'll be damned," said Altog. "Though you know, Salty, it might have been safer to ask Lera to check it instead of risking your hand."

Salt looked at him, embarrassed. "I guess you're right. I keep forgetting it's a bigger team than just our squad."

"Anyway, you'd best get that to Inky. I'll let Wheeze know what happened."

"Thanks, I'll catch up with you guys as soon as I can." Salt wrapped the sword up again and went back to the palace as quickly as he could. The weapon might not be a real Firesword, but, given the trouble the real one had caused him, he couldn't be too careful. Inksharud was in Gurt's usual place in the map room. A large map of the city was painted on a wooden table. The wall was dominated by a huge painted map of Bialta. Stacks of notes and lists were scattered about it and every other available surface in the room.

Inksharud looked up as Salt walked in. "Surprised to see you back so soon."

"I found a funny little trinket in a shack in the slums. Thought you might want to see it." He dropped the oilcloth and drew the sword.

Inksharud's jaw dropped. "Not a second one!"

"It's a fake. Pretty damned good copy, though. Whoever made it must have had a real one in their hands at some point. I wouldn't do this with the real one," he said and closed his left hand around the blade.

Inksharud considered for a minute "The color of the flame is wrong too. The real ones burn green, not orange. It's pretty impressive, even if it doesn't burn anything. . . . I'll pass it on to Lera. She should take a look."

"Is this something we should tell the Dreth about?" Salt asked, resigned.

"Can't see what business it is of theirs. This isn't anything they lost. All kinds of weapon sellers try to convince their customers that the poor blades they're hawking are Dreth steel. I guess it was only a matter of time before someone tried it with a Firesword. Truth be told, there's nothing illegal about this. If a merchant had it for sale in the market, we wouldn't have a problem with it at all. It was probably just being sold by shady characters to help convince buyers it was real." He shrugged. "We may even put it back once Lera's seen it. You can't be too careful with new magic."

Salt nodded. "Relieved to have it off my hands for now anyway."

"I can't blame you. I'll take care of it from here. Feel free to take the rest of the night off. Your patrol is nearly finished and isn't expecting to hit anything big tonight."

"Thanks, but I'd rather get back to them. I'd hate for my squad to be shorthanded if they ran into a surprise."

"Good for you, Salt. Don't let me keep you."

***

Yajel watched the Night Guardsman leave the castle. *Without my sword.* That was twice the Night Guard had taken everything from him. They had destroyed his team, killed his lover, and stolen his Firesword. The old anger still bubbled inside him. It had kept him going over the past months and pushed him to recover from his terrible wounds, to rebuild himself and dare to reach for more than a pathetic existence in the Muds. Selling fake Fireswords had been Banjax's plan. And one he had only reluctantly agreed to at the time. Since he survived his execution that plan had been all he had left. It had taken him months to find a mage capable of doing what he needed. Few were the unlicensed mages who had even half of Banjax's skill. *And then that damned Guardsman comes along and steals it from me!* Finding him walking out of the palace alone was an opportunity Yajel wasn't about to pass up. Then he saw the misshapen hammer strapped to the man's back. There was no denying the origin of the weapon. *So you've been beyond the black wall and been rewarded, human.* He hesitated for a moment, despite being unarmed himself, then retreated into the shadows. There was no telling what the mortal could do with such a weapon. *But now I have a face for my hatred. I will not relent, human. I will destroy you utterly for what you have done to me.*

***

The city was in turmoil after the attack in the crown district. The Arcanum was heavily involved in the search efforts. Demons and less recognizable things patrolled the skies and the streets. Robed men and women moved in groups hunting for traces of magic.

Nial ducked around a corner as another patrol passed by. *There are so many of them. We should probably just hide with Uncle Skeg until it all passes by. No more hunting for a while.*

Reluctantly, Zuly agreed. Her drive to hunt had increased since their encounter with Amon Kareth. She seemed determined to harvest as many souls as possible now and was becoming impatient with Nial's rules about who they would hunt and why.

The girls heard a scream from the next street over. Nial hesitated for a moment before moving toward the sound. *Let's check it out quick, then we can go and hide.*

There was a loud crash and most of a house fell inward, followed by more screams. They dashed over and wove their hiding spell around themselves as they stopped. A creature of some sort was crouched over the corpse of an old woman, noisily devouring her. It had fishlike scales and squirming appendages that held up a fat gray body and a mouth that was altogether too large for its size. It bit off another mouthful and swallowed with a gurgling shudder that spattered droplets of blood all around it. *A demon,* thought Zuly. *Not a kind I recognize. And it is not bound.* Nial was horrified.

We have to stop it, Nial thought. *Those mages have already moved on. If we don't do something, it could be too strong for them by the time they get back.* The spell of hiding dissolved as they rushed toward the thing. *No magic,* Nial cautioned. Though the thing was more than a match for a normal human, it really didn't stand a chance against Nial and Zuly, strengthened as they were by their collection of souls. They grabbed two of the limbs on the thing's left side and pulled them off. The beast squealed and pulled away. They pinned it down with one foot and took a firm grim of its head. The squealing rose in pitch, a nauseating smell rising from its body as the demon panicked and thrashed around. Silence returned suddenly as with a grunt of effort, the girls ripped the slobbering head from its body.

Stinking ichor rained down around them. Zuly saw something move out of the corner of their eye and rushed at the new threat. In the heat of the moment, the girls barely recognized the Night Guardsman who had walked Nial home months ago. Zuly smashed him aside and sent him flying into a wall. *Should we kill him?* Zuly asked. *No! He was nice to us and his squad can't be far.* The man struggled to get back to his feet. Zuly knocked him down again, not quite as hard as the first time, then they launched themselves over the wreckage of the broken hovel and out of sight.

***

Salt walked into the barracks limping slightly. His nose was obviously broken again, one of his eyes was purple and swelling shut, and both his lips were split and bleeding.

Krigare chuckled when he saw him. "So what happened to you, Salty? Try to pay the wrong woman for a roll in the hay?"

Behind him Min wore a hard smile. "Nothing that exciting. He just decided to pick a fight with a Chosen of some sort."

"Bastards should be made to wear signs," Salt grumbled in mock annoyance. The others laughed.

Krigare smiled. "And what fun would that be? Besides, we've dealt with Chosen before. Remember the tip about not taking them on by yourself?"

Turning back to Min and Altog, Salt countered. "Well, you lazy shits could have helped out a little then."

Min's smile broadened. "And miss seeing you get your ass handed to you by a girl half your size? Never! Besides, she ripped that rogue demon in half before she went for you, so I think she deserved a break."

"There was something familiar about that girl. I could swear I've seen her before," Salt said.

Brolt shrugged. "That might explain why she reacted to seeing you like that. I'd say we were lucky she seemed more eager to get away than stay and fight. That girl wasn't like any Chosen I've seen before."

Inksharud shrugged. "Well, if all she did was kill a demon, we've got no reason to worry about her. Go get cleaned up and get some sleep. I'm sure the ladies will have plenty for you to do again tomorrow."

***

"We're not going to be able to go out for a while are we, Uncle?" asked Nial, after telling Skeg about what had happened.

"Not if you can possibly avoid it, girls. There's simply too much at stake, and far too many people hunting for you, even if they don't know who or what they're really looking for." He looked at them seriously. "Now, are you girls going to tell me what's wrong? You've been upset since you came back from Karethin, when you should be overjoyed! You survived! And more, you've crossed out the last name on Shade's list!"

Nial went pale and looked away from him at once. "It's nothing really. Nothing important." Uncharacteristically, Zuly cut her off, saying in a dead voice, "The demon lord attacked us while we were in his realm. We carry the spawn of Amon Kareth within us."

Skeg sat back, stunned. "That fucking son of a syphilitic goat." He breathed with barely suppressed anger. "I'm sorry, girls. I had no idea. I . . . I didn't even know that was something demons were likely to do." He shook his head. "I don't know what to say. Is there anything I can do?"

Nial felt a wave of warmth and affection for the strange old mage. Skeg wasn't afraid. He wasn't going to tell them to leave as she had feared. He only wanted to help them. "I don't know, Uncle. It's growing fast and we really don't know what to expect."

"You'll just have to stay here. Make sure you're near the circle in case that scum tries to contact you again. . . . And when the birth comes, I'll be here for that, too."

Nial and Zuly, in perfect agreement, ran over and hugged him tightly.

After a time, they moved apart. The girls' body language was shifting back and forth in a way that told Skeg they were having a heated discussion. They barely noticed him as he moved back to his accustomed place behind the counter.

A few moments later their eyes snapped back to him, and Nial nodded sharply as if deciding something.

"Are you girls all right?"

"Fine, Uncle. We just decided it's time to share a little project we've been working on with you." They gathered up their books and moved to their spot in the back room, pulling the curtain closed behind them.

Skeg shook his head, confused but grateful the girls' spirits seem to have lifted so quickly. *Two of them in there and one a demon. They are tougher than you'll ever know, old man.*

CHAPTER 19

Lord Irem 's voice rose above the buzz in King Arlon's council chambers. "Dealing with the Tolrahkali invasion is not enough. If a city-state dares to attack us, none of the great nations will respect Bialta. We need to send a message to all of the North. Once we mobilize one of our larger armies, we need to make more use of it than just crushing these upstarts. Conquering Tolrahk Esal would be a start, but won't leave an impression. They are, as I said, only a city-state, large perhaps for one city but hardly a fitting target if we want to send a message to the Abolians or Keralans." Various voices joined him in calling for blood.

King Arlon just shook his head. He cleared his throat, and the assembled council members turned their attention to him. "Expansion is a noble goal. I cannot deny that. But do all of you forget why our great nation has not expanded in centuries? Have you also all ignored the very important fact that the Tolrahkali soundly defeated us in our first battle? A battle where we outnumbered them two to one? Have you also forgotten just how many mercenary companies are based in

Tolrahk Esal?" The king paused and looked at each member of the council in turn, letting the silence draw out and making each of them feel his full displeasure.

"You all speak as if conquest is a simple matter and will solve all our problems. Conquest is never easy. The price paid for it is always more than expected. We have an invasion to deal with and all you can talk about is the need to send a message. . . . In which direction would you have our armies march?" He turned his gaze on Councillor Corvuy. "North to the Hillmen? They have nothing we could ever use, and nothing but a desert beyond their mountains. They serve us well where they are."

The king's eyes moved on to Lord Irem. "To Dreth then, cousin Harold? And repeat the folly of mad King Furnis? If anything, the Dreth are stronger now than they were then, and we weaker. I know you've traveled to the Free Cities on more than one occasion yourself. Do you really think it's realistic to march our entire army through that desert? How many men would we lose to the sands before even engaging them?"

His gaze swept across the council table. "Or should it be west to the Abolians? They test us constantly though we've repelled them time and again. They have more soldiers than any nation that small has any right to, even with one of their factions being mixed up in that war with Sacral."

"So should it be south to Sacral?" He let the word hover giving the supporters of this idea time to hope for a different verdict. "A city held by a goddess who ousted the Dead King himself and is surrounded by miles of the emptiest, most barren land in the world. Only the most foolish of men become involved in wars with gods. From all accounts they have already chewed up the Abolian Red Army and have come through it stronger than they started."

"Which only leaves us with Keral," he said, finally looking at Lady Demir. "Our one stable ally on the continent. Our greatest trading partner and our doorway to the South."

"Why trade when we can take it all? We can have our own access to the South!" insisted Lady Demir.

King Arlon's frown deepened. "And just how eager do you suppose those kingdoms will be to trade with us when we conquer their ally? Will you then conquer them, too? How many men do you think we will have left when we are done with the Tolrahkali *and* Keral? Few enough that Aboleth will take a bite out of us?"

The king shook his head in disgust. "I will hear no more of this foolishness. You all speak like children who have heard too many stories of knights slaying dragons. Times have changed since King Altaren forged this mighty nation by unifying the city-states of Bialta. Our paths to prosperity are trade and knowledge. I will listen if any of you have suggestions relevant to either of these courses of action." The councillors looked at one another sheepishly, like schoolchildren being caught at something they weren't supposed to be doing.

"As for our armies," the king continued, "I do agree some sort of message needs to be sent. I want to overwhelm the Tolrahkali. I want their force surrounded and destroyed to a man. Any further repercussions will be discussed when we have dealt with the problem at hand. Now, how many troops can we marshal to deal with them? We made the mistake of thinking the Eastern Army would be more than sufficient. I do not intend to lose any more of our forces to these mutants."

The bickering and arguing among the councillors started up again almost immediately. King Arlon sighed deeply and massaged his temples. He felt like an old man today. His kingdom was being torn apart, and there seemed to be nothing he could do to stop it. Threats were neutralized only for two more to appear in their place. Even Bialta's legendary resources were being strained to the breaking point. Perhaps he could persuade the Abolians to sign a peace treaty. Not a permanent one, of course—their insane religion would never permit such a thing. But perhaps offering to move the border a small way in their favor would entice them to sign a very carefully worded agreement. If he could free up much of the Western Army to help with the Tolrahkali, they should be able to overwhelm them no matter how strong they had become individually. He should ask Gustave to put as many scribes and diplomats on the project as possible, just to make sure the Abolians couldn't slip through a loophole in whatever treaty they signed. Dealing with them was always hard since the three ruling factions had so much autonomy and each had an army of its own. *At least the Reds should be eager to sign if the news from Sacral is true.* The lands near the Abolian border were nearly useless anyway. The scrub grass was barely good enough to raise goats on. Some of the border forts would need to be stripped if not destroyed if they moved the border that far, but it would probably not be necessary. The Abolians weren't likely to refuse even a small tract of land after being frustrated in their incursions for so long. *I'll have to really push the Arcanum to help as well. They may not even argue too much for once. One of their own has been killed, after all, and they will want to prove their superiority over the warlocks. Gods, my headache is never going to go away at this rate.*

He was thankful for men like Gurt, who took some of the pressure off him. His childhood friend had proven to be his biggest ally and most loyal supporter. Men like him were too rare in the palace. With him gone there wasn't enough idealism and honor to fill a thimble in his whole court. If only he hadn't had to send him away.

Enough time wasted with these fools. Time to get things done. King Arlon walked out of the room without a word to the council members, his two Crown Knight bodyguards following on his heels.

***

Matchstick hissed behind him, and Dantic reached out to allow the construct to pour him another glass of wine. He had succeeded beyond all hope, but because of a little cosmetic issue, most of the Arcanum was unwilling to even look at what he'd accomplished. The enchantment had worked despite his last-minute slip. The marionette—dressed in a smaller version of his own formal robes—moved about and performed basic tasks for him without needing to be asked. His mistake had caused only minimal damage to the project—a consequence of a backlash of energy when the weave was released too quickly. Half the marionette's face was a blackened mess, and the servant's ability to speak had been reduced to a barely audible hiss. Hence the name he had chosen for it. *Still more than anyone else could have managed,* he thought bitterly. The truth was he was enjoying having Matchstick with him. It was helping him in any number of ways by anticipating what he would need and bringing it to him at just the right moment. *I probably would have succeeded in making a construct perfectly had I already had him.* There was little point in thinking along those lines though. His modest reserve of funds had been entirely depleted by his first effort. He would need to find a new way to best Bagwin.

And then, as if on cue, news of the Tolrahkali attack spread through the halls of the Arcanum along with tales of the death of Mage Lasven—one of Bialta's most famous warmages. *Not the kind of opportunity I was hoping for, but beggars can't be choosers.*

As expected, an official call came to all the Arcanum members for volunteers to join the king's army and bolster its magical power. Dantic made sure he was the first to volunteer and even managed to have himself appointed leader of the Arcanum force. *That fool Bagwin even voted for me. He's probably just glad to get me out of here for a time. Probably hopes I'll get myself killed while I'm at it. But if I pull it off, there won't even be a point in counting the votes when I return.*

His young supporters had flocked to join him. They crowded into his rooms, eager to help. He sat among them as Matchstick busied himself serving refreshments. "The more mages we bring along, the easier the job will be, and the happier the king will be in turn. If we do enough, he'll probably donate enough funds to the Arcanum to make that ridiculous Silver Servant project meaningless."

One of the youngest, clearly nervous about the prospect of violence, asked, "How many other mages do you think will come? It can't just be the ten of us, can it?"

Dantic yawned. "No, Edward, it won't just be us. A few of the old warhorses won't be able to resist coming along to relive their glory days. Just as well 'cause the truth is—we can use them. We're younger and smarter than any of them, but we'll need to see what they do so we can do it better." The assembled youths nodded at his wise words. "I'll need you all to help recruit more mages though, the stronger the better. We'll need a big turnout to impress the king."

There was a polite knock on the door. Dantic waved his hand and the door opened smoothly. One of the Arcanum servants stood outside. "Forgive my interruption, Archmage, I was told you were now in charge of the war delegation."

Dantic waved impatiently for the man to get to the point. "A mage from outside the Arcanum has presented himself at the doors and is offering his assistance against the Tolrahkali."

"Outside the Arcanum? Where is he from? Keral? Aboleth? One of the other Free Cities?"

"I believe he said he was of the Oviyan tribe from the far side of the Great Desert, sir."

"A savage? Here?"

The servant stood silent, unsure if he was expected to answer.

"Send him up in an hour or so. I'll need to finish conferring with my colleagues."

The servant bowed and closed the door behind him.

"You're not seriously thinking of bringing a tribal along, are you?" asked one of the younglings.

"Of course not. The last thing we need is some illiterate buffoon getting in our way when we're trying to coordinate rituals. But in this matter I represent the Arcanum and we have to keep up appearances. I'll let him wait for a suitable length of time, then I'll speak with him, show him that we're beyond whatever little tricks he thinks will be of use to us, and send him on his way."

He leaned back in his chair with a look that said he was willing to suffer the stupidity of his lessers because he was such an exceptionally patient man. The assembled mages all nodded to one another at his words again.

They continued speaking for nearly another hour before he asked them to leave. "I do need to meet with the witch doctor, after all." They laughed as they filed out of his rooms.

A few minutes later there was again a polite knock on the door. Dantic sat straight in his chair and picked up a thick sheaf of paper as if he had been interrupted reading it. Then he again used his power to pull the door open. *I wonder if opening a door will be enough to impress the savage. Just being in the Arcanum is probably overwhelming the poor fool. He's probably used to mud huts.*

The man who stood behind the same Arcanum servant didn't fit Dantic's expectations. He wore embroidered silk robes of a deep blue that would have been the envy of many of the more fashion-conscious members of the Arcanum. He had no tribal tattoos, piercings, or talismans. Though his coal-black skin clearly marked him as an outsider, here was a sophisticated man of pride and confidence, not the cowed savage Dantic had expected. The look of irritation on the man's face was also clear.

He walked into the room uninvited, pushing past the servant and Matchstick, who was offering a glass of wine. He looked at the papers in Dantic's hand, the slightest hint of a frown showing on his ageless face. The look made Dantic feel young and foolish for a moment before anger pushed to the fore. *If the damned savage thinks an expensive robe and a lack of respect is going to get him anywhere with me, he's mistaken.*

"So, Oviyan, what is it you want with the warmaster of the Arcanum?" *Hmm, not a bad title. I may need to keep it.*

"Warmaster now, is it? You Bialtans and your titles. Is that in addition to mage, and archmage?" His tone was increasingly angry. He stopped suddenly, then with visible effort, the man calmed himself. "I apologize for my words, Warmaster Dantic. I am not accustomed to being kept waiting, and I fear I have let my feelings get away from me. Let us start again if you will." Dantic shrugged as if the outburst had been beneath his notice.

"My name is Kishan Nikhil. I am the kladic of the Oviyan. I have come to offer my assistance in your efforts against the Tolrahkali."

"You'll forgive me if I don't know what that means, Kishan. Your tribe hasn't been one of the subjects of any of my studies.

Now, why is it you want to help us and what do you expect in return?"

The anger returned to Kishan's eyes. "I am not some mercenary. For better or worse, Bialta has been my home for several years. Honor demands I assist in her defense."

Honor . . . Gods, he's one of those. "And just how do you propose to do that?"

"Kladic is a title among my people much like archmage is among yours. We are particularly gifted in deceiving the senses, in—"

Dantic held up a hand to stop the man speaking. *Though I'm sure it was a very well-prepared speech.* "So you do tricks and illusions. That may help in tribal squabbles, but we're talking about fighting the Tolrahkali and their warlocks. I just don't see how you will be of any help. There isn't even enough time to train you to assist in our rituals so we can put you to better use."

"Then I see that the command of the war effort is in the hands of a fool, and there is little hope of winning the coming confrontation." Dantic's face flushed in anger as Kishan continued. "To enlighten your small mind, I will give you a demonstration."

Dantic embraced his talent and prepared to defend himself. There was a flash of light and Dantic instinctively wove a shield around himself. But no attack came. Instead of one Oviyan mage standing in front of him, there were now three. Though they clearly shared the same ancestry, each was somewhat different and moved independently.

Kishan's voice sounded from all three. "Which one of us would you attack, Warmaster? Would you waste effort on all three or take your chances? I can do this for full platoons of soldiers."

A rift then appeared in the air between them. A demonic creature pulled itself through and jumped down onto Dantic's desk, scattering papers in every direction. Despite the shield protecting him, Dantic jumped to his feet, knocking his chair down in his haste to distance himself from the creature.

The beast faded away, and Kishan once again stood alone in front of him. "And sight is only the most obvious sense I can twist to my advantage."

"I can taste fresh apple as if I were just biting into one," Dantic exclaimed, despite himself.

Kishan nodded. "Not the taste I would offer an enemy, of course. I could have half an army emptying their stomachs with little effort. And the weave is subtle enough that your senses and shield did not even alert you to it."

Dantic dropped his shield. Irritation, surprise, and fear were all blown away as the implications of what he'd just seen sank in. "I owe you an apology, Kladic Kishan Nikhil. You are correct—ignoring your offer would indeed be the worst sort of stupidity."

The mage nodded, the fire in his eyes undimmed. "Most outsiders make the same assumptions you harbored a few moments ago. A kladic is not a trickster or an entertainer. Attention to detail must be absolute. Even among those with the raw ability, only the rarest of students are able to walk my path. My arts are sufficient to mislead all but the strongest and most paranoid of minds. Providing the spells come as a surprise, it is a rare thing indeed for anyone to see through my weaves, even among the greatest of mages. Warlocks are legendary for their single-mindedness, so I doubt that a taste or a smell, no matter how bitter, will affect them as much as it will the Tolrahkali foot soldiers. . . . But misleading them into unleashing their fires on empty ground, or perhaps even on their own forces? Now that is something I do not doubt I can accomplish."

Dantic stood up and walked around his desk. He held out his hand to the blue-robed mage. "Welcome to the war effort, Kladic Nikhil."

The kladic hesitated a moment before taking the proffered hand.

Dantic was internally ecstatic. *This little addition will win us the war, I've no doubt. I'll just have to work it so that I get the credit. Lucky for me the kladic came to me first.* "Thank you, Kladic Nikhil. Now, if you will excuse me? I will need to reconsider possibilities and rework our strategies significantly to make the best use of your skills. I am calling a war council tomorrow at dawn for all the mages who have elected to join us, as well as a few representatives from the king's army and their accompanying priests. Will you be joining us alone? Do you have any apprentices or attendants?"

The man shook his head. "My art is too demanding for more than a single apprentice to be taken at a time, and she must remain behind to preserve my teachings should I fall."

"Of course. I will assign a senior Arcanum apprentice to attend to your needs while you are with us."

***

In the weeks that followed their arrival in the underground city of Ischia, the realities of their new life started to sink in for the Sacral refugees. The homes they were settled in were oddly similar to those they had left behind, if a little larger and newer, but this was not home and the rules here were far different.

Jenus had to admit a certain fascination for the Gling'Ar city. The walking corpses performed much of the menial labor, but that didn't mean the living inhabitants were indolent. Each and every person he saw, human or otherwise, seemed to be occupied for much of the day pursuing some activity or other that could benefit the city as a whole. The refugees who practiced a trade or engaged in some form of teaching or learning received more generous supplies from the walking corpses. They were also invited to take part in the markets or were offered roles as scribes or teachers in the city's many libraries and schools. But while effort was rewarded, idleness was barely tolerated, as some of the less-active refugees soon came to realize as their rations became increasingly plain.

Ischia filled a number of roles within Gling'Ar society. It was a refuge, a place of learning, even a warehouse and trading hub. It was becoming clear to Jenus how one central element could be an agent of change for a nation. One hidden city helping the tribal giants to rise, to unify them around a solid core. *And what does that make Sacral? A single inward-looking city built around a lie and the conceit that we are all the descendants of heroes.* From what Jenus had learned, the Gling'Ar had been little more than the savages he had taken them for a few hundred years ago. It was shocking that they had come so far in such a short time. *While in Sacral, nothing changes.*

Jenus made every effort to keep his people motivated and his soldiers in fighting form. He led training sessions every morning and again every afternoon, giving himself little time for anything else. And yet every day that passed, fewer of his men came to join him. There was no denying it—he was losing his people to the Dead King, every one of them seduced by the opportunities that Ischia offered. Those without families, or those lucky enough to have their families with them, were the first to go. The rest bled away in a slow but inexorable trickle.

It took a few months, but the inevitable happened and Jenus found himself alone when he came out to train. Traven had been the last to abandon the pretense of military discipline.

I have failed them all, Jenus thought as he stubbornly moved from one form to another. He finished his routine and headed for home. *Even I'm starting to think of Ischia as home,* he realized. Jenus watched his people going about their lives. A handful spared him a nod or a wave as they passed. Most didn't even acknowledge his presence. They were busy with their new lives—sharing a drink with friends, preparing meals, going about their trades, or busy trying to learn one. There was no place for human fighters in this city. They were simply not as suited to the task as the Gling'Ar. He wondered if he would be tired enough for sleep to find him tonight. As often as not, regrets gnawed at him well into the night.

Lost in his dark thoughts, Jenus almost didn't notice a group that had formed in front of the home of one of his countrymen. The assembled men and women whispered and argued in obvious shock and anger.

"Jenus! Thank the Silent God you're here! Banok's house is empty! The Gling'Ar must have taken him!"

Jenus was shocked. Banok had been one of his soldiers. "Gone just like that?" he asked.

The man nodded. "There was a tussle of some sort between him and his neighbor last night, and now here's his house cleaned out as if he never lived there."

"Did anyone see anything?" he asked the crowd. The faces all looked back at him in silence. One of his men was just gone. That he was a difficult man—one even deserving of harsh discipline on occasion—changed nothing. Banok was his responsibility, and the Dead King would answer for his disappearance.

Jenus walked resolutely toward the central temple. None of his people followed him. Either they had given up all hope for freedom and all confidence in their leader, or they had integrated too fully into their prison. *It is a prison, dammit! For all of that bag of bones' words about being accepted and given freedoms!*

Four Gling'Ar stood at the end of the street. Four dead Gling'Ar with gleaming steel weapons and armor. The only thing that linked the hulking figures with the human dead more commonly used as laborers were the featureless iron masks that hid their faces. *Figures that they would use the big guys as fighters.* "Where is Banok?" he demanded of the undead guards. "I know someone with a working brain can hear me! What have you done with him?"

All four undead nodded to him in an eerily similar movement. One of them stepped aside and pointed up the road. Jenus stepped past them, his outrage giving him the courage he had thought lost.

He was swallowed up by the crowds of the greater city, its teeming marketplaces and busy streets. The variety of people in Ischia was astounding. Jenus had to hold firmly to his outrage to avoid being distracted by the exotic clothes and disparate races. Part of him regretted keeping himself isolated among his countrymen as he had until now. Then another faceless dead Gling'Ar, only half seen beyond a group of arguing merchants, repeated the same curt nod and pointed him on. Each time he turned, there seemed to be another of the dead things watching him with their eyeless faces, herding him along without bothering to move. *So many of them . . . as if the living army of the four-armed giants wasn't bad enough.*

Finally, Jenus was led to a living Gling'Ar. This giant carried no visible weapon at all. He was dressed much as the noncombatants in the outside villages had been. "Human, you seemed eager to speak with one of us, so I have come to meet you. I am Grodol."

Almost forgetting his anger, Jenus mumbled, "Banok is gone. Where is he? His house has been cleared out with no word to any of us."

"That is what has you so worked up? Your people are welcome to live among us. But that does not mean we will tolerate lawlessness. The human you speak of attacked another inhabitant of Ischia and has been punished. He will not be returning to you." As if to illustrate his point, a group of human animati moved past them, pulling a heavy cart that would have been more suited to a team of oxen. Jenus's mind swam—*Dead. Just like that. . . . And worse than dead.* Jenus felt his stomach turn over. *They turned him into one of those things! He deserved to be punished but this?!*

"What gives you the right to kill one of my people?!" he demanded, the anger returning.

The Gling'Ar looked down at him impassively. "Remember where you are, human. Your anger means nothing here. I hear Warchief Sonum gave you a little demonstration already. He may be the greatest of us, but he is hardly the only one ready to deal with the likes of you—a half-trained runt of a Warchosen."

Jenus ground his teeth.

"Your man was guilty of stealing from his fellows. Worse, he physically harmed someone who refused to hand over a part of what they had earned through honest work. All crimes in Ischia carry the same sentence—death."

"With no trial? With no warning?"

"No trial is needed. The Dead King's justicars can divine the truth of any situation. They will have listed all the items stolen, as well as the names of those wronged, in the annals of justice. If absolutely necessary, you can speak with them and confirm the truth of the events. But there will be no apologies or exceptions to the king's justice. Know this, human. This is a tolerant and open city. But we will not accept the type of selfish behavior that is so common in human society. Everyone in Ischia earns what they get, be it wealth and luxuries, or an iron mask." Grodol gave Jenus a nod, his movements perfectly mirroring those made by the undead Gling'Ar around the city, and walked off. Jenus was stunned. *Could Grodol be controlling all of them?*

Disturbed, Jenus wandered back toward more familiar parts of town. He met a few of those who had told him of Banok, but only managed a shake of his head when they asked him for news.

Mage Marean was just entering his home as Jenus was passing by. The old mage looked into Jenus's eyes and invited him inside with a wave of his hand. Jenus mumbled his thanks and walked in. The whole of the entry room was devoted to silk weaving. A profusion of beautiful cloths hung from every part of the room. *The old man's been busy.*

"Welcome to my home, Jenus. I hope you are well. It has been a long time since you sought out my counsel."

"Thank you, Mage Marean. I . . . don't feel the need for counsel often these days. My duties and responsibilities seem to be evaporating."

Marean nodded to him and gestured for him to take a seat. "And yet it looks like you carry more on your shoulders than ever before. You spend too much time on your own or waving a stick around, Jenus. It's time you accepted that we won't be leaving this place anytime soon."

"I can't bring myself to do that. Not yet anyway. And besides, what else could I do? Fighting is all I know."

"It is never too late to learn. I hadn't tried my hand at silk weaving since I was a boy and my apprenticeship was interrupted by the discovery of my magical talent. That was more years ago than you have been alive."

Jenus gave a noncommittal shrug.

"Ischia is wondrous, Jenus. Would you believe I barely resent the binding of my talent anymore? I miss it, of course, but to live in such an incredible place! The society the king has built is amazing. People prosper in both knowledge and culture—Gling'Ar, humans, and other races I don't recognize, all working together for the benefit of all . . . and being well rewarded for their efforts! Even the poorest of craftsmen live better than most of our people back in Sacral. That such a thing is possible!"

"But they enslave the dead! How can you admire them?"

"They who show their prisoners more kindness than we offer those who live in the Black in our own city? Who invite us to join their perfect society? And they do not enslave the dead, Jenus. They simply make use of the bodies of the fallen, put them to work. Similar to animating a statue but far more efficient. The masks avoid the dead being recognized by their loved ones. For all that corpses are useful, the Dead King is not cruel. As is usually the case, reality has little in common with stories."

Jenus sighed in frustration. "It's all still too much for me to accept. Some part of me still believes I'll be going home one day."

"It is your choice, of course. But if you ever feel the inclination to learn my trade or a more scholarly pursuit, you will always be welcome here."

CHAPTER 20

It took hours for the army in Darien to assemble, and longer yet to get under way. The Night Guard were left lazing on a hill overlooking the South Gate while they waited. Salt and Inksharud leaned up against a tree and watched the Arcanum delegation slowly move out to join the rest of the army.

"The Arcanum sent more mages than I expected," Inksharud said to Salt as they watched the robed men and women walk past in small groups.

Salt looked them over, shaking his head at the long and often elaborate robes and cloaks they all wore. "Not much like Lera, are they?"

Inksharud laughed. "Aren't many like Lera in the whole world, I bet. Tell most mages they should learn to use a weapon or wear armor and they laugh in your face and maybe show you some little magic trick they think will impress you. That's the Night Guard's biggest advantage when dealing with mages in my opinion. Still, it doesn't mean this lot don't know what they're doing." He pointed toward one large group that was walking by. "See the short stocky guy in the black dress?" Salt grunted. "Well, he's the youngest-ever Arcanum archmage. Passed his Fifth Order at twenty-three. They expect he might make it to Ninth in another decade—most powerful mage the Arcanum has trained in a thousand years. The guy in the blue dress next to him is some kind of tribal they all seem really interested in. Most of the others are pretty strong too, and they're carrying all kinds of sources and anchors." Salt just looked at him with a raised eyebrow. The Dolbari laughed. "I don't know what any of that means either. It's just what the ladies told me earlier."

Salt grinned. "Well, like you said, at least there are a lot of them."

It was another hour before the mages were all assembled and settled into their wagons and carriages. *I guess I need to become a mage if I want to avoid riding.*

"Well, Salt, it looks like you'll be under way shortly. Now that the robes are organized, the generals will make their way out. You should spend a couple hours on the road before you need to make your first stop."

"How many soldiers are down there, would you guess?" Salt asked, looking out over the ranks that choked the road as far as the eye could see.

"Don't need to guess. There are about twenty thousand fighting men and women, two hundred mages, and about fifteen thousand cooks, drovers, smiths, cobblers, armorers, and various others in support roles. That many more will join you on the road when you meet up with the Western Army, and half that again when the Northern Army makes its way down."

Salt shook his head. "So many. Not leaving anything to chance. Not that I'd want the job of trying to keep this mess organized."

"Good thing you won't have to. Gurt sent word: you'll be in charge of the Night Guard contingent marching south, which only amounts to twenty of you, so you should be able to manage well enough till you meet up with Gurt." He punctuated his words with a mocking punch to the shoulder that left Salt's arm numb. "Just don't let any of those officers down there think they can order you around. You answer to Gurt and the king and no one else. Got it?" Salt nodded. "But try to avoid making enemies of any generals if you can avoid it. Politics usually falls on Gurt, and he won't thank you for making his life any more complicated than it already is."

***

Beren sat in silence as the rest of Maura's council discussed the various reconstruction efforts and changes they were implementing across Sacral. He rarely offered an opinion. Unless it was something he could help doing with his own two hands, or something that might pose a threat to Maura, he wasn't really all that interested. The focus of his existence had become very narrow, and he didn't reserve a lot of room in his mind for more than Maura's well-being and regrets. He hated how his relationship with Maura had changed. He knew holding back was hurting her. He knew she wanted to help him any way she could. And if anyone in this world could understand what he'd done and why, it was Maura. But he just couldn't. The loss of their son had come as near to breaking her as it had him and he just couldn't allow her to share his burdens. *She has so much on her shoulders already.*

Beren realized that Captain Harrow was speaking. ". . . I found five more priests after finishing the interrogation of the first. Those helped me find two more." He took a deep breath and everyone could see how much the interrogations had cost him. "I am now reasonably sure that no priests remain within the prison." Beren felt a surge of gratitude toward the captain.

Here was a man who took threats seriously. Who would help them make it through whatever came next and who always did what was necessary to safeguard the city and Maura.

Corwin cleared his throat. "The question remains—what do we do with the rest of the prisoners? It's all very well that Captain Harrow is confident that no more priests are hiding among them. But the prisoners themselves are dangerous enough, and we've received no request to ransom them back, or any word at all from Aboleth. If I may repeat my earlier suggestion—a painless death for them, and an end to one of our biggest worries." Karim, Jerik, and Harrow all started to repeat their own opinions.

"I have had enough of death," said Maura. "No two of you can agree, so that leaves the choice to me—we're letting them go." Corwin started to argue, but she shook her head and he let her continue. "Each and every prisoner will be given the choice of returning home or staying in our city. If they choose to go, we'll give them enough food and water to make it through the Wastes. We can even allow them to take a couple carts to carry the supplies if enough of them want to go. You'll be in charge of that, please, Karim. I will let them leave if that's their choice, but I don't want them taking any more than absolutely necessary to get them home alive. We just don't have enough to spare." She looked around at all of them to make sure there were no more arguments. "Any of those who decide to stay will get to help with the reconstruction and farm work. Captain Harrow? That makes them your responsibility. They are to be treated the same as any citizen of Sacral with one exception—none of them are allowed to join the People's Army, and they are not to own any weapons or armor."

"As fair a compromise as we're likely to reach and one that'll leave me with my conscience clear," said Karim, nodding his approval.

"There is also the matter of what is happening beyond the Wastes," Sevren said. "As important as our efforts to restructure Sacral's military are, I think we should also consider diplomacy going forward. Our neighbors to the east—Bialta—are apparently being invaded by a city-state from the desert beyond. None of the surviving mages in Sacral are very adept at long-distance scrying, but we've been able to detect the use of war magics across the southern part of the country and it seems that very large armies are on the move. Larger even than the forces the Abolians sent against us." He stood up and walked over to one of the overly decorative maps that hung on the council chamber's walls and pointed to the blank expanse that showed beyond the Icespine Mountains on their map. "The invaders are coming from somewhere out here. From what little we know of the outside world, Bialta is reputed to be one of the stronger nations on the continent. A gesture of peace toward them might stand us well. Especially when they are experiencing difficulties."

Corwin looked shocked. "Peace? Like our efforts with the Abolians? Look at where that got us."

"I'm not suggesting we send them soldiers, or get involved with their war in any way. I just think that if we were to send an envoy to Bialta and maybe south to Keral, it might help us understand what is happening in the world around us so we aren't surprised again. Besides, I'm fairly sure the Abolians would have attacked regardless. Our gesture of support just made things easier for them."

"My lady, on a related note," said Corwin. "Have you given any further thought to taking the crown? An envoy has to represent someone, and we will need a ruler as well as a strong army if we want to dissuade others from attacking us." There was a chorus of agreement from everyone assembled.

"My love," said Beren. "I agree with them. Enough of walking back and forth from our little house to the palace every day. You should be here and be protected all the time, not just when you're in the council chamber making decisions."

"You want to move in to the palace? To leave our home?"

"It's not our home anymore, Maura. It stopped being our home when the Abolians took our son from us. Now it's just a house full of sad memories. Please, love. For me, move into the palace and let Harrow and the other Warchosen protect you as they should. It's their duty and they'll feel better for doing it."

"But . . . I can't. We've already been over this. I'm just a normal person."

"You already are our queen, Lady Maura," said Corwin, "in fact if not in title. The only complication is the status of your husband. . . . I do not believe the people will be so quick to accept him as king."

Beren looked up in shock. "I won't be the king. I'll just be the queen's husband. Nothing more."

"I am quite relieved to hear you say that, Beren," Corwin continued. "I've been researching the subject quite thoroughly these last days, and naming you the consort of the queen seems to be a rather simple matter in our laws—proof that we've had a ruling queen at least once in our history, though I couldn't find her name."

"Besides, the people could use a celebration," Jerik said. Maura stayed silent, unable or unwilling to say anything more.

Harrow stood up. "I think Maura's silence is as close to an agreement as we're going to get. We are all in agreement?" Everyone but Maura nodded. "Then, Corwin, since you are the showman among us, would you be willing to plan the coronation?"

The little man's eyes lit up. "Oh, I can't wait. I still haven't had a chance to show you just what Corwin the Magnificent can do."

***

Dawn was only a short hour away. Skeg flexed his fingers and marveled at the complex patterns Nial and Zuly had woven within his flesh. The process had been . . . uncomfortable. At times it had even challenged Skeg's legendary pain tolerance. He had lain on the floor for hours trying not to move while the girls used their magic to push mixtures of minerals and herbs into his body and then molded them into the patterns required to shape his raw talent into something useful—they had carved a pattern object into his flesh.

"Try it out!" Nial said. "We're sure it will work, Uncle," she said brightly. "Just remember to hold your fingers out exactly like we showed you."

The back wall of Skeg's shop was blank stone and was as solid as could be found in the Muds. Skeg held out his left hand and carefully moved his fingers into position. Feeling as excited as the night he had consumed the imp, he pushed a modest amount of power into his arm. Instantly, blue flames burst out of his palm and hit the wall with a dull thud. The flames dispersed when they hit, leaving behind a star-shaped black smear on the stone. Skeg laughed in delight. It was so easy. He tried again and again with varying levels of power. After only minutes of practice, the back wall of the shop was a blackened mess and Skeg felt like he was throwing flames as naturally as if he'd been born to it. His new wellspring of demonic power finally had a purpose beyond making him a little stronger physically. *I wouldn't have had enough power to throw fire more than once or twice before consuming that imp. Now it's nothing.*

He turned to the girls to thank them, his voice even more hoarse than usual. "Girls, I . . . I don't know how to thank you for this."

"You already have, Uncle," Nial answered with a bright smile. "Besides," added Zuly. "We're just getting started. We have a couple more surprises we've been working on for you." Inwardly, Nial was stunned to hear Zuly speak so freely and fought not to show her surprise. The combination of a project to turn their minds to and the support of Uncle Skeg seemed to have helped her come back to herself, if only while they were in the shop.

Skeg walked over to Nial and pulled her close. It was the first time he could ever remember voluntarily hugging anyone. "You girls will make a real mage of me yet," he whispered, trying to ignore the feel of their already swollen belly and everything it represented.

The next night, Nial and Zuly were waiting in the shop when Skeg came down from his room.

"We worked out something a little more complicated for your right arm, Uncle. We think you'll like it."

"I'm sure I will. So what are you giving me now?"

"Patience," answered Zuly. "We'll show you after it's done. Now lie down and don't move. We've taken a lot of materials from your shop for this and you don't have enough of a lot of things for us to try again."

Skeg did as he was told. This pattern took longer to complete. He heard the dull sound that warned of customers at his door several times and ignored it. It was quite maddening, lying there waiting for the searing pain running through his arm and shoulder to pass. Nial and Zuly were totally absorbed in their work. Neither one of them spoke at all. They just made small movements to pick up another pouch of components they had prepared and placed it against his skin. More often than not, they only used their talent to do everything. It almost felt like they were just staring intently at him for hours. Only rarely did they even blink.

Hours passed. *It must be hours.* He felt like the bones in his arm were on fire. He was gritting his teeth, trying not to react to the pain. Finally, Nial stood up slowly and dusted off her dress.

"We're done, Uncle!" Nial smiled down at him. "We think you're really going to like this one. It's more useful than the first weave we made for you, but we thought you needed a way of protecting yourself before we did anything else."

Skeg pulled himself to his feet. He was trembling. Zuly looked him up and down. "You need to feed before we show you how to use it. Sit up against the wall there and rest. We'll find you a meal."

Before he could argue, they were gone. The shop door closed behind them. Skeg had always been a patient man. He'd devised an almost excruciatingly slow path to power for himself, but now he was like a child waiting for his name-day gift. He would have argued with Zuly about his need for a meal. Her abrupt manner just showed that she had anticipated him. He was part demon now, and if there was one thing Zuly understood, it was his hunger.

The girls stepped out into the street and let out a slow breath. So far they had managed to hide the impact the pregnancy was having on them from Skeg, but it was only a matter of time before he noticed. There was an urgency in the spawn of Amon Kareth—it grew far faster than any mortal child. Their stomach seemed to be expanding every day now. Their partially demonic body was coping with the rapid changes, but the spawn's needs were draining the girls' strength in ways they didn't understand. Though their wellspring of power was undiminished, and the souls of their victims still brimmed with untapped energy, they always felt tired, and moving around was becoming increasingly difficult. Nial felt a mix of fear and curiosity when she looked down at their rounded belly, but the feelings from Zuly were more extreme and clear—loathing and disgust. The spawn was a living reminder of what Amon Kareth had done to them. It occurred to Nial that the feeling of helplessness that Zuly associated with their attack was possibly the hardest part of the ordeal for her to overcome.

They moved around the Muds cautiously looking for any potential victims and hoping to find an animal of some sort they could take back for Skeg. The uproar they had caused in killing Gunnar Danekor hadn't blown over as they had hoped. Groups of mages and armed soldiers still patrolled every part of the city. Not only were they having trouble dodging the patrols themselves, but the increased traffic was scaring their usual prey into hiding.

Yet another group was approaching—six city watchmen escorting three Arcanum mages. Nial quickly pulled a weave around them to hide them from sight as they crouched on the edge of a rooftop. *This is pointless*, complained Zuly. *We've been out too long already.*

Nial agreed. *I guess we could just buy something for Uncle Skeg. There's a market not far from here.* Then they felt a surge of magic—formless but powerful—radiate from their belly. The girls froze, their heart beating faster. The Arcanum mages stopped dead, looking around for the source of the magic they had felt. *That thing's going to get us killed.* Zuly slowly drew the Soul Knife out of their belt and prepared to fight. They stayed unmoving for a long time as the mages tried to locate the power they had felt, but eventually they moved off.

The girls slowly relaxed. The last thing they wanted was to kill more Arcanum mages and stir things up even more. *We just need to stop hunting for a while,* thought Nial.

Not hunting isn't enough. We're going to have to get farther away from the Arcanum. If the spawn is already doing this, it could be much worse as it gets bigger. We can't sit in the ward circle forever.

Skeg's pain was already ebbing by the time the girls returned with their customary cup of blood for him. He drank it down as quickly as he could swallow—an obedient child gulping down his dinner so as to be allowed dessert.

"Do you feel better, Uncle Skeg?" He nodded, wiping the blood from his lips with the back of his hand. "Now, this pattern is a lot more complex. We worked on the idea for a long time, and it's not quite so easy to use. To start with, two patterns are linked in this one. If you hold your fingers out in the same position as we showed you for the flames, you will pull an object to yourself like this." The empty cup flew from the floor next to him into her hand. "Now take it back."

Skeg smiled. The cup flew out of her hand and over to him. He caught it deftly. "Thank you again, girls. You've given me another skill of yours that I've always envied. And, again, it's so damned *easy* to use! I can barely believe it!"

"We're not done yet Uncle. Make a fist now and try it."

Skeg placed the cup on the floor and pointed his fist at it. A little surge of power sent the cup skidding across the floor. Like a child with a new toy, Skeg sent the cup flying away from him and pulled it back again and again.

"We're so glad you like it. We wanted to finish it before we had to leave." Nial smiled sadly. Skeg stood blinking at her in surprise. She tried again. "We have to leave Bialta; we have to get as far away from the Arcanum as we can."

"I'm sorry, girls. I'm just surprised and sorry to hear that. What brought this on? You know you can stay with me for as long as you need to."

"Something happened while we were hunting earlier." She looked away. "Being pregnant is slowing us down, and we don't know what'll happen when it's born." The tears were streaming down her face now. She looked straight at him finally. "The thing inside us . . . we felt its power. We've been trying to pretend everything's normal . . . but I'm scared."

"Are you sure?" The tears just kept falling as she looked at him miserably. "I'm sorry, girls." Skeg continued shaking his head. "Of course you're sure. And you're right to get out of Darien, and maybe even Bialta. It will only be a matter of time before we attract the wrong sort of attention. Stay here. Sit in the circle. I'll bring a few cushions to make you more comfortable. Don't leave the shop any more than you need to. I'll only need a few hours to prepare, then we'll head south and aim for the border."

Tentatively Skeg reached out and squeezed their shoulder. Their whole body started to tremble. Skeg let go and rushed out of the shop. He had a thousand things to do and no time to do them. Luckily, he had planned for the day he'd need to make a hasty escape. It was only prudent given the illegality of his chosen profession. Skeg had amassed a small fortune in the years he'd been running his shop. He had dipped into his savings a lot these past months, but there was more than enough left to move and set up elsewhere, perhaps to even allow himself to live in a little more comfort. First though, he'd need to find a safe place for them to hole up until the child was born. *Trouble will follow the child.* But Skeg's view of all things demonic had changed since meeting Nial and Zuly. If he was honest with himself, he'd admit that he was looking forward to the birth. He already thought of the baby as his grandchild. *And, the Muds are no place to raise a baby.*

The girls sat in the warded circle and waited with Nial gnawing on their fingernails. The last few days had proven to them just how important it was for them to get out of Darien—the thing growing inside them was now almost constantly radiating powerful if formless magic. *It's all so unfair!* Nial liked to think they had made a difference here. That they had made the worst part of this sprawling city a little safer for the poor people who had to live here. She didn't want to leave. She didn't want to leave her home or even her father. Even if he refused to look at her. *It's all because of Amon Kareth!* At the thought of the name, wordless anger and hatred bubbled up from Zuly. The child within them stirred. Nial shifted uncomfortably. *At least Uncle Skeg is coming with us.* Zuly calmed slightly and the child settled. *It understands so much already,* Nial thought to herself, careful this time to keep her thoughts private. She let out a long sigh—surely other women didn't have to deal with so much to carry a baby.

Skeg finally came back into the shop. Nial realized with a start that they'd been dozing again. It was becoming harder and harder to stay awake for any length of time.

"Everything's ready, girls. I have a cart outside packed with most of what we'll need. I have a few things here that I want to grab, but we'd best be off as quick as we can. A contact of mine is working at the South Gate. We need to get there before the shift change."

Nial nodded at him sleepily. It was so hard to keep their eyes open now. "We'll get you settled in the back of the cart, and I'll just pop back in to grab a few things."

A large horse-drawn cart nearly filled the alley. The two dun-colored horses harnessed to the cart snorted impatiently. Skeg helped the girls climb up and got them settled in a hollow he had obviously prepared for them. He surrounded them with soft bundles, cushions, and blankets. "You should be able to relax here. The cart is almost as heavily warded as the shop." Nial only managed to look at him in surprise. "This is the cart one of my contacts uses to sneak supplies into the city for me." Skeg hopped off the back of the cart and went back inside.

Nial couldn't help feeling a twinge of jealousy at how freely he moved. *I don't understand how this pregnancy business works. I can lift a grown man with no effort but my own body seems almost impossibly heavy.* Their eyelids slid closed again.

The cart jolted and Nial opened her eyes with a start. The sun was setting beyond some hills. Fields and farms extended off in every direction. "Uncle Skeg?" He was sitting in front of them wearing an oiled rain cloak and a floppy wide-brimmed hat. Overall, the outfit might have made him stand out less on the road, had it not been so warm and clear out.

"I'm glad you're awake. Are you feeling any better? You've barely moved since we left Darien."

"We're all right. Still tired, but better."

"You just rest for as long as you need to. We'll stop to rest the horses at the next inn, but there's no reason for you to move. I'll get us something to eat as well if only to keep up appearances." Nial managed to give him a little smile as she drifted off to sleep again.

Days passed in a blur. The girls kept nodding off, unable to keep their eyes open for more than a few minutes at a time. Occasionally, they would look up and see Skeg's ever-present shape in front of them, guiding the wagon. They were so grateful to him. Skeg had left his shop, his city, everything he'd known and worked to build in his life. All of it for them, a girl and a demoness who'd just happened to walk into his shop one day. He'd taught them and helped them far more than he needed to. They knew for a fact that they'd cost him far more business over the time they'd spent together than they'd ever brought him. They shared more than knowledge now, of course. In a strange way they were kin, both of them carrying the essence of Karethin demons.

Skeg shook his head and looked around with bleary eyes. His head was hurting. He felt dizzy. *Nial and Zuly!* He'd left the cart pulled up next to an inn to find something to eat, desperate for an easing of the hunger after days of not feeding. He'd handed a silver coin to the innkeeper to keep an eye on his niece who was fast asleep in the back of the cart, with the promise of more when he returned. The man had been skeptical of the arrangement but had reluctantly agreed once he was handed the promised coin and saw that there was more where it came from. And then . . . Skeg remembered nothing. He tried to move and came up short. His arms were chained to the wall behind him. Long enough to let him slump against the wall but too short to bring his hands together. The wall behind him was made of long planks that let in a faint breeze from outside. He strained against the chains, but the pain in his head made him give up before he could split the boards. Skeg heard dogs barking outside the building. Then a door creaked open and a light shone in, forcing Skeg to avert his eyes.

"Well, look what we got here. The thing's awake, Jax. Let's see what it is." A dog whining was his only answer. "Dammit, Jax, get in here." More keening from the dog. A burly man walked in to what Skeg realized was a small barn. He wore mud-stained breeches and a simple homespun shirt. His head and bared forearms showed an impressive network of scars. He looked down at Skeg with watery, piggish eyes. The blinding light was nothing more than a single lamp he carried. When Skeg tried to focus on anything, he felt like the world was tilting under him. He shook his head, trying to clear it.

The man glared down at Skeg from a safe distance half-way across the barn. "You're not fucking human, are you?" He waited a moment for Skeg to answer, then continued. "You sure as hell heal faster than any man I've ever met before. An' I was in the Legions so that's sayin' something. And your smell is freaking out my dogs. None of them will come near the barn with you in here. Even my Jax won't come in, and he's as mean as a helldog."

"Let me go," Skeg whispered. His head was clearing slowly, but he was still feeling weak. *The shit must have hit me with something. Goes to show, magic isn't everything.* He felt strangely calm. He'd been attacked and taken prisoner, but he was sure he could get out of it given time to recover. His body was starting to tremble, but more from hunger than weakness.

"Now why would I want to do something like that? I find you creeping around my fields in the dead of night. Seems to me you had some bad intentions. Especially now I see how my dogs are reacting to you. I think I'll wait till morning and get the guards in here. You some kind of freak?" He picked up a heavy shovel. The flat of the blade was crusted with dried blood.

My fucking blood, thought Skeg. "Listen, I don't mean anyone any harm. I was just passing through. Didn't even know I was on your land. Just let me go and I'll be on my way. No harm done." He pulled himself to his feet, leaning against the wall.

"No harm? You freaking bounce back in a couple hours from a shovel to the head that should have killed you. You're not natural, and the guards are going to want to see you. I might even get a reward for catching some dangerous freak thing." He waved the shovel menacingly. Skeg reacted more by instinct than by intent. Pain exploded behind his eyes as he drew on his power. *Pain be damned.* Skeg made a fist with his right hand and sent a surge of power out, knocking the man's shovel out of his hands and slamming it against the far wall so hard it embedded itself in the wood. The he opened his hand and *pulled.* He grabbed the man around the throat as he stumbled forward, and let a trickle of power seep into his left hand. Blue flames flickered in his palm.

"Last warning," he told the farmer through gritted teeth. "Otherwise I'll just burn you and the rest of this place to the ground and walk out."

The man didn't say a word. He was trembling and Skeg could smell urine.

"I'm running out of patience. Take off the chains now and I'll walk out of here. Like I said, no harm done." Skeg was feeling the hunger growing in him. Using his power was only making it worse. He realized he was looking at the man he was holding more as food than as a person—actually enjoying his fear. He was disgusted with himself. The man was fumbling with his right manacle. As soon as it fell off, Skeg pushed the man back and removed the left chain himself.

"The guards don't scare me," Skeg said. "But if I find them hunting me, I'm coming back for you. You won't catch me by surprise a second time. If I come back, I will raze this whole village. You understand me? Every man, woman, and child will burn alive. Every fucking cow and dog." The man sat in a puddle of his own urine and nodded, his piggish eyes looking everywhere but at Skeg.

Skeg left the barn. It was all he could do to keep on his feet and not vomit from the intense searing pain in his head. He could hear the farmer weeping in relief. Outside, the dogs howled. *I've got to get back to the girls. They'll be missing me. And I still haven't found anything to eat.* They couldn't get out of Bialta fast enough. The lands south of Darien were far too crowded for Skeg's liking. He stumbled through a field and almost collided with a cow. Hunger flared inside him and before he knew what he was doing, he had his arms wrapped around the animal and his teeth planted in its neck. The cow screamed and thrashed. Skeg's demonic strength and hunger proved to be stronger. Hot blood gushed into his mouth and he drank hungrily, the blood pumped out of the animal by its frantically beating heart so much sweeter than the cold cup Nial used to bring him. By the time he had finished, the cow was dead and he had practically ripped its head completely off its body. He looked down at his gore-caked clothes in disgust. *I'm becoming a monster. I can't let my hunger get this far ever again. If that hadn't been a cow . . .*

CHAPTER 21

The Bialtan army was making good time. They had moved down toward the Ragged Coast where the Icespine Mountains met the Black Sea. If the Tolrahkali were going to move through in any sort of numbers, this would be the place. It was the only pass that would accommodate wagons. No matter what abilities and strange equipment they might have developed, they must still be bound by the normal needs of an army—food, equipment, basic supplies.

The Arcanum worked its divinations and detection spells. Most were unsuccessful. This wasn't much of a surprise. They had expected the Tolrahkali force to include a number of warlocks who would be hard at work trying to obscure the presence of their army. Swarms of magically bound lesser demons were also sent out. Few were able to find anything. Those that did were quickly destroyed.

The war effort devolved into an infuriating game of cat and mouse. Lost magical servants provided some small clue as to where enemy troops might be. The Western and Northern Armies were split off from the main force again to increase the chances of finding the invaders as they swept across the countryside.

The Southern Army was still a week from the Ragged Coast when their first scouting party vanished. "Ten good men mounted on fast horses don't just disappear. The scout units always keep eyes on one another, and that's not including the Arcanum's . . . things," growled General Felkin as Gurt passed the information on to him.

"I agree, General. There must be some trace out there. I'll pull the Night Guard back from the vanguard and have them search."

"Do so, Commander. And find out how they did it. The Tolrahkali have drawn blood again. I mean to make them pay for it. Whatever resources I can provide to you and your men are yours."

Gurt saluted and left the tent. *The gold skins must have more mages than expected to keep the Arcanum blind. Not weak ones either.*

Salt led two squads of Night Guard to search for the lost men. As it turned out, they weren't difficult to find. All ten mounted scouts had seemingly had been drawn into a small hollow just out of sight and killed so efficiently that not one soldier or horse had a chance to call for help or scream. Salt looked around at the bloody corpses. "Anything, Min? Brolt?"

"There's a hint of sorcery all the way around the hollow," Brolt said. "As for killing them without making a sound? That looks like it was just a blade through the lung . . . on every one of them at almost exactly the same time."

"This is becoming less *fun* every minute," Salt grumbled. "Which way did they go?" Min pointed off into the distance. Salt turned back to the rest of his team. "Seely, report back to Gurt. We'll hold here and wait. I'm sure he'll want to bring in more men if we're going farther from the main column."

The trail left by the Tolrahkali was obvious and deliberate to a trained tracker. It led like an arrow to the village of Sweet Trees, famed for its orchards. Not wanting to leave anything to chance, Gurt led the whole of the Night Guard force, all one hundred and twenty-six of them, to investigate.

Smoke rose in plumes from the charred remains of houses. The Guardsmen fanned out and moved in fast and low from three sides. But it quickly became clear that not a single Tolrahkali remained for them to fight. The village had been ransacked and left to burn. The villagers themselves had seemingly been led to the town square before being systematically butchered. Bones were stacked randomly—those that hadn't been split for the marrow. Even the Guard were shocked by the savagery the attack had shown. The loss of their scouts was no more than a means to show off the killers' handiwork. All Salt could think was, *The people have been eaten!*

The trail that had led so clearly to the village vanished beyond it. Not even Lera or the Night Guard scouts were able to find the least trace, either mundane or magical.

Gurt was quick to organize a corpse detail. "I want all these bones stacked together. Lera will fire them with magic. We don't have time to sort through them all and bury them, but these people deserve better than having their bones left out for the birds to pick at. Any of you who follow a god and want to say a few words over the pyre are welcome to. Now move, people. I want this done and us on the way back to camp in half an hour."

For weeks they maneuvered and followed false trails. The Arcanum grew so frustrated at losing their magical servants that they refused to send any more out. "You'll simply have to rely on your scouts, General Felkin," insisted Dantic. "We simply cannot continue wasting our efforts on scouting. The time and effort involved in summoning even a minor demon and binding it with any level of certainty is not something we can easily do on the move. Unless you are suggesting leaving us behind?"

"No. Of course not, Archmage Dantic. But I need you to find a way to neutralize their advantage. Tell me how they are managing this? Dammit, it has to be magical. No army can move with such speed and with no supply train. They've been running circles around us for weeks and haven't even bothered taking much in the way of supplies from the villages they're raiding."

"I don't have an answer for you, General. I wish I did. We've even got teams of researchers working on the problem back in the Arcanum, but so far none of the possibilities we've considered seem even remotely possible."

"Could they be teleporting? Flying?"

"Teleportation is highly unlikely. There are only a few documented cases of mages able to perform that type of magic in all our recorded histories. Even if they did have someone capable of creating that kind of weave, it would take time to build a gate large enough to send an army through and they wouldn't be able to move it around with them either. We've considered flying as well. One of my colleagues guessed that they might have created a flying fortress of some sort, but the power required to create such a thing, much less control it and keep it in the air, would be astounding. Every single Arcanum member would have to work on such a project for years with no guarantee it would even work. No, General, the solution either isn't something we've considered, or it's not magical at all."

The general turned away in anger and called for the scout captains to assemble again.

The Bialtan army was growing frantic as frustration and anger mounted. For all their numbers they felt increasingly helpless as word spread of further atrocities committed by the invaders. Scouts had now confirmed a dozen villages and even a midsized town had been attacked. Each one had been devastated, their populations dead to the last. The generals grew more reckless as time went on, sending out more and more contingents of scouts. The Night Guardsmen were constantly on the move, half of them on patrol at any given time. They were approaching the Keral border and just about to set up camp late one afternoon when scouts reported they had found a solid trail. It had been partially obscured, but it seemed like a large group had been through the area.

"Thank the gods," Gurt said with a sigh. He gestured to one of his ever-present messengers. "Get the Night Guard together. All of them." The man took off at a run. Gurt paced impatiently in front of the command tent. He didn't have long to wait. The frustration of not being able to close with their enemies was affecting the Night Guard as much as anyone. They assembled in short order. All of them looked at him eagerly.

"We finally have something!" Gurt announced. "I want each squad to go out as soon as the last of the light fades. Fan out from south to west and see if you can actually get eyes on the slippery bastards. If you meet small groups and can do some damage, I'll leave that decision to your squad leaders. Just don't get carried away; we won't be able to get any support to you if you stir things up too much. I'll be handing out tokens for you to carry tonight. Lera and her friends from the Arcanum have cooked up some sort of enchantment that should make it easier for you to sneak around unnoticed."

Lera nodded. "The weaves should last until morning. They will help hide you from most senses, but they won't hold up if you're standing right in front of someone. Archmage Dantic and his team are putting the final touches on them now, so they'll be ready by the time you head out."

Gurt looked at them in silence for a moment. "It's time for us to turn the tables on these invaders and who better to do it than the Night Guard. Make me proud. Now go get ready. You leave in an hour."

Salt's squad found the enemy camp about an hour before midnight. The Tolrahkali army filled the valley with their campfires. Salt directed his men down the hillside trying to keep as low as possible. "We going for the baggage train then?" Brolt asked in a whisper. Salt shook his head. "Getting close enough to get a reasonable count is going to be hard enough. They have too many men out."

"Flyer!" hissed Min. The squad dropped to their bellies. A few tense moments passed while the creature and its rider passed overhead.

Slowly, slowly they made their way down to the camp. They crawled on their bellies as often as not, sneaking between patrols as much by luck and boldness as by skill. The flyers passed by overhead at odd intervals.

Early guesses of the invaders' numbers seemed to be accurate—the Tolrahkali army seemed far too small to challenge the Bialtan force. Min and Brolt estimated no more than ten thousand fighters in the camp, as well as support units and slaves. *But then there's no guarantee this is the only camp they have in the area,* Salt thought. Rows of supply wagons were visible, each harnessed to strange creatures that were covered in the same chitin the Tolrahkali warriors used as armor. A large number of the flying creatures were being tended to on the edge of the camp. A group of thirty were preparing to leave, each carrying two warriors. *Well, that explains how they're outmaneuvering us. Our whole army's probably been chasing raiding groups that they've been moving around on those things.*

The ground shook as a unit of heavy cavalry moved in from the opposite side of the valley. It was more of the strangely equipped Tolrahkali soldiers, but these were mounted on monsters. Covered as they were with the same red-black chitin, it was hard to tell where the mount ended and the rider began. They were clearly similar to the pack animals though these were a more warlike variety. Their horns glinted in the firelight like swords, and their breathing, as loud as bellows, sent clouds of steam into the night air. Packs of the lizard dogs the survivors of the Eastern Army had told them about darted around the cavalry. Salt counted at least a hundred mounted soldiers in that one group. *And I'm sure that's not all of them.*

"Good enough," he whispered to his squad. "Let's get out of here."

By the time Salt and his squad made it back to camp, the sun was just starting to lighten the horizon. Other squads were drifting in around them. Gurt met them in the same spot outside the command tent, obviously not having slept at all while they were out. He took the time to speak with each squad leader individually before sending them all off to rest.

Gurt gestured for Salt to join him in the command tent. At this early hour it was deserted. They sat down in camp chairs and Gurt poured them each a cup of wine from a jug that had been left on a side table.

"The numbers of soldiers and *things* in that camp aren't what's bothering me. It's the fact that the squads that went out to inspect their trail said that the Tolrahkali haven't moved any large number of men for a few weeks at least. That means you were right about them using flyers to ferry troops and maybe even warlocks around to keep us confused and chasing our own tail. I'd guess the bastards just followed the coast south until they got to where they are and made very little effort of hiding their actual trail."

"So you think they're just toying with us until we realize where they are and come to meet them?"

"That's my feeling. And if they're waiting for us, I wouldn't want to give them any advantage we don't have to. So really the question is, Do we move in on them with just the men we have here with us or do we pull the Northern and Western Armies back to us first and risk losing them again?"

Salt shrugged. "If I've learned anything since joining the Guard, it's that doing what an enemy wants is never a good idea."

"I'm glad you agree. I may need your help convincing the general that we should sit on our hands for a few days and make sure we have every soldier we can get before we move on the bastards. Even if we get word of fresh attacks elsewhere."

Once the armies came together, the Bialtan force was by far the largest they had assembled in decades. And now here they were, nearly fifty thousand soldiers with a full contingent of Crown Knights and nearly the full complement of Night Guard ready to mete out justice. The Tolrahkali were pinned down near the border with Keral, seemingly unwilling to invade a second kingdom and fight a war on two fronts. Countless scouting parties had reported in, and the Arcanum had confirmed their findings—the Tolrahkali were mustering to meet them at last, moving out of the valley they had been hiding in and onto a wide, flat plain—the clash would come in the morning.

Salt walked through the camp for most of the night, unable to settle. Everywhere he passed, the troops seemed nervous but in good spirits. They outnumbered their enemies at least five to one and would finally be able to slake their thirst for vengeance. No matter what strange equipment the Tolrahkali might have, it was hard for anyone to argue with odds like that. The Arcanum contingent and the presence of the near-legendary Night Guard didn't hurt morale either.

Salt was pulled out of his reverie by a scream. Shouts joined in and soldiers scrambled to put on their armor and ready their weapons. Salt stopped a messenger who was running past. "What happened?"

"An attack on the mages, sir. They're in our camp!" Then he was off, intent on delivering his news to whoever he reported to.

Salt jogged toward the central camp where the mages and commanders were billeted. The whole place was in chaos. Soldiers were running. Officers were ordering them about to little purpose or effect. Fires were burning in the crushed remains of four large tents. A shimmering wall of blue-white energy surrounded the main command tent.

Salt swallowed. The tents had belonged to the Arcanum. They had been ringed with wards above and beyond those that protected the whole encampment in anticipation of a preemptive magical attack against the army's mages and officers. And yet despite the obvious precautions the Arcanum had taken, as well as their presumed magical superiority, the heart of their encampment had been breached and it had cost them.

"Night Captain Saltig, sir!" called one of the soldiers, recognizing him.

I guess it's time to earn my pay. "Report, soldier."

The soldier saluted. "The attack came just a few minutes ago, Night Captain. Four mages were killed, and Archmage Dantic was attacked before he managed to drive off the attackers. He joined the commander and Archmage Lera in the command tent and then that wall of magic appeared."

"And the attackers? How many made it out?"

"From what we've been able to piece together, all of them, sir. There's talk of them being the Drokga's mage hunters."

"If that's true, they're living up to that title. It will be our job to make sure we don't make it so easy next time. So who did we lose?"

"I'm not sure, sir. The other mages took care of the bodies."

Salt nodded. "Good work, soldier. Get this lot organized. I want a guard of fifty outside the command tents at all times from now on. Send a messenger and have the full Night Guard and all the scout captains join me here." Salt walked over to stand in front of the command tent.

Four mages lost. The Tolrahkali had played their hand masterfully. They'd let their enemies move into position arrogantly, thinking their advantages too great for their smaller foe to overcome. *And they send a handful of men to kick our teeth in the night before our first real battle.* Part of the Bialtans' magical superiority had been lost. Even the surviving mages would be looking over their shoulders and jumping at shadows from now on. The glowing power put into the shield around the command tent was proof of that. No telling how much of the army's magical effectiveness would be lost because of this one attack.

Salt sighed. There would be precious little sleep for anyone tonight after all. Gurt was probably locked in the command tent along with the other senior officers. Keeping order fell to Salt. As the Night Guard and scouts started to show up, he sent them out in teams to search for any trace of the intruders.

Two hours before dawn, the great wards flickered out and Gurt emerged from the tent. "Thanks for keeping an eye on things out here, lad. It's going to be a long day for all of us. It's been decided, we're finishing them today. No routes, no second battles. We crush them here and now and don't let them try anything like this ever again."

Salt nodded, unsurprised. "I take it there was talk of moving on Tolrahk Esal again?"

"Come morning, if you can believe it. Lots of anger in that tent last night and it hasn't cooled much in the past few hours." Gurt stretched and Salt heard a dozen pops from the old lord's joints. "Go get some rest, lad. Orders have already been issued to form up for the attack. The Guard will need to be on its feet and ready to fight as soon as the sun's up."

Salt nodded his thanks and went off to find his bedroll. The Night Guard camp was quite different from that of the surrounding soldiers. The tents were the same, as was most of the equipment. What was missing was the palpable tension and nervousness that Salt had felt everywhere else. The Night Guard had faced so many horrors that the prospect of a battle was nothing. That didn't mean they were complacent though. Salt noticed pairs of Guardsmen moving around the camp together, acting as unofficial sentinels. Every man and woman was fully armored and had their weapons close to hand, though most dozed while they waited to hear when and where they would be needed.

**

Dantic sat in the corner of the command tent and tried not to listen to the incessant whining of the other mages. Their confidence had taken a real beating after the night's attacks. The wards set up around the army, and more specifically around the mages' camp itself, would be considered excessive by all but the most paranoid practitioner—even given the proximity of an enemy army. . . . And yet it seemed the Tolrahkali mage hunters were able to ignore the most powerful of magical defenses. They had proven their ability during the night by cutting down several very capable members of the Arcanum. Dantic thanked the gods the kladic hadn't been the target of the attack. The surprise they were preparing for the invaders was hopefully still intact.

Dantic shivered as he recalled how the inhuman thing had shrugged off his power. *If I hadn't thought to hit him indirectly. . . .* The mage hunter had walked through Dantic's strongest weaves and almost completely ignored the wall of power he'd tried to trap the monster in. Dantic could clearly remember the assassin's smile as he realized Dantic was both helpless and paralyzed by fear. Then a small pebble flew out of the dark and struck the Tolrahkali in the forehead. The man flinched at the impact and looked around for the source of the attack. The minor distraction gave Dantic the time he needed for self-preservation instincts to kick in, and a little bit of panic if he was honest with himself. He threw up a massive torrent of stones and dust from the ground. The stones were far more effective, not to mention near impossible to dodge given the exaggerated scope of Dantic's panic-fueled weave. Pelted with an unending stream of wind, stones, and dust, the attacker had no choice but to retreat.

We're more vulnerable to these hunters than the least of Bialta's soldiers. Dantic herded the remaining mages into his tent and summoned up a swirling wall of magic and sand to protect them. With the extra time to think about what he was doing, the wall was a much more refined version of his earlier spell. The magic component did little more than keep the sand moving. The tiny grains of glassy stone were whipped up by incredible magic winds and roared around the tent so fast that it would strip the flesh off anyone who moved too close. *Probably won't do much against armor, but they have to have some exposed skin. The real question is how many of the others will be able to manage a weave like this.* They would just have to make do now that he would be able to tell them not to use their power on the attackers directly . . . or he would if the lot of them ever calmed down enough for him to speak. He sighed and lifted his cup for Matchstick to refill, numbly wondering who could have thrown that stone that undoubtedly saved his life.

***

After his last misadventure, Skeg didn't dare leave Nial alone again. Relieved at having found her still asleep in the cart in front of the inn, he disposed of his bloody rain cloak and washed off as well as he could in a rain barrel behind the stables before handing the innkeeper an extra handful of silver coins. After that, Skeg stopped eating entirely and struggled through each day to control the ravenous hunger that prevented him from sleeping or even thinking clearly for longer and longer stretches. As the Keralan border approached he was desperate to stop. Every moving creature that caught his eye made his mouth water, whether it walked on four legs or two.

"Uncle? When did you last feed?" Nial asked him the next time she woke. "You look terrible."

"It's been a few days anyway, probably more. I've been hoping to see an open air market on the road where I can pick up a live animal, but we've been missing market day in every place we pass."

"You're close to losing control, Uncle. I can feel it from here."

A farmer stepped out in front of the wagon, waving at Skeg to stop. "I represent a mutual acquaintance. A house has been prepared for the two of you." The man indicated the road ahead. "Please, my friends, allow me to lead you there. Food and shelter are not far now."

"I don't know anyone in the area, *friend*. And I seriously doubt anyone I would want to accept a house from lives in this town."

The smile on the man's face didn't waver. "Well, in that you would be wrong, Mister Skeg. Not that there is any need to worry. The rather shady individual I represent owes the young lady a significant debt. He wanted me to tell you how impressed he was with how his two previous payments were put to use and furthermore how she went above and beyond in executing her last task for him. His home is much the cleaner for her efforts. And while he had expected to provide an altogether different reward, recent events soon led him to the conclusion that a new home would be needed, one far from the capital. While he understands the need, he was sorry to see the two of you leave as you had a not-inconsequential cleansing effect on the entire region, an effect that he is grateful for above and beyond the services that you performed on his behalf. I am to give you further assurances that you will not be disturbed by any unwelcome third parties so long as you reside in this village."

Sure as hell doesn't talk like a farmer. If I didn't know any better, I'd think the man was Arcanum trained. Skeg looked over at Nial sitting in the back of the cart. *Not like we have much choice.* Skeg sighed and nodded.

The house turned out to be a simple farmhouse, well built by local standards, but not to the point of making it stand out. The farmer offered to help in unloading their wagon but nodded and walked off with a wave when Skeg declined.

Skeg tentatively stepped into the house, both hands extended in front of him, ready to unleash his magic. They may be desperate and all but out of options, but he still didn't trust Shade or his gifts. The house was simple and included a large vegetable garden and an enclosure that housed dozens of rabbit cages. All in all, it was a house you might expect to find in any number of small towns throughout Bialta. But clearly great effort had gone into preparing it for Nial and Zuly's arrival—nearly every part of the floor, walls, and ceiling were carved with elaborate wards. Row after row of them circled out from a central point in the main living area in an elaborate profusion. *It must have taken months to do this. Even if there was a team of powerful mages working on it.* Skeg swallowed. *Shade knew we were coming this way weeks before we decided to leave Darien.* It was a chilling thought, but they had nowhere else to go and there was no denying the hunger any longer. Skeg pulled a rabbit out of its cage and sank his teeth into its neck.

Life was turning out to be rather pleasant in their adoptive village. Nial and Zuly were relieved to be out of the cart. They curled up with a pile of blankets and cushions on the floor in the center of the wards and spent the bulk of their time dozing in relative comfort. In fact, the house was far nicer than any Skeg or Nial had ever lived in. They had minimal interactions with their neighbors, who were all outwardly friendly and didn't show too much interest in what Skeg or Nial were up to, which suited them just fine.

Just don't get soft, Skeg told himself. It was too easy to forget that this home had been given to them by Shade, and a couple weeks' leisurely travel was certainly not enough to put them beyond his reach.

Just as he was finishing that thought, Skeg walked into the house to find Shade standing across the room. "What are you doing here?" he said. The tone of his voice brought the girls out of their doze. They moved awkwardly, propping themselves up as they prepared to defend themselves.

The masked figure made no move.

"Well, Shade? What do you want now?"

"I applaud your caution, Mister Skeg. Trust is something that should never be given too quickly. But do not fear, my motivation for coming is, as ever, curiosity. I have no demands, no new tasks for you. I was simply curious to see with my own eyes how my three friends were settling in to their new home."

Skeg looked sideways at the runes around the doorway.

"Oh, come now, Mister Skeg! Your own runes could not keep me out before, why do you now imagine that I would be barred by those carved by my own hand?"

Zuly growled. "We finished the work you gave us. We owe you nothing now."

"I see you haven't learned nearly as much as I might have hoped since our last meeting."

Shaking his head, Shade continued, "Foolish children. You owe me everything! It was my nudge that allowed the two of you to find each other. A she demon—lost in the nether, doomed to starve until her hunger consumed her. One among many. . . . And a dying child, a shining spirit rising out of Darien, admirable raw talent reaching out for salvation. I wasn't close enough to intervene directly. And so, with few options available to me, I chose. A small nudge in the right direction and the two of you took care of the rest. I admit I didn't have high hopes of a positive result, but you both managed to surprise me." He looked over at Skeg: "Little takes place in my city that I am not aware of. And yes, it is *my* city. I am by far its oldest inhabitant, though it was not my first home. Every so often something new comes along to make existence interesting again. I made use of your talents for a time, and I enjoyed watching you work. You may not know it, but the effects of your hunting will likely endure for some time."

The featureless mask looked back and forth between Skeg and the girls. "I am, as I said, here to satisfy my curiosity and also to offer my assistance should I be needed when the time comes. I know as well as you do who the father of that child is. You will need my help. I imagine you don't know any better than I do what will come of the child itself. Whatever it is, it is powerful. More powerful than its mothers? I can't say yet. At the moment of birth, you will be at your weakest. Even though there are two of you in that body, the pain and effort will likely distract you. And unfortunately, your *uncle* is not quite up to the task." He looked down at them in silence for a moment. "So there you have it. It is me or nothing. The choice is yours. You don't need to decide just yet. I think we'll have a few more days before the inevitable. I will spend a little time around the house now and then. Try not to overreact to my presence every time, won't you? I'll just be double-checking the wards and perhaps reinforcing them. You never can be too careful when you deal with gods and demon lords." Shade walked toward a wall and just faded from existence.

"Is he gone?" Nial asked, her voice shaking.

Skeg shook his head. "There's no way to know." He ran his hand over the warded stone of the wall. "He may be right. I don't think I'll be able to help enough." He kept his back turned to the girls. "The decision is yours, but for what it's worth I don't think we have a choice."

CHAPTER 22

The day of the battle dawned with the vast majority of the Bialtan force having spent a sleepless night. The Tolrahkali army awaited them as the sun crept over the horizon. Tactics would play a small role in this battle. The invaders had chosen the field of battle and, again, it was a choice most strategists would scratch their heads over. The numerically smaller force had moved to confront the greatest army in the known world in a relatively clear area near the border, the trees of the Keralan forests darkening the far side of the green plain. But the lesson of the Eastern Army had not been lost on the Bialtans. The attack and losses they had suffered during the night only reinforced the conviction that there was more to the Tolrahkali than numbers. The day's work would be bloody, none doubted that.

Salt stretched and tried to rub the fuzziness from his eyes. *I've never been so tired in my life, and now I have to lead the Guard into their first war. The gods really must have gotten together and decided to screw with me in every way possible. . . .*

Fighting was something the Guardsmen did often and well, but a war?

The thousands of warriors arrayed across the field from them didn't make a sound as the Bialtans struggled wearily into their own formations. The Tolrahkali stood unmoving and patiently waited, seemingly unwilling to fully capitalize on the advantages their night attack had won them. The message was clear—we can outmaneuver you and disrupt your forces at will, but we won't need any of that to crush you in open battle.

The Tolrahkali made no pretense of secrecy. The bull-like cavalry units were neatly arrayed on the west flank of their foot troops, with the lizard-dogs massing around them. The flying creatures and their riders patiently waited in the rear or already circled high overhead. Every Tolrahkali soldier was completely engulfed by the strange armor that was quickly becoming the defining symbol of the desert city-state.

Salt had found himself put in charge not only of the bulk of the Night Guard, but also an equal number of Crown Knights to bolster their numbers—two hundred men and women all told. The remainder of the Night Guard joined a large unit of heavy infantry acting as support for the Arcanum and the command group. The rest of the Crown Knights formed their own elite unit.

The glowing overconfidence of the Bialtan army was gone. *Probably a good thing,* thought Salt. He'd rather the men and women at his side fought with a healthy dose of wariness instead of charging heedlessly into battle convinced of their own superiority.

There was little point in the Bialtans trying to be overly creative or subtle with their battle plans. Though they were certain they could still block any magical scrying, thousands of troops simply could not be hidden from airborne enemy scouts on an open plain. The foot soldiers were placed in the center of the field, the much-vaunted longbows behind a screen of cavalry on the eastern flank, and the bulk of the remaining horses set to counter the Tolrahkali cavalry on the west. Both the Crown Knights and Night Guard units were too small to deploy alone and would both be held back as relief units to bolster the line where resistance was hottest.

Salt watched the last units edging into position. *It won't be long now.* Horns sounded on both sides and banners were raised before the armies thundered toward each other.

***

Dantic stood proudly in his pavilion with Matchstick next to him. The open-sided tent would keep the sun off him and a small group of the most senior mages, as well as make them a less tempting target for any of the enemy flyers that might fly overhead. Not that he'd bothered to share that idea with those not fortunate enough to join him inside—most of the other mages stood in neat ranks to either side of the pavilion with the support troops massing around them.

He couldn't admit it to anyone, but Dantic was nervous. More nervous than he'd ever been. He rubbed his wet palms against his robe and hoped no one noticed. Through all the planning he'd never expected to be put in any real danger, certain that the Bialtan army and the Arcanum would make short work of the invaders. But the Tolrahkali and their warlocks had surprised them time and again. His doubts started to multiply—doubts about the abilities of his team, doubts about facing the warlocks, and even doubts about his own magical prowess.

Dantic watched in morbid fascination as the two armies came together and people started to die. He shook himself. *Just don't think about any of that. Concentrate on what you know.* He looked over to the kladic and gestured for him to proceed. Kishan nodded and closed his eyes. Delicate strands of magic started to spin off into the air around him as he prepared his weaves. It would take a while for all of his spells to be ready. Dantic had asked him to launch everything he had in one massive attack to make the most of the surprise factor.

Time to soften up the enemy while he gets ready. "Begin the attack on all points of the Tolrahkali line," Dantic called out. "Start slow." The instructions were repeated up and down the line, and mages started weaving their magic, calling various forms of energy and fire down onto their enemies.

Dantic had never actually seen war magic used against real people. The idea of killing had never appealed to him and the idea of burning hundreds or thousands of people to death with his magic was sickening. Since he was in command of the assembled mages, he had set himself the task of protecting them should the warlocks attack them directly. He fully expected the Tolrahkali mages to attempt some sort of major attack early on, and he had prepared extensively. He had a number of shield spells prepared and set in spell anchors ready to activate at a moment's notice. *If all goes as planned, the warlocks will fail early on in battle and we can be done with all this and go home.*

***

The battle was going badly. Salt knew it. The realization was dawning on more and more faces as the fighting wore on. Every one of the Tolrahkali warriors was a nightmare to fight. They were inhumanly fast and strong, fought with amazing skill, and were almost impossible to kill, short of chopping them to pieces. Only Bialta's superior tactics and organization had kept them on the field this long. They fought in tight, mutually supportive formations while the Tolrahkali fought as individuals. Damned talented individuals, but individuals nonetheless.

Still, the tiny army of desert warriors was mauling a Bialtan force several times their size. *Even if they lose,* Salt thought, *they've made their point. No one will be quick to dismiss Tolrahk Esal again.*

The Night Guard had been moved to the front several times as pushes by the Tolrahkali, or worse, charges by their monstrous cavalry, had torn holes in the Bialtan lines. After the most recent wave, the Guardsmen had been left virtually alone holding the center of the field. They only managed to hold because their enemies were more eager to prove their individual prowess than to capitalize on the Bialtan force's weakness. When the desert warriors confronted the Night Guard, the fights would quickly break out into duels. The Guardsmen were acquitting themselves well in the exchange, a testament to the skill and dedication of their weapons master. Then the tide of the battle shifted and Salt found himself cut off from the front line with most of his men between him and the enemy. He watched in helpless frustration as Brolt dueled what could only be a Tolrahkali Warchosen. She moved like a dancer, light on her feet and fluid in her movements—a true artist, beautiful and lethal in her chosen profession. The chitin armor moved with her lithe body like a second skin, long black hair protruding from under her helm and trailing down her back. Unlike most of the Tolrahkali, a steel-bladed longsword gleamed in her hands.

The clang of her blade as it struck Brolt's sabers rolled across the field. Even only half seen between the press of bodies, Salt had to admit he'd never seen a duel like it. Brolt never called on his talent in training, and rarely in the field. But for this duel, Brolt was giving his Godchosen talent free rein, and the result was astounding. Salt lost sight of them as the tide of the battle shifted again. He pushed forward, determined to help if he could, or at least to do his share of the fighting.

He caught sight of the dueling Chosen again just in time to see Brolt dart in and swing from both sides. His blades buried themselves deeply in the Tolrahkali's sides below her rib cage and stuck. Without slowing, she brought the pommel of her sword down toward Brolt's head. A long spike had extended from the pommel. It barely missed his face but dug deep into his shoulder above the collarbone. A kick to the chest sent him sprawling. She hung her own weapon on her back, then clumsily pulled his swords out of her sides and dropped them on the ground. She turned her back on the Bialtans just as Salt managed to push through to the front, and walked back through her own lines, the other Tolrahkali warriors parting to let her through.

Salt felt like he was going to be sick. Brolt hadn't been the first to fall today, but he'd been the first from Salt's squad and the loss cut deeper. *Don't give up yet. He could still be alive.* Salt pushed forward, swinging his sword at the nearest Tolrahkali, but he was badly outclassed. His opponent quickly disarmed him and sent his sword flying off into the melee. Salt pulled Bretuul off his back and swung the hammer in a wide arc in front of him as he fell back a step, hoping to give himself a little space more than deal any real damage. The Tolrahkali warrior saw the attack coming and swung his own blade up in a lazy parry. But Bretuul was not a normal hammer—it collided with the Tolrakhali's chitin sword like a boulder hurled from a trebuchet. The sword exploded into shards and the hammer sheared the man's arm off at the shoulder.

Salt and his opponent stood looking at each other in shock for several moments before Greal stepped up behind the Tolrahkali and buried his tulwar in the back of the man's head. He gave Salt a nod and moved on to find his next opponent. Salt was stunned. It was the first time he'd actually swung his hammer at a real person. *That was just wrong.* Night Guardsmen were struggling with the Tolrahkali warriors all around him. *I guess it's no worse than what the Tolrahks are using. . . .* Still, it made him feel dirty. *Live with it, Salt,* he thought. *Those are your people dying around you.* Salt stepped over Brolt's body to meet the next enemy, while Wheeze and the other medics moved up behind him to recover the fallen.

Salt lost track of time. The smell of shit and sweat mixed with the iron tang of blood and other less identifiable stinks. There was nowhere to turn that didn't offer new horrors. The Tolrahkali kept pressing forward, and Salt swung the Demon Hammer around him in broad swipes. Blood and worse erupted from their bodies when Bretuul struck even a glancing blow. Their strange armor couldn't save them from the power of the Dreth-made weapon. Salt's leather armor was slick with gore.

It felt like an eternity before the Night Guard was able to pull back, relieved by a cohort of heavy infantry supported by the remnants of the Crown Knights. Salt's crew was near the point of exhaustion. They stumbled to a relief post, dragging or carrying their wounded. The sounds of battle were still all around them. It was surreal to be there, so close to the front, able to hear the screams of the wounded and dying and yet able to sit and pour a cup of water over their heads and try to control their pounding hearts. Salt looked around the group. Fewer than half looked like they'd be able to return to the front without an extended stint in the healer's tents, and far too many hadn't made it back at all. His mind was too numb to be able to figure out who was missing. He guessed he had about fifty soldiers left in some sort of fighting form. The squad healers moved among them, unable to rest themselves until they had taken care of their comrades.

***

The warlocks were proving to be surprisingly good at providing magical defenses for the Tolrahkali army. Dantic was getting progressively more frustrated and desperate as time went on. *They haven't even tried their fire magic. Destruction is all they're supposed to be good at, everyone agrees. And yet however many are out there, they are preventing us from making any attacks despite our numbers . . . and doing absolutely nothing in return.*

Dantic had tried to entice his opponents to attack, dropping all but the most basic of defenses on their own side. He'd tried directing the Arcanum's attacks toward the back of the enemy's lines where he suspected the bulk of the warlocks would be stationed. But nothing. Not the simplest offensive move and not a single Arcanum spell showing the slightest effect.

The tactic was rarely used. Only defending was not a foolproof strategy in any form of combat. A time would come when an attack would slip through, and there was little that could compare to the devastation caused by a large-scale attack spell.

But the warlocks were simply not making any mistakes. Each and every attack was masterfully blocked or simply taken apart before it could cause any damage to the Tolrahkali forces. Dantic had expected at least a portion of their magic to be neutralized, but he'd still assumed he and the other mages he had recruited would have a more tangible and direct impact on the war effort.

The generals sent messengers more and more frequently to Dantic demanding magical support for the failing ground forces. The plan had been to ramp up the size and frequency of magical attacks to overwhelm the warlocks before giving the Oviyan the signal to launch his own spells.

The kladic had prepared an appalling number of complex weaves, each made up of countless strands of exquisite delicacy, and was holding them all within his power, ready to unleash them at the most opportune moment. But as more time passed without any sign of weakness from the warlocks, the kladic continued to weaken from the strain of holding them at the ready.

Dantic watched another wave of magical attacks streak toward the Tolrahkali—only for them to fizzle out or be taken apart before making contact. The mastery the warlocks were displaying took his breath away.

He looked up at the flyers. They had mostly ignored the flying creatures since the start of the battle. The arrows they dropped were little more than a minor annoyance compared to the bloodshed being caused by the Tolrahkali foot troops and cavalry. Then it occurred to him—the warlocks were all flying. Not just a couple of them, *all* of them. Being closer to the Bialtans was giving the warlocks more time to notice and unravel the spells flying toward their army. It wasn't a huge difference, but when countering magical attacks, a second was an eternity. And they were doing it while minimizing the risk to themselves by not standing at the back of their army's lines where they were expected to be. He cast his sight up to get a closer look at one of the flyers. Two riders rode the strange beast. One was clearly in control of the creature and dropping bundles of arrows at opportune times, while the other didn't seem to be doing anything at all. *The armor is wrong. The second one's armor isn't the same as what all the warriors are wearing.*

Dantic checked another flyer and then a third. He counted fifty warlocks. If they were all of the Tolrahkali's mages, they were showing a level of skill that put Dantic to shame, outclassing over two hundred Arcanum mages as they were. *But let's see how you do when I take away your little advantage.*

"Signal all the Arcanum mages—drain all sources as needed. All-out attack on the Tolrahkali flyers now!" The call was again repeated, and the mages around him all pushed themselves to their limits, sending a dizzying flurry of spells up at the flyers. He saw magical shields flare as spells struck the warlocks' defenses. Dantic threw caution to the wind and prepared his own attack. Casting it high, he angled the weave to strike blades of intense heat down at a dozen of the flying creatures. The spell slashed down and neatly cut through the body of three of the strange creatures even as it bounced off the others' shields. The wounded flyers dropped from the sky, taking their riders with them. The survivors started to scatter.

"Press the attack!" he called.

***

A messenger flag flashed above the command position. Salt's eyes widened. "All right, guys!" he shouted. "Command is saying the west flank is about to collapse and we're to push into the gap." The soldiers around him looked at him as if he had just sprouted a second head. "Don't look at me that way. I'm sure the generals have something up their sleeve that they're about to pull on the sand-eaters. Maybe they'll even get us some magical support. Gods know it's about fucking time the mages pulled their weight in this fight. We move forward in five, people."

Glum nods were their only response. Everyone still able to pulled themselves to their feet and readied their weapons.

They moved west and forward toward the mass of Tolrahkali foot troops.

The Tolrahkali didn't seem to be weakening. If anything, they looked fresher than the Bialtan relief troops, even though they'd been fighting all morning. The western flank was indeed crumbling. A huge Tolrahkali in the heaviest armor Salt had ever seen was literally cutting through all resistance on his own with a huge chitin sword. The rest of the armored fanatics rushed in to follow him. Blow after blow found their mark, but whether the Bialtan attacks cut into the carapace or bounced off the incredibly heavy armor, the giant didn't slow at all. Salt watched him casually smash Tsoba out of his way and neatly slice the head off Seely with the return swing. And then Urit was in front of him. The giant battered at him relentlessly, but the stubborn Night Guard would not give an inch. He was disarmed repeatedly, his shield cracked in half, his armor split, his blood soaking the padding beneath—but he just calmly drew the next weapon from his extensive personal armory as it was needed and stood his ground. The Bialtan troops rallied around him and started pushing back.

Salt was finally able to drive through the crowd to support his friend who was slowly being cut to pieces. He swung the Demon Hammer toward the oversized Tolrahkali from his unprotected side. Bretuul smashed into the warrior's chest hard enough to lift the giant off his feet and send him tumbling back into the Tolrahk lines. Everything seemed to slow down, both sides pausing as they watched the huge champion pull himself back to his feet, his limbs seemingly not responding properly. His breastplate was shattered—shards protruded in all directions around the impact crater Salt's blow had created in the center of his chest. With great effort, the warrior reached up and pulled the helm off. The head beneath was laughably small—average sized, Salt realized. More pieces followed, and the incredibly thick armor was pulled off to reveal a normal-sized if undeniably odd-looking man with overly long arms.

"You broke my carapace, Bialtan. I did not think such a thing possible. But no matter—it only slowed me down. Now we will see if you are worthy to stand against Nasaka Jadoo."

Slowed him down? Oh shit. Salt raised his hammer and prepared to defend himself.

***

The tide had indeed turned. Dantic saw more and more spells make it through to smash into the warlocks' shields as they tried to escape. But beating them back was taking everything the mages had. His only hope was that the kladic's delicate work would pass unseen amid all of the crackling power. He nodded to the desert mage just as he joined the offensive himself—throwing spell after spell toward the warlocks. He held his breath as the kladic's strands of power snaked out. He lost sight of them himself and feared they had been torn apart like so many of their other weaves. . . . Until the Tolrahkali army went berserk and turned on itself.

***

Salt barely managed to fend off the Tolrahkali's first flurry of attacks. *I'm not going to survive long against this thing,* he realized. The man's blade seemed to come at him from all directions, and it was all he could do to frantically fall back. The only advantage he had was that Nasaka was avoiding parrying any of his strikes. He was dodging them entirely, clearly understanding the consequences of being hit with the Demon Hammer. Not that it was a great advantage. Nasaka flowed around Salt's frantic swings as if his bones were liquid and always, always he came back with a complex counterattack. Urit moved back up to stand next to Salt, unperturbed by the loss of half his weapons or the blood leaking through his mangled armor. Urit and Salt slowly moved apart trying to catch Nasaka between them even as the rest of Salt's company swept past to intercept any other Tolrahkali warriors. Nasaka Jadoo just laughed. With a smooth motion, he scooped up Seely's rapier from her dead body and moved directly between them as if it had been his intention all along. His attacks came faster and faster, pushing back both of the Night Guardsmen and scoring glancing blows on Salt's shoulder and Urit's left leg. Then the Tolrahkali army went insane. All around them warriors started screaming in rage and pain and either started attacking each other or even hacking at their own limbs—trying to peel the armor from their bodies.

Nasaka Jadoo screamed in frustration at those around him. "It's nothing more than a spell! Trickery! You weak-minded idiots!" But the Tolrahkali were too far gone. What had moments earlier looked like a crushing defeat for the Bialtan armies turned into an all-out rout for the forces of Tolrahk Esal. Chitin-armored soldiers streamed past as they fled in panic, and more Night Guard moved up to support Salt and Urit.

Nasaka backed off in a smooth motion. "You may have won this battle with your tricks, Bialtan, but the war will be lost far from this place." Then he fled through the crowd just as the Bialtan troops charged after their retreating enemies. After the mauling they had experienced at the hands of the golden-skinned invaders, the men and women of the Southern Army were not inclined to mercy. All semblance of order was lost as the Bialtans seized their advantage and cut down every Tolrahkali they could reach, while maddened Tolrahkali mounts rampaged around the battlefield killing indiscriminately.

As soon as the Tolrahkali broke, the Night Guard backed off and regrouped. All but a few exceptions—Greal was pushing forward, cutting through as many of the invaders as he could. Even through the mask, Salt was sure the man was smiling. *Sick bastard. I need to pull him back.*

The man was so drunk on slaughter that he didn't hear Salt the first two times he was called. As his captain jogged up beside him, the older man growled and swung his rusty tulwar in a savage killing stroke. Another head rolled and Salt was sprayed with blood. Greal's next swing slashed out wildly. Salt only narrowly managed to parry the blow with the haft of his hammer. "Back in line now, Greal!"

The man's eyes narrowed, and for a moment Salt wondered if he would try to kill him. Then with obvious effort, the leather-masked Guardsman stepped back and lowered his weapon. He turned and buried his blade in the back of a wounded Tolrahkali who was crawling in the dust nearby before moving back to his squad. *He's completely losing it.* Salt looked up as the ragged remnants of Bialta's cavalry thundered past toward the Tolrahkali camp.

***

"Harold? What do you think you are doing here? These are my private chambers and I do not recall giving you leave to enter."

"Well, Your Majesty, I didn't think you would agree if I had asked, so I just let myself in."

"Don't give me that—there are Crown Knights posted at every door. Who let you in?"

"I need not mention names. Just know that some of those knights are smart enough to know which way the wind is blowing, and ambitious enough to serve the true king of Bialta."

Arlon's anger went cold. He'd always known Irem was reckless and power hungry. But this?

"Ah, so you understand. Your time ruling over us has ended. You've kept our great nation stagnant and slowly shrinking as you barter away our lands to the likes of the Abolians when we should be expanding! We are the greatest power on the continent and we should be reveling in that superiority! Sharing our greatness with our lessers and taking them beneath our wing . . . whether they want our guidance or not. For too long we've been ruled by a king who is unmanned by fear."

King Arlon bristled despite himself. "You raving idiot! Don't tell me you believe all that crap! We're not in the council room and you don't have an audience to impress. Now get it over with. My best days as a warrior may be long behind me, but I will not make this easy for you. Fear has never ruled me, Harold, but no ruler should ever be entirely without it—if not for himself then for his country and its people. Our days as a dominant military force on this continent are long over, if you'd just wake up and notice. We are being invaded by an upstart city-state, by all the gods! Not Aboleth, not Keral—the bloody Tolrahkali! And they are winning! And you would lead us to war? Against the whole of the known world?" He spat at Lord Irem, his face twisted with contempt. "You disgust me. You may have been able to corrupt enough of my guards to get in here tonight, but you'll never be able to rest easy with those same men guarding your sleep. Your reign will be both short and unpleasant, I have no doubt." He looked around curiously. "So what's it to be? Poison? A dagger? How are you going to blame this on one of our enemies?"

With a smirk Lord Irem moved toward him. "Nothing so obvious as that." A long blade started to grow through his palm. The king's eyes widened in surprise.

"You were quick to believe that the knights would turn on you, when in fact all they did was allow an unarmed man in to have a private word with his cousin—they searched me quite thoroughly I assure you. Unfortunately, we will be interrupted by a Tolrahkali assassin. They will probably blame the same team that is even now taking care of your family. You are right that the Tolrahkali are winning. But, then, the invasion is a necessary evil—a cleansing if you will. We also had to ensure that a number of potential obstacles were far from the capital for a time. Once the might of Bialta is united with the power of Tolrahk Esal, the entire continent will fall before us. Not even the Dreth will be able to stop us."

The king threw his book at Irem, but the fleshcarved lord just batted it aside and ran him through. After letting the corpse slump to the floor, Irem very carefully sliced open his own cheek while looking in the mirror. *I've always wanted a scar. Just the thing to give me that daring look.* Then he cut his other arm almost to the bone before picking up a heavy wooden table one-handed and casually throwing it through the window. The warded glass shattered under the impact. *My short time spent abroad with that disgusting creature Carver was most certainly worth the discomfort.*

When the Crown Knights burst in moments later with swords in hand, they found Lord Harold Irem bent over the corpse of the king sobbing and holding his wounded arm close to his body.

***

Shade felt the coup coming before it happened. The burning ambition and resentment at the heart of Harold Irem was something he had become very familiar with over the centuries. He could feel the end approaching, and seethed in silent frustration as the moment drew nearer. All his servants were out of place, be they unwitting pawns or friends and voluntary allies.

He had mobilized nearly all his resources to deal with the birth and the attack in the South. Now there was no one in place to guard the king he had so carefully groomed for the throne. There was no telling what damage a fool like Irem could inflict before he could be removed. Everything had been progressing so well too. The Arcanum had become more open-minded and far less accepting of the abuse of nonmages, the Night Guard had been formed to weed out the darker elements that had a habit of hiding in larger human populations, and all under a king who genuinely cared about the well-being of his people. *And now he's dead. What a waste. . . .* So much has been lost to give the child a chance at life. It would have been more prudent to destroy it and its mothers, but he'd been unable to resist indulging his curiosity. He would just have to do everything he could to ensure the birth went smoothly and Amon Kareth didn't interfere. *It really is all too rare for something truly new to come into the world. I can only hope some good eventually comes of it.*

EPILOGUE

Jenus moved from one stance to the next, shifting smoothly and without thought. The familiarity of the training was small solace. It was so familiar he barely had to think about what he was doing, and that left his mind free to wander, his conscience unrestricted to twist around and torture him. *Maybe I should see if Ischia needs a drover.... At least I'd be doing something useful then. ... If Ischia has animals that aren't undead anyway.* His barrel stave was knocked out of his hands before Jenus realized he wasn't alone.

"Well, well, so you're the fallen champion Sonum's been telling me about." The man who spoke was human and quite a bit shorter than Jenus but incredibly bulky. He was also visibly armed with at least a dozen daggers and knives hanging from his belt and several weapon harnesses. "Good to see you aren't getting lazy. That stubbornness you've shown since you got here is actually a trait I value in my apprentices."

"Apprentice? What are you talking about?"

"Well, maybe 'apprentice' isn't the right word. You really aren't suited to joining the Crows. Far too open and honorable to stick a knife in someone's back, I wager. And, besides, you're still breathing, so you're not really eligible." Jenus's skin went cold—here was another of the city's undying elite. "But since you obviously aren't willing to give up your calling as a warrior, we figured someone should train you. It's plain for any real Warchosen to see that you haven't reached your potential. I'd guess no one in Sacral was a challenge for you. So it's time to push your boundaries a little and see what you're capable of," he smiled darkly. "And who better to do that than Rahz the Insane?"

***

The death of King Arlon sent shock waves throughout Bialta. Not only had the nation been invaded and a vast number of its people killed in horrific ways, but even the king—the protector of the realm—had been cut down in his chambers at the heart of the palace by assassins from a small city-state. Rumors were flying across the country. Villagers were fleeing from imagined threats and moving en masse away from the borders, fearing both the remnants of the defeated Tolrahkali army returning from across the Keralan border and a fresh invasion directly from the desert. A report had even come in from the north coast of a fishing village's residents becoming convinced that they were next and committing mass suicide to spare themselves from the pain of being eaten alive.

Gurt was visibly shaken by the news. Not only was Arlon his king, but also his childhood friend. "I've received news that the king was lost to Tolrahkali assassins along with most of the royal family. The king's cousin has taken on the role of regent for King Aroten until the boy comes of age—our king is now a boy of five." Salt was stunned. The news had killed any relief that the war with the Tolrahkali appeared to be over.

Gurt shook his head. "It gets worse. The regent is overreacting as badly as any of the peasants. He's made all kinds of commands to boost the army. He's ordered me to triple the size of the Night Guard. Each Guardsman is to take on two initiates and help teach them. He's also reinstated the penal legions—any citizen convicted of pretty much any crime is getting pushed in. Apparently he's got troops going through the Muds grabbing every able-bodied person they can lay their hands on and pushing them into service. And he's ordered all of us down here to return to the capital. We're only to leave a skeleton force guarding the borders and mopping up this mess until he's done *restructuring* the army."

Salt felt a chill run down his spine. Nasaka Jadoo's parting words echoed in his mind: "the war will be lost far from this place." He had been eager to return home, a safe place to mourn their losses and a return to familiar routines. But what would they be returning to now?

***

"It's time!" Nial gasped.

Skeg broke out in a cold sweat. *The baby is coming.* The thought swirled around in his head again and again. After all the waiting, after all the preparations they had made . . . it was both terrifying and exciting. Nial's expression was grim. She didn't speak—no more needed to be said.

The runes around the girls were already glowing as if under sorcerous attack, each concentric ring dimmer than the ones within but slowly brightening. Skeg's palms were wet with nervous sweat that he couldn't seem to rub dry no matter how much he tried. His worst fears were already proving to be well founded—the child's great power was challenging their wards and the birthing had only just begun.

They had taken elaborate measures to prepare for an attack by Amon Kareth, scribing their own wards and augmenting Shade's work wherever they could. But the power beating against their magical defenses was coming from within, not from the child's father. Skeg poured every ounce of his power into the innermost ring in a desperate attempt to strengthen it. Sweat started to bead on his forehead. The wards were getting too hot. Even with Skeg's help, they wouldn't last. He held on for as long as he could, before switching to the next ring, then the next. Each one failed faster than the last as the power at the core of the circle grew and Skeg's strength waned. Nial and Zuly were almost invisible against the glare of the incandescent wards as they heated up and burned deeper into the stone floor.

Where the hell is Shade?

Another ring of wards flared into blinding light and faded as they shattered. The shock hit Skeg like a physical blow. The stone floor was glowing brightly; the blankets the girls were lying on had already burned to ashes.

A grinding sound was building as the house's foundation threatened to shatter from the immense strain. *What is this child? How could it be doing this?* For the first time, Skeg's misgivings overwhelmed his hopes.

The house shook more violently, as if something huge had just landed on the roof. Skeg looked around in a panic to see the wards on the outer walls and ceiling glowing brightly—all of them. *Amon Kareth is here!* He was at a loss as to what to do. The wards on the floor were smoking as the stone was slowly being eaten up by the incredible heat. The air in the house was like a furnace. Skeg's talent was already nearly exhausted.

And then Shade was there. He appeared out of nowhere to stand next to Skeg. Power poured out of him into the failing defenses—barely, just barely holding the whole together.

Skeg took a step back only to be brought up short by the wave of heat radiating from the wall behind him. Each breath he took burned his lungs. He stood with his legs set wide and did the only thing left to him—he drew whatever shreds of energy were left in him and tried to bolster one last row of wards somewhere in the middle of the room. He was vaguely proud to see the ward dim slightly as he countered the strain it was under. Blackness was crowding the edges of his vision.

His last thought before consciousness faded entirely was just to wonder which way he'd fall and so which set of wards would burn him up. Just as he blacked out, he thought he saw Shade flicker and fade from view as his own well of power ran dry.

Skeg woke up to birds chirping. He felt like he'd been beaten within an inch of his life. For a moment he thought he was a child again. There had been far too many mornings like this for him back then, when he was alone and weak. Memory returned in a rush and he sat up with a start. Pain burst behind his eyes and his vision went black. His chest and arms hurt horribly. It hurt to breathe. *Hell, it even hurts to think.*

He tried to get up again, more slowly this time. Spots floated in front of his eyes. He slumped against the wall with a sigh. Two rings of wards had held. *Only two. And I'm outside of them,* he realized with a start. *I guess I'm lucky old Amon wasn't interested in a half-trained reject of a mage.* The rest of the floor was a mess of ash and melted stone. The roof looked to have caught fire at some point in the night as well; there wasn't much of it left. The birds Skeg had heard were perched in the rafters fanning their feathers in the setting sun. *Setting, yes. The light is coming from the west. It's been a whole night and a day.*

Nial was lying in the middle of the room. Her clothes had completely burned off, but she was curled around a little baby that was clutched to her breast, sleeping peacefully.

It looks perfectly normal, Skeg thought, stunned. Whatever he had expected, it wasn't a healthy-looking little boy.

His thoughts shifted to Shade and to what he thought he saw. *Bastard's not human. No real surprise there, but a spirit? Or something not fully solid? Now that's something new to go on. I don't think I've ever heard of a spirit being a mage.*

He dragged himself to his feet and went in search of a blanket for the girls. He found one in his room that was only partially scorched. After covering up the girls and their son, he did the best he could, bandaging the burns on his arms and chest and then stepping outside in the hopes of clearing his head. *Demonic hunger or no, I feel the need for a good stiff drink to wash the taste of burning magic out of my mouth.*

He struggled with the front door for a moment before it fell out of its frame. *I can't believe I'm alive.* His disbelief only grew when he looked outside. If the inside of the house had taken a beating, it was nothing compared to what had happened outside. The ground all the way around the house had been fused to glass. Wisps of smoke still rose slowly from the cooling embers. The vegetable garden was gone; the rabbit cages, blasted into a heap of ashes. Even the fence around their little property was scorched, though the heat hadn't been fierce enough there to melt the stone.

A few townsfolk walked quickly past, eyes darting to the destruction as they hurried to get some distance between them and the danger. Skeg even saw the next-door neighbor leading a laden wagon away from his house, his entire family and all their belongings piled inside.

The farmer who had initially welcomed them to the town was just leading a rickety-looking cart up to the house. "This is the best I could do on such short notice. But we need to get you and the girl out of here as soon as possible."

"Go? Where?"

"Does it matter? What happened here last night ruffled a lot of feathers. If the army and the Arcanum weren't occupied down south, this place would be swarming already. Think, man—Amon Kareth broke into the world at this spot!"

Skeg's blood went cold. The ordeal must have numbed his mind. Every mage and power on the continent would be rushing to find out what happened and to make sure the demon lord didn't break through again. *He's right. We need to get out of here as fast as we can.* He looked at the farmer and nodded his understanding.

The man looked relieved that he wouldn't have to argue any further. "Don't worry about bringing anything or looking through the rubble. I'll take care of that and send anything I can salvage to you later. Just get in the cart and get moving. We have another house prepared for you, but it's a couple days' travel, and we don't have another warded cart."

"Another house?"

"We couldn't be sure which road out of Darien you'd take, so Shade prepared a few options. Now get moving!"

From inside the house Skeg heard the baby cry.

THE TIDE OF MADNESS

The following excerpt is from Craig Munro's forthcoming novel *The Tide of Madness*. Track its development on Inkshares at inkshares.com/books/the-tide-of-madness

The island of Aspro was a corpse, the remains of a primal god, an elder being who walked the earth when the world itself was but newly formed. The white sand that made up the bulk of the landmass was one of the deadliest poisons known. The touch of a single grain against the skin would turn a grown man into a screaming lunatic for a few short moments before he started spewing blood and died. Not even plants were immune to the white sands. Not a blade of scrub grass, not a mushroom or a clump of moss was able to live on the island. That didn't mean it was entirely barren, however. Aspro had several rivers and multiple deep turquoise lakes that held an abundance of fish and other aquatic life. The poison, as deadly as it was, became inert through contact with enough water. Life had also found a way to spread across the two great mountains that dominated the island—life that had crawled out of the ancient corpse itself. These creatures, one and all, fed on fish or on one another. The most common were reminiscent of large eagles and a derivative of the cat family, though they had neither feathers nor fur. Like every creature that drew breath upon the poison shores, they had a thick, chalk-white hide and pupil-less milky-blue eyes.

Outsiders only rarely ventured close to Aspro—sea captains and crews driven as much by desperation as by greed. A few small jars of white sand lifted carefully from the beach could pay off a great many debts . . . so long as a stray gust of wind or a careless movement didn't bring a screaming end to the expedition.

Ruin looked around sadly at the vestiges of her once-vibrant village and the inbred remains of their herd of steeds. Only a dozen yurts were set around the standing stone that was the heart of the tribe. Her people couldn't see themselves for what they were, for what they had become. But the Bright Dreams came to Ruin often and showed her the past—the tribe had been greater and stronger than any of them could now imagine, their herd numbering in the hundreds. Proud warriors and hunters had competed with each other in battles for dominance. She could see them as clearly as if they stood before her, mounted atop their savage white steeds, casting bone spears in their endless struggles. Theirs had been one of the largest villages on Aspro. It had counted over a hundred families, children spilling out of every home. Now there were no younglings left at all. . . . Hers was a fallen people. They had been set on an almost incomprehensibly slow path to dissolution in the far past.

The Bright Dreams did not forget. They had shown her the blue-skinned darklanders who didn't fear to walk in the land of light. Who had come to them in the guise of traders and had taken the bulk of their herd, not just from her village, but from every village on Aspro. The loss of their four-legged brothers and sisters was the start of their fall. But the dreams had also shown her a way forward, a way to reclaim that which was taken so many generations ago and restore the balance.

Ruin understood why the dreams spoke to her more clearly than to anyone else. She was the strongest hunter her tribe had seen in an age, the fastest with a spear, the quickest to learn the skills and knowledge of her people—she was born to her purpose. *Tonight is the night I take the first steps along my path.*

She left her yurt and looked up at the sky. The land around her glowed, reflecting the stars and moonlight all around her. Her kill from her evening hunt hung outside the yurt, deep-red blood still dripping into the sands. Ruin drew her bone dagger and cut a slab of meat off the haunch. It steamed in the night air as she bit into it. She made a point of eating as much as she could. Her journey would not be an easy one and there would be no fresh meat where she was going.

She would enter the dark cavern between the mountains. She had seen what lay in the deepest depths of the darkness. The dagger—if a blade half again as long as her arm could be called such—was roughly hewn from a jagged crystal, the handle wrapped in rough hide. It waited for her in a deep pool of murky corruption—the rotting blood of the dead god. The weapon was old beyond imagining. It was the first tool created on this world for the sole purpose of inflicting murder. There was power in symbols, and the symbolism of this most ancient weapon crafted to kill a god held a power few would dare to wield. *And with it I will bring vengeance to the Dreth!*

***

Salt sighed loudly. Life just couldn't seem to return to the nice simple routine from before the war. Not that anyone in their right mind would call a Night Guardsman's life simple or routine. Soon they would split up his squad and lump him with a bunch of new recruits—volunteers from Bialta's other military forces. Worse still, the Arcanum's special investigator had been permanently assigned to assist Salt in carrying out his duties.

Altog adjusted his sword in its scabbard impatiently. "We really have to wait for the guy in the dress?"

Salt shrugged. "His fanciness Mage Holit Nobesid is now a member of our squad. We'll all just have to get used to it. Count yourselves lucky. Most of you will be moving on to other squads or leading your own in the next few weeks. I'm stuck with him."

As Holit Nobesid came huffing up to join them wearing his usual elaborate Arcanum robes, Salt turned his back and set off. "Come on, we need to get moving. We've got a lot of ground to cover tonight."

"Night Captain, a moment to catch my breath if you will—"

"So? Where to, Salty?" Min interrupted.

Salt smiled and gestured for her to walk with him. "Gurt gave us a good one. We're heading up to the temple district. He wants us to check out a new cult. Their god has some name I can't pronounce, but they also call him 'the Blood God' if you can believe it."

"Sounds like a friendly bunch," said Altog.

"We going to clear them out?" asked Min.

"Not tonight, anyway. We'll just poke around a little and maybe introduce ourselves to these new priests. There's been some talk about them making people not wake up for a price. The ladies think there's something to it. So if need be, we'll push them a little and try to get a reaction. They're in the ruins of the temple of Basat if any of you guys know where that is."

Min groaned. "Figures you'd come up with a reason to drag us there."

Salt looked at her in confusion.

Altog laughed. "Basat was Bialta's very own homegrown god of pleasure. These cultists have got balls. There aren't many who'd try to set up shop in another god's temple. Basat wasn't really scary, but the consecration was real. Even if he doesn't have any followers around here anymore, they still risk pissing off the god of perverts' shade if there's anything left of him."

"God of pleasure, huh? How come I never heard of him?" Salt asked with a grin.

Skye laughed. "His cult died out at least a hundred years before you were born. The faithful didn't get a whole lot of work done and ran out of gold pretty fast. Charging for their services wasn't part of the creed apparently, but all priests need followers to throw coins at them every once in a while."

Min nodded. "Still, the old goat had real power. The fact his temple's stayed empty for so long in the heart of Darien is proof of that."

The walk to the temple wasn't long. The old stone building Min said was their target was an imposing structure. Salt shivered when he saw it. Old statues of people in various states of undress and enjoying a variety of excesses had been defaced. Faces and limbs had been hewn off, and each had been splashed with blood. Simple altars made from rough stone had been set up against the outer wall at regular intervals.

"Min? Holit? Either of you getting anything off this place?"

"It crawls, Salty," said Min. "There's power here. But it feels more like sorcery than any god." Holit nodded his agreement while numbly wiping the sweat that was streaming down his face with a handkerchief.

Salt looked at the temple with distaste. He didn't much trust priests at the best of times, but this place looked like it

was openly flaunting blood sacrifice. "Keep sharp, everyone."
The fact that no sarcastic comments answered his words was
proof enough that the whole squad felt as he did.

While they were watching, a nondescript man walked
up to one of the makeshift altars with a squawking chicken
clutched in his hands. He pushed the bird down onto the stone
and cut its head off with a quick chop of his belt knife. Steam
rose off the altar as blood pooled beneath the spasming bird.
The man shook a few last drops out of it, then walked back the
way he had come.

"That's disgusting," said Min, looking at the pool of blood
with a handful of dirty feathers floating in it.

"I don't know," answered Altog. "Nothing worse than you'd
see from any marketplace chicken seller. If you grew up on a
farm, you'd be used to worse."

Min rolled her eyes. "It's still out of place in this part of
town, and the chicken seller doesn't rub the blood and shit on
the walls. Besides this new god isn't calling himself the Lord
Harvester or the Great Lost Farmer—"

"Let's head in," cut in Salt before their argument could
escalate.

No doors barred the entrance to the temple. The wide hall
Salt and his squad walked into was starkly empty and meticulously clean. *Not a speck of dust, or a drop of blood, or any
loose feathers for that matter.* Two guards wearing blackened
steel armor and long red cloaks stood at the far side of the
room. Both were armed with wickedly barbed spears. Their
helms completely obscured their features. Only their eyes were
visible—black irises surrounded by whites so severely bloodshot they looked pink from a distance.

The guard on the left pounded the shaft of his spear against
the floor when they came in. Salt stopped a respectful distance
from the guards and waited while his squad filed in behind him.

A moment later, a woman swept into the main hall from the opposite doorway. She wore long deep-red robes elaborately detailed in gold thread. They trailed along the floor behind her like a spreading pool of blood. Her face and hands were colorless and translucent. Salt could easily see the network of bluish veins beneath the skin. Her head was perfectly hairless and her eyes matched the hue of her robe—nothing but dark pupils floating in pools of blood.

"Good evening. I am Sakku, Ninth Bride of Ansharukan. To what do I owe the pleasure of the Night Guard's visit?" Her words were mocking, but her face and tone didn't betray anything.

As devoid of emotion as a corpse, Salt thought to himself. "I'm glad you know who we are. . . . We're just curious, really," he answered lightly. "And of course a name like the Blood God does spark a few concerns with some of the more squeamish inhabitants of our fair Darien."

"All are welcome within our halls, Night Guardsman. Many of the locals have already embraced our presence and make regular offerings on the altars outside. If some few find our practices distasteful, we can hardly be unique in that offense."

"And you're content with chicken blood, are you?"

"And so we come to the root of your concerns. I appreciate you not wasting time. I will answer simply, though you likely won't believe me—we do not take the lives of thinking beings within these walls. All blood is welcome, be it from a king or an earthworm. The red river of life flows through us all and is the domain of the great Ansharukan. The faithful offer what they will, be it a few drops from their own finger or a torrent from the throat of a lamb. This is a place that celebrates life, not death."

Salt looked around the room again—a room so totally devoid of life it might as well be part of the Silent God's domain. "And where did you come from? I assume you came in by ship?"

"Of course. We are from the Empire of Gho far to the south. The great Ansharukan rose from among our people. We travel to share his many blessings."

"And you just picked Darien to set up a new temple?"

"Is it not the right of any temple to establish itself in this city? Do we have to espouse flowers or commerce to be accepted? Darien and indeed Bialta as a whole are the envy of many lands. It was a logical choice."

"Are all faiths welcome in Gho?"

"There is only one god in Gho. Since the ascension of Ansharukan, no false gods have risen to contest his dominance over the archipelago."

"Still, priestess, rumors have been going around that if I want to make someone stop breathing, you are the right person to ask if I am willing to pay the price."

"You will find that I never leave the confines of my temple, Night Guardsman, nor do any of my guards." She cocked her head suddenly, as if hearing something no one else could. Her eyes snapped back to Salt. "Now if there is nothing further you require of me, I must return to my meditations. You are, of course, welcome to remain for as long as you wish. My guards might even welcome some new sparring partners if you would like to pass the time. Be forewarned—they always practice with bare steel—Ansharukan welcomes all offerings both intended and accidental." With those parting words, she swept back out the way she'd entered.

Was that a threat or what passes for humor in Gho? Salt looked at the others, who shrugged. He jerked his head toward the door and they filed out without another word, the guards watching them with unblinking eyes.

"Creepy bastards, aren't they?" said Altog.

Salt nodded. "Her answers were oddly specific, don't you think?"

"Yeah," said Min. "Only within these walls? And she and her guards never leave the temple?"

"I'll ask Gurt to put some eyes on them," Salt said. "It might be a good job for some of the new recruits. In the meantime, I'll ask Lera and the ladies to do a little more digging into this cult and Gho in general. I don't think I've ever met anyone who's been there."

"Those people aren't what they say they are," Brolt said.

Holit nodded sagely, having only just managed to get his breathing under control again. "It's not like any temple I've ever been in or near. The flavor of the power here is all wrong."

"So she's a mage, not a priestess? Or is it the guards? Wouldn't be the first mages we've seen wearing armor."

Holit didn't take the bait. "I didn't feel anything from the guards while we were in there. But there's definitely traces of sorcery or something very like it clinging to the priestess."

Salt waved them forward. "We're not going to get anything more done here tonight. Come on, guys, let's get to the next name on the list—I want to be back at the palace before dawn."

ACKNOWLEDGMENTS

Writing this story was a very private and personal experience. Turning it into an actual book has been anything but. From the first readers of my early drafts to all those who helped fund my book, there is a staggering number of people I need to thank for their help and support in making *The Bones of the Past* a reality.

A few names stand out in particular: my wife, Margo, who has kept me sane and supported me every step of the way; my sister Kirsty, who was one of my first readers and one of my biggest promoters during my Inkshares campaign; Laura and Cyril, my sister and brother-in-law, who spearheaded the sales effort and moved more books than I thought possible; my brother, Keith, who introduced me to Inkshares in the first place and did his fair share of marketing for me as well; and of course my parents, Scott and Elaine, who were right there with the rest of us promoting my book to friends all around the world.

I was also greatly helped in my efforts by a number of fantastic friends including Mathieu, Sara, Isabelle, and Eddy, who led the sales efforts in France; Dave for his marketing advice and for allowing me to promote my book at the Wizard's Tower; Sebastien for jumping in and helping when I needed it most; Karim for helping me create the Gling'Ar; An Song Ok and her family for their generous support and help getting copies to so many of my friends and former students in Korea; half the island of Ireland—an astonishing number of friends, family, and complete strangers who all pitched in and preordered a ton of books; and so many others I just can't list them all without filling more pages than I already have with my story.

Then there are all the incredible people at Inkshares and Girl Friday Productions who took my manuscript and turned it into a real book. Special thanks go out to Angela Melamud, who so patiently answered all my questions and kept me and the project moving in the right direction, and my developmental editor, Lindsay Graham Robinson, who absolutely overloaded me with work (in a good way!) and whose invaluable insight helped me take my story to the next level.

And finally, thank you to each and every one of you who preordered, ordered, or walked into a store and bought this book. I am grateful beyond words and I truly hope you enjoy the time you spend in my world.

ABOUT THE AUTHOR

Craig A. Munro has worked in a variety of fields, including government, language instruction, tech blogging, and construction—all while completing a couple of years of med school at the University of Nice and eventually earning a BSc from the University of Ottawa (yes, in that order). He has lived in countries across Europe, North America, Asia, and the Middle East and has recently returned to Ottawa, Canada, where he pushes paper for the federal government. *The Bones of the Past* is his first novel.

LIST OF PATRONS

INKSHARES

Inkshares is a crowdfunded book publisher. We democratize publishing by having readers select the books we publish—we edit, design, print, distribute, and market any book that meets a preorder threshold.

Interested in making a book idea come to life? Visit inkshares.com to find new book projects or start your own.